The 'Wild Edric' Saga

Novels by same author =

Book one = The Shieldwall.

Book two = The Broken-Shield.

Book three = Aelnoth.

Book four = The Warrior king. (This Book)

Book Five = The Red King.

Best Wishes

[signature]

The above books belong to M. J. Hands and Mr, J.T. Hands who are identified as author's and sole owners of the copyright of these works in accordance with section 77 and 78 of the Copyright, Designs and Patents Act 1988.
All rights are reserved. No part of any of these publications may be reproduced, stored in a retrieval system, or transmitted in any form or by any means, electronic, mechanical, photocopying, recording, or otherwise, without the prior written permission of the Author's.
Any person who commits any unauthorized act in relation to these publications may be liable to criminal prosecution and civil claims for damages.
A CIP catalogue record for this title is available from the British Library.

Whilst these works are fiction, many of the characters, battles and place names are real.
The people portrayed in these books lived, loved, fought and died in the 11th century; in their attempt (be they Norman, Welsh or English,) to survive in the turmoil of what was then England and Wales.
Other than those long dead warriors and their kinfolk, there is no semblance to any other person, living or dead.

A number of words in this book have been taken from a USA dictionary and may seem to be incorrect to British readers.

LOCAL VOCABULARY VARIATIONS.

Thee = You.
Thou = You.
Be = Is & Are.
Yourn = Yours.
Taint = It is not.
Me Hlaford = My Lord.
A Nithing = A Nothing= A nobody= A worthless person.
Beof = Beef.=Cows= Cattle.
Mutton = Sheep= Lamb'
A Quarrel= A bolt or an arrow from a Crossbow.
A Poniard= A slender dagger.
A Saex = A short sword. Something akin to a Roman Gladius.
Small beer= Is a second brew of beer. Not the best beer.
Unt = Is a Mole.
Upper Wommer'= NOT a local. A stranger.

THE WARRIOR KING.

CHAPTER ONE.

I had searched every farmstead, hamlet, town and village in Mercia in vain, before I widened my search into the Welsh valleys.

I had ridden my old stallion into the ground, building a pyre with my own hands.

I cried like a baby as I had watched the flames consume him as his savage soul drifted with the hazy wood-smoke that mingled with the bitterly cold Welsh mountain air on its way upwards towards Valhalla.

It had taken eight weary days for me to walk out and emerge into the land of the English again and it was during that trek down the damp valleys that I was eventually forced to accepted the fact that my Lovely Godda, who has been lost to me these dreary years that perhaps she had not really been a true Queen of the Light elves.

Maybe she had been nothing more than a mere woman who had left me and did not want to be found.

Oh! Leaving Wentnor and everyone and everything I held dear, except my beloved Godda, had been the most difficult thing I could remember doing. I had been extremely sad at leaving my two sons, Godwin and Aelnoth, but I had convinced my-self that as

Godwin had reached the aged of 20 and was as strong as an ox, he would be able to cope with my small fortress at Wentnor and would care for his fifteen year old brother Aelnoth well enough.

I was tired, footsore and ragged when I rang the bell at the door of an Abbey near the river 'Dore' in the hope that the monks would take pity on a near starving man and throw me a crust of bread, but when the small portal in the studded door was flung open, the monk merely looked me up and down with obvious distain and when his eyes rested for a brief second on the battle-sword that was slung over my shoulder and then to my Saex which were the only possessions I owned, he uttered a scornful. 'Be gone' and the tiny door was slammed shut in my face with a loud thud.

I was more fortunate when I reached the four houses that made up the hamlet of Abbey-Dore, where a kindly housewife who was washing clothes outside the door of her cottage bade me sit on her stool. She brought me a piping hot bowl of thin broth which she thrust into my hands saying, 'there thee be old fellow, get this down yer gullet 'afore me husband returns, for he do not like oi feeding beggars.'

That bowl of broth gave me the strength to walk a little farther along the overgrown path, until I discovered an empty dilapidated cottage where I spent the night.

The cooing of doves in the rafters woke me soon after dawn and much to my surprise I found that I was not alone, for there not two feet from where I had slept, I was startled to see the ragged hairy figure of a man who had apparently joined me during the night and lay sound asleep on the same bundle of damp straw that I had lain upon.

I rose to my feet and exclaimed 'What the hell do you think you are doing sleeping in my bed next to me?' forgetting for a brief moment that I was no longer the lord of the manor, or the fact that I looked equally as my scruffy as new neighbour.

The man slowly sat up and shook his head in an attempt to clear it of an erotic dream he had been having. 'Taint no more your bed than it is mine,' mumbled the still sleepy man.

'In fact it be more mine than yorn, since I bin sleeping 'ere for the past three months.'

I was somewhat taken aback at being chastised like this by a grubby peasant, but suddenly realised that my own attire. My unwashed face and my unkempt hair was probably grubbier than my former bed-mate.

The man rose to his feet and although he was unshaven and bedraggled, I could not fail to note that the man was eight or ten inches taller than myself and was probably some twenty years my junior.

It was only then that I noticed that his right arm ended just below his elbow causing me to guess that he had lost his arm in battle, but I felt it prudent not to mention it.

'My apologies to you.' I said in a friendlier manner. 'The cottage seemed to be empty when I arrived last night.'

The man nodded and gave a half smile.

'That's alright. Tis a cosy enough place and the thatch is solid enough. Mind you, the thatch has collapsed in the other room.'
'You surely inner an 'Upper Wommer'? He said to me in such a broad accent that I didn't really know what he was asking.
'What on earth is an 'Upper Wommer'? I asked.
'An Upper Wommer' is a man who is not from this valley.' He answered, as a wry smile crossed his pockmarked face, which silently said to me that everyone with a brain in his head ought to know what an 'Upper Wommer' was.

I avoided to answer the question and asked 'Do you have any food to spare?' I asked.
'No.' He answered, shaking his head as if to prove that he was not lying.
'Not to worry,' he said. 'Follow me. I have a nose for food. Never go hungry that's my motto,' and he led a way through the doorway that did not contain a door.
I followed him around the back of the cottage, and then through an overgrown path that had once been a cultivated garden from which two old apple trees and a large patch of mint struggled for existence through several beds of nettles and docks.
We passed through a hole in what had once been a boundary fence, for I could see where someone had laid the hedge many years ago, but it was now overgrown, and at least 15 feet high.
I followed the man through woodland that had been coppiced at least ten years ago and through meadows

that were now dotted with thistles, nettles and all kind of weeds, we exchanged a few words.
'I am called Edric.' I said.
'What's your name?' I asked.
'I am Wilfred of Kent,' he answered. 'Although I am a long way from home and doubt I shall ever see Kent again.'
'Oh. Why's that?'
'That's a long story. Maybe I shall tell it to you one day.'
'Were you in the Fyrd?' I asked, for his clothing, or what remained of it, and his bearing seemed to indicate to me that he had once been more than the down and out peasant that he appeared to be.
'Might have been,' he answered. 'What's it to you?'
'You be 'askin a lot of questions for an old tramp.'
'Of course I know you are not merely an old wolfs-head like myself,' he added, ' as only a warrior who carries a long-sword over his shoulder and a Saex in his belt can survive to your age, if he is either very good or very lucky.'
'Which are you?'
'Lucky.' I answered slightly shocked at Wilfred's speech and his logic.
Before I could ask him more questions that were beginning to flood my mind, he suddenly stopped as we reached a meadow which contained four tethered milking cows and a small flock of black faced sheep.
'Here we be.' He said with a sigh as he pointed towards the far end of the second meadow where I

could see a small village and the type of castle that most of the villages in the area seemed to possess.

As we neared the village, I could see that the castle itself was in a state of disrepair and many of the thatched cottages were green with grass and mould and in sore need of fresh Thatch.

'Bernard and his brother Edward live there. Oh and of course Her Ladyship. I were forgetting' Her.' Said Wilfred, as he nodded towards the Castle, but they have let things slide a bit since old Lord Percival died.'

I followed my newly found friend past most of the houses in the village and was rather surprised when he began to stride manfully up the slight rise that led to the castle.

However as we neared the iron studded gate, he suddenly veered to the left and skirted around the outside of the structure, to halt some half way around the fort when he reached a very small Sally-port that lay partially concealed behind a thick holly tree.

He banged lightly on the door with the haft of his eating knife and waited a few moments until the door was gingerly opened by a rotund woman who smiled sympathetically at Wilfred, but the moment she turned her gaze towards me the smile left her face and she shook her head, saying, 'Now Wilfred I don't mind giving YOU a bite to eat now and then, as you were a brave lad to have followed his lordship into Wales, but the boys would flay my back raw if I feed any more waifs and strays.'

'Send him on his way before the boys come down and find him here.'

'Come now Sarah,' said Wilfred in a friendly tone. 'Surely a kindly soul like yourself would not send a starving man away from your door, for the sake of a dry crust or two?'

'He is merely another good fellow who is down on his luck, like my-self, and he is called 'Edric.'

'Please dear Sarah. Just one stale loaf and maybe a slice or two of that boiled ham that has made you such a famous cook.'

'Just this once dear Lady and I swear by all that's holy that I won't bring him here again.'

'Oh all right then. Quickly now! Bring him in before some busybody sees him.'

She stepped to one side and held the door open whilst I followed Wilfred into a short passageway which led into the Castles kitchen.

The Kitchen contained a bread oven, a stone cooking range upon which three pots simmered and bubbled sending out clouds of steam and the delicious aroma's that sent my weary mind back to the old kitchen at Wentnor, where Godda used to make me the most delicious food long ago, causing my mouth to begin to water as my mind flitted between apple and blackberry and plum pies.

Both Wilfred and my-self sat on three legged stools on opposite sides of the table and were each given a wooden trencher that was almost immediately filled with a steaming hot stew consisting of slices of ham and an assortment of vegetables and half a small loaf of brown bread.

'There thee be old fellow. Now eat it up quick like and be on thy way afore we be found out.'

I must admit that despite burning my mouth and my gullet, that was the finest meal I had eaten for many a long day, and to show my appreciation I scraped the final drops of gravy from the trencher until a starving dog couldn't have licked it any cleaner.

Wilfred nodded towards Sarah and smiled as she said in the same country dialect that Wilfred seemed to speak in an odd sentence or two, before he returned to what I would describe to as being the normal language of England.

'Well,' she said, 'He bolted his fettle quicker than an 'unt' disappears down an 'unt' ole.'

He nodded his consent, but I was forced to ask.

'What did she say?'

She said that you ate your fettle (meal) faster than a mole disappears down a mole-hill.' He said with a smile.

As we both rose from our stools to leave, profusely thanking Sarah for the food, the door was flung open as the two brothers Bernard and Edward burst into the Kitchen.

I immediately assumed that the two well-dressed young men were the 'boys' who were the owners of the castle, and noted with some concern that the right hands of both of the brothers speedily went down to rest upon the hilts of their expensive looking swords which hung upon their left hips.

'Let's kill these two near-do-gods who have invaded our kitchen and are eating us out of house and home,' snarled Edward as he gave a wicked smile and gazed towards his brother. His brother immediately nodded and almost in unison the two young men drew their swords.

To say that I was not afraid would be a lie, but my mind was saying to me that despite my ripe old age of 55, or whatever age I was, even in my rather weak and ragged condition, I could still take on two striplings like these, or even double their number and still win.

Oh I was aware that at my age, I was perhaps a little slower than I had been in my youth, but with the numerous battles and single combat fights that I had fought, I knew from bitter experience that any fight is a dangerous business and I have seen many a champion warrior slain by a common slave and have also seen proven warriors killed by horses, slain by serfs with a cudgel and die in more ways than I can recall.

I was very reluctant to fight these two good looking brothers and realised that the long-sword that was still in its sheath over my shoulder was much too cumbersome a weapon to use here and my hand reluctantly fell to my short Saex.

Nevertheless, it seemed that I was about to be forced to fight for my supper in the confined space of this steamy kitchen by two untried youths who were under the impression that the slaying of my companion and myself was naught but a youthful prank.

My hand was still on the hilt of my Saex as I leant backwards to allow Edwards long-sword whistle past my chin.

My Saex parried Bernard's sword which plunged past my right shoulder and whilst his sword was still behind me I stepped forward and bashed the fair headed youngster between his eyes with the hilt of my Saex, sending him senseless to the floor.

Edward gripped his long-sword with both hands and raised it upwards for a downward cut, but the swords momentum suddenly ceased as it was imbedded in a ceiling beam and was snatched out of his hands, leaving his hands empty as they appeared in front of his startled face. He found himself staring wide eyed and open mouthed at the space where his sword should have been.

My Saex pricked his neck and I said with a smile. 'Now I think that should be the end of this nonsense and I have no wish to kill or even to hurt you. Indeed I would merely like to thank you and your staff for inviting us into your lovely Castle and offering us a bite to eat.'

Without further ado I returned my Saex smoothly to its sheath and turned to leave.

Edward looked up at the sword which was still lodged in the beam and angrily grabbed the haft and wrenched it out, resting the point on the floor as he watched me turn around to leave.

His gaze turned to his brother, who was sitting on the floor against the kitchen wall, shaking his head in order to clear it from the stars that blurred his vision.

'Halt.' I heard a stern voice demand.

I halted half way through the door and turned fearing to see the two brothers on their way to continue the fight or perhaps worse, I had an uneasy feeling that one or perhaps both of them had crossbows aimed at me. `

My intuition was wrong, thanks be to Odin, for as I faced them, Bernard was standing by Edward and was still holding his unsteady brother up and he spoke, not to me but to Wilfred who was standing behind me.

'Wilfred,' he said, 'I have known you for most of my life and know that you lost the best part of your right arm in the service of my father, when he took you and the rest of our men on his disastrous foray into Wales.'

'Here-to, I realise that I have not treated you with honour, and as I am the eldest and the rightful heir to 'Wolf Hall.'(Sir Percival had liked to be flamboyant and had been of a melodramatic nature) I will allow you to live here with us in the castle if you will agree to carry out a few simple chores for us.'

Wilfred paused for a moment and switched his gaze towards me and with a stare that I could only think of as being cold. 'As for you.' He said as he looked at me and paused for moment, before he blurted out. 'I don't even know your name.'

'What IS your name?' but before I could answer, he added. 'You look like a wolfs-head or perhaps you are a fugitive or deserter from some lord or army?'

'Which are you?' He snarled.

'Nay.' I did not call him Lord, for my blood was still slightly up and I, who had been called 'Lord' for most of my life did not deem this untried youth, who I had just bested, had earned the right for me to call him 'Lord.'

'I am neither a Wolfs-head nor a fugitive or a deserter, but I am a man who is known in my own country as 'Edric' and I am also a man who you see in this sorry state, due to the fact that I have been searching throughout Mercia and the seven Kingdoms of Wales for my wife who has been taken from me.'

Edward only seemed to have heard only the word 'Edric' but little else of what I had just said, for he glanced at his brother who had at last reclaimed his senses and he said. 'Edric. Edric,' he repeated rubbing his chin in thought. ''Tis a common enough name. I know of at least three men such named, here on our estate.'

'There is Edric the Thatcher. Edric the Nash who lives at an'ash, and old Edric the ploughman. 'How else are you known?'

CHAPTER TWO

'Edric the Savage.' I answered honestly, in the hope that these two youngsters had not heard of me.

Neither of the brothers seemed shocked at my name, but the blond haired one asked.

'And are you a savage?'

'Oh I have been known to get quite angry now and again.' I answered in a lame attempt to evade going into details.

'It would seem,' Bernard said. 'As I look at the two swords you are carrying and the way that you bested my brother and myself, that it would appear to me that you are a man who has fought in a Shield-wall?'

'Is that not so Edric the savage?'

'I have fought in a number of battles including a Shield-wall.' I answered calmly.

'And did you win?'

'Always.' I answered.

I could see that my answer had shocked both of the youngsters, but I simply ignored the questioning expressions that crossed their faces.

'And are you a Christian?' Edward asked.

I avoided answering him and asked. 'May I ask how do you intend to treat Wilfred in order to better his lifestyle?'

Bernard answered my question, as we could all see that my question had been an unexpected ploy, and it was blatantly obvious to me that his brother had not given his previous statement much thought.

'We shall take him into our service and we will house him and feed him, as if he were still one of our household warriors.'

'How many men do you have?' I asked.

'Only four, since his lordship lost six men in Wales.'

'How remiss of me,' he said, for we must not forget poor Wilfred here.'

'But of course. He is no use to us as a warrior now that he has lost his right hand.'

'Well, that is not really true.' I said, speaking rather hastily and without considering the possible consequences of my short statement.

Bernard had already seen a possible opening here and caused me to think that he was the younger of the two brothers and as the law decreed he would not be the new Lord of 'Wolf-Hall one day, but he was certainly the brainier of the two.

'Could a man of your obvious experience train him to be a warrior again?' he asked.

I rubbed my chin as if I was considering the possibility and thought that such a task may solve a number of pressing problems.

By training Wilfred would allow him to earn his keep as well as bring up the numbers of household warriors up, especially as I would be lodging here, and in doing so I would be bringing the tally up in able bodied men who would be here to defend the castle.

'I would like to see your other men.' I stated.

The two brothers looked at one another and after what seemed to be a long silence.

Bernard responded to my unexpected demand. 'Of course,' he said. 'Follow me.'

He turned to exit the door through which they had emerged half an hour ago.

I followed the two brothers through the door and up a flight of half a dozen stone steps, emerging into a sunlight forecourt of perhaps a one hundred paces square area of cobblestones.

The courtyard was surrounded by a ten foot high wall and a recently thatched manor house, as well as two further cottages and a partially completed Barn.

As we walked across the cobblestoned courtyard I became aware that the castle had originally been built of wood. Probably, I assumed shortly after the conquest and the wooden structure had been replaced with a larger and sturdier structure made of cut stone a few years ago.

The stone had probably been scavenged far and wide, for most of the stone seemed to be square, so I assumed that it had been scavenged from one of the many Roman Villas and out-houses that had been abandoned when the Romans had left Britain two or three hundred years ago. These old buildings all stood roofless and derelict.

The Roman buildings had been left uninhabited because both the Britons and the Saxons shunned such places, believing them to be haunted by spirits of the dead and fit only for sheep and cattle.

The castle now stood solid and proud upon the man-made mound that Lord Percival had forced his peasants to build when he had arrived here some forty years ago.

Edward and his adopted brother Bernard appeared to be very alike.

I learned some- time later that both of the youngsters were eighteen years of age. They were the same height and carried themselves with the same kind of raw confidence of fit and healthy youngsters, in fact their gait could have been mistaken for the kind of strut that is usually contributed to proven warriors who have fought and overcome a number of their enemies, but that had not happened in their case.

I learned that they had practiced each and every day since the age of five, and might be called experts by other men who spent their days at the plough or hedging or ditching, or doing any of the other activities that most other young men did day in and day out, but neither Bernard or Edward had ever struck a blow in anger, let alone slain a foe-man.

Edward was English and was some ten months older than Bernard.

He had been found abandoned in the forest by Bernard's mother where the babe had been left to be devoured by wolves, as was the way of many English families who felt that an extra mouth to feed would be an impossible burden for the family to bear.

He had been brought up by Bernard's mother as a son of her own blood, and had grown into a strong and robust young man.

Bernard and Edward seemed to me to have been born into the wrong bodies.

Edward was English, and most people would have expected him to be fair skinned and have fair hair, like the majority of the English people. But he was dark skinned and had a head of thick curly black hair.

Bernard on the other hand, being a Norman should have been of a darker hue, as was the majority of his father's Norman neighbours, and yet he possessed hair that was platinum blond and skin as white as the driven snow.

They did not lead me into the Manor house, but walked past the front door and halted at the doorway of one of the small cottages that nestled to the rear and slightly to one side of the Manor house.

'There.' Bernard said as he pointed towards the cottage.

'You two can live there. It is empty, and has been so for some considerable time, but the thatch is good and one of the side walls may need a little attention, but I think you will both be comfortable enough there.'

He looked first towards Wilfred and then at me, noting the sour look on my face.

'Well' he said. 'It's not that bad and I will get one of the servant girls from the Manor to cook and clean for you.'

'It will be fine.' I said, remembering the many wet and cold nights when I had slept in the open with nought but a cloak between the elements and myself.

I walked the few steps towards the front door of our new abode but halted and turned to face the brothers

'I would like to see your housecarls?' I said in a pleasant tone, using the old English way to describe household warriors who were retained by a Lord.

Edward turned and placed his hands around his mouth and bellowed at the top of his voice. 'Hugo. Hugo.' He repeated.

'Up here. Now and bring those other three layabouts with you.'

I was somewhat shocked at his tone and the phrase that Edward had used to describe his retainers, but allowed my thoughts to pass as I waited for the four men to appear.

A long silence followed his orders until I heard the sounds of movement and doors being slammed shut in the adjoining cottage.

The door was eventually flung open and three half-dressed men staggered out as if they had been pushed forward by a fourth man. They stood rather shamefaced before their two Lords whilst still adjusting their clothing.

'I am not at all surprised you came back from Wales with your tails between your legs if these are an example of the men you took with you.' I said shaking my head in disbelief.

The brothers both snorted in anger and their hands flew to the hilt of their swords but their hands remained there and allowed my insult to pass, as their thoughts and indeed my own thoughts were interrupted by the appearance of one of the largest and most formidable looking individuals I had ever seen since the days of my youth, when I had met and fought with Ivor half-face and his equally enormous brother.

'This is Hugo,' Edward said quietly, as Hugo stood in front of the three other more or less normal looking housecarls.

'Hugo and you can live in the same house.' Bernard uttered with a smile.

The three other men appeared to be of average height and aged between twenty and thirty.

They were all dressed in dirty leather shirts and trousers, held together with strips of leather that had been tied into a knot to hold their trousers up.

I also noted that the younger of the trio had a long knife tucked into his belt, whilst the other two had Saex's sheathed in reasonably well kept sheathes,

Hugo, however, was far from the run of the mill housecarl, for he stood some six feet eight inches in height and looked to be as heavy as two or even three of his fellow warriors put together.

He had greasy hair that fell in tangled knots onto his shoulders, where they merged into his full, untrimmed beard, which was flecked with white.

I guessed that he was probably aged around mid to late thirties.

'Who's this?' demanded Hugo.

'This is your new sergeant at arms.' Edward stated quietly.

'I think not.' The gigantic Hugo snarled.

'I did not leave sunny Picardy and travel all this way to this cold dreary place to be ordered about by some Old Saxon has-been.'

He swaggered the few paces towards me and thrust his face into mine, causing me to turn my face away and wrinkle up my nose in order expel the smell of stale beer and other noxious odours that assailed me.

Despite my age, my mind spun with the possibilities of an encounter with this big bully, telling me that whilst I was confident of beating the man.

My mind also told me that it would be very unwise to kill him, as he seemed to be the only man amongst this sorry lot of so called housecarls who looked as if he could fight.

My unwise pondering was interrupted as Hugo grabbed me by the top of my ragged jacket and literally lifted me off my feet with one of his huge hands, and flung me forward, bowling Edward, Bernard, the one armed Wilfred and myself over, leaving the four of us in a heap.

'I am the Sergeant at arms here.' Hugo grunted. 'And no grey-bearded Saxon is going to take my place.'

I untangled myself from the other three men and as I stood, I took my battle-sword from my back and withdrew my Saex, dropping both of the weapons onto the cobbles.

'Is that so?' I asked and stepped towards him.

I had already noted that he carried no weapons.

He crouched down and took up a fighting stance with his arms held out wide and in doing so he made himself appear to be even larger than his already enormous bulk actually was.

His face was now on the same level as my own, and I was standing upright.

I leapt into the air and kicked him under the chin with all of my might, causing his face to shoot backwards and sending him onto his back as his head hit the cobbles with a deep thud.

Neither my kick nor the thump of his head on the cobbles had knocked the man out as he merely sat upright and rubbed his chin.

He stared at me and an evil smile briefly crossed his ugly face.

My own thoughts at this moment in time were rather mixed, for I realised that with the skill that my old mentor Vorta had knocked into my thick head when I was a youngster, together with my battle experience, I could overcome and probably kill this gigantic man, but that may be a serious mistake, as the two brothers who were standing on the side-lines watching the contest, would probably not want their best housecarl slain and killing him could cause my own death if I did slay the brute. (Of course I was still without my weapons, which glistened on the cobbles some twenty feet away.)

But apart from that, I had also reached the conclusion that this man-mountain who I surmised had achieved his reputation as a warrior from his sheer size and brute force and not from any particular skill or finesse with weapons, told me that I ought to beat him within the next few minutes, before his strength or a lucky blow overcame me. Then, with a little luck, I may be able train him properly in tactics and weapon-craft so that in a shield-wall, or in a real battle, he could literally be unstoppable.

As he scrambled to his feet, I stepped to one side of him and kicked him on the back of his right knee, which was one of old Vorta's favourite ploy's and one that I had rehearsed many times before but had never carried out in anger.

My kick ought to have brought the giant to his knees, but it appeared to have little or no effect on the man, for when he rose to his feet and turned to face me, all I could detect was a very slight limp.

He was obviously annoyed at being injured by who he thought to be an old man, and he bellowed out a loud roar.

He charged at me like a bull, rushing towards me with his arms outstretched in the hope of catching me like a fish in a net.

I ducked under his outstretched arms, kicked him again behind his knee, and I added to his impetus by jumping and landing with both of my feet in the middle of his back, causing him to crash face forward into the sandstone blocks of the wall.

I sat upright and looked towards my advisory in anticipation of continuing the bout, but I was rather relieved to see the hulking body of Hugo lying flat on his face, completely unconscious.

Both Edward and Bernard held their hands out to help me to my feet and as I rose I could see that both of the brothers had wide grins across their faces.

'Christ's Holy blood.' Edward exclaimed with gusto. 'No living man has beaten Hugo since he was thirteen years old, when his own Father whipped him for killing his elder brother in a fit of rage.'

'I think his brother had bullied him when he was a child.' Bernard added as he walked over to Hugo, who was in the process of wakening from his brief sleep and had begun to sit up and rub an enormous lump on his forehead.

Bernard helped Hugo to his feet and watched with a sympathetic face and a kind word, as Hugo shook his head and simply stood and stared at me.

I thought that he might renew our contest and attack me again, but thankfully my fears seemed to be unfounded as the giant walked the few paces towards me.

His face, which appeared to be made of skin and bone with no real flesh, but his strange bull-like face broken into what struck me as being something between a silly smile and a grimace, causing me to prepare myself for his second attack, but much to my amazement, he grasped me with both of his huge hands and stroked my shoulders like a man caressing a pet puppy.

He released me and stood back a pace.

He held his right hand out and repeated his rather bewildering smile.

'Come.' He said. 'I'll show you your new home.'

I followed him into my so-called new home, which turned out to be a one roomed shack that contained a fireplace, a table, two chairs and one bed.

'That's my bed.' Hugo said gruffly. 'You will have to sleep on the floor.

Bernard who had followed us and stood in the doorway said, 'Oh, don't you worry about that. I'll get old Arnold to knock a bed up for you before night-fall.'

I was to learn that Arnold was an old greybeard who seemed to be a general handyman, and a man who could do pretty well anything from attending the large vegetable patch, to repairing and making anything to do with woodwork or masonry.

'In the meantime.' Bernard added. 'Come with me and meet the real power in 'The Wolf Hall.'

CHAPTER THREE

I followed Bernard and Edward as they strode casually across the cobbled courtyard and through the iron bolted door of their Manor house.

Bernard paused for a moment and turned towards me saying quietly. 'You are about to meet my old Mother and I suggest that you act politely and reverently towards her, as I can assure you that she can be a savage adversary to those who anger her.

He turned and entered the room before I was able to respond and left his grinning brother and myself in the doorway.

The still smiling Edward ushered me through the door where I could see nought but an empty room with a large polished oak table with benches on either side, plus a servant girl who was standing behind a high backed chair that was placed close to a roaring fire.

I thought to my-self. How on earth has that chair not caught fire?

The fire threw its welcoming light into the otherwise darkened room.

Edward walked over to the fire and stood with his back to the fire, facing the chair.

'Mother,' he said in a very civil voice. 'I would like you to meet Edric.'

He turned and beckoned me forward and as I approached I heard him say to his Mother. 'Edric is to join us and he is to take a position with us as our new 'Sergeant at arms.''

A husky voice asked 'What happened to Hugo?'

'Is he dead?'

'No Mother.' Edward answered. 'Edric beat him in a fight and he was forced to stand down.'

'I thought that mountain of a man was invincible.' She said.

'So did I Mother. So did I' he repeated with a shake of his head, 'but Edric beat him.'

'My god.' She exclaimed.' He must be good.'

I was now standing alongside Edward and was shocked to see. Not the haggard old crone that I had expected, but a very attractive lady, who must have been aged somewhere around my own age, or maybe a little younger.

She was sitting with her legs together as her one hand fondled a ginger cat that was purring so loud that I could hear it from the four or so feet away from where I stood.

Her other hand rested upon a small tapestry that she had been working on.

She looked up at me and my heart sank as I realised that here I was, a Lord with countless holdings and hundreds, if not thousands of people at my beck and call and yet I was standing here like a serf, presenting myself to a lady as If I was a landless peasant begging for my supper.

I suddenly realised that I had not washed for many a day. My greasy hair hung down my neck onto my shoulders. I probably stank like a farm dunghill and I was wearing the same ragged and unwashed clothing that I had worn for the best part of two years.

I was suddenly brought back to reality and forced to disconnect myself from those startling blue eyes that stared back to me, as Edward nudged me in my ribs and said. 'This is my Aged Mother. This is 'Ella.'
'The Lady Ella to you my good Edric,' uttered a husky voice that came from beyond her ruby lips.'
 I knelt like a yokel ploughman and stooped downwards towards her, pressing my unwashed lips upon the back of her hand.
 'I am honoured my Lady.' I grunted like an oaf and stood in order to make a speedy getaway.
 She smiled and in an aloof manor she said. 'You may leave us.'
 I turned to go but was brought to abrupt halt when she said in a stern voice.
 'Not you Edric. I wish you to remain.'
 I was left alone with the Lady Ella and her Maid.
 'Pray sit.' She said in a pleasant voice. 'I would like to know more about you if you are to become my Sergeant at arms.'
 I was trying to assess this strange lady whilst at the same time I was determined to tell her as little as possible about my-self and my past, lest I upset her and get ordered out of this hereto comfortable position of bed and board that I had found myself in.
 I lied. 'My Lady I am merely a soldier of fortune, searching for my lost wife and I have unintentionally stumbled upon your good-self and your two sons.'
 'And I think that you are stretching the truth Messier'.' She spat with unexpected venom.

'Or, maybe you are taking me for a fool, and that I am not, for a blind man on a galloping horse can see that you are not an ordinary man-at-arms.'

She rose from the chair and faced me with those startlingly blue eyes that gazed from out of her un-pockmarked face.

'Certainly, your clothing is filthy and worn, she said snootily, 'but it is still the cloth of a Nobleman, and your ornate belt, your boots and your sword could not possibly be owned by a peasant, or even a soldier of fortune, unless that soldier had slain and stripped a dead man of his possessions.'

Before I could argue against her logic, she continued. 'Is that what happened Edric?' Yet again she answered her own question before I could speak saying, 'I think not.'

'Shall I tell you what I think.'? She asked.

By this time I knew it would be futile to try to speak, so I merely stood with my own face some three feet away from the Lady Ella who clasped her hands together and said in a voice that a moment ago had been snooty and aggressive, but now sounded as soft as the voice of a purring kitten.

'I think that you are a warrior of some standing, who is very much in love with your wife.'

'She is a wife who you have upset and who has left you.'

'You are now full of regret and grief stricken.'

'You now wish to find her and assure her of your undying love, but after two long years of searching, you have reached the conclusion that she is either dead or does not wish to be found, and finding someone who does not want to be found is nigh on an impossibility in our turbulent Kingdom of England'.

She paused for the space of perhaps fifty heart beats before she continued.

'Edric,' she said quietly so that despite the fact that there was no one else in the room, she would not be overheard.

'I will be completely honest with you. Despite the fact that I rarely leave this castle, I have heard of a man with your name who lives in the western part of Mercia and he is named as 'Edric the Savage by us Normans.'

'This Edric was married to a Welsh Princess who suddenly disappeared.'

'The Edric who I am speaking of, was one of the few English Nobleman who has been allowed to keep his land and his title, and that alone tends to narrow it down to a very small number of such men.'

'This man Edric was a warrior of note, and that again leaves even fewer Saxons left in that category since the Battle of Hastings, when the Cream of Harold's England were either slain or have been forced to ply their trade abroad.'

'Your ragged, yet expensive clothing and your obvious skill with your weapons tell me that you are this Edric. But fear not, for despite being a grieving widow I am still an old romantic and I do envy you for the love that you have for your wife.'

'May I say that as long as you stay here and cause us no harm, then I will assure you that your secret is safe with me?'

'You are, of course free to go and resume your quest whenever you want, but it is my wish that you remain with us here in 'Wolf Hall.'

I would like you to train my housecarls in the arts of war. I think you have heard of our disastrous foray into Wales, where my impetuous husband lost not only his own life but also the lives of half of our men and left me with Hugo, a one armed man and three other useless near-do-wells.'

I merely nodded and refrained from remarking on her very logical assumption of our situations, for indeed the five men, all who I had seen, I knew I would be hard pressed to turn them into trained warriors, which did cause me to hesitate for a moment.

Certainly, I had trained many men in the past and had succeeded in making most of those men into reasonably good warriors.

These five posed rather unusual problems in their own individual ways.

Admittedly, Hugo was a bull of a man, but whether he could accept discipline or not and decided to resist my authority was a moot point. With his obvious strength he may well be able to overcome perhaps two, three or even more adversaries in a fight, but even his strength would not save him if his obvious ego caused him to break our own shield-wall, which would probably cause him to be surrounded and slain by more disciplined warriors. His death would then allow our enemies to pour through and slaughter his fellow warriors.

I felt that I may be able to train Wilfred of Kent to learn how to fight using his one remaining arm, but I surmised that from what I had seen of the three other men, they had appeared to be lazy and indolent, caused me to decide to give them a trial period of perhaps a month, and if they did not show signs of improving, then it would be better to send them on their way and find more promising recruits.

'My thanks to you Lady Ella,' I said. 'I will be honoured to stay for a while and train your men.

'Then that is settled.' She said, and returned to her seat, causing me to stare as the light from the fire caused her hair that I had first thought of as being rather dull and brown, to glisten with streaks of dark gold from the flames of the fire.

Without turning to face me, she said in the same savage tone that she had used before. 'You may call me my Lady Ella.'

I turned and left the room.

'Edric.' She said in a stern voice.

I halted and turned.

'I have just had a thought.' She remarked as she turned in the chair and faced me.

'I am left alone in this castle on too many occasions when the boys are out hunting, or when they spend nights away in the village, wenching with the village maidens, and think that I would feel much safer if I had someone like your good-self here, so I will allow you to sleep in the spare room, here in the castle. '

I nodded my head and mumbled my thanks to her, but she merely continued, saying.

'I shall instruct one of my thralls (Servants) to make the room ready and tighten the strings on the bed in order for you to be able to 'sleep tight.'

'I will also find some of my husband's old clothes for you to replace those dirty rags you have been wearing for the Good Lord know how long.'

From hearing her mention 'The Good Lord' I immediately knew that she had been converted to the new religion of the white Christ and as I left the room, my mind tussled with the possibility of her changing her mind about allowing me to remain as her 'Sergeant at Arms' if, or when, she found out that I was both a Pagan and a Christian or perhaps something between the two.

*   *   *

I am usually a man who can fall into a blissful sleep from the moment my head hits my pillow, but on that particular night, perhaps it was because I had been sleeping rough for most of the year, or perhaps my mind was racing with my fight with the gigantic Hugo and the other odd things that had happened to me since I had been wakened by one-armed Wilfred of Kent in that abandoned cottage.'

As I lay awake, I watched the moon through my open window.

The moon slowly reached its zenith, and as it do so, I imagined a shadow flitting across the moon, causing me to immediately lie still, apart from my right hand which shot down to the hilt of my Saex that lay at my side, fully expecting to be attacked by someone, and my mind immediately flew to the gigantic figure of Hugo.

 It was a warm night and I had long discarded my sheepskin fleece which lay in a bundle on the floor on the right hand side of my bed.

 I heard a gasp and a muffled squeak which told me that my intruder as a woman; as she stumbled over the sheepskin and fell flat across the lower half of my body.

 My hands fell upon her shoulders, which were unclothed and I pushed her sideways as gentle as I was able, so that she lay facing me.

 'Wait there.' I mumbled, 'while I light a lantern.'

 My fingers seemed to have a mind of their own as I struggled with a flint in order to light the oil lamp.

 I shielded the lamp with my hand until it was fully ablaze, and walked over to the bed to see my intruder, and what I saw when I gazed towards her, totally shocked me, for it was not one of the serving maidens, who I had assumed it to be, but it was 'Her ladyship' herself who lay, naked on her back smiling up towards me with a smile that I can only describe as lecherous.

 'Lady Ella,' I said in a voice that seemed to have grown in my belly and had made its own way upward, to utter the words in a voice that I swear was not my own.

'Sir Edric the Savage.' She said back to me in her cultured Norman tongue.

'How now? Sir Edric?' She added sulkily.

'I think you already know 'how now.' I said as I lowered myself onto the bed and lay beside her. I placed my arm around her body where I could feel her heart beating wildly like a drum.

I think my own heart was attempting to rival the heart of my newly found bed-mate as she straddled me and plunged herself onto me, causing her to growl and tremble so much that I thought I had hurt her.

'Sorry.' I mumbled. 'Have I hurt you? It is such a long time since I have been with a woman.'

'Shall we stop?' I asked, hoping that the answer would be 'NO'.

'No. Gods blood No! I too have not had a man since that stupid husband of mine left me to go raiding in those bloody Welsh hills.'

'The stupid old bastard!' She spat.

'No don't bloody well stop. I will bloody well kill you if you stop now.'

I thought she was jesting although the other side of my brain told me that she was not, and I said to her. 'I didn't know that Norman ladies swore and knew such words.

'You would be surprised if you knew Norman ladies' she said.

'Our habits and our knowledge in the department of love would put a brothel full of Saxon whores to shame.'

We continued, slowly at first, until the fire in my loins caused me to throw caution to the wind and I humped her like a wild stallion serves his mares on the mountains back home.

The faster I went the louder she moaned and groaned, until after our second series of climaxes, we both lay exhausted side by side panting in order to catch our breath.

I roused myself a couple of hours later and turned to face her in the hope of a return match, only to find her side of the bed cold and empty in the darkness of the early morning.

I awoke after the best night's sleep I had experienced for a long time, to a dawn and the sound of larks, as well as thousands of other birds singing their dawn-chorus.

Long ago I had started my day without eating anything before mid-day, so I dressed and strode out of the still silent house and into the two separate dwellings where the men slept, waking the sleeping men by stripping them of their sleeping sheepskin beds and shouting for them to rise.

'I'm going nowhere until I have broken my fast.' Growled one sleepy man, as he rubbed his unruly mop of greasy brown hair and attempted to locate a flea or a louse in his equally greasy unkempt beard.

The other men all growled and grumbled their agreements with him and as I did not want to make my first day as their new Sergeant at arms too difficult for them, so I relented a little and accompanied them to the kitchens.

I sat down and joined them in a tankard of small beer and a piping hot bowl of porridge.

After a much longer breakfast than I had intended. I ushered them out of the kitchen and into the cobbled courtyard and then across to a fresh pile of timber that I had noticed the previous day.

I selected ten likely looking pieces of ash branches and pulled them out, laying them in front of my men saying. 'You and I will spend the morning cutting and whittling these branches into wooden swords before we start our training, as I think it may be unwise to start hacking at one another with iron swords.'

I stooped down and picked up the nearest branch to me, and then I walked over towards the castle wall. I sat down and started to cut the wood into the correct length and shape of an English Saex until after an hours cutting, it began to resemble a short sword like the Saex that I habitually carried in my belt.

I stood and stretched my aching back before I walked over to the four men to inspect their efforts.

One armed Wilfred of Kent was still in the process of cutting his wood by holding the length of it with his feet and hacking away with his eating knife into what resembled something more like a club than a sword.

I patted him on the shoulder and said.' Don't worry too much Wilfred, I think that a spear may be of more use to you and I assure you that I will make you into a good spearman.'

I walked on to the three men who were sitting apart from Hugo and laughing and chatting amongst themselves.

All three had produced something that resembled a Saex and whilst two of them resembled clubs.

However one of them looked so realistic that if I hadn't known it was made of wood it could easily have passed for the genuine article.

I took the wooden sword from him and studied, it saying to him. 'That is good.' Can you make me a dozen more like it? Can you do that for me?'

'Of course I can.' He answered. 'I was taught wood carving by my father, and I can churn out as many of these as you want.'

'Excellent. How are you called?' I asked.

'I am named Ethelwulf.' He said with a little flourish of his hand.

'Good! Ethelwulf.' I said, 'I shall call you Ethelwulf the Woodman.'

I turned to the other two and looked at their 'Swords' shaking my head at their poor examples of woodcarving.

'Those are not too good are they lads?' I said to them. 'None-the-less. We will leave Ethelwulf here for the rest of the day and you two can join me in a pleasant walk in the countryside.'

'You too. Hugo.' I shouted to Hugo who was still sitting where I had left him with his face turned up towards the sun that had broken through the thin clouds.

'Where are we going?' Hugo mumbled unhappily.

"I would like you four men to show me the extent of Lady Ella's estate.' I said, 'and we may be able to find a few straight poles which we can turn into spears.'
'Lead the way.' I said, and Wilfred led the way across the cobbled courtyard towards the open gate, followed by my-self and my four new recruits.
We crossed two meadows and a newly ploughed field, waded through a shallow stream and into a large patch of natural woodland where I could see Oak, Ash Sycamore and Hazel.
'Find a good stand of Hazel,' I said, 'and cut as many strong poles about as thick as your wrist and as long as Hugo and three thick pieces of sturdy, straight ash poles and bring them all to me at the edge of the wood.' 'Off you go now.'
A large pile of Hazel and Ash wooden stakes were assembled within a couple of hours and although I was forced to discard four or five pieces that I felt would not serve the purpose of being used as either a spear or one of the appropriate stakes that I needed, the pile was still large enough to provide each one of us (including myself) with a load that would test the strength of each of us in the next hour or so, in our effort to carry them back to the Castle.

We piled the wood close to the wall, where I told the men to take the rest of the day off, with the exception of Ethelwulf who I asked to remain behind by promising him a couple of tankards of ale if he would stay behind and continue to carve as many swords as possible until the darkness of the evening would stop him.

In fact it took Ethelwulf the complete afternoon and two further days of carving before he had reduced the pile of wooden stakes to a large pile of kindling that lay alongside twenty wooden swords and ten poles that resembled spears.

The brothers Bernard and Edward had been watching our antics with smiles and remarks that we could not hear, and I felt sure they were relaying our progress on to their mother.

I had not seen her Ladyship since our encounter in my bedroom, although I suspected that I did see what resembled a face that peered out of the opened window on a number of occasions.

CHAPTER FOUR

 The day I started the training was something of a farce, for Hugo broke two wooden swords on two separate occasions when he missed the sword of his opponent, causing his own two swords to shatter when they hit the cobbled courtyard
 After two days of solid and very frustrating training, I came to the conclusion that 'Hugo the giant' and 'Wilfred one arm' would be my spearmen whilst the rest of the men would use swords.
 I made this decision which I thought would not only for train the men with their chosen weapons, but it would also serve to train both groups of how to attack and how to defend themselves from enemies who were armed with swords or spears.
 The willow shields which I had asked the two maidens and two of the older women to make, eventually arrived, giving the men more confidence but alas less courage, for the men cowered behind their shields to such an extent that I was forced to bellow at them, swearing that unless they obeyed my orders and became more aggressive, I would take the shields off them and would order them to fight without the shields.
Progress was slow but sure, to such an extent that after some two weeks of sword and spear exercises

plus numerous hours in hacking away at the stakes which had been sunk into the courtyard, I felt confident enough to reduce the weapon training to a couple of hours each morning, so that I could lead them out into the countryside each and every afternoon on a forced march, in order to build up their stamina.

 I used my time during these marches to change my position from either leading the men from the front, to marching behind them in order to urge the laggards, and to march alongside the men in order to familiarise myself with them.

 I was surprised to learn, especially so from the one armed Wilfred of Kent that the 'Lady Ella' was neither a recluse or the disabled person I had thought her to be, and had a long standing feud with her nearest neighbour, who was a Norman Knight with the title of 'Sir Ralph De La Pinion.'

 Wilfred informed me that 'La Pinion' was much disliked by his tenants and serfs, as well as most of his Norman neighbours whose lands and estates he coveted.

 He had met with the Lady Ella on several occasions since her husband had been killed, with offers, as well as threats to add her estate to his own much larger estate.

 I also learned that the two brothers periodically went through periods of Love and hatred.

  There were times when they were the best of friends, whilst at other times they seemed to have arguments and periods of dislike turning to total hatred, which sometimes lasted from days to many months.

Within a couple of months I had recruited an addition two young men to swell our force to seven.

I studied my men as they stood in a line before me and assessed them.

My eyes went from the large figure of Hugo, to one armed Wilfred of Kent, and then to 'Ethelwulf the woodman.' 'Ubba the Mercian.' Leofric and the two new boys, 'Frithoft' and 'Sigard.'

Both Frithoft and Sigard were eighteen year old twins and who I had chosen from the ten or so young men who lived on the estate, considering them to be the most suitable to join my small force, purely due to their size.

The two of them were big young men who looked as if they could be aggressive and handy men to stand next to in a shield-wall, and it was only much later that I learned that they were sly, lazy and untrustworthy.

I spent an hour or so lecturing the men as we sat in a semicircle near the training posts, relating on to them as much knowledge as I could from my vast experience of the wars and the battles that I had experienced thus far in my life,(which Incidentally I did NOT divulge to them in any detail).

I tried to instil into them the basics skill and knowledge needed in order to stay alive, like discarding your scabbard before a battle, thus eliminating the outside chance that it could snag on any likely obstacle or else trip a man up at a vital moment in combat.

I explained that is never wise to pass a wounded man on the ground, no matter how badly injured he may be, for even a wounded (or a one armed man could kill you as you pass by) this brought a smile or two from the men as their heads all turned towards Wilfred one arm.)

I informed them to keep their hair and their beards short for many a warrior's hair or his beard had been the cause of his death when his hair or his beard had blown into his eyes at a vital moment during a battle.

Many of the village boys came to watch us as I taught my small army the ways of war.

Some boys came and watched for a few minutes before they got bored and wandered off, whilst others stayed for perhaps a couple of hours, but there was one boy who was perhaps eleven or twelve years of age who arrived on time, each and every morning when we appeared, and he remained until I called a halt when the light began to fade in the late afternoon.

This boy was not particularly big, but he was sturdily built and stood straight.

His shoulders did appear to be a little wider than most boys of his age and his red hair stood out wild and unkempt like a large banner on his head.

'Aha,' I thought to myself. 'He is obviously of Albian blood,'

He carried a stout quarter-staff, which I noticed was invariably with him or along-side him wherever he sat and he used it with vigour as he rehearsed all the moves that I taught my spearmen.

I called 'Wilfred one-arm' over to me.

'Who is the boy? The one with the red hair?' as I nodded towards the boy.

'Oh that is young Cnut' he said. 'He is the son of old Aelbert who was killed in Wales.'

I nodded and ambled slowly over towards the youngster.

I stood beside him and asked. 'How often do you come to watch us practice?'

'Every-day.' He answered in a serious voice.

'Are you any good with that quarter-staff of yours?' I asked?'

'I am very good.' He replied in a voice that had not yet lost its childhood squeakiness, but in a tone that was full of the confidence that a man usually finds in men who have already proved their worth in battle and not in a voice that one would expect to find in an untried ten or twelve year old youth.

'But it's not a quarterstaff.' He said. 'It's a spear, but I haven't got a head for it yet.'

I looked down at him and smiled, but as he looked back towards me, I could see no sign of humour in his face, only a grim look of utter seriousness.

'I'll tell you what.' I said with a smile. 'I will have one of my men fix a spearhead onto the shaft, if you can beat one of them in single combat with that stick of yours.'

I knew full well that he would jump at the challenge, but before he could answer me. I added. 'Which man would you like to challenge?'

'He looked up at me and said. 'All of them.'

'Yes I understand that, but which of them would you like to fight first?'

He strode a couple of paces away from me.

He halted and turned to stare directly into my face.

His own face began to redden and match his fiery hair. 'All of them at the same time.' He said.

Now that sent my mind whirling, for if I allowed him to join combat with them all at the same time, then he would surely be knocked senseless or even killed within a few minutes, and yet, if by some miracle his luck held and he was good enough even to injure one or two of them, then with his big ego, he would be likely to harm one of the more promising of my men, even the gigantic Hugo, which would damage the confidence not only out of Hugo himself, but would also dishearten the rest of them.

'I think you are being a little optimistic to say the least. 'I said to him, 'but if you insist on being so rash, I will keep 'Hugo' and 'Wilfred one arm' in reserve, just in case that by some miracle you manage to beat the others.'

'Off you go.' I said in a voice loud enough to be heard by all, and the cocky little child swaggered away from me and stood in the centre of the training ground holding his quarter-staff in readiness in front of him.

'Right lads,' I said to the men.

'Only use the flat of your swords and the butt end of your spears and give this big headed idiot a couple of blows, just enough to hurt him, but try not to damage the silly young fool too much, as I have taken a bit of a liking to the arrogant little sod,

The four men strode wearily towards the boy and spread out around him.

Ubba was the swordsman who was proving to be reasonably good with his sword, whilst Leofric, Frithoft and Sigard swaggered forward, carrying their iron spears and shields.

Although, I was to recall later, that at the precise moment of his attack, I was not quite sure whether I momentarily moved my head or blinked, but within the twinkle of an eye Leofric and Sigard were flat on their backs, either dead or unconscious, whilst Ubba backed away in horror from this child who crouched as he stalked towards him with his quarter-staff in the same position that I had seen him in before I had blinked.

I still find it difficult to understand exactly what happened next, as I have never seen any living thing move so fast, except perhaps a feral cat, that I had once seen catching a bird in mid-air when I was a boy, and that was so long ago that I had quite forgotten about it until this very moment in time.

The memory of that incident was brought back out of the depths of my mind when this boy appeared to dance in the air and bring his quarter-staff down on the unprotected head of Ubba whilst at the same moment as he landed on his two feet, he swung the staff around catching Frithoft on the side of his head and sending him into a heap alongside his three equally unconscious friends.

Cnut gazed towards me with a glance that I can only describe as being 'Arrogant,' with his left hand he casually reached up and brushed a long wisp of his greasy red hair out of his eyes, before he swaggered slowly back towards me.

'Wow,' he said in his squeaky voice. 'I really enjoyed that.'

'Can I have a go with 'Hugo' and one armed Wilfred?'

'I'm pleased that you have had so much fun,' I said, as I was still in some awe at what I had just witnessed, 'but I think you have done enough damage to my men for the time being.

'Now,' I said. 'You will expect me to honour my word by providing you with a spear-head to fix onto that quarter-staff of yours.' I added sarcastically.

'Thor alone knows what havoc you will cause then.' And shook my head in genuine despair as I really was not sure what I should do with this infant warrior.

Yet again, he broke my chain of thoughts by saying. 'Thor. Now that's who I want to be like. I shall slay any man who attempts to oppose me and I shall soon exchange this puny spear for a hammer and be like the Mighty 'Thor', Himself.'

I placed my arm around his shoulders and slowly guided him towards the manor- house, where I thought would be safest place for this dangerous young man.

If. I reasoned. I were to allow him to sleep in the hut with the other men, then his arrogance could cause a situation that could easily lead to him to end up with a knife in his ribs whilst he slept, whilst on the other hand, if I allowed him to live with and mingle with the other men, their lack of enthusiasm could undermine his confidence and I could lose a promising young warrior.

The boys, Edward and Bernard preceded us before we reached the front door and waited in the hallway for Cnut and my-self.

'We were watching you on the rehearsal field.' Bernard said quietly.

'And to say the least, both my brother and I were impressed with your performance,' added Edward.

'Indeed we were,' said Bernard, adding, 'especially so for a ten year old boy.'

'Eleven.' Cnut growled under his breath.

Yet again, I was struck by the grown-up tone and manner of this angelic looking red haired boy, as well as his demeanour, whatever age he was.

CHAPTER FIVE

Richard was born on a bright September morning at Beaumont Palace in Oxfordshire, which one of the most prosperous shires in England.

He was the third son of the young King Henry of England and his mother Matilda of Saxony.

It had been a difficult birthing for Matilda and had caused the midwives much concern before the screaming child was finally birthed.

The four midwives plied their trade with silence and efficiency.

There were many other people in the birthing chamber, for it has long been decreed that when a queen is on her birthing bed, there must be many credible witnesses present in order to guarantee that the succession to the Kingdom is correct

There were gasps of awe and surprise as the senior midwife handed the newly-born child to his mother, for none of those present had seen such a large child born before.

Over the next few years the gigantic child developed into a daring four year old who rode a full sized horse with the skill and dexterity of a Knight of the realm.

His tutors were amazed that by the age of six he was fluent in the languages of the people of France, Normandie and 'Limousine.'

He composed poems in the language of Limousine and although it is thought that during the first eight years of his life he learned the language of the English, not through his tutors but from his servants and lackeys.

He deemed the English language the tongue of peasants and nithings, and as such, he deigned it unworthy to use.

His Tutors schooled him in the manners of Norman/French society.

His Father recruited a special blacksmith, who was employed simply to make him a new suit of armour each and every year, in order to protect his huge body that seemed to grow twice as fast as the other youths of similar ages.

Specialists taught him the way of the Sword, and of the mace and the lance.

He was instructed in the intricate ways of the joust, so that before he had reached the age of sixteen, he had unhorsed most of his father's knights, sending two men to their graves and countless other untried youths home to their Fathers Chateau's with broken limbs and wounds, which would prevent them from riding at the tourneys for many months to come.

His Father became aware of the situation only when one of his close 'Equerry's' complained that Prince Richard had Injured the 'Equerries' own son and many other boys, so much so that Prince Richards Father feared that his son would ruin the cream of his up and coming Knights to such an extent that it could impair his ability to wage war and fight off the many Barons who envied him his lands and titles.

CHAPTER SIX

Cnut's Father 'Aelbert' had never wanted a daughter and he had treated 'Brungilda' with scorn and contempt from the moment she was born.

He had forbidden any of the village midwives to attend her birthing, and had personally helped with her birth. Biting through her umbilical cord as at the same time as he was cursing her for being a girl.

It was her Father who had announced that his wife had given birth to 'a healthy boy,' to the few friends who had gathered outside the cottage door.

'We shall name him Cnut' he said proudly.

'He will be named after our long dead ancestor 'King Cnut' who ruled England many years ago.'

They had all heard him boast of his supposed link to the Danish King many times in the past and although most people doubted the lineage, there were one or two of his special friends who believed him and nodded in agreement.

'Brungilda' had lived as a boy with the name of 'Cnut' for all of her childhood years.

She had played with the village boys. She had hunted with them and from an early age. She had out-ran them and out matched nearly all of them in their wrestling bouts as well as all of the childish and youthful war-games that village boys needed to do in order to build up the skills and muscles needed for those turbulent times.

Years of strenuous exercise and training had honed 'Brungilda's thin body into rather immature and yet tough muscular body that had become the envy of many of the boys, causing most of them to find friendships with other youngsters, leaving 'Cnut' isolated and disliked.

'Cnut' had learned never to disrobe to swim, or to wash in the heat of the summer. He swam fully clothed under the pretext of 'washing my clothes as well as my body at the same time,' he shouted, as he splashed in the stream that bordered their village and he never allowed anyone near enough to see the parts of the body that would reveal his secret.

'Cnut' had watched this new 'Sergeant at arms' with avid interest, as the man assembled and drilled the few men left in the castle after his Lordship's disastrous raid into Wales.

As 'Cnut' followed the men's manoeuvres on the side-lines, he completed their moves and actions with ease, so much so, that his whole body surged with energy and urgency that was completely alien to him.

'Cnut's mind flew back to those early years of his life. He hated his Father who eventually told him that 'Cnut's Mother had not survived his birth.

In later years Cnut was told that she had died from the lack of basic knowledge, which one of the many Village midwives would have experience and could have prevented her death, if they had been allowed to attend the birth.

'Aelbert' had given the tiny child, and she spent her first two years in the arms of a grubby wet-nurse, who had been bribed into secrecy.

'Cnut' was shaken out of his thoughts by the stern voice of the new Sergeant at arms.

'Follow me.' I said to 'Cnut' and he followed me to the Manor house and through the door to the room where the Lady Ella spent most afternoons working on her tapestries.

We were ushered into her room and found her sitting close to a roaring fire (despite the summer heat) working on a huge, half completed tapestry.

She looked up and dropped her needle onto her lap, gazing in amazement at us, as if she had not seen either one of us before, which was of course not the case, for I had been a regular visitor to her dining table and I felt sure that she must have seen young Cnut on many an occasion, as I had often seen her standing at her window and looking down upon myself and the other men practicing in the training field..

I was rather surprised with the reactions from both her ladyship and Cnut for whilst 'Her Ladyship' seemed to be totally enamoured by the red haired little boy who had entered her work-room. Cnut shrank back into me with a fear that I thought he had not possessed, and indeed he should not have possessed, for Lady Ella's face was full of a love that she had thought had deserted her since the death of her husband.

She bent forward and ruffled his unruly red hair and gently stroked his cheek, cooing and clucking like a broody hen.

   'Cnut's body was shaking as he cowered to such an extent that he was forced to retreat behind me seeking the protection of my own unwashed body.

   'Come now my beautiful boy,' she said as she kissed him gently behind his ear, nestling her face against his grubby, sweaty neck.

   'Oh my Good Lord,' she clucked. 'The poor child is frightened of me.'

   'Why so young man?' she cooed. 'I won't hurt you.' She straightened her back and walked a few paces towards a table where I could see a dainty plate, and a pile of fancy cakes.

   She took two of the cakes and walked back towards him, holding the cakes a few inches from his face.

   'Here, my lovely boy.' She said softly, smiling a smile that suddenly filled me with jealousy, as the thought of my own lovely wife, the beautiful 'Godda,' flooded back into my mind.

   'Godda' had also been a lady who had possessed the skill to bake similar delicacies, causing my own mouth to fill with saliva and remind me of my quest to find the wife who had deserted me, these long years past.

   It was a quest that I had sworn to carry out, and yet here I was in the company of people I did not know and in truth, and in fact many of whom I actually disliked and I had all but forgotten my oath since I had moved into 'Wolf Hall' where every waking hour of every day had been taken up with the training of my small band of no-hopers.

I silently swore to myself that as soon as I had trained these men to a point where I felt they could hold their own against a similar or even a larger number of opponents in battle, I would leave 'Wolf Hall' and resume my quest to find 'Godda.'

I pushed them hard over the next twelve months.

I led them on gruelling marches carrying shields and weapons, insisting on a full hour of weapon training without food or water before leading them back to the fort by a different and more difficult route.

Eleven year old 'Cnut' turned to be the finest man with any weapon the youngster could lay hands on, except for the long-bow, but he was also the most obedient member of the group, who was willing and able to learn and absorb all of the new tactics and moves that I attempted to teach them.

'Cnut's inability to use the 'Long Bow' was no surprise to me, for to become a successful archer usually meant that a man needed to be trained from childhood. Commencing his training as early as four, so that by the time he reached age of thirteen, and deemed ready to join a company of archers, he would have developed arm muscles and shoulders that would be half as big again as a normal boy of that age, who would then be able to launch ten arrows into the air in the space of a minute, from arms and fingers that would be as hard as blacksmith made steel.

CHAPTER SEVEN

I vividly remembered that final day at Wolf Hall; as I lolled against the steering board in this this creaking old cargo ship in the hot sun.

I remember walking across the cold and wet courtyard towards the Manor house.

It had rained hard for most of the hours of darkness causing me to soak my newly acquired goatskin boots as I walked through the large puddles towards the door.

Lady Ella had summonsed me just as I was about to lead my small army out into the forest of Dean on a training exercise and I was not best pleased to leave my men idling the morning away, sheltering from a spot of rain.

'Ah there you are Edric,' she had said with what I recognised as one of her forced smiles.

I had seen that very same smile before, which looked something akin to a lady being introduced to a total stranger, causing me to guess that something was amiss, especially so, when she invited me to sit and partake of a glass of red wine, that she usually kept in a locked cupboard and was used rarely, except on very special occasions.

She was a pretty enough woman. Indeed many men would think her to be beautiful, but I think that life itself, or perhaps it had been the death of her husband, had twisted her, and somewhere deep inside her, his death had left her warped, bitter and manipulative.

She had long abandoned her habit of inviting 'Cnut' into the manor house, abandoning him as a child would discard a rag doll.

  She rarely spoke of him.

  She emptied her glass and as if she was clearing her throat she said.

'My son and I have been talking,' as she nodded towards Bernard who was seated by the window, 'as you are well aware, both Bernard and I are both committed Christians.'

  She paused for a moment before she continued. 'We have decided to answer the King Richard's call to gather warriors and send them on a crusade to free Jerusalem from the non-believers.'

 'We have been asked to send our finest warriors to support his summons.'

 'My son Edward will lead you, but he will need the support and advice of a proven warrior to act as his second in command and I can think of no man better qualified than you, my dear Edric who could be that man.'

 I was rather stunned by this sudden turn of events and as my mind told me that this move could simply be a ploy to expel her adopted son 'Edward' from her domain, in order that her natural son 'Bernard' would be free to inherit the castle and estate without any objection from 'Edward.'

  She continued. 'Oh I shall allow 'Hugo' to accompany you. He is as strong as an Ox and will be as good as six men in a battle, should you need him.'

 'You can also take 'Ubber' the 'Mercian.'

'Take the twins 'Frithoft' and 'Sigard.'
My heart sank a little as she uttered the names of the gigantic twins, who were, in my opinion nothing more than a couple of layabouts who went through the motions of doing what they were told to do, but seemed to excel at nothing.

'Sigard' could use a long-bow reasonably well, whilst his brother was little more than a bully.

They are both good men.' She said. 'They are as big as oxen and they should be good if you get into a fight.

'I will have to keep my eyes on those two,' were my immediate thoughts.

Lady Ella continued.

You can also have young 'Cnut,' who my son tells me is something of a born warrior.'

'He has consistently beaten everyone who has challenged him, except you of course.'

Her statement thwarted my own effort to interrupt her and I was just about to question if it would be wise to send me on such a mission, as I had been brought up in the old religion of 'Thor,' 'Woden' and 'Freya' and had little knowledge of the new religion of 'Christianity' that was sweeping through Europe.

'How could I, who am a believer in the old Gods, lead men on a Christian crusade?' I asked my-self?

'Lady Ella's mention of 'Cnut' caused my mind to jump from religion to the question of 'Cnut,' who, with his obvious talent for weapons, had caused me to have visions of greatness in the boy, who I considered to be a potential slayer of men with the possibility of rising to be a leader of men, or even a 'King.'

My mind flew to the old Norse God of Hell.' Loki,' whose image appeared in my tiny brain and laughed aloud at my silly meanderings.

Oh I was aware that our new 'King.' 'Richard.'

He, who was being called 'Coeur-de-Leon,' had left England some months ago with an army, in order to conquer the holy-land and to take back Jerusalem from the Saracens on what I think was probably the third crusade that had left Europe in the past ten years.

Looking back now, I can see that I had missed my opportunity to say 'NO' to the Lady and had fallen neatly into her trap.

I had been caught off guard by this scheming, beautiful woman, like a lovesick child and was left speechless as she smiled at me, before she reached onto the small table that was beside her divan, bringing the imported and refilled Roman glass of red wine to her lips, which she sipped daintily and gazed beguilingly up at me. over the rim of the glass, looking at me with those startling blue eyes and her famous smile that reminded me of a wolf looking up at me through the bloodied ribs of a recent kill.

At that particular time I had no knowledge whatsoever of a second meeting that she held that evening, when she had spoken to no less than three potential assassins, promising them satchels of silver shillings providing that none other than themselves returned to their homeland hale and hearty.

CHAPTER EIGHT

The Battle for the control of the Castle and township of Taillebourg would be a difficult thing to achieve for any veteran of warfare and siege tactics, but without the training and aggression shown by the sixteen year 'Prince Richard of Normandie.' it would have been an impossible undertaking.

His Knights and his warriors had reluctantly followed 'Prince Richard' into this particular battle, despite the fact that very few of them held any hope of success in the taking of this stout Citadel.

'Poitou' was the centre of a rich district in the Duchy of Aquitaine.

The Castle itself was perched upon a high rocky outcrop and surrounded on three sides by towering cliffs, as well as being encircled by a strong wall.

The village of Taillebourg stood out-side the walls of the citadel, and consisted of a small cluster of cottages, workshops and houses, that were encircled by another thick and high outer wall, which consisted of three separate layers of stone.

The approach to the village was a narrow twisting roadway which came to an abrupt end when it met the single massive gate, which barred the way into the town.

'It does look like a difficult nut to crack my Lord.' A Knight uttered.

'Indeed it does, answered the Prince.'

'That is probably why my Father chose his third son and not his heir to take this assignment.' Prince Richard added.

'Nay, my Lord.' The Knight answered. 'He chose you because you are the best.'

'You had better not let my Father hear you say that, or he will have your guts for garters.'

'I see no place flat enough for us to place our Trebuchet.' He added.

'Then we shall have to make one, will we not?' Prince Richard said drily.

'Make camp in these meadows, only after the men have raised a protective marching camp in readiness for any attack that the enemy may attempt during the night.

'I know my Knights and men-at-arms think of me as an untried youth,' he thought to himself, 'but few, if any of them have had the training and lessons in warfare and tactics I have had over the last ten years.'

I well remember the hours upon hours when my tutor 'Alain of Gascoyne' laboured over the manoeuvres and tactics of the Roman legions, and especially the necessity of construction a marching camps when the legions were on the march or engaged in siege warfare.'

He walked outside his own tent that had been erected in the centre of the camp and walked a few paces to the ditch. He nodded with satisfaction as he noted that the sods of turf were being carried by masses of sweating men, who would throw them on the soil, in readiness for other men, who would pick them up and lay them in double thickness in readiness for the thousands of stakes which, in turn would be driven into them, in order to erect a barrier that would be impassable to attackers, other than a large and determined battalion of assailants.

He retired to his tent and with a contented groan he lay on his ready-made cot.

He had steeled himself against the noise from the camp and dropped off into blissful sleep.

By noon on the following day his engineers had levelled a long piece of uneven ground to allow his Trebuchet's and Mangonel's to be placed.

After consulting with the Sergeant in charge of the four siege machines, he ordered them to be placed within the limit of their range, which would allow them to reach the village itself and the wall.

There were three main reasons for these orders.

(One.) He wanted to demonstrate to the Knights on the battlements the destruction that his siege engines could cause by demolishing the outer wall and the village.

(Two) By destroying the outer wall, his army would have a ready-made entrance into the enemy's defences, as well as an area where he could station his siege engines?

And. (Three.) His Father had stressed to him that he would prefer to take the Castle of Taillebourg intact.

He tried to recall his Father's exact words and remembered him stressing that the Castle was too good to be destroyed, and it would make an ideal base for one of his sons to use, in order to control the entire northern sector of Aquitaine.

Thus, Richard thought that the destruction of the village and the outer wall would dishearten the defenders to such an extent that they may sue for terms.

The village ceased to exist after three days and three nights of bombardment.

'Prince Richard' gave the order for two of his machines to be dismantled and to be taken up the narrow causeway towards the flattish area that had once been the village.

Of course he knew that many of the missiles that had been hurled at the village and the outer wall, had missed their targets, but his tutors had stressed time and time again that the psychological effects of the sound of the huge rocks hurtling through the air and crashing literally anywhere all day and all night, would keep the defenders awake and unsettle them for the coming fray which they all knew was about to happen.

The Prince assembled squads numbering hundreds of men to widen and straighten the trackway that led up to the outer wall.

The men laboured throughout the night, hacking away with hammers and chisels and hurling the rubble into dips and holes in the old trackway, in order that the siege engines would be able to reach their destination by daybreak.

By dawn, after a task which many of Prince Richards Knights had considered to be impossible, the Mangonel and the Trebuchet were in their positions on a small portion of level ground, a mere one hundred paces away from the inner Castle walls.

'Prince Richard' was amazed that the Castle itself did not possess any anti-siege equipment, but after a short meeting with some of the older of his Knights, he was assured that this was not an unusual occurrence, for, they assured him that in some circumstances such as this, the defenders deemed their Castles to be so impregnable or had been built on such unassailable crags or escarpments that the need of such things were totally unnecessary.

He asked himself during the night what he would do if he were the custodian of such a castle, if he had found himself in a similar position.

He had immediately answered his own question.

'I would sally forth and destroy my enemies' siege engines.' He had muttered.

The moment he had been wakened by his esquire, he had ordered his Senior Knights to attend him.

He was in the middle of devouring his second pork sausage when the three Knights arrived.

'Assemble half of our army and have them make ready for battle and to follow me.'

'I shall be hidden just fifty paces behind our siege engines, behind that bend which caused us so much trouble yesterday evening.

I shall be ready to repel the Knights who I anticipate will sally forth out of yonder gate and attempt to destroy my siege engines.'

'I shall lead fifty Knights, and we will hold our ground until you can relieve us, and then ,with the help of god, we will defeat those rebellious Knights and follow them into their stronghold and drive them before us, back into the guts of Taillebourg.'

'Sir Albi,' he said. 'I would like you to select fifty young Knights who have not yet seen battle and who are the second or third sons of better known Lords, as they usually tend to be fearless and eager to earn praise from their Prince.'

'If they live long enough,' muttered a gnarled Knights

'Prince Richard' said naught, but he knew exactly what the man had said to be true.

The siege engines only had time enough to load and hurl a single missile before the huge iron bolted gate of Taillebourg was flung open, allowing a phalanx of mailed Knights and men to erupt out of the fortress.

'Prince Richard' allowed them to reach the siege machines and engage in battle with the defenders, who he had placed around the machines, before he led his fifty men around the loop of the newly made road and into the attackers.

His men were outnumbered by the attackers by three to one, slaying and overcoming a few of the attackers. The remaining attackers seemed to lose heart, causing their foray to stall, and as he had anticipated. The Prince continued the battle as they retreated back to and through the still open gate.

Reinforced by the warriors who he had held back, hidden from the defenders. They followed their Prince into the Fortress, whence they spread out along the walls and into the citadel itself forcing the Lord of the keep to emerge and bend his knee to 'Prince Richard.'

CHAPTER NINE

The past seven weeks of constant travel blurred into nothingness.

But that vital meeting with Lady 'Ella' was still vividly implanted in my mind as I stared wistfully into the azure blue of the Mediterranean Sea.

As I gazed into the wake of the ship, I thought of the first time that I had met Godda.

She had been dancing in a circle surrounded by her sisters as the white petals of May blossom drifted downwards from the Heavens to settle onto her shoulders and her white blonde hair.

She seemed to have floated over towards me and had uttered my name.

'Edric.' She had said, in that husky voice of hers.

'You have come at last.' She had whispered in my ear.

A hand on my shoulder shook me out of my dream, causing me to shake my head and I found myself staring into the weathered face of the Captain.

'Forgive me from waking you my Lord,' he said, 'but you were tottering and I feared you were about to fall overboard.'

I stared at the far horizon and the blurred shoreline that was probably a mile away, seeing pretty well the same scenery I had seen on countless days aboard the ship, which was one of twenty-seven other ships transporting food, as well as dozens of crates containing Pigs. Sheep. Goats and Chickens

The ship was also crowded with Men who had been recruited to swell the Kings army, who lazed against the side of the ship, totally bored at staring at the sea and the faces of their comrades who stared back with the glazed eyes of bored men.

Stacked in the hold and in any other nook and cranny were weapons and round barrels full of arrows.

Many of the round barrels contained so many bundles of arrows and arrow-heads that at the beginning of the voyage I had been afraid that they had been stacked too high and would cause the ship to capsize and drown the lot of us.

Thank goodness that had not happened, for the weather had been kind to us and we had not yet lost a single ship out of our small fleet.

*   *   *

I looked across the crowded ship and up into the billowing sails that sped us on our way, and then looked down into the bowels of the ship where I could see the ungainly figure of Hugo, who was fast asleep on top of some sacks, and then I gazed towards young 'Cnut' who way sitting close to 'Ubba.'

They were both staring, silently towards the prow of the ship where 'Edward' stood, staring into the misty blue horizon.

The large frames of the twins 'Frithoft' and 'Sigard' were sitting together with their heads bent low in deep mumbled conversation, discussing something so important, which they wished to keep to themselves.

I was also staring into the azure of the sea and shook myself to force the beautiful face of my lovely wife Godda out of my mind, for it seemed to me that each and every day my mind wandered again and again into the lost love of my life.

'Cnut' caught my gaze and rose to walk over to me.

'Lord Edric,' He said, which was the first time that I had been addressed as such for more than three years, causing me to believe that he and the other men had been talking about me in my absence.

As he sat beside me, I ruffled his shock of red hair, pleased to have the company of someone to talk to. Even a child like this.

I was rather shocked again as he continued in a very adult way, especially so for a eleven year old youth.

'Lord Edric,' he repeated.

'They tell me that you have been in this warm sea before? And may I ask you that on that particular occasion were you attacked by Pirates?'

'If that was so?' He did not wait for me to answer but continued.

'Do you think there is any chance that we could be attacked again?'

I did feel like relaying on to him my past experiences, neither did I wish to frighten him or any of the other crewmen who were within hearing distance, so I took a long time in answering his question and when I finally spoke, I asked him. 'Would you like us to be attacked?'

'Oh Yes I would.' He answered quickly and I could almost see his enthusiasm racing through his body and leaping out of his mouth as he uttered the words.

As I had known the boy for over a year, I knew full well of his eagerness to fight and to kill a man.

Indeed, his eagerness to fight and to kill, was very unusual, especially in such a young boy.

Each and every man I have known over the past 50 years, including my-self, had no such feelings. We are all very reluctant and fearful before we go into battle.

Most men touch the Crosses or Hammers that hang around their necks and pray to their God, be him the 'Christ God' or 'Odin' and plead for protection.

Any Battle, especially the dreaded 'Shield-Wall' is a fearful place.

It is full of blood and the screams of battle from men killing or being killed.

It is a place of blood and guts that can cause a warrior to trip and if a man trips or stumbles whilst he is in a 'Shield-Wall' then his next vision would be in the afterlife.

If that man is a Christian then he will be escorted into Heaven with Angels singing soft songs of joy, but if he is what the Christians call 'A Heathen,' a man who believes in the old Saxon Gods and dies with a weapon in his hand, then he will be transported to 'Valhalla' by the Valrykes, who are beautiful rose lipped maidens, where he will spend eternity singing bawdy songs and drinking ale with his friends and the warriors who have preceded him.

The fleet spent the winter in a sheltered bay near the port of 'Salerno' on the island of 'Sicily,' where we few men from 'Wolf Hall' met and dwelt in squalor with an army of men from every corner of Northern and central Europe.

It was in 'Salerno' that we lost Edward.

He had left the camp one evening with half a dozen other men, to walk into the grubby town that had grown from a sleepy fishing village into a rowdy town, brimming with drinking dens and brothels, which now seethed with drunken sailors and warriors from the fleet, as well as women of all shapes and sizes who had made their way from all over the island, willing to do pretty well anything to please the men in order to earn a single copper coin.

I questioned the men who had accompanied 'Edward' into the township, learning that when they had arrived in the town, 'Edward' had mumbled something about going to one of the bars and had wandered off alone.

None of the men could remember the name of the bar, despite the fact that even as I questioned them, I realised that they had probably all been drunk last night and no amount of threats managed to clear their still befuddled minds into telling me more. Never-the-less, I gathered every single man who had left with him and ordered them to follow me back into the town, where we forced our way into locked rooms and empty bar-rooms, turning over drunken men who lay where they had fallen the previous night, in an attempt to find our missing friend.

We searched the town again on the following day and scoured the surrounding hillsides and dry river beds on the third day, to no avail.

'There are a number of things that could have happened to him.' I said, as 'Cnut' and I sat in front of a fire, where we waited for a goat to cook on a grill. 'There is always the chance that he is alive and well, and has fallen for one of the women in the town and simply does not want to be found.'

'Oh I think someone had slit his throat and buried him somewhere in one of the gullies up there.' Answered 'Cnut,' which was a typical response from the youngster, as I could-not think of a time when he had said something funny or positive, and seemed to be a boy whose mind seemed to dwell on death and the killing of men.

I decided to remain in port for one last day before I gave up the search and walked casually into the town.

I walked slowly up and down the few streets and into the shanty town that had sprung up on its outskirts.

I had halted and was about to give up my search when I noticed a grubby man lounging in a doorway and I could see that his head was nodding downwards onto his chest, but as his eyes opened and he saw me. He suddenly shook him-self awake and disappeared into his doorway.

I distinctly heard him lock and bolt his door.

I thought this rather strange and hurried to his door.

I thumped the door with the hilt of my Saex.

I waited and thumped again, much louder and for a far longer time.

I shouted and kicked the door and was met with an eerie silence.

I stepped back a pace and ran forward, hitting the door with my shoulder and making no impression other than to hurt my shoulder.

I ran around to the rear of the house and immediately kicked the door in, which shocked me a little, as I had fully expected the rear door to be made of the same sturdy wood as the front, but after a second effort, the door was off its leather hinges and hanging inward at a wry angle.

I was about to sidle past the damaged door when I noticed a flash from the darkness within the room and hastily moved to one side. My move was not a split second too soon; as a heavy war spear literally tore through the sleeve of my jerkin and sped onwards to embed itself in the ground some fifteen feet away.

I carried no shield and it may be deemed stupid, or maybe brave, but non-the-less, like an idiot, I dashed into the darkened room, fully expecting to find two or three ruffians waiting for me with drawn swords, but to my amazement and also to my great relief. (I immediately whispered my thanks to Odin and to the Christ God,) when I saw a middle-aged man and a grubby woman standing at the far wall of the room.

The man carried a battered old shield which was emblazoned with the arms of the old King of Cyprus, whilst the woman carried a year old infant wrapped up in a dirty blanket.

I walked carefully towards them, half expecting a hidden opponent to be hiding behind a half-hidden curtain, covering what looked like a hidden room.

The couple cowered and moved to their left in order to allow me with my gleaming Saex to have access to the drape, which I swept to the floor with my Saex and jumped to one side in order to deny any assassin access.

I carefully put my head around the doorway and just as speedily snatched it back and I uttered a loud sigh of relief, as I could not see an assassin or a group of armed men.

But I did see that the bundle of rags which was lying, trussed up like a goat ready for market.

I moved over to the bundle and heaved it to a sitting position, revealing the battered and bruised figure of Edward.

I glanced over to his two captors, and motioned with my Saex. 'Untie Him.'

'Be quick about it and don't make any funny moves or my Saex 'Bloodeater' will rip your heart out.

I had always resisted the usual practice of warriors to name their weapons and had not ever even thought of a name for the silver embossed Saex, which my Lovely wife Godda had given me in happier times.

As Edward was too weak to walk, I personally carried him back through the town and down to the ship.

The ship's crew clapped and shouted their approval as we boarded the ship and fussed over the still weakened Edward who I lay in the tiny cabin that usually served as the Captains quarters.

CHAPTER TEN

An unusually early and warm spring tide brought King Richard and the rest of his fleet to Salerno.
 The King held a meeting immediately after his arrival, ordering his Knights to glean as much food and other essential provisions from the township and from the surrounding countryside in order to sail for Cyprus in seven days- time.
   I had been put in charge of a small foraging party.
 During our first day out, we searched a number of farmsteads but found that all of them had been emptied by previous search parties.
 I led my men down a green valley towards a particularly wealthy looking farmstead that was five or six miles out of the town.
 I learned from one of the Geonese crossbowmen who were accompanying us that King Richard was furious with a man called 'Isaac Commenus' of Limassol, who had slain the crews of three of his English ships, which had been driven onto the shores of Cyprus during the last storm of the winter.
 This knowledgeable archer also told me that this 'Isaac Commenus' who called himself the 'King of Cyprus' had also captured the sister of King Richard as well as his bride-to-be, 'Berengaria.'
 'Berengaria' was the daughter of the King of Navvare, and her abduction caused King Richard to swear that he would teach the man a lesson'
 'Not only will I teach the man a lesson,' the King swore, but I will conquer the Island and bring all the

warriors in Cyprus with me to the Holy Land to fight for our cause.

The thoughts that had entered my head disappeared when we neared the farm-house where I could see a small crowd of men waiting for us.

I halted my men in front of the farm where we were confronted by a large prosperous looking individual, who wore a silver torque and a number of silver arm rings.

He seemed to have brought his entire work-force with him and they stood behind him, armed with knives, sickles and pitch-forks.

The man drew a curved sword from its sheath and snarled 'What do you band of ragamuffins want here?' as he pointed his sword towards me.

'We have been commanded to take provisions for our army from you. Willingly I hope, but if it is to be by force, then so be it.' I snarled back to the man, for I had taken an instant dislike to the fellow and I too was quite eager to see whether or not young 'Cnut' would live up to the swaggering bravado which had begun to annoy me as well as the rest of my men, especially those of us who had experienced warfare.

The prosperous looking man appeared to mellow a little and his hereto aggressive voice and stance changed to one of subservience.

'I have little or nothing to give, except an old mare who is past her best and a few bags of oats.'

'Other than that,' the man moaned in a subservient voice,' we are near starvation our-selves.'

'Oh we need a lot more than that.' I said manfully.

I could see he was about to argue and was rather surprised when he lifted his curved sword a little, but then he hesitated.

I had seen the man's eyes move from the large form of Hugo to the diminutive body of 'Cnut,' who stood apart from the rest of the men. Cnut was standing with his legs akimbo and the heavy metal hammer that the Blacksmith at 'Wolf Hall' had fashioned for him.

I could see the boy's annoyance of having to listen to all this talk, whilst his one and only thought was the hope of exercising his skill with this new weapon of his, which he practiced with for at least four hours each day since he had had the damned thing, appeared to be slipping away from him with all this silly talk, causing him to seethe with annoyance that he not yet been allowed to kill a single man.

The landowner's eyes stayed on the small figure of Cnut for a mere second or so, and he could see the sadistic evil that was oozing out of the boy's narrowed eyes, telling the landowner that to fight the giant as well as this evil looking red-haired boy would be nothing short of a stupidity.

Of course, he assured himself, he would certainly not be in the fore in any fight that occurred, but even then, there would be a good chance that he could be wounded or even killed.

I saw the landowner look again at the huge figure of Hugo who towered over the rest of my men and he shook his head in amazement, as he obviously thought to himself, how could he have been stupid enough to even consider resisting this bunch of savage looking foreigners?

He sheathed his scimitar and stood to one side, bowing his head to the inevitable.

We loaded a confiscated wagon with ten bags of barley which we had found hidden under some straw, and we drove twenty four sheep before us (being exactly half of the sheep we had found on the farm) and had left the furious red faced man hopping mad when we left his farmstead, loaded down with meat, bread and provisions, which had been 'willingly' given by the unhappy farmer.

The landowner had little choice other than to 'willingly' help us, as I had twenty, tough armed and hungry warriors in my command, whilst the landowner, who, by the look of him, would have been a hard and a cruel man to deal with in normal circumstances, but at this moment in time, he possessed a force of eleven workmen, (and half of them had iron slave collars around their necks,) plus three other men who were probably members of his family.

Thus I surmised that he had obviously mused the thought over in his mind, whether or not to resist us, and had reached the logical conclusion that firstly he might be injured or even slain, and even if he and his men did prevail, he would probably end up with at least half of his men maimed or slain,(and new slaves would be expensive to buy.)

When we arrived, the docks were a melee of noise and chaos, with sailors loading the waiting ships with crates and sacks full of fruit and foodstuff, sheep, pigs, chickens and ducks with their legs tied, who all seemed to be baa-ing, honking, clucking and honking at the same time.

These noises blended in with cursing, grumbling armed men who were hauling themselves up and onto the waiting ships, where it seemed to me they would be hard pressed to be able to find a space to stand, let alone sleep.

My men, myself, our sheep and our cartload of provisions were quickly and (much to my surprise) efficiently distributed amongst the waiting ships, so that within the space of the next hour, our own ship joined the rest of King Richards's fleet and set sail southwards.

I lost count of the number of monotonous days we spent at sea, but I think it was probably nine or ten.

Edward of Wolf-Hall had made a full recovery and swore he could man an oar to help with the rowing, but I persuaded him to rest and he joined me as we watched the other men take the strain on the oars.

We halted at the Grand harbour in Malta for a full day.

The harbour and its buildings were quite spectacular with stone towers and high walls, which surrounded the complete township.

The people seemed to be friendly, and crowded the ships and its long harbour walls with men, women and children selling everything from fruit, clothing, weapons, (including armour and shields) as well as slaves of every age and colour imaginable.

Two days later the fleet had an overnight stop in the beautiful Bay of Matala which was a large sheltered bay on the lush green island of Crete.

During the voyage we encountered hundreds of merchant ships plying their trade in this placid blue sea, and one misty morning we were approached by fifteen ships that flew no flags, and possessed the grim look of a pirate ships about them.

They were sleek and high in the water and brimming with armed warriors.

This small fleet came to within half a mile of our own fleet before they realised that they were heavily outnumbered in both ships and men, and sheered away rowing vigorously towards the eastern shore.

We were stiff and tired, hungry and thirsty when the large island of Cyprus appeared on the horizon, but our troubles were put behind us when we were ordered to make ready to land, causing hurried excitement, as we scrambled and pushed our way to where we had left our weapons and armour.

I found it difficult to untie the leather thongs that bound the large bundle which contained my own mail and helmet, due to the crush of other men who were struggling into their own chain mail, or other men who were in the act of finding and checking their weapons.

All of the ships had their oars out and were rowing as hard as they could in order to counteract the off-shore wind and ebbing tide that seemed to be doing its level best to prevent us from reaching the shoreline.

It was mid-afternoon when the prows of our ships finally drove into the sandy beach to the west of Limassol.

Ours was not the first ship whose prow crunched up onto the beach and as I leapt over the side of the ship I landed in the knee deep water, before I commenced to make my way onto the beach and up towards the bushes.

The undergrowth grew right up to ten paces from the sea-line.

I was forced to halt by a cursing crowd of armed warriors who were either waiting to enter, or were attempting to push their way through the tangle of undergrowth that hid the interior of the island from our view.

Suddenly, as if by some unseen signal, a cloud of arrows flew out of the bushes catching our men off guard, as many of the men were either standing on the small strip of beach between the ships, or the bushes, whilst other men were still in the ships or in the act of disembarking.

I instinctively shouted 'Shield-wall' and noted with satisfaction that nearly all our own men who were within my vision, ceased their forward rush and slung their shields to the fore, so that the residue of that first deadly flight of arrows ceased to strike my men down and thudded harmlessly into our shields.

I glanced to my left and to my right where I could see ships crews disembarking.

I watched men forming into tight knit groups of warriors with their shields to the fore, as they approached the bushes, which grew like a thick barrier in front of us

Our men formed into a wedge shaped formation which we had rehearsed time and time again before we continued our advance up towards the tree-line.

'Cnut' could be seen peeking out from behind Hugo's massive shield.

I entered the undergrowth at the head of my men and eventually halted in the centre of a cart-way that appeared to have been cut through the vegetation which ran adjacent to the coastline along the entire length of the beach.

We formed tightly knit groups of warriors in the cart-way, fully expecting to be attacked, but there was no sign of any opposing force, neither was there any sign of the bowmen who had showered us with arrows that had slain and wounded a number of warriors.

The small figure of 'Cnut' made his way through the crowd of warriors and stood beside me. He was followed by his erstwhile companion, Hugo.

'Our enemy is there.' Growled Hugo and he nodded towards the hills.

We followed his gaze to see a scattering of men making their way through the thinning trees, upwards and along the side of the hill towards where we assumed the township of Limassol would be.

I looked down at 'Cnut' and could see that he was still fuming with anger.

'What's the problem?' I asked.

'My Lord.' He said in his strange, high voice.

'We both know that was not a real battle and I have drawn Bretwalda.'

He waved a short Saex that he had named 'Bretwalda' aloft, 'and I swore I would not return her to her nest unless she tasted blood.' He said.

Without a further word he pressed the blade of his new sword across his left arm, drawing a long trail of blood, which he wiped on the leg of his breeches before he returned the cleaned sword to its sheath.

'So!' I thought to myself. 'After all the trouble I had, making that damned hammer for him. The silly young fool has swapped it for a Saex.'

I began to lead my men onwards, following the flow of men who had started to march in a westerly direction towards where we assumed the town would be.

I mumbled to myself at the sheer nerve of this untried boy, who yearned for battle and for blood, who had named his sword 'Bretwalda.'

Of course I knew that 'Bretwalda' was the name that the old tribes of Albia had given to the overall chief of all the tribes on our island of Britain.

I glanced behind me and was pleased to see that our ship's crewmen, including my few men from 'Wolf-Hall' were still behind me, and noted that the left arm of 'Cnut' had a strip of cloth wrapped around his self-inflicted cut.

I glanced at the Saex which he carried in a sheath.

I noted that his eyes never remained in one place for more than a few seconds.

I realised that he had seen the strange look I had given him, and he must have noted the questioning look that had probably crossed my face.

My thoughts had been correct and he answered my question before I could ask it.

He said in his gruff yet still unbroken voice. 'Hugo preferred my war-axe, so I swapped it with him and he gave me this Saex in return.'

I thought to myself that the war-Hammer would be of far more use in a battle if it was in the hands of the gigantic Hugo, rather than the slight figure of 'Cnut' who had never been in a real fight.

Now, I thought, providing 'Cnut' could fight within the shadow of his large friend, then he too might survive and be of some use to our cause.

Our army filtered through the large jumble of mud houses, which gave way to larger houses made of stone. We were eventually brought to a halt where thousands of our men had halted and standing and gazing at a medium sized fortress.

We could see the standard of 'King Richard' flying from the one and only tower.

A large number of noblemen eventually emerged out of the fortress and after speaking to their sergeants at arms, they began to arrange the army into more orderly formations.

My troop were assigned to areas of the township where we were ordered to lodge with the residents of the houses wherever possible, and although our small group did manage to crowd into a small cottage.

The vast majority of our army spent the night sleeping under the stars.
 Dawn found us sitting around the fire waiting for a large pot of oatmeal to boil.
We were joined by one of the King's servants who informed us that the Castle and the township had been left empty by 'Isaac of Limassol,' who upon the sight of our fleet, had speedily vacated both the castle and the township, and had fled with his troops to a fortified hilltop some six or seven miles away, where, even as the man spoke, the man informed us, King 'Isaac' and his men would be toiling through the night, digging ditches and repairing their long neglected fortress.

CHAPTER ELEVEN

 Each man was given a half filled bladder of water, which we were told should be used with great care as had to last us for at least four days.
 I slung what looked like my sheep's bladder filled with muddy looking water over my shoulder to join my shield, as well as my blanket and meagre belongings, before my men from Wolf-Hall and myself marched out of the township and along a cart-track that was to lead us to Isaac's fortress.
 It took the army over four hours of marching over some of the rockiest terrain that I had ever seen to reach our destination.

We had trudged through dry river beds and over scrubland that was splattered with rocks and boulders before we reached the Citadel.

The complete army had halted at a position that was just above the tree-line, about half way up a steep hill, where some of the leaders of each section were ordered to move to another part of the hill in order to surround the entire hillside.

The whole camp was roused at dawn by 'Sergeants-at-arms' shouting their orders, ordering us to assemble, fully armed with weapons and clothed in our chain-mail shirts and our helmets, which fewer than half the army seemed to possess.

My small contingent was assigned to a place in the front ranks by a Knight called 'Sir Guy of Blurignan,' although no one I spoke to, knew where or what 'Blurignan' was.

Sir Guy called his 'Sergeants-at-arms' forward and we gathered around him as he sat proudly on his shiny black stallion.

'We have been given the privilege of leading our army to take yonder fortress.' He shouted at the top of his voice, in the language of the Normans, which I understood and probably half of the other dozen or so Sergeants also understood, but it was a language that was totally alien to most of my men, as well as many of the other men who were within listening distance.

'I want two volunteers to come up the hill with me to inspect their puny castle, so that we can take the place without too many casualties.'

'You and you will do.' He pointed to me and to a burly looking veteran who stood a few paces away.

'Come.' He ordered and nimbly dismounted his steed.

'Have either of you two had any experience of scouting?' He asked

The other man shook his head and I said confidently 'Yes. I Have.'

His eyes bulged and his face changed to the colour of a red fox and he snarled. 'When you address me you address me as 'My Lord.' He snarled.

True, I had momentarily forgotten that I was merely another man in this army, and not the Lord I had once been, so I swallowed my pride and mumbled.

'Yes My Lord.' 'Please accept my apologies my Lord.'

He seemed to calm down a little and nodded and then grunted. 'Follow me.'

He led the way up the hill, through the sparse trees and bushes that eventually gave way to a variety of large and small rocks.

We could see the fortress high above us.

We followed Sir Guy a little way up the hill and crouched behind him as he halted behind a large boulder.

'It looks easy enough.' He said haughtily.

'All I can see a bit of a ditch with a few stakes in it and a rickety old wall.'

'The gate looks strong enough my Lord.' I said.

'And the two stone towers seem to be well built and they are bristling with defenders.' I added.

'Perhaps there is another gate or a part of the fortress that is less well defended on the other side.' I suggested.

I saw his glare and I realised that I had, yet again forgotten to add the words. 'My Lord,' and I hastily added. 'My Lord.'

'Go and Look.' He growled.

'You go round that way.' He ordered the other Sergeant and then he snarled at me.

'You can go around that way.'

I turned and went down the hill until I reached the tree-line, where the defenders had ceased clearing the scrub and trees, or perhaps they had not had enough time to do so.

I stealthily made my way around the hillside.

The enemy fortress seemed to be in a reasonable good state of readiness for much of the circumference of the hill, until I noticed that their wall and the ditch suddenly ceased to exist as a steep pinnacle of rock jutted out of the hillside, causing a sheer rock-face to soar high up the hillside, replacing the defenders man-made obstructions.

Hereto, I had noticed that the fortress had numerous warriors patrolling the perimeter, but I could only count two men who sat high up on the crag, overlooking the steep pinnacle of rock that had replaced the moat and the stakes.

Sir Guy and the other sergeant joined me and stared upwards at the fortress with its wall and sheer cliff-face which soared above us.

'Well, we can't get up there, so I suppose it will have to be a frontal assault on the gate.' He said gloomily.
I didn't think the man realised just how costly a frontal assault would cost us in men and materials.
'My Lord.' I said to him in a quiet voice.
'I think I could scale the cliffs. I could take out the two sentries and have a hundred men up there before dawn, which would allow us time to take the gate and hold it until you and the rest of our men could relieve us.'
'With a bit of luck we could take the place without the loss of too many of our men.'
'A hundred men? He spluttered.
'Don't be so bloody stupid. '
'You are an old man and couldn't get up there yourself, let alone take a hundred men up there with you.'
'I think I could my Lord.' I answered and added.
'Anyhow what have you got to lose?
'Just a single old man.' I answered my own question and emphasised the word OLD, and then I added, 'I have climbed steeper cliffs than this, so I can assure you that we could take this fort with a minimum loss of men.'
'I agree. 'You won't be much of a loss.' Sir Guy snarled in a reluctant voice.
'What I will do is return here with you at dusk and I shall wait at the bottom until I see if you reach the top. 'IF you reach the top.' He added sarcastically, 'and if you reach the top and dispose of the guards. Then your one hundred men can follow you up.'

'I will be waiting in the dark near the gate,' he added sarcastically, 'in the hope that you can open the gate and let my men in to take the fort.'

*   *   *

It took me over three hours to select my one hundred men, and after much pleading I reluctantly allowed 'Cnut' to join the other selected young men who all assured me that they had scaled cliffs or high trees before, and who were eager to join me in 'an exciting raid.'

 I was careful not to explain when or where my raid was to be, for I there is always a chance of enemy spies infiltrating a camp such as ours, which had numerous hangers of in the forms of local men and women who had joined us in order to perform mundane tasks as washing, cooking, collecting firewood as well as scores of people selling all kinds of foodstuffs, many of which were unfamiliar to our northern European palates.

 Dusk was approaching before I had gathered my volunteers.

 I had also amassed a number of balls of string and twenty three heavy ropes which all had to be transported on mules for the journey to our assembly point below the cliffs.

Sir Guy stumbled into our dark camp on what seemed to me to be one of the darkest moonless nights I could remember.

'Are you ready?' He muttered quietly.

'I am, my Lord,' I said and pointed to the man who I had chosen to follow me on my climb.

'This young man will follow me once I have reached the top.' I said.

'He will make the climb if I fall.' I said.

He grunted in a noncommitting way.

I tied the three balls of string onto my belt and started my climb.

Despite the fact that I had studied the escarpment in the daylight and had more or less chosen the route I intended to follow, the climb was one of the most difficult and trickiest climbs I had ever attempted, for the rock face was pretty well sheer and the rock itself was crumbly and weather worn, to such an extent that the hand and foot-holes were few and far between.

Using all my skill and avoiding a number of possibly falls, I eventually reached the top and lay for quite a while sweating profusely and gasping for breath, cursing myself for volunteering for such a risky climb, and doubly so, as I was beginning to realise that I was no longer a young man, and well past the age when most of my childhood friends had already left this world.

Clouds flitted slowly across the dark sky.

An owl hooted and a nightingale, which I had unwittingly silenced, started to sing again. I took these as good omens and raised my head above the few tufts of grass that the grazing animals had abandoned half eaten.

 I could see no sign of the two sentries who I had seen patrolling the top of the cliffs during the day, so I crawled on my hands and knees towards the fire which seemed to indicate the end of the cliffs and the recommencement of the stockade.

 The two sentries were sitting on the ground around a fire and as they were both facing the other way, I managed to crawl silently through the sparse vegetation towards them.

 I eventually reached them and could see that the man who was the farthest away from me appeared to be asleep, whilst the other man seemed to be holding a stick with a piece of meat on it over the fire.

 I rose and as I was reluctant to slay two more or less innocent men, so I brought my Saex down, striking the man over his head with the flat of my weapon and with a nudge from my left hand caused him to grunt and fall sideways alongside the fire.

 The noise of his fall caused his fellow sentry to waken with a start and rise to his feet.

 As he stared aghast at the prone body of his friend, I clouted him around his ear as hard as I could with the flat of my Saex, sending him to join his companion by the fire.

 After dragging them a couple of feet away from the fire, I tied both unconscious men up with their own belts, stuffed a gag in both of their mouths and left them in a sitting position back to back.

I ran back to the escarpment carrying a burning stick from the fire and holding on to one end of the balls of strings, I hurled all three bundles down to the bottom of the cliff whilst still holding onto the vital ends of the balls.

A tug on the loose string told me that the men at the bottom had attached a rope to the string, so I pulled up the first rope and a few minutes later pulled up the other two ropes.

After securing all three ropes around the stub of a large tree, I waved my still smouldering fire-stick and felt the ropes tighten as the first men began to climb up.

The one-hundred men climbing up three ropes took so much time that I was fearful that dawn would break and we, or the two guards who I had tied up, would be discovered, which would end up by us being eliminated by the several thousand warriors who occupied the fortress, but luck was with me as I assembled the men who had made the climb into a wedge shaped formation.

I ordered them to sling their shields off their backs and bring them around to the front.

This was done without any noise other than one man who suddenly developed a nervous cough.

He was speedily shut up by a number of his fellow warriors, who shoved several scraps of cloth into his mouth, causing him to splutter and gasp for breath, but he eventually controlled his coughing and silence returned.

'Draw your weapons.' I ordered in a quiet voice.

What seemed to me to be a long loud sigh that issued from our men as they drew their swords from their fleece lined scabbards, causing me to stare in the direction of the stockade, fearful that the noise had been heard by our enemies, but after a long silence I realised that thus far, we were safe.

I turned to face the men. 'Shields to the fore and follow me,' I said quietly, 'and I don't want to hear so much as a whisper from you until we reach the gate.'

I led them some fifty feet away, parallel with the stockade, as I knew that there would be guards patrolling along the top, who fortunately would be looking in the other direction, and would not be expecting trouble to arise from within their own stockade.

We made our way carefully and silently through and around the mass of sleeping men in their hastily constructed tents, reaching the inside of the gate a little earlier than I had planned, as the sky was still dark, with the dawn nothing more than a slight lightening of the sky in the east.

We were twenty feet away from the gate when a shout broke the stillness of the dawn.

The shout was followed by a sparse shower of arrows that thudded into our shields, with the exception of a single arrow that had been aimed speedily from an archer who had not pulled the string of his bow to its full extent, thus the arrow failed to reach the height of our shields and thumped into the thigh the small figure of 'Cnut' who was some paces in front of the main body of my men, sending him sprawling onto the ground.

Nevertheless, the impetus of our charge sent us hurtling into the six guards whose duty it had been to guard the inside of the gate.

They had no chance and were slaughtered where they stood.

The sentries on the walkway had been shaken out of their lethargy and pelted us with a steady stream of spears and arrows from their high perches.

Several of my men were hit before I could organise us, so that approximately half of my men were facing their front in a shield-wall, which was three men deep, whilst the rest of my men had raised their shields above their heads in order to protect us from the deluge of spears, arrows and boulders which were now being thrown onto us from above.

Then with the help of two other sturdy looking youngsters, we three men heaved the two heavy locking bars from the inside of the gate and pulled the double gates open.

To my dismay, no sound or person appeared out of the gloom.

I ran twenty or thirty feet down the cart-way and, oblivious to a shower of arrows that skimmed and danced along the gravel and swished past my head, I shouted at the top of my voice.

'TO ME.' I bellowed. 'TO ME.'

'The gate is open.'

Nothing happened for a long moment, but then a roar echoed from out of the gloom, as a solid mass of Sir

Guy's men emerged out of the darkness and sped towards me, suddenly engulfing me as they passed by, heading for the gate.

A cloud of arrows rose from our own men and soared over the open gates landing into our enemies who were racing towards their open gates.

The shower of enemy arrows appeared to meet at the apex of their flight, to mix with and then separate with a much larger flight of arrows that had risen from the ranks of our own men, with the exception of a single arrow, which swished past my ear and embedded itself in the chest of one of my own men.

The heads of Sigard and Frithoft' stood out from the ranks of our own archers. Sigard cursed quietly to himself as he saw the man he and his brother had been paid to kill.

I re-joined the battle.

The newcomers speedily relieved my men who were by this time heavily out-numbered, and were in the process of being overwhelmed and cut down.

Our reinforced army immediately eased the pressure on my men and began to drive their now panicking enemies before them.

Hundreds of fleeing men were cut down as they attempted to run up the slight rise, in order to find safety in the 'Inner-keep' which stood in the centre of the stockade, but most of the fugitives suddenly realised the futility of their flight, as the gates of the 'Inner-keep' were slammed shut before they could reach them.

They ceased their flight and threw their weapons on the ground, kneeling with their heads bowed in surrender.

Our men thronged into the fortress, scrambling to be the first to rob and loot the hundreds of kneeling defeated warriors, fighting and arguing amongst themselves for the right of looting some of the more wealthier looking prisoners.

Showers of arrows sped from the 'Keep' thudding into our men and their shields now that they were massed between the 'Keep' and the stockade.

I looked around in desperation to find Sir Guy, who I surmised must be amongst the crowds of our men who were sheltering behind their shields, but could see no sign of him, and knew that this situation was speeding out of control.

I realised that unless some positive action was immediately taken, then we would be forced to vacate our newly won ground or be slain by the arrows and spears which seemed to intensify with each passing minute.

'Hold your shields up and form a shield-wall two men thick.' I yelled, 'and you men at the back. Hold your shields above your heads and form a tortoise, then you must all shelter under the shields for the time being.'

'You men in the rear,' I shouted.

'Sling your shields onto your backs and follow me to the stockade.'

I ran down to the stockade followed by hundreds of anxious men.

'Dig down here with your spears and swords.' I shouted pointing to the bottom of the stockade.
'Bring those carts up here.'
'Cut the stakes from the stockade loose and lift them so that they are in front of the carts,' indicating a dozen or so empty carts that had been abandoned along the inside of the stockade,'

Men quickly dug out and cut loose the eight feet long stakes that formed the stockade and I ordered them to place them and tie them in rows across the top of the carts, thus constructing a large number of small movable fortress, which could now protect the men behind them and could be pushed upwards towards the 'Keep' with its single wooden gate that stood a mere seventy five paces away.

When the first row of five carts reached a level piece of ground some thirty feet from the gate I was rather surprised when the showers of arrows, many of which had been embedded thickly into the front of our logs suddenly, ceased, causing me to order them to halt.

I suspected that a large attacking force would immediately issue out of the fortress.

However, after what seemed to me to be an extremely long wait, I was astounded when the gates suddenly opened and the figures of three white robed individuals emerged, rather than the body of armed men and the charge of horsemen that I had expected.

The three white robed men carried nothing other than green olive branches as a sign of peace.

I looked behind me and studied the horde of our armed men and the immobilised protective carts, which had all ceased their advance up the hill.

I searched in desperation for Sir Guy or some other leader who would be able to approach the three white robed men and negotiate with them or even accept the surrender of the fortress.

Nothing happened for a long moment until there was a stirring amongst our men, who eventually moved to one side in order to allow three heavily mailed and armed men to push their way through them.

I recognised the man who was in the rear of the three mailed men as they came nearer to me, for it was none other than Sir Guy, but it was not until the men reached me that I recognised the emblazoned coat of arms which the third man carried on his shield, or the blazoned arms of England on his breast-plate, which slowly penetrated my mind, telling me that I was staring with my mouth agape into the face of 'King Richard of England.'

He looked down towards me with a haughty look, for although I have always been a tall man, he was taller than me and his startling blue eyes stared through a face that contained nought but a small fair beard and a moustache which surprised me further, as his moustache was cut in the English style, and not clean shaven, as is the style of Normandie.

'Is this the man?' Asked the King in the tongue of Normandie?

'It is. My lord King.' Sir Guy answered quietly.

'But he is an Englishman,' Growled the King.

'You did not reveal that fact to me.' He added in a quieter tone

'And it appears to me that this man has conquered this fortress whilst you were away from the army? Which I had left in your safekeeping,' he snarled as he looked at the now cowering Sir Guy,

'Err , I was searching for you my Lord King.'

'And you left my army without a leader.' The King snarled.

'That Sir Guy, is unforgivable.' He growled.

'I should take your estates in the Kentish lands from you and add them to my own.'

'But he did take the castle my Lord.' Sir Guy spluttered.

'As I knew he would, my Lord King.'

'He is an experienced warrior my Lord King.'

'He fought against us at Hastings.'

'Did he by God?' The King exclaimed in a grim manner.

'And did you slay any Normans? The King asked, as he turned his head towards me.

'I did your Majesty.' I said.

'How many?'

'I really don't remember your Majesty.' I answered truthfully.

The King's face broke into a smile and he gave me a hearty slap on my shoulder.

'My God, Now that's the answer I would have given.'

'Your Englishman appears to be a good leader AND an honest man.' He added as he glowered again towards Sir Guy.

'Follow me.' He ordered, as he pushed past us and began to stride up the incline towards the three white robed men, who had halted some fifteen feet away.
'We shall see if we really have captured this fortress or not.'
'These damned foreigners can be slippery fellows.'
'As for you, my dear Sir Guy.'
'If these three fellows do surrender the fortress to me, and release my sister and my Betrothed unharmed, then I may just allow you retain your lands in Kent and Blurignan, but if they do not, then I may have to rethink my decision.'
The three men advanced a few steps towards the King.
'Do you speak French?' he demanded.
'A little my Lord.' The youngest of the three white robed figures answered.
'Good.' The King said. 'You have approached me seeking terms, and remember this. IT IS YOU WHO IS HOLDING THE OLIVE BRANCH?' 'NOT ME!!' He hissed as his mouth twisted into a downward snarl.
'IT IS YOU WHO IS SUEING FOR PEACE.
'Are my sister and Berengaria unharmed?' He demanded, in a quieter tone.
'They are both safe and well my lord. The man said.
The King continued before they could answer, saying.
'My Army outnumber you by at least two to one and we have the means to crush your tiny fortress within this very day.'

I would rather not be forced to, but I could put your entire garrison to the sword, so I DEMAND that you surrender your fortress immediately to me.'
'What say you?'
The man answered slowly. 'My Lord King.' He said
'Isaac Komnenos.' The King of Cyprus' is willing to cede this fortress and the entire island to you one condition.'
He hesitated for a long time searching for the right words.
'He is a man who is not known for his generosity and he has been a harsh ruler of the island and the people have no love for him.'
'Therefore he says that you may do as you will with his warriors.'
'You may slay them.'
'You may sell them and their wives and children into slavery if you so wish.'
'He also has his wife and his harem and children within the fortress.'
'His one condition is that he must have your oath, as a King of a Christian country.
'That you will not to put him in irons;' and you will allow him to sail away from the island unharmed and in peace.'
'I will agree that Komnenos can leave Cyprus, and I will allow him, and him alone to leave Cyprus. NOT IN IRONS,' King Richard emphasised.
'His three wives and their children must remain here, in Nicosia in order to show good faith that he will never return with an army.'

'Providing he adheres to those conditions, I will allow him to sail away.'

'NEVER TO RETURN,' he said loudly.

Before the emissaries could reply the King abruptly turned and began to walk away, but he hesitated for a moment and half-turned towards them and said in a loud voice.'

'THE FORTESSS IS TO BE VACATED BY NOON ON THE MORROW.'

CHAPTER TWELVE

I was merely a single man in the large English and Norman army who had assembled by mid-morning in the valley below the fortress, although for a reason unknown to me, I had been assigned not in front of my own unit, but to a large group of Norman noblemen who stood in the centre of our host, some thirty paces or so ahead of our army.

The gates had been opened before the dead-line of noon and the first people to leave were the ordinary citizens who had taken shelter before our army had encircled the fortress.

A troop of gaudily dressed warriors emerged from the gate and I could see that they were escorting two un-veiled ladies in their midst.

'Ah!' Exclaimed King Richard loudly. 'I see my sister Joan and Berengaria.'

'So, it does appear that the old despot is keeping his word.'

They were followed by over five hundred warriors who King Richards person guard ushered to the left, where they were ordered to place their weapons on the ground in front of them and to remain where they were until ordered otherwise.

'Next to emerge through the gate were members of the Ex-Kings household who could be recognized by wearing expensive looking bright yellow clothing.

They were closely followed by a large number of even more expensively dressed women, with a large gaggle of children of all ages.

I heard King Richard say loudly to his noblemen.
'Who are they?' It was a question that was followed by a long silence before one of the younger men said quietly. 'I think they must be the woman and children of the Kings harem My Lord King.'

'So many.' He uttered in astonishment.

'I had no idea he had so many wives.'

'How many do you think Lord Askey?' he asked, only to be answered by a shake of the head from the astounded Norman Knight.

I am afraid that before I could stop myself, my annoying habit of counting the numbers of birds in a flock. The number of animals in a Herd, and the number of men in a group, took over my normally sensible and logical brain, and I blurted out;

'There are four hundred and twenty-one wives and forty eight children my Lord.'

He turned sharply and stared at me and twisted around.

He snarled to his scribe who was standing slightly away from the noblemen.

'Go and count them and we shall see if this know-all Saxon is correct.'

The black-robed scribe scuttled around the noblemen and ran towards the women muttering profanities under his breath.

The ten men escort of the Berengaria and Joan halted and allowed the two ladies to step away.

They both hastened towards the King and threw their arms around him in their happiness and relief.

'Follow me Lord Chames.' Said the King, 'and bring your men with you,' as he strode manfully ahead of Lord Chames who began to shout at his 'Sergeants at arms,' who in turn, ordered the hundred or so of the men who Lord Chames had brought with him on the crusade.

'You women and children from the fortress are free to return to your homes.'

Shouted Lord Chames, causing a loud sigh of relief emitting from the throng, who immediately began to disperse and make their way homeward.

The King halted about thirty paces before the warriors of Komnenos, who stood in an unorganised crowd beneath the walls of the fortress.

He heaved his huge sword off his shoulder and drove the point of it into the ground before him,

'You men,' the King bellowed at the top of his voice.

'You are all my prisoners, and as such I now have the power of life and death over you.'

'However, as I am a King of a Christian country, our Lord Jesus Christ orders his followers to be merciful and to forgive our enemies.'

'As this is the case, I will grant life to each and every one of you, but as a Warrior and a leader of Warriors, it would be foolish of me to allow you to leave this place as fully armed as warriors and sworn enemies, who could do me and my people harm in the future.'

He held both of his hands out to his sides as if he was in submittance and saying to them. 'What would you do if you were in my position?

And then he said. 'I have given this matter much thought.'

He moved uncomfortably before he continued.

'I have decided that I shall offer you all to join me as warriors in my crusade here in Cyprus, and in the holy-land as free-men, providing you kneel, here and now and swear on the Holy Bible to become Christians and to fight for me in any battle I see fit to undertake.'

Some of the white robed warriors shouted, whilst others turned towards their friends and spoke in more humbled tones.

Twenty seven of them snatched up their weapons. (Yet again, my annoying habit of counting things streaked through my brain.)

And these twenty seven zealots raced towards the King, screaming curses, but the King had anticipated their move and the archers who he had placed in the rear of his army sent a cloud of arrows aloft which decimated the attackers with the exception of one heavily armoured man who, despite being struck by two arrows, continued his charge and sped towards the King, but again the King had anticipated any such move and he snatched up his two handed sword and when the warrior was within six feet of the King, the King swung his sword and decapitated the man whose head appeared to jump off his body, while his body took one additional step before it toppled at the feet of the King.

King Richard replaced his now bloodied sword into the ground and held his hand aloft in an attempt to silence the still arguing enemy warriors.

The noise slowly abated and he said again in a loud voice. 'Whilst I admire these men,' indicating the fallen warriors.

'Their bravery was in vain.'

'Indeed, they attacked me before they had even heard my terms, for whilst I said that I will grant life to each and every one of you, and I will indeed grant you your lives.'

'Those of you who join me will leave this place alive and well, but those of you who decide not to join me will also be allowed to leave this hill, as I promised, but those men will only take their left hands with them, for your right hands will be struck off, so that you will never be able to take up arms against me again.'

The silence allowed me to hear the harsh cackle of crows, and the screech of Kites and the chatter of magpies that were already assembling overhead.

The scrawny black robed figure startled the King as it appeared in front of the King, who was still awaiting an answer from the captives, causing the King to take a step backwards, fearing an assassin.

'Wha. What,' exclaimed the startled King as he looked down and suddenly recognised his scribe.

'They number four hundred and twenty-one wives and forty eight children.' My Lord King.

'Ha. Is that the number the Saxon said?' He snarled into the face of the cowering scribe.

'Exactly. My Lord King. Exactly.' He repeated in a quivering voice.

'King of the English. Sixty-two men have refused your offer.' said a loud voice.
The King was slightly shocked by the number.
He said loudly. 'Let them step forward.'
Sixty two men moved out of the crowd of sour faced prisoners.
'Executioners.' Said the King and six men armed with razor sharp axes moved towards their prey.
Twenty eight of the sixty-two men carried weapons in their hands and they immediately bunched together and charged towards the King and his retinue.
A second cloud of arrows swept over them as a harvester cuts a swathe of oats at harvest time, leaving a single man standing, with no fewer than four arrows in his chest, causing him to slowly sink onto his knees, where he hovered for a few brief moments before he fell face forward onto the rocky ground.
The executioners had merely paused under the arrow cloud and began to continue walking, almost casually towards the remaining thirty-four men.
Screams and muffled moans pierced the air as the pile of severed hands grew and the maimed men were ushered off by the executions towards a blazing fire, where their stumps were thrust into the blaze in order to prevent the men from bleeding to death.
Clutching their Bibles, six priests were sent forward to convert the remaining men whilst the King and his Norman Knights including myself walked up the rise towards the ex-wives and concubines, as well as the white faced ex-King Komnenos, who had been watching the whole procedure.

All of the women wore a piece of coloured cloth that covered the lower half of their faces. (I was to learn later that it was called a 'Yashmak,' and the more important the wife, then the more costly was the silken Yashmak she wore.) The children were aged anywhere between their early teens to newly born babies, and apart from one child who was screaming his or her head off, they were completely silent.

King Richard reached the women and halted a few feet away from them.

'Take off your masks.' He ordered.

No one obeyed him.

'Your Majesty,' said one of his noblemen quietly.

'I don't think they can understand you.'

King Richard turned towards us and asked. 'Do any of you men speak their language?'

No one out of our small gathering stepped forward.

'I speak English and a little of the tongue of Normandie.' A quiet female voice said from a female who was standing behind the centre row of the women and children.

'Come forward.' He commanded, and the front and second row of women stirred, revealing the form of a woman dressed in the style of Arab women.

She walked the few paces and stood in front of the King.

'Remove the veil.' The King ordered.

The woman reached up and pushed her hood back and unhooked her veil to reveal the startling blue eyes and the lined, ancient, and intelligent face of European lady.

The King and his retinue, including myself were stunned by this unexpected turn of events, and I am sure that our silence and the awed look on our faces told the lady of our shock, but before any of us men had gathered our thoughts, the lady said in the tongue of England.
  'I am called 'Ludmilla' and I have been in the harem of Komnenos for more years than I care to remember.'
  'I was once his number one wife, but that was in my beauty years.'
  'I was replaced thirty years ago.' She added.
  King Richard had spent the first eight years of his life in England, but for most of his adult life he had lived on the continent of Europe, and had merely stepped foot on English soil a couple of times since he had inherited the title of Kingdom of the English. Thus he did have knowledge of the English language, but as a matter of pride he simply refused to speak it, considering it a language of serfs.
  He said haltingly. 'Ludmilla,' but he was rudely and yet politely interrupted as the woman who said. 'Your Royal Highness.' 'The people here do not know me by my old name of Ludmilla, as they seem unable to pronounce my Mother tongue, so that for the last thirty or so years, I have been forced to dwell amongst them, they have called me 'The lady Fatima'.
  'For the past twenty five years I have held the post of the head lady of the Harem so I can tell you the names, ages and lineage of each and every one of the ladies and their children who stand behind me.

I could see by the Kings face that he had been slighted by this women who had interrupted him, but I could almost read his mind, and I surmised that he realised that the knowledge that this particular woman possessed regarding all of the women of the Harem, as well as the knowledge of where they came from. (Perhaps his agile mind was already considering either ransom or alliances.)

Perhaps he was thinking that her knowledge of the Island of Cyprus. Or maybe the Islands strategic position in the centre of this inland sea would be invaluable to him.

Whatever his reasons were, he allowed her rudeness to be temporary accepted.

'What can you tell me of him?' he said to her, as he turned his head and nodded towards the previous King of Cyprus.

She stared towards Komnenos and she spat in the dust.

'He is a pig who slew his own brother and his cousins to ascend to the throne.'

She paused for a moment as if she had been struck dumb but then she added with scorn.

'He treated his people and his warriors as if they were all animals.'

'He tortured them and had men slain for merely looking at him.'

'I think it is truthful to say that we would all be happy to see him slain, here and now, in front of us.

'We are the people who he has ill-treated and abused.' She added scornfully.

'I think you will not gain the respect or the loyalty you seek from the people of Cyprus, by allowing that monster to sail away, as free as a bird.'

 'We have all heard the rumour that you have sworn an oath that you will allow him to sail away and you have promised that you will not clap him in irons or harm a hair of his precious hide.'

 'I have also heard a rumour that he has swallowed enough diamonds and gemstones to purchase an army of mercenaries.' She added with a grim smile.

 I saw King Richard gaze down to Fatima and noticed a sly smile cross his face. 'You are quite correct dear lady, but you should not forget that I am a Norman King and as such, I have been dealing with spies and traitors since I was a child,' he said, and turned his gaze towards one of his executioners who was a few paces away.

 'Come.' He said.

 The man stepped forward and held out a medium sized leather bag to the King.

 The King refused to take the bag and slapped the man across his face, causing the man to drop the bag and take a step backwards.

 'Gods blood man,' the King exclaimed. 'I pay you to do my bidding, not to do menial tasks like this myself.

 'Pick it up,' he ordered and gave the bag a mighty kick which sent the bag to the feet of Komnenos.

 The man staggered over and picked up the bag.

 I half expect the bag to contain a couple of snakes or a handful of scorpions, so I was surprised to see the man bring forth a heavy, solid jumble of what looked like silver.

'Put them on.' The King ordered.

After a moment of thought the executioner sorted the things out to reveal a thick, solid bar of silver, with a thick silver ring on each end.

He grabbed the right hand of Komnenos and thrust one of the rings around his wrist and pulled up the left hand of the startled ex-King and thrust his left hand into the second ring.

He then snapped the ends shut and left the startled man standing and staring at the silver manacles that had been forged especially for him by the Royal Blacksmith who had spent all of the previous night, collecting and forging the one and only silver handcuffs that he had ever encountered in his long and busy life as a Blacksmith.

'Yo', You swore you would not put me in irons and would allow me to leave the island without doing me harm.' The man groaned.'

'I said that I would not put you in irons.' The King snarled.

'Are you in Irons?'

'Are you in Irons?' He growled for a second time.

'No. But.' Komnenos sobbed.

'No ifs or buts,' the King growled. 'I gave you my word that I would not put you in irons and you certainly are NOT in irons, and I certainly WILL allow you to sail away from Cyprus but I did not mention either Oars of Sails. DID I?'

'I have arranged to furnish you with a boat, in order that you may leave the Island as soon as my men can escort you to the coast.'

'You will, as we agreed, be totally alone and there will be no Sail or oars, so you will be at the beck and call of the tide and of your own God.'

The executioner and a couple of King Richards's noblemen escorted the sobbing ex-King down the hill and through the waiting ranks of our army.

'Now my loyal Noblemen, you may ponder over the question as to why I should not have this despot slain rather than waste so much of our silver in order to fulfil my oath.'

'However, before you addle your own minds with that question, I have pleasure to inform you that by adhering to my oath, I have proven to our men that my oath, in fact the very oaths that we, as leaders of this Christian crusade swear, are sacred oaths and should never be broken.'

'Let me also assure you that I have not used a single speck of your silver, but I have used a very small portion of the silver that my men captured from the two carts of treasure that this vile man was attempting to smuggle through our lines in the small hours of this very morning.'

'I shall, as you would expect, keep all of the captured gold, which will help me feed and clothe our army, but I will share the rest of the treasure with your good-selves this evening when we are safely embedded in yonder citadel.'

The Noblemen cheered loudly and the warriors who were stationed too far away to have heard the Kings words joined in, causing the surrounding hills and valleys to echo with their happy voices.
 'Now for another thing that will please you.' The King said, as his face changed in the blink of an eye from the grim face of Killer into the face of what I would have called the face of 'Loki,' who was the Old Saxon God of tricks, and of deceit and playfulness,' but for a brief moment I was forgetting that I was merely half-a Christian as well as a half pagan, amongst these thousands of ardent Christians who would probably lop my head from my shoulders if they knew my true thoughts.
 The King led the way up the slight incline towards the waiting women and children who had been the wives and playthings of Komnenos.
 'Ludmilla.' The King said loudly, obviously preferring to call her by her Northern name, rather than that of an Arab.
 Ludmilla obediently trotted up to stand beside him.
 'Bid them take off their veils and their head coverings.' He ordered.
 She immediately nodded and spoke to them in a jumble of words which I thought sounded more like the braying of a donkey than the voice of a human. Nonetheless what-ever she said had the desired effect and the women began to unhook their veils and push their hoods back so that the hoods hung over their shoulders and down their backs.

The removal of their veils and head coverings altered the women from what had, in my opinion, been more like a group of black hooded crows, into a large cluster of women ranging in ages from thirteen to seventy or even eighty years of age.

Most of the women possessed jet black hair, like that of a raven, whilst a few of them had hair of lighter shades of black, brown, auburn, and red, with half a dozen women who had hair the colour of northern Europeans, ranging from light brown to blonde.

'Now as you are my bold Norman Knights who took this citadel perhaps I ought to give you the first choice from these beauties who stand before you.' The King said in a genial voice.

The Knights pushed before me and started to stride towards the waiting women.

'Wait.' The voice of the King roared.

'You did not have my leave to stampede up the hill like a herd of love sick cows. 'Just allow me a second to consider the matter.' '

'Which of you scaled the cliffs and threw the ropes down?' He asked in a sinister and sarcastic voice.

His question was answered by a stony silence.

'Which of brave you Knights helped one hundred of our men to scale the cliffs and who, may I ask, slew the sentries and opened the gates?'

No one answered, but I did notice that a few of them briefly glanced towards me.

'And yet it is you, and you alone who have failed to earn the right to dash up to these women and select the youngest and prettiest of them, before the man who both your good-selves and I know did earn the right to have first choice of the booty.'

'Lord Edric.' He said loudly, and despite the fact that I was one of the few men who had not rushed forward. He then said in an even louder voice, presumably, I surmised so that not only the Noblemen present could hear him, but also loud enough for his voice to carry to most of his army, who were assembled some one hundred paces away.

He beckoned me forward and said to me.

'You have a slow count up to one hundred to mingle with the women and select two of your choice.'

'Go.' He said, and added as he nodded towards the other noblemen.

'You others may each seek out and choose one women for yourselves to use as a Wife, or as a concubine or merely as a servant or a slave, once Lord Edric has returned to us with his choice.'

I was rather shocked by this turn of events and stumbled up the slight incline towards the hundreds of waiting women with my right hand on the hilt of my Saex, as I could see that many of the female faces, who had or were still in the process of removing their veils and head dresses, glared at me with obvious dislike, even hatred, and I knew from past experience that sometimes the female of the species can be far more deadly than the male.

I walked slowly to and then around to the right hand side of the women, noting that very few of them looked to be older than perhaps thirty-five or forty years of age and I passed by a clutch of dark skinned women, for I had never had anything at all to do with black or dark skinned women.

I headed for a small crowd of eight women who looked as if they had originated from northern Europe, hoping that perhaps one of them may speak English or even Norman/French.

I thought that if I could find one of them who spoke either English or even Norman/French then, at least I would be able to converse with her, which would make life a little more pleasant for me.

I halted before this group of women.

'Do any of you ladies speak the tongue of England or Normandie or Frankia?' I asked in English. This brought an immediate response as the faces of two of the women lit up and both said 'Yes, I do.'

I looked at them in a new light, perhaps looking for a woman in the image of my beloved 'Godda' whom I still dreamed about most nights.

Her image began to swim before me again, probably caused by the sight of these two reasonably good looking young women, stirring something within me that I had presumed I had lost many years ago, and although these two young women did not have the tall stature of Godda, the one who appeared to be the eldest of the two did possess the same slender face of my wife and had similar bluey/green eyes and hair that was fair enough to be classed as blonde.

I shook my head as if to clear Godda from my mind and noticed that the hair of this woman was greasy and sweaty looking, which I thought may have been caused by her standing in the hot sun for most of the morning in what looked like thick black clothing and a hood.

The other woman looked so alike that she could have been her sister, but her otherwise pretty face was covered in blotches and marks that looked like she had suffered from the pox during her childhood.

'Come with me.' I ordered them, as I turned and walked back towards the King and the group of Norman Lords who stood by him.

As soon as I reached the group, the King nodded to me and said. 'Ah I see you have chosen two beauties.'

He then turned towards his entourage and said quietly. 'You may go now,' and the noblemen let out a collective howl and like a pack of hounds after a fox, and they charged up the slope and into the flock of cowering women.

'Stay with me awhile.' The King ordered, and my two newly acquired womenfolk and my-self remained with him, fifty or so paces away from the mayhem of screams, shouts, cries of triumph and grunts of pain as the Norman Lords scrambled and fought with one another over the possession of the ex- Wives and playthings of the former King of Cyprus. '

'I am sure you have heard of my dislike of you Saxon people.' Said the King, 'But I feel no enmity towards you personally, in fact, although I have only met you a few days ago, your action and your honesty have made a good impression upon me.'

'You devised a daring plan to take this fortress and despite the risk to your own life, you carried your plan out to perfection without the loss of a single man, whilst those Normans who were supposed to be leading you, dithered and dallied and took no action what-so-ever.'

'I was also impressed by the fact that you speak Latin and the God given language of Normandie.'

'You have proved to me that you are also numerate, when you counted the number of women and children long before my own scribes had any idea of their numbers, causing me to consider that you could be an asset to me, should any of my Norman Noblemen try to cheat me.'

He again looked down to me from his great height, for despite the fact that I am over six feet tall; he towered above me by more than six inches.

'I plan to sail to the Holy-land as soon as the winds favour me and I was seriously considered leaving you solely in charge of Cyprus, but I have been advised by my learned councillors that such a move would undoubtedly cause ill-feeling amongst my Norman's and my Frenchmen, for they would feel insulted to be ruled by an Englishman, so I have decided to leave 'Richard de Barniville' and 'Robert of Thornton' with you to act as Governors.'

'However you are to be the senior Governor in order to mediate between the other two Governors, who I am told are both ambitious men, who dislike each other with a hatred that is barely under control, and those two capable and stubborn men will take a lot of controlling.

The fourth Governor will be 'Guy de Blurignan,' who will take five hundred of my men, in order to subdue the rest of this island before Sir Guy joins me in the Holy-Land in a few months' time, or earlier, should I need the support of him and his men.

I had a difficult time sleeping that night and spent a large part of the hours of darkness dreaming of Godda.

At first, my dreams were of happier times, of when we had first met and fallen in love.

I recalled the times when we had ridden over the Long Mountain to the township of Streeton, on hot and balmy summer days that were so hot that we had oft-times been compelled to halt, in order that we and our ponies could slake our thirst at a spring that was near to an old shepherds hut, half way across the hill.

It was a spring that never dried up and brought forth the most cold and delicious water imaginable.

Alas, my dreams of those happy times turned into a nightmare and I could see my beloved standing at the prow of a Long-ship, which was being driven across a wild sea by a ferocious storm, heading uncontrolled towards a cluster of black rocks that protruded out of a foaming sea, and despite the efforts of the ship's crew, who, for some unexplained reason, had not lowered the sails.

The oarsmen were rowing their hearts out, but their puny efforts were totally in vain as the ship was driven onto the rocks, hurling the crew and my own beloved in all directions.

I could see the distressed face of Godda as she fought valiantly to stay afloat in the turbulent sea, and

although she was an excellent swimmer, her cape and leather clothes dragged her under the churning sea.
 I watched in horror as I saw her face disappear in the foaming sea.
 I wakened and rose from my bed to a wet and rainy morning with ferocious wind that howled through the tree-tops, sending leaves and branches in all directions like the deadly bolts from crossbows.
 When I pulled my shirt over my head, I walked, as was my habit, over to the window where I could see that the usually tidy lines of shipping had been blown into clusters of ships whose anchor stones had been uprooted in the storm caused no fewer than five of King Richards small fleet lying on their sides on the beach.

CHAPTER THIRTEEN

Within the week the astonishing organisation of the Norman King and his advisors forced my rather unwilling mind to admire them, for King Richard had not only had his damaged ships repaired but the entire fleet had sailed from the island with just over two thirds of his men and his horses and equipment.

Sir Guy-De-Blurignan marched inland with an army of five hundred Knights and men-at -arms, leaving me with less than one hundred men to control Limassol.

My secondary task was that of completing the building of the fortress and subduing the people of Limassol and its surrounding district.

I had installed myself in an abandoned Villa with my two newly acquired women and two English men-at-arms, who acted as bodyguards.

I also commandeered two additional men who could assist me in the overseeing of the masons and workmen, who in turn laboured under the eyes of a skilled Norman master- builder who answered to the name of 'Clushto.'

Whilst I did not particularly like Clushto, he was a fastidious man who worked from dawn to dusk on the construction of the castle.

My two new womenfolk were named 'Alaina,' who was the elder of the two, and 'Edith,' who was eleven months younger than her sister.

Both of the women had been captured by Barbary pirates when they had been travelling from the estate that belonged to her Father.

Their Father had recently been granted a small township near the Devonshire township of Brixham.

The pirates had realised the value of two young women, who were, apparently still were chaste and untouched.

The Pirates had carried them to the Island of Cyprus where the ex-King had purchased them a few days before he had vacated the city of Limassol and retreated to his fortress in the hills.

The third female member of my newly established household was the ex-main lady of the former Kings harem 'Ludmilla.'

She had simply followed me down to Limassol without my permission and installed herself into my household.

It was 'Ludmilla,' who set about cleaning and organizing the two servants who 'Ludmilla' had found in the streets of the town, and had ordered them to assist her into cleaning the dirty, almost derelict Villa with such efficiency that within hours the house was clean and fit enough to be lived in again.

I admired her efficiency as well as her local knowledge and allowed her to stay.

That first night in my new abode was one of celebration with my old friends from Wolf-Hall, plus half a dozen men who I thought had performed particularly well over the past few days.

I am afraid that I celebrated a little too well on that particular evening and ate and drank much more than I had intended, as every one of my guests seemed to insist that I drank more of the delicious wine, as we raised our glasses to celebrate our victory.

Hence, sometime during the early hours of the following morning I finally staggered to my sleeping quarters, after leaving most of my clothing strewn across the floor and I flopped down onto my bed where I immediately fell into a deep sleep.

Most nights I prayed to Thor, Odin and the White Christ to send Godda back to me, but none of the Gods answered me, or sent my beloved Godda to me, however on this particular night I was so inebriated that I could not remember doing any such thing.

Nonetheless, much to my astonishment, the figure of Godda did appear before me as I lay on the bed.

She walked across the room; casually shedding her clothing on the way so slowly that it appeared to me that her clothing floated silently to the floor as if her clothing had been made of gossamer or silk.

When she reached my bed, she threw aside my sheep-skin fleece and lay beside me as she had done a hundred times before.

She kissed my neck and then stroked my chest and my waist before she descended to my groin as she had also done so many times before.

She slowly straddled me and lay upon me with her beautiful face hovering an inch or two above my own face, and then she kissed me with a kiss that lingered so long that we seemed to be fused together.

The kiss, which I swear no other man in the universe could ever have experienced, sent blood surging through my veins so fast that I feared that I would explode.

She then pushed herself onto me and I entered into a new domain that seemed to be a wonderland of feelings and sensations, which surged through me, not just my own body, but I knew that it also surged through her body, not once, not twice by three times until she withdrew, leaving my loins, my legs and stomach hot, wet and sticky.

The next thing I can recall is waking from a deep sleep and throwing my arm over to the other side of the bed in order that I could cuddle my beloved Godda again, only to sit upright with a start, when I realised there was-no one beside me, but there was a small patch of blood in the space where my beloved Godda had lain.

I was still in a state of euphoria and stupor as I fumbled with my clothing and I was still in the act of tying up the horn toggles on my shirt when I entered my Dining Hall.

The three women-folk of the household Ludmilla Alaina and Edith sat at one side of the table whilst Hugo and Knut sat opposite them.

I could see by their empty platters and the remains of a roast goose, that they had already eaten, but I seemed unable to figure out why all five of them were simply gaping at me as I advanced towards my seat at the head of the table.

'Lord Edric.' Hugo mumbled who was seated next to me.

'Your flies,' and his eyes dropped to my crotch, where, when I looked down, I could see that the toggles that should have been secured, had not been touched and my crown jewels were plain for all to see.

'My apologies.' I mumbled, and turned my back to the audience and corrected my error.

I sat down and took a long drink of the watered-down wine provided for me, despite the fact that I was still red-faced and embarrassed.

I speedily finished my meal and left the table without any further explanation, and I walked away to go about my daily business.

On the second day of my new position of the main Governor of the Island, the large figure of Hugo was ushered into my hall.

'Ha, Hugo' I said as I walked forward to greet him.

'It is good to see you my friend. What brings you here, out of your cosy billet in the town? I asked.

'It is not good news sir.' He grunted, 'Dire news.' He added.

'Little Cnut. He's very sick.

'The arrow,' he explained. 'It has gone bad.'

'I think he is dying my Lord.'

I had seen men die from mere scratches from arrows which, I had always assumed had contained poison.

'Ludmilla.' I shouted and within a few minutes the slight figure of Ludmilla appeared in the doorway.

I explained the situation to her, causing her to utter the terse statement of: 'Bring him with me.'
 'Quickly.' She snapped.
 She spun around on her heels and disappeared, leaving Hugo and myself staring into an empty doorway.
 Ludmilla was proving to be invaluable, for she knew the names of each and every merchant, not only in the town of Limassol, but also in each valley and fishing village on the island.
 She could guide either my-self or my master builder 'Clushto' where to find, and what would be a fair price of foodstuffs, materials and manpower needed to complete the building of my new fortress.
 The slight figure of the red-haired Cnut arrived on a stretcher carried by two of his friends from Wolf-Hall.
 He was hastily carried into a small room by Hugo, directed by the ever efficient Ludmilla.
At least half of my English warriors were from the north of England, which meant that most of their ancestors were of Danish or Scandinavian origin, therefore for many of them. Their first language was still that of the Vikings, so I more or less understood the garbled dialect of the English language spoken by one of my Sergeants-at-arms.
 He was a large broad shouldered man who answered to the name of 'Thorgil the shield-bearer' who had been working on the main tower of the Fortress, under the master builder 'Clushto' and who, had under my personal orders, been keeping a watchful eye, not only on 'Clushto,' but also a number

of other construction workers who possessed the opportunities of stealing an odd bag full of valuable iron nails or an odd plank of sawn timber now and again to resell in the city.

'Thorgil' touched my arm and indicated that he needed to speak to me and I followed him to the far side of the Fortress which was in its final stage of completion.

'Lord Edric.' He said to me. 'I have overheard 'Clushto' ordering three additional cartloads of ten inch long nails.'

'You know my Lord.' He said as he held his hands out to the length of the nails which were needed to secure much of the structure needed for the building of the walkways that allowed defenders to walk along and fight upon, if and when the Castle was attacked.

'Well my Lord.' He added. 'I know for a fact that 'Clushto' has already completed the main buildings and the walkways and that he intends to declare that the Fortress will be completed by the 'Asgaut of Astrid'. (In the language of the Vikings the words 'Asgaut of Astrid,' meant the third day in the Month of May.)'

'So why? I asked myself. 'Has he ordered three complete cart-loads of ten inch long nails? when no more are actually needed?'

'And the only conclusion is that that I could reach was that he was probably in collusion with a number of blacksmiths and others who will turn each and every one of those nails into knives and spearheads and use those weapons against us.'

'Thank you for your information.' I said to Thorgil.
'Sit here and have a glass of this tasty Greek wine while I send for 'Ludmilla.'
'She has eyes and ears everywhere on the island and I am sure she will be able to tell us more information regarding our crafty friend 'Clushto.'
I explained the situation to Ludmilla, who listened quietly and avidly nodded her head a couple of times.
 I have never trusted 'Clushto' she said, 'and I have long suspected him of salting a few coins off the top of the pile, but I had no idea that he was embroiled in this sort of treachery.
 'However, I have been aware of his connections with the 'Guild of the iron-makers,' who the previous King of Cyprus made into wealthy men, due to the vast numbers of spear-heads and arrow-heads, as well as the armour that they made for him and his personal guards.'
 She dropped her withered face down upon her chest, covering her face so that all I could see was her mane of silvery white hair, causing me to think that she had fallen asleep.
 She remained in that position for the space of one hundred heartbeats before she suddenly shook her head and stared wide eyed up towards me.
 'Where are the nails now?' she asked.
 I had no idea where they were so I looked towards Thorgil for an answer.
 'I believe they are still in the process of being forged into weapons my Lord.' He answered.

'Where are the forges?' I asked him and stared at him as I said in a whispered voice.

'Where will the smiths turn them into weapons'?

'I. I don't know my Lord.' Thorgil stammered.

'My Lord.' Ludmilla said quietly. 'I have spies inside the Castle and in the street of the Iron- makers and I will bring you the names and the whereabouts of the nails by this time on the morrow.'

Ludmilla arrived at the same time on the following day just as I had completed my daily tour of the castle.

I ushered her into a quiet spot where she told me her news.

'My Lord.' She said quietly.

'It is as I suspected. My spies could find no trace of the three carts in the Street of the Iron-makers, but they have managed to trace the carts and their owners after bribing them with a silver coin or two.'

'I have been led to understand that they had been instructed to take the carts and their contents to an isolated farmstead half way up the Troodos Mountains, where there are a large number of forges glowing with activity.'

'Good.' I said quietly.

'Can you lead us there?'

'Nay, My Lord. I am too old to make such a journey,' Ludmilla said with a grimace and a shake of her head.

'I would not survive such a journey, but I do have a servant who was born in the mountains, and he has agreed to lead you to the place.'

'I would suggest my Lord,' she added quickly. 'That you leave when Limassol is asleep, maybe past the hour of mid-night and take a strong party of warriors with you, for the place described to me as seething with men and activity.'

*   *   *

Thankfully, the night was slightly overcast, with clouds skipping slowly over a new moon when the last of my men arrived.

They had filtered to our assembly point in ones and twos.

Our guide was a young Greek, who was getting more and more agitated as the time ticked by. He swore quietly in a language that he had assured me was the tongue of Normandie, but he gabbled away at such a fast pace that I found it very difficult to understand. However, I did sort of decipher that he was worried that our destination was a good three hours march away, and he was afraid that any further delay would mean that we were likely to reach it after the sun had risen.

We were led by the guide, who was closely followed by huge figure of Hugo who I knew to be not only enormously strong, but when we had dwelt at 'Wolf-Hall', he had been a man who had almost routinely gone out pouching most nights and therefore should be used to finding his way about in the dark.

I appeared to be the only man amongst us who began to find it difficult to keep up with the other twenty five young and fit young men who I had chosen.

Our guide led us up a much frequented road-way, which half a mile later turned into a well-defined track, which speedily turned into a rock strewn track that wound its way up a boulder strewn hillside.
  After two hours of treacherous walking through this rugged landscape, my suspicious mind caused me to wonder whether or not our guide was leading us into a trap.
  I was the last man to join my fellow raiders at the top of yet another rocky hill, where my men rested the crest of a smaller rise, looking down a series of several valleys.
  I was about to halt him and accuse him of treachery, when he paused and held his hand aloft, causing me to stop and catch my breath.
  I watched him stoop down and point to the ground.
  He beckoned me forwards and I pushed my way through my waiting men and joined him.
  'See my Lord.' He said.
  'They had to clear these boulders here in order to get the carts over this hill.
  They failed and I can see the carts down there.'
  I looked down the hill and could see the carts directly below us.
  One of the carts had been emptied but the other two were still piled high with metal. 'It looks like they are waiting for the dawn before they bring up more donkeys to carry the metal down to the forges.'
  'Where are the forges? 'I asked, as I could see no sign of cottages or forges?

'Oh they are well hidden, but if you follow me down the hill you will be able to see them.'

'We had best be on our way down.' He said.

'The dawn is almost upon us and you did say that you wanted me to get there you here before first light.'

'I do,' I said. 'Lead the way.'

The way down was steep and precarious and I could see why mules or donkeys would be needed to carry goods and other things up and down the mountain-side.

Never-the-less, we followed the boulder strewn trail downward, almost to the valley floor before I could see any sign of habitation.

I eventually noticed several slight clouds of smoke which I had first thought to be the morning mist rising from the valley floor and then I noted that a narrow channel had been cut along the mountain-side which suddenly ceased as the thin channel of water vanished into the earth.

I halted and held up my hand to halt my men and was suddenly startled by the braying of a donkey, causing me to recall that some tribes in the Welsh mountains used donkeys as well as dogs and geese as sentinels.

I motioned to my men to spread out along the mountainside in readiness for me to give them the signal to attack.

I noticed that the braying of the donkey had alerted the men in the underground caverns, causing two men to emerge from two of the gorse covered entrances.

Both men carried drawn swords and gazed warily up and down the valley and then they looked to their left up the mountain-side, before the nearest man to me, gazed directly back into the entrance from which he had emerged.

 He looked up to the hillside which we had just descended and upon seeing my-self and my men. He stared, opened his mouth to shout a warning, but before the sound came out of his mouth he suddenly looked down at his chest and fell to the ground with two arrows protruding from his body.

 The second man was more fortunate, for he too was shocked, not only to see my men and my-self standing above him, but also by witnessing the fate that had befallen his comrade, and a mere second after he started to run back into the doorway from which he had emerged, a covey of arrows thudded into the very ground where he had stood.

 At the top of my voice I shouted 'Shields.' And each man, including myself swung our shields from around our backs to cover our chests.

 I yelled again.' Follow me' and I leapt off the hillside to land on the narrow strip of moss covered grass in front of the three half hidden doorways, through which the two men had appeared.

 This was an unexpected turn of events, as I had anticipated the iron-workers and the forges would have been in either cottages, or at least some hastily constructed shelters, but I was forced to rethink my strategy, now that I had discovered that the forges and my foes were dug into what looked like a labyrinth of tunnels.

I shouted to the men who were hovering near to the centre and far right tunnel.

'Men.' I shouted.

'Half of you go and cut as much bracken and tree branches as you can and stack them in front of those two tunnels so that we can smoke them out.'

'The rest of you men are to hold your positions around the cave entrances.

'I go in,' grunted the forever belligerent Hugo, as he licked his lips and prepared to charge forward.

'Nay Hugo,' I said as I placed a restraining hand on his massive shoulder.

He looked down at me and gave me the impression that he was going to ignore my order, but when I placed my other hand on the hilt of my Saex, he snarled something in the back of his throat and spat on the ground near to my feet, before he relaxed a little.

'Come, old Friend,' I said.

'If my ploy fails, then I may well have need of you and your strong right arm.'

I left ten of my men guarding the entrances whilst the bulk of my men foraged far and wide, up and down the mountainside as well as up and down the stream, bringing back armfuls of dry bracken, logs and branches of dead and decaying wood.

Only when the two outer doors had been blocked, did I order the men to fill the centre door, for I visualised a dozen bowmen waiting in the dark in order skewer us with arrows, if we were to walk casually in front of the two outside cave entrances.

 The fires were lit and were burning fiercely when I told the men to push the burning debris further into the cave entrances and then to throw green leaves and ferns onto the already smoking pyres.

 Some smoke blew back out of the caverns, but much of it remained inside and no fewer than four plumes of smoke blew out of half-hidden air-holes, which had been drilled into the caverns some way up the mountain-side.

 'Go and cut some turfs,' I ordered, 'and block up those holes.

 A few brief moments later, after a lot of swearing from one or two of the men who found the turf difficult to dig, the holes were blocked and the men returned to their previous positions surrounding the cave entrances.

 Coughing and spluttering in an attempt to breath, no less than nineteen men emerged out of the entrances holding their weapons above the heads as a sign of surrender.

 'Stand over there.' I shouted, indicating a spot where eight of my bowmen stood with arrows locked and ready to shoot.

 'Leave your weapons on the ground.'

 The defeated men looked at one-another before one surly man threw his sword to the ground with a grunt, followed by the rest of them, until the once silent valley rang with the clash of metal crashing on metal, as knives, swords, and axes crashing to the ground.

'Are there any men left in the caves.' I shouted to the group of disgruntled prisoners.

'None' growled one of the men.

'May-be or may-be not.' I said, as my men began to tie the prisoner's hands and passed a long rope looping each man together in a long line.

'We will wait a-while for the smoke to clear and then we shall see.

'Give them all a drink,' I ordered, and three of my men walked slowly to the nearby stream and filled up their water-bottles.

My men returned to give each of the prisoners a swig or two before they returned to sit on a small knoll overlooking the prisoners.

I told two of the men to tie up the captured weapons into two bundles in order to carry them back to Limassol.

I stood and ordered half of my men to follow me into the caverns, whilst the other half waited outside, guarding the prisoners and they stood by the cavern entrances in case any further men emerged into the daylight.

I led the way with my shield up and my Saex at the ready

We stood in the gloom for several minutes in order to adjust our eyes to the sudden alteration of the light before I led them further into the caverns.

I had ordered my men to swing their shields from their backs to the frontal position, as my men usually carried their shields on their backs whilst they were walking in order to leave their hands free.

I made sure that they were ready and led the way down the dark passageway and around the first corner.

We were in the act of emerging into a large cavern where I could see two forges glowing in the darkness.

Two arrows thudded into the front of my shield.

Despite me gazing in the direction from which they had been shot I could not see the archers.

I stepped back into the tunnel and speedily organized my men into forming a 'Tortoise' which was a formation that I had seen the Normans perform when they rehearsed their tactics on their practice grounds.

The 'Tortoise' meant that my men and my-self were completely covered by shields from our front, sides, top and rear.

I led my men out of the tunnel and past the dying fires of the forges, then across the cavern towards the tunnel where I thought the archers might be.

I was correct in my assumption, for arrow after arrow thudded into our shields, causing no injuries.

We reached the entrance of the tunnel and found it empty, so I formed a shield-wall four men deep and moved forward, ready to meet our foes, but after what seemed to be a long and cautious advance we found no exits and no foes. `

We cautiously moved forward until we reached a small cavern that contained a further forge, but it was not until I led my men approximately half way across that particular cavern that we found three archers hiding at the far side of the forge.

My ten men and my-self surrounded them, causing them to reluctantly throw down their weapons and kneel before us.

I ordered my men to bind their hands in front of them, before we set off down the tunnel.

I asked them in a menacing way. 'Are there any more of your people down in these caves?'

All three men shook their heads, but my suspicious nature made me to ask again, to no avail, as they continued to shake their heads.

'If that is the case,' I growled. 'If I find anyone else down here, I will flog him and you three to within an inch of your lives.'

But they still continued to shake their heads in denial. So I drove them before us down the tunnel and out into the open air.

I assisted my men to load the three carts with the three forges and sacks of spears, whilst and the fourth donkey carried two unused sacks of iron nails

The hike back to the castle was more difficult than our outward journey as we were all loaded down with weapons and other equipment.

On arrival we unloaded our booty onto the cobblestoned courtyard of the castle walls where half a dozen of my men to escort our captives to the newly constructed dungeons.

I intended to keep them in the dungeons for a day with-out giving them either food or water.

I did this purposely as I wanted them to sit and worry before I let the large figure of Hugo interrogate them.

I ignored Ludmilla as I walked wearily past her in order to swill my sweaty face in a bowl of clean fresh water that was waiting for me.

 I had left my dirty clothing on the floor, and changed into something more presentable.

 I walked then walked back into the room where I knew she was waiting.

 'Well Ludmilla,' I asked.

 'What is it that is so important that you seem eager to tell me?'

 'Have we been attacked?'

 'Has King Richard been killed or has he ordered my men and my-self to join him in the Holy Land?

 'Nay Lord Edric,' she answered.

 'It is that I am very concerned about the person you called 'Cnut.'

 'Damn and blast.' I exclaimed, as I stood with a mouthful of half-chewed roast goose and the remains of the leg of the same goose in my right hand.

 'Has he died from his injuries?'

 'Could you not save him from death for the few days I was gone?'

 'No, no.' she stammered. 'It is not that my Lord.

 'It is that when I say I am concerned about him. I mean. He is not a He. He's a She.'

 'A she?' I spluttered.

 'What in the Devils name do you mean?

 'He's a She?'

 'You are not making sense.'

 'He is one of my best men. He is a savage and a bloodthirsty little devil.'

'Have you had too much wine or are you taking that 'juice of the poppy again?'

'No my Lord Edric,' she said aggressively, 'absolutely not.'

'I will show you,' she huffed, and turned on her heel and strode towards the door.

'Follow me to the Infirmary.'

I had little option other than to follow her, but only after I had snatched up a silver tankard of red wine, which I sipped as, I followed her to the 'Infirmary.'

I arrived to find to find Ludmilla standing over the bed of the lad I had known of as 'Cnut.'

'Look', she snapped, as she flung the bed-cover off the half delirious youth, to reveal the body of a maiden below the weather-beaten, familiar face of 'Cnut.'

'Is that the body of a boy or a girl?' She said snootily.

'No.' I was forced to admit.

'It is definitely a girl.' Now cover her up.' I added quickly.

'By Odin's Holy blood,' I spluttered, because this was a turn of events that I had never considered, or could ever have visualised.

'What the Devil can I tell the other men? 'I spluttered.

'They all thought the boy was a warrior of legend.'

'He was their mascot and was always ready for a fight.'

Ludmilla interrupted me, saying. 'I have known of her gender from the first moment I saw her, and have thought long and hard of how this could be dealt with, so if you would allow me, my Lord.'

I grunted and nodded my head as I was still too shocked to speak.

'I will suggest to you what I think would be the best way for you to handle a situation such as this.'

'If I were you,' she said quietly, 'I would not tell your men that she is a girl, as I think that would upset both the girl herself, and a lot of your men.'

'After all, from what I have heard, the girl has an aggressive nature and a skill with all kind of weapons that few, if any of your men can match, and may I ask you, that as a warrior of note? Would you like to be beaten by this stripling of a girl?'

I nodded and grunted in agreement with her.

'So?' I said, 'I shall continue to call her 'Cnut'?

Ludmilla shook her head but gave no answer to my question, so I asked her.

'Would you consider it to be wise if I were to install her into my personal guards, here in the castle and dissuade her from mingling with the men?' I asked?

'Nay my Lord,' said Ludmilla with a shake of her head.

'Install her into your household by all means and give her a room to herself in order to allow her a little privacy' but I do think some people, including the girl herself would object if you were to isolate her from the men.'

'After all' she has got away with it so far, has she not?'

'How long is it that she has been 'a man amongst men,' if you will excuse the pun?'

'More than two years.' I answered reluctantly.
'Then I am sure that it would be safe enough for her to continue the pretence and continue to mix with the men,' she said

She turned and walked away, leaving me standing by the bed of this half-awake extraordinary person.

'What was all that about?' asked 'Cnut' groggily.

'I was rather reluctant and unprepared to answer her, but I realised that she had probably guessed what Ludmilla and myself had been talking about, so I told her in detail, what we had decided.

She made a grimace or two and scowled a couple of times before her small mouth turned into a smile, and the occasional nod of her head told me that, not only did she agree to go along with our plan, but her smile and her loud sigh also told me that our discovery that she was a female, had been something of a relief.

'Ludmilla has told me I will be well enough to get up and walk a little on the morrow.' She said quietly, 'so I will soon be able to join you and the men within the week.'

I nodded, grunted the word. 'Good,' and left and slowly walked back to my own quarters in order to make arrangements to accommodate 'Cnut' when he returned to duty.

CHAPTER FOURTEEN

After a quick bite of dry bread and a leg of cold chicken, I visited our captives from the caves, who were now packed into my largest cell.

The large cell was adjacent to a small cell which contained 'Clushto the builder' and six of his accomplishes.

I had ordered the guards to supply 'Clushto' and his co-conspirators with bread and water, but to give nothing at all to the other prisoners until they had been questioned.

My second in command, 'Guy-de-Blurignan' and his men returned the following morning.

They crowded into the fortress like the conquering hero's that they were, for Guy and his men had subdued each and every town, outpost and village on the island.

He had slain countless Saracens and had forced much of the remaining population to renounce their religion and allow them-selves to be converted to that of the Christ child.

He had also turned every Mosque into a Church.

I strode forward to meet 'Guy' as soon as he had dismounted from his horse and I was pleased to notice that he greeted me with no animosity what-so-ever and he kissed me on both of my cheeks and hugged me, as is the way of these strange Norman Nobles.

We agreed to meet in the Great Hall of the Castle at sunset to celebrate his achievements.

I sent messengers to the other two Governors, 'Richard-de-Barniville' and 'Thomas of Thornton,' inviting them to join us.

Striding into the Great Hall at sunset caused me to falter for a moment as all three of my fellow Governors had already arrived and were seated on the two sides of the table with a stranger who I did not recognise.

I noted that they had left the chair at the top of the table empty for me.

I sat and viewed my three fellow Governors and the stranger.

Guy rose to his feet. 'Lord Edric.' He said as he looked directly towards me.

'As a friend and a fellow governor of this lovely Island, I stand in awe of this Castle which you have completed here in Limassol, and I commend to you the enterprise that you have just completed, when you hunted down and captured the leaders of an uprising that could have put all our lives in jeopardy.'

'I salute you and raise my glass to you, and ask my friends here to stand and drink to your success, as well as to our own successes.

He placed the silver cup to his lips and drank, but whilst he drank I did notice a slight grimace of reluctance briefly cross the face of Richard of Barniville, but his face speedily altered into a smile, as he turned and raised his glass to me.

As we sat down again, I noticed that my third in command, 'Thomas of Thornton' had remained standing.

I knew that he and the remaining guests had all drank the toast to me and yet he still remained standing with his goblet still raised as he stared directly at me.

'Lord Edric,' he said as he smiled what I considered to be a genuine smile.

'Pray forgive me for the discourtesy that I have shown to you, but I can assure you that I am your genuine friend and an ardent admirer of you.'

I beg your forgiveness, for I have not shown you the good manners that are expected of me as a Norman Lord, for I have failed to introduce to you this young man who is sitting uninvited at your table.'

He turned towards the man and said in a whisper, which I heard anyway. 'Stand up.'

The man stood and faced me with a smile beaming across his young face.

'May I introduce you to my nephew? 'Robert,'

'Robert is also from my Manor of Thornton, in England.' said Thomas, 'and I ask you, my Lord Edric, for your pardon, for I had intended to introduce him to you earlier, but did not find the opportunity, and I ask for your forgiveness and lack of courage as well as for my lack of good manners.'

Before I could answer, Thomas continued. 'My Lord,' he said, 'Robert is the eldest son of my brother, who was slain at Hastings and he has lived with me as my adopted son since that day.'

'He is a strong young man who I have schooled in the arts of warfare and weaponry to such an extent that few men can better him on the practice field.'
'I ask your indulgence to allow him to join me in my fiefdom here on Cyprus.'
I could see his nervousness, as the goblet which was still held high was shaking so much that I feared he would drop it, so I rose and asked him to sit down, and as soon as he was sitting and had regained some of his composure I said. 'My dear Thomas, I thank you for your honesty and I am delighted to welcome your nephew Robert into our ranks.'
As you are probably aware, despite the fact that I have recently eradicated one nest of conspirators, I am certain that they will not be the only people who will rise against us, so I feel certain that we will find a good use for his strong right hand.'
I remained standing, as I had not finished speaking to them.
'My Lords' I said 'Today I received a letter from our King and in that letter, King Richard has commanded that you. My dear friend 'Guy' and you 'Richard' are to gather your men and to sail immediately to the port of Tyre in the Holy-land, where you will meet with a troop of the Kings Knights, who will escort you to King Richard.'
I paused for a moment in order for them to absorb the news before I continued.
'My Lords,' I said again. 'I must stress to you that the King has marked your departure from Cyprus as, 'Immediate' in his letter on no less than two

occasions, so I must insist that you make your preparations to leave on the ebbing tide on the morrow.'

'I can do no more than wish you 'Gods speed, and say to you that I wish I was going with you.'

I sat heavily onto my sturdy oak chair and took a long drink of red wine from my ornately carved silver goblet.

* * *

I was up and dressed before dawn and I strode out of my front door into the still darkened sky and the fresh off-shore morning breeze.

I entered into a world of shouts from Sergeants-at-arms and noisy men, intervened by the cries and wails of womenfolk, and the neighing of horses as they fought and resisted being forced to walk into the sea in order to wade out to one of the many ships which were anchored in the shallow bay.

The horses neighs of objection was echoed by the noises of other livestock who protested as they were forcibly hauled onto a small fleet of boats that were in the act of rowing them out to those ships, who had been unable to anchor on the shoreline.

The fleet sailed on the ebbing tide and slowly vanished into a hazy, hot day, leaving the bay empty; with the exception of a few fishing skiffs and a sea that looked like it had never possessed a ship of any kind.

I was lost in thought, as I paced along the walls of the fortress in a vain attempt to come to terms as to how I was going to control the complete island with the limited number of men left to me.

Ludmilla must have seen me pacing the ramparts and I did notice her climbing the steps upwards to join me.

'Lord Edric. She said. 'I can see you are troubled and thought I may be of some help?'

'Ludmilla.' I said. 'I have been an English Lord for most of my life, but in this army of Normans. Well mostly Normans. I am not really a Lord, despite the fact that the King has honoured me by making me the senior Governor of this Island.

'Alas,' I added, 'I find myself in something of a quandary.'

'I do thank you for your concern, but my problem is that now the rest of our army is, or soon will be in the Holy-land, and I am very concerned, because I do NOT think that the King has left me with enough men to hold on to Cyprus.'

'How many men do you have?' She asked.

'91.' I answered and added. 'And that includes 6 men who are in the infirmary.'

'Pray allow me a little time to consider the matter. 'She said with a wry smile, 'and I may be able to advise you as to what would be the best course of action for you to take, when we meet for our morning meal.'

I was in the act of finishing my breakfast the following morning when Ludmilla joined me at the table.

'Forgive me, my Lord, 'She said, 'I had a restless night

and to be totally honest with you, I was unable to find an answer to your problem and have no option other than to agree with you, when you said that you do not have enough men to keep control of the Island.'

'I too had a restless night.' I said, 'but I think that I have found an answer to our problem.'

'How so? My Lord?' She asked.

'I have already sent riders to bid Sir Thomas and his nephew to attend me here.'

'In fact he should be arriving within the hour, and when they do arrive, I shall tell them that I am going to allot a fiefdom to each of them and that after they have met with me, they must immediately ride to the Port of 'Larnaca,' where Sir Thomas will remain and build a castle in his new fiefdom, which will allow him to control the Port and the town.'

His nephew 'Robert' will take half of their men to the only other town of note, which is the township of 'Nicosia.'

'Robert will establish his own fiefdom there and he must also build a fortress in order to secure that town and that part of the Island.

I shall tell them that as soon as they arrive at their assigned fiefdoms, then they must contact all the ex-warriors in their fiefdoms, who fought for the previous King of Cyprus, and recruit all the young men from the Greek Christian families who dwell in their areas.'

'He must re-train them in the arts of warfare so that they can support us in our quest to quell and rule the island.'

'My Lord, she said, 'I totally agree with all you have said and really do think that you will have solved almost all of your problems, but if I may be so bold my Lord, perhaps you have missed one vital thing.'

'What?' What?' I growled. 'What have I missed?'

'Well my Lord Edric,' she stammered, for she had never seen me when I was annoyed or in one of my bad moods.

'My Lord,' she said quietly. 'At least half of the Islanders are Saracens and if troubles do arrive, then it will come from them and not from your Greek Christians.'

'Oh, I have thought of that,' I said smugly.

'Both Sir Thomas, Robert and my-self will ask our Christian recruits to sponsor and suggest some of their special Saracen friends who they think they can trust, to join us, in order to keep the peace on the Island.'

'After all,' I added. 'They did mix and live in harmony before we conquered the Island. Did they not?'

Sir Thomas burst through the door puffing like an old billy goat, followed by his nephew who looked as fresh as a daisy.

They both sat at the table where they were offered a glass of the local wine.

'Well, my Lord Edric,' grunted Sir Thomas as he emptied the glass and held it out to be refilled by a servant.

'What is so important that you have ordered us here at this ungodly hour?'

I thought it best to ignore his rudeness and told him my plans, and although he nodded and grunted a couple of times, I could see that he was not a happy man.

However, his nephew Robert beamed with joy when he realised that I intended to install him into a fiefdom of his own.

'That's all very well,' grumbled Sir Thomas, 'but how in God's name do you expect us to hold down the complete northern end of Cyprus with fifty men?

'Christ alive, we will both need ten times that number to do a job like that.'

I tried again to reason quietly with him and explained to him that I would be left with less than half of my existing force.

I explained to him that if he and his nephew followed my plan, then the number of men who I had assigning to them could be doubled within a few weeks.

'Recruit men from within the old King of Cyprus's old guard.' I told him.

'The old Guard had originally been made up from both Christians and Saracens.' I snarled at the silly old man.

'These are men who have already bent a knee's to King Richard and had, as such, already agreed to serve him.

'I have selected a few men,' I told him, 'who will be help for both of you and they are waiting for you in the courtyard.

They include a master-builder named 'Clushto' who was instrumental in building this fortress and I would like him to oversee the building of both of your fortresses, which must be erected in commanding positions, and be completed within the following twelve months.'

'Your Fortress, Sir Thomas, must overlook the Port of 'Larnaca' before 'Clushto' moves on to the township of 'Nicosia.'

'I would suggest to both of you that you keep him in chains and guard him at all times with at least two guards, for he is a canny fellow with an astute mind, as he was one of the main instigators in a local rebellion, which I only just managed to 'nip in the bud' before it had time to blossom.'

'When I was in England we used to send 'Town Criers' out into the towns and villages to inform the people of events and news.' I said to them.

'I will be sending 'Town criers' to visit every town and village in Cyprus, to order all the warriors who served the ex-king, as well as any other young and fit young men who wish to join us, to meet me here in Limassol.'

'You Sir Thomas will be in the main square in Larnaca and you Robert will be at the docks in Nicosia at the dawn on the last Sunday morning of this month.

I shall be leading most of the patrols from here and I will travel far and wide throughout the Island.'

'Obviously, I will be visiting both of you from time to time.'

The beaming young man who was followed by his still grumbling Uncle stood for a moment before they walked slowly out into the courtyard and strode over to inspect their men.

I did notice that during the time that the two men inspected their recruits that both men appeared to be reasonably pleased, and chatted happily to each other as they mounted their horses and rode through the Castle gates.

There was a lot of shouting from the two 'sergeants-at-arms' who rode, straight backed and with their heads held high, as they followed their new Lords and led their new troops out of the main gate.

When I returned to my room, I found Ludmilla sitting at the same chair near the fire, which was exactly where I had left her throughout the whole confrontation with Sir Thomas and Robert.

I could see that she had something on her mind, so in order to hear what she had to say, I asked her.

'I can see that something is bothering you dear lady, so spit it out and we can both get on with today's business.'

She smiled a wry smile and rose to her feet in order to face me. 'My Lord,' she said in her quiet voice, which had been influenced by the language of the Saracens as well as the fact she had not spoken the tongue of the English for more than forty years.

'It is not something that is worrying me, but it is something that I may be of help to you in your quest to build an army here in Cyprus, so that we will all be that much safer from invasion or a takeover from the Saracens who still outnumber us Christians.'

'Quick then, tell me what is on your mind.' I said as I thought that I had already found a solution to our problems and was eager to be outside sorting out my men, who seemed to be sitting in the sun or gambling.

'Well my Lord Edric.' Said Ludmilla, 'as you know, I was the main advisor for King Komnenos when he was in power, and I was privy to all, or most of his meetings.'

'As a result, I personally know the names and whereabouts of most of his officers and Generals, who, with the greatest of respect do know the territory, the water courses and the Wells on the island better than you newcomers, and if we could recruit some of the better Officers, they would be most helpful in helping you in your quest to recruit and build a new army.'

'After all, My Lord.' She added. 'What good are large regiments of warriors who are without leaders who can speak their own language?'

'They cannot follow orders if they don't understand what is being said.'

I was somewhat taken aback by what she had said and could see nothing but good sense and good things coming from her short statement, so I walked slowly towards her and stood within a few feet from her and looked down into her sincere face.

'Dear Ludmilla,' I said. 'Pray forgive me for my foul mood.'

'I seem to be beset with problems and I have been neglectful in asking your advice.'

'You have jolted me back into reality by your very presence and your knowledge, which you have gained over those many years when you were a captive on the Island.'

'I will order a carriage for you and will ride my favourite nag with you in order for you to introduce me to the younger and more up to date Generals and Sergeants.'

'Heaven knows, my stallion and my-self both need a few hours off from these petty petitions that I seem to have lumbered my-self with here in Cyprus.'

'Lord Edric.' She intervened as I was about to leave the room.

'I do think it is a little late in the day to start journeying abroad, as the sun is high and I am no longer the young slip of a girl I used to be.'

'I think it may be wiser to rise early and travel in the cool of the morning.'

'As you wish my Dear,' I said, as I had momentarily forgotten that she was an old woman, many years older than my-self.'

'I will meet with you first thing in the morning.'

After a hurried breakfast, I walked out into the courtyard to find Ludmilla seated comfortably under a parasol, on a small carriage with a dun coloured mare standing in the morning sun, in readiness to pull the carriage.

Chatting to her was Hugo and the small figure of 'Cnut' who had now recovered from His/her illness and was fully fit and very eager to resume his duties.

After a brief greeting we were off.

Cnut trotted along happily as his small mare alongside my own stallion as we followed her carriage.

We rode out of the gate and into the township where we halted twice, to be introduced to two middle aged ex-generals of Komnenos, and after a short time of speaking with them, they both willingly agreed to re-join my new force.

I was told that the next man was younger and was both a staunch Christian as well as a man who had been cashiered out of the army by Komnenos for suggesting some modern alterations of his army.

After a tiring journey which took all of the remaining daylight hours we arrived at an isolated village that had been built on the top of a steep incline, half way up Mount Olympus, in the Troodos mountains.

We halted before a small but sturdy gate, which was opened within a few minutes, to allow a young man of perhaps thirty years of age to stride manfully towards us.

He was dressed in the casual wear of mountain men and a black woolly hat that allowed his black hair to hang out in every direction, to such an extent that I failed to understand how the man could see.

As if the man could read my mind, he brushed his hair across his forehead revealing two startling blue eyes which emphasised not only their colour but also the deep tan that covered his young intelligent face.

'Welcome my Lord.' The man said.

'We have been watching you for the past hour as you made your way up towards us.'

Before anyone in my party spoke, he added.
'Of-course I did recognise you my darling Mother and bid you welcome to my humble abode, which I have re-named. It is now called= 'The Eagles Nest.'
'I assume you have brought with you, either the man who is the new King of Cyprus, or one of his minions.'
'I am neither.' I blurted out for I had been shocked when I realised that the man was speaking to me in the language Of Normandie.
'I am not the new King of Cyprus nor am I one of his minions. But I am the new overall Governor of the Island, who has been given the honour of keeping the peace of this Island and to protect it from any Invaders.'
'Oh I know all that.' The man said.
'I have eyes and ears everywhere, and know you for a Christian and I also know that you are a man of good intentions.'
I hesitated for a moment, thinking to myself that either he had been misinformed about me being a Christian, or perhaps he was attempting to trap me, and did not really believe me to be a genuine Christian.
For in truth, I still spoke to the old Gods as well as this new Christian God who died on the cross, and still wore both a silver Christian cross around my neck which clashed silently with the iron hammer of Thor when-ever I moved.
'Your Name sir?' I demanded in a rather gruff tone.
'Forgive me my Lord,' Ludmilla said rather quickly.
'I have not yet introduced you to my son 'Stavros.'

'Stavros is a Christian and one of the best Generals in Cyprus, and he is a man, who in my opinion is exactly the right man to serve under you in your quest to subdue any risings or invasions, to and help you keep the peace on the island.

I was rather shocked when I heard her declare that Stavros was her son, and stared for a moment at her, where-upon she smiled and nodded, as if to confirm what I had heard was correct.

I nodded in return and held my right hand out to Stavros, whose grip was firm and friendly.

'Come, Lord Edric,' Stavros said, as he led me through the open gate and into his small stronghold.

'Come and see my stronghold here on mount Olympus.'

I held Ludmilla's arm in order to assist her across the cobbled courtyard.

She turned her head towards me and said. 'Pray forgive me my Lord for leading you here to my son, but I really could not find the words needed to say that despite the fact that he is my son, he still is the most loyal and able men you will find in Cyprus.'

'Stavros was fathered by the Father of the late King Komnenos and I hid my pregnancy from him by taking to my sick-bed for eight months, and after his birth I bribed one of the Eunuchs to smuggle him out of the Harem and take him to this place, where he could be reared safely into man-hood by one of my trusted friends.'

'Have I displeased you my Lord?' she said quietly.

'Not at all.' I answered.

'In fact it is exactly the opposite.'

'I rather like your son and feel that he is precisely the man I had hoped to find here.'

'Cnut' walked with the two horses and followed a groom who led the horse and cart towards the stables, where Cnut had agreed to spend the night, snuggled up in a horse blanket on a soft bed of straw.

Ludmilla embraced her son in a clinch that lasted several minutes, and after they had parted we both followed Stavros through a stout iron bolted door into his private quarters.

We were assigned to separate rooms.

My room contained a bowl full of clear mountain water, a towel and a fresh robe in the old style of the Saracens who had ruled the island until the arrival of King Richard a few months ago.

The following morning I entered the dining hall, to be met by Stavros his wife Aglaia, who were sitting at a table that was literally filled with all types of meat, ranging from roast pork, (which was a meat that I had not tasted since leaving England, due to the annoying habit of the Saracens and their minions, of not eating any meat made from the body of a pig.)

There were platters of roast fowls of several varieties, sliced beef and huge platters piled high with chunks of freshly baked bread, plus the unusual bowls of foaming beer, which both astounded me and pleased me, as beer had thus-far been unobtainable here in Cyprus, due to every village on the island containing a vineyard and every village had a distillery.

Hence everyone from the nobility, down to the lowliest peasant and his family drank huge quantities of locally produced wine.

I had just reached my seat when the door was flung open to allow the large figure of 'Hugo' to enter, closely followed by the tiny form of 'Cnut,' and Ludmilla.

I did notice that both Hugo and Knut immediately reached over and grabbed a roast quail and plonked the browned birds onto their wooden platters.

A loud growl from Stavros halted both men as they were about to bite into the breasts of the birds.

Stavros then clasped both of his hands together, bowed his head and spoke loudly in the Language of Cyprus.

The two offending men dropped their birds back onto their platters and dutifully hung their heads until Stavros had completed his speech thanking the white Christ for the food.

We were on our way back to Limassol within the hour.

Stavros led the way on a small mountain stallion whilst the remaining men, including Hugo and myself, who rode behind him on sturdy mountain ponies that trotted, sure footedly down the mountain sides, which we had wearily trudged up the previous day. When we reached the township, we were greeted by cheering crowds of citizens.

We rode through the gates where we found squads of new recruits being trained by the Sergeants who I had personally appointed a few days ago.

However, I did notice that there were an additional number of new sergeants who, I thought must be men who I had hoped to attract on my recent recruitment drive.

After I had settled the men in an empty room in the castle, I asked Stavros to join me in my quarters, and as soon as I opened the door to enter, I was confronted by 'Alaina' and 'Edith' who stood as if to bar my way into my own home.

Both women stood with their heads hung down and their hands clasped together.

'Alaina,' I said sharply.

'What is amiss?'

'Why do you deny me access into my own Keep?'

'Are you mad to bar your liege-Lord entry into my own Keep? I growled.

'My Lord Edric,' Alaina sobbed as she dropped to her knees.

'Pray forgive us but I could think of no other way other than to tell you such dire news before you heard it from someone else.'

'News.?'

'What news?' I demanded, as I pushed my way past the still standing Edith and assisted the slight figure of Ludmilla to a chair near the fire.

'What damned news?'

'Spit it out girl. What bloody news?'

'My Lord. The King, my Lord.'

'Oh my God.' I exclaimed, fearing the worst and already visualising the dire and complicated

consequences which could occur on the death of King Richard.
'Is the he dead?' I shouted in a loud voice.
'No. My Lord Edric.'
'The King is not dead my Lord,' she whispered in a voice that quivered with fear.
'The King is here?'
'What do you mean girl?' I shouted into her face.
'Here?'
'Here in Limassol? Here in Cyprus?' Dammit Girl where is the King?'
'The last thing I heard about the men, he was in Italy.'
'No, my Lord. He is here my Lord.'
' Here in Limassol.'
'He is bringing his bride-to-be through the crowds to join us here in the castle, even as we speak my Lord.'
'His bride-to-be?' I said.
'I thought he was already married.'
'Apparently he is not married my Lord.' Alaina said quietly.
'I believe his new fiancée is a noble lady named 'Berengaria' of 'Navarre.'
'Navarre.' I exclaimed, as I was rather shocked, as I had heard of Navarre, and from what I had been told, it was region full of wild tribesmen who had been at war with each other, as well as with the people on the borders of Spain and France for hundreds of years.
'That sounds about right my Lord.' Ludmilla said in a quiet voice, who had risen from the chair where I had deposited her a few short minutes ago?

'And I would wager this gold ring here.' She held her hand aloft in order to show a thick gold ring which glowed in the firelight, 'that the dowry which King Richard will have demanded will be hundreds, if not thousands of wild 'Basque' tribesman to join him on his quest to conquer the holy-land.'

No sooner had she spoken than the door was flung open to admit, not only King Richard but his bride to be, but no less than a dozen of his guards and noblemen.

'Did I hear the word 'Basque' mentioned?' He said in a loud voice.

'You did my Lord, and may I bid you welcome.' I said in the bravest voice I could muster.

'We have only just heard of your landing and had no idea you would be visiting us so early and with the Lady 'Berengaria' at your side.'

'We were not sure what sort of accommodation or food your-good-self and her Ladyship would prefer,' I lied.

'Oh, I see.' He uttered civilly, and said.

'Fear not my Lord, for she has been cooped up in a tiny ships cabin for the past two weeks, so anything here in the castle will be a welcome change.

'As for the food, well I am sure any good food, cooked in the normal Norman way will be acceptable.'

Before I had time to respond, he walked the few paces to the table and plonked himself down at the head of the table.

He thumped his fist down on the table, shouting at the top of his voice. 'Wine!'

'Bring me wine and bring enough to slake the thirst myself and my men.'

He motioned me forward and pulled the chair next to him half way out from under the table.

'You! Lord Edric. Come and sit with me, for I need to hear from you how well or maybe, how not too well, you and our people are faring here in Cyprus.'

After explaining to him my plans for recruiting men and building strong-holds at strategic points all over the Island, he emptied his second glass of red Cypriot wine.

He stretched his feet out and lay back on his chair which creaked as his weight tested the old chair to its limits.

'Oh, I have to admit, I have received several reports from my people over the past year, and you have confirmed to me that all is in order here, and that you have acted as I had expected you to act.

'How are the small fiefdoms that you granted to Sir Thomas and his nephew Robert?'

'Are they prospering?'

'They are. My Lord King.' I answered.

'Both men have used my own master builder, who has built this sturdy fortress and the fortress that belongs to young Robert now who controls the port of Nicosia, which is bringing in all sorts of goods and foodstuffs from abroad, as well as taxes that will go into your majesties own coffers.'

He nodded, grunted and began to partake of the fruit, meat and pastries that had been placed on the table.

As soon as King Richard finished eating, he emptied his fourth goblet of wine and stood.

 Every man in the room, including myself stood, whether they had finished their meal or not.

 'Come Sir Edric.' He said, as he walked towards the door.

 'I would like to see some of those new men of yours perform.

 'I will inspect some of them as you put them through their paces.'

 I forced myself to halt quickly to avoid bumping into the King who had halted some six feet into the cobbled courtyard.

 His retinue bunched up behind us and mingled with half a dozen of my own men from Wolf-hall who had been lolling against the wall, idly watching a large squad of new recruits being drilled.

 The recruits were ex-warriors from King Komnenos men who had rallied to my call, and were all spearmen who carried a spear and a shield, as well as a short sword which was nestled in scabbards around their waists.

 Upon seeing the King and his retinue appear in the doorway, the 'Sergeant at arms' shouted the order of, 'about turn,' and the men dutifully turned to face us.

 I did notice that as the new men faced us, they apparently realised that they were facing King Richard, causing some of the men to smile whilst others stared forward in indifference.

 However the faces on a number of the men turned into what could only be described as snarls and the twisting of men's lips, which automatically sent my sword-hand down to my Saex.

The Sergeant then shouted. 'Salute the King,' and held his own spear high in salutation, which was perhaps not quite the right thing to do under the present circumstances. Indeed I could see by the scowls on the faces of many of the men that it was a step to far.

I glanced towards the King, who was standing by my left shoulder to see if he had seen anything suspicious, to no avail, as he was still smiling and waiving his right hand towards the new recruits.

Suddenly, four men from the front row levelled their spears and with wild yells, they screamed something indescribable, which seemed to emit out of their long black beards and raced the few paces towards the King.

The King's own guards were packed into the throng of men lodged in the doorway, behind his noblemen, and despite the fact that they tried valiantly to shove their way through a concentrated block of men who were standing directly behind the King, they failed for several vital minutes.

The leading attacker threw his spear and had it been allowed to follow its true course it would have struck the King in his chest, but I used a tactic which I had learned when I was a boy from Vorta, who had been my own mentor and friend when I lived in a cave with four other boys.

I stepped two paces forward and sliced through the spear with my Saex before it reached its target.

Alas, the best plans of men do sometimes go astray, and this was one of those unfortunate times, for as I sliced the shaft of the spear in two, the front part of the spear which contained the nine inch long spearhead, swung around and clouted me around the ear and the side of my face, sending me to the ground in a pool of my own blood, whilst the sweet songs of birds echoed loudly in my befuddled brain.

As I regained consciousness, I lifted my head and mumbled.

'How is the King? Is he safe? 'I stammered.

My eyes cleared to a sea of faces who stared down at me and the man who was nearest to me cupped my head in the crook of his arm and as my eyes turned to him I saw that it was no other than King Richard himself.

'Aye. Sir Edric. I am safe, thanks to you and your men. Gods' truth, that Giant of a fellow nearly hacked one of the assassins in two with a single blow, and that tiny 'Troll' of yours simply danced around the other two as if they were standing still.'

'He literally carved them to pieces at a speed that mesmerised them. In fact it mesmerised all of us. He was so damned fast.'

'Only once in my lifetime have I seen a performance like that, and it was in my beloved Normandie, and I watched in amazement as that tiny weasel danced around a buck rabbit, which was twice its size, before the Weasel dashed in and killed it, and then dragged it off to its lair.'

'What is the child's name?

I was so shocked by the suddenness of this question that I nearly blurted out the real name of Brungilda, but I faked a cough and stopped my-self as I said.
 'He is named Brru. He is naught but a child who is called 'Cnut the small.'
 'He accompanied me from Wolf-Hall in England.'
 The King nodded and carried on speaking as if I had not spoken and said.
 'Oh. By the way, when I asked Ludmilla about the attackers, she informed me that it was obvious to her that those three men should not have been allowed into our army.'
 'She told me that she thinks that many of the men have refused to shave or to have their hair cut, and have not only refused to accept our true God in Jesus Christ our Saviour, and she feels certain that they are still ardent believers in their own false God.'
 'Thus I have issued an order that every man must shave off his beard in order to remain in our Christian army, and I must order you, here and now to disarm and cast adrift any man who refuses.'
 'Is that what you would have done?' The King stared directly into my eyes as he asked the question,
 'Indeed it is.' I lied.
 'Oh, said the King in a casual tone and turned to leave.
 'Now let us get you into the Hall and I will have my personal Medic have a look at that cut.'
 'It looks a bit gruesome.'
 'I shall spend the rest of the day hunting.'

'I would invite you to join me, but with that cut on your head, it would be nought but a painful ordeal for you.'

'If I can find the time, I shall call in and see how you are in a couple of days' time.'

I was quite relieved when the King had gone, for in truth I did have a momentous head-ache and the cut seemed to be burning a hole from my cheek-bone, and right hand side of my skull.

The King had assigned his own personal Greek Medic to care for me and after examining me, he walked out of the room, returning a few minutes later to administer to me a small drink of something that I thought smelt and tasted like cats-piss, although in truth, I have never really tasted cats-piss.

Cats-piss, or no, I was asleep within the blink of an eye and when I was wakened by the same Medic. He informed that the hour on the sand clock was already past mid-day on the following afternoon.

'You mean to say that I have been asleep for a day and a half? 'I asked groggily?'

'You have indeed my Lord.' The Medic answered.

'And the swelling is considerably less.' He added.

'How do you feel?' he asked.

'My head is still a little fuzzy. 'I said as I tenderly felt my forehead and ventured a little into my still blood caked hair, 'but I doubt I shall be leading my warriors on their usual tour in the hills this afternoon.'

'I have been told by the King that I must have you up and about within the next three days, as he has arranged his marriage to the lady 'Berengaria' at mid-day on Wednesday, which is now a mere two and a half days hence.'

My head began to spin again as I struggled to absorb this last bit of news, so I said to the Greek.

'Well I do wish the King good fortune, but what has his marriage got to do with me.'

'I feel certain he will not want an Englishman to mingle with his Norman nobles who will be attending his Wedding.'

'You could not be more wrong my Lord,' he said almost in a voice that seemed to be so quiet that I thought he was afraid and was whispering.

'He has specifically asked for you by name and he has assigned a special seat for you in the front row of the Church.'

'Damn.' I swore for I could think of nothing worse than being the only Englishman amongst a host of snobby posturing Norman Lords.

I slept for the rest of that day and had something of a restless night as the Medic seemed to waken me each and every hour, in order to change the dressing on my face and my head.

He also administered me doses of his sour tasting concoctions each and every hour.

My head felt much better during the daylight hours of Tuesday and I slept well during Tuesday night.

I believe that the Medic came to see me a number of times during the following night, although I not really aware of his presence.

However, I was wakened not long after sunrise on the Thursday morning by a flurry of servants, who brought me a bowl full to the brim of some sort of porridge which contained a generous helping of honey.

 This was the first food I had tasted since the incident, and it was a meal that I enjoyed so much that I literally licked the spoon and the bowl so clean, that I swear it did not leave a single grain of food for the Kitchen dogs, who habitually follow the servants as they brought the empty chargers out of the dining hall to be washed.

   Three other servants carefully laid out a large choice of clothing, which in truth, I would have been hard to have provided for a guest, or indeed for myself, in my so called 'Glory days,' when I had been a Lord of thirty-six manors.

 'Thank goodness,' said the diminutive figure of Ludmilla as she joined the small throng of people who had invaded my room.

 'Now we can dress you appropriately and you will stand out like a star amongst that dreary crowd of Normans.' She said haughtily.

 She immediately took charge of the proceedings and discarded garment after garment until she found what she assured me was the correct clothing to wear at the coming ceremony.

 I was not at all thrilled at her choice but she poo poo'd me and over-ruled my own choices, when I reached for a number of less gaudy clothing, saying. 'Oh, for goodness sake my Lord, you cannot attend a Kings wedding dressed as a beggar.

'Neither can I attend a Kings wedding dressed up like a dog's dinner.' I retorted, but in the end we both compromised a little and I left the room dressed in a green Tunic which was edged at the neck and the cuffs with silver, held at the waist by a wide polished leather belt and a large silver buckle, plus matching green and blue Hose with a dark green cloak, plus matching green sued boots.

CHAPTER FIFTEEN

I made sure that I was one of the first men to enter into the Chapel of St George, which would at least allow me to be sitting, when the other Noblemen took their places, and I would not have to parade along the aisle of a packed Chapel, where I thought I would be stared upon and looked down upon as an Englishman, and as such, as an outsider amongst many of the men who had probably known each other for all, or maybe most of their lives.

The babble of voices and the noise told me that the Church was being filled by Noblemen and their wives, although thus far no one had yet seen fit to join me on the front bench.

The front benches on the opposite side of the church was already filled with the Brides family, which consisted of her widowed mother, who wore black as was the custom, and what looked like several other females who I also assumed were aunts, (who were also in black) but the dearth of menfolk was obvious, for I failed to see a single member of the male line of her family, until my eyes fell upon a single middle aged Knight in the fourth row.

The noise in the room slowly abated into a silence, and I could hear the noise of metalled footsteps striking the stone floor.

The spaces alongside me suddenly filled up with 11 heavily armoured Knights who plonked themselves heavily down onto the pews without giving me a single glance.

I suspected, correctly as it turned out, that they had been pre-warned of my attendance.

The silence was broken by the footsteps of the King and his attendants as they strode manfully up the aisle.

The eerie silence continued as the King and his 'Best Knight' stood in front of the priest who had been waiting silently by the lectern.

Silence prevailed whilst we waited for the appearance of the Bride to-be, who, I was told later, always purposefully kept the groom waiting as a sign of protocol and of her own virginity.

The silence was broken as the heavy oaken door was flung open to allow the Bride and her retinue of maidens to enter the Church.

She was escorted by an elderly Knight, who I assumed to be her Father, as well as six bride-maidens and at least four other members of her family.

The faces of everyone, including my-self turned to take our first look at the lady who was to be our Queen, and as she was escorted towards the altar the congregation reverently rose to their feet, and as she reached them, each of the ladies lowered their heads and politely curtseyed, whilst the men solemnly bowed their heads in respect.

I too lowered my head, having had the mere spit second to see the face of 'Berengaria' beyond the silken threads of her veil, and I was totally shocked at the face that stared directly back into my eyes, for it was the face of my own true love.

It was the devastatingly beautiful face of my wife. 'Godda.'

It was the face of my wife who was the 'Queen of the light Elves.'

Perhaps it was the shock of that beautiful face, or perhaps Ludmilla had been correct when she had literally forbade me to attend the wedding, for she had told me time and time again that the wound on my head and my face were still inflamed and she had insisted that I was not fit enough to attend the wedding.

Whatever the reason? My head became fuzzy and my sight blurred.

I felt myself falling into the steel-clad body of the man beside me.

'What in the name of God is going on? Boomed the baritone voice of the King as his right hand flew to the ornamental golden ceremonial sword that hung at his waist.

A lady in the congregation screamed and fainted into the arms of her escort and virtually every man in the first three rows snatched up their ceremonial poniards (for no man with any weapon other than a small ceremonial knife had been allowed to enter the Chapel).

The men rushed forward to the Knight who I had fallen into and who lay with me in a tangled heap in the narrow aisle between the seats.

I, of course knew little of what was going on, for although I do not think I was unconscious. I could certainly hear the shouts and the mayhem which my fall had caused.

King Richard had abandoned his bride to-be at the altar and had pushed his way through the crush of men who looked down at me.

'Oh it is my faithful Englishman.' He said bluntly.

'It is Sir Edric.'

'I knew he had not fully recovered from his wound.' He lied.

'Quickly now.' He said loudly. 'Get him up and carry him out into the fresh air.'

'Now, for the sake of Holy Jesus, let us get on with this wedding business.' He said loudly.

I sensed myself being carried down the aisle, past staring faces and out of the door, where the Knights who were carrying me, laid me down against one of the newly laid grave-stones, before hurrying back into the Chapel to resume attendance of the ceremony, which each and every one of them were all reluctant to miss. For this was the wedding of the year. Was it not?

Not a Knight amongst them was willing to miss the wedding between the most famous Warrior King in Europe and the most beautiful women in Christendom?

It was a wedding they would be able to boast about to their grandchildren when they were old men.

A short time later I watched enviously as the King and his Bride walked out of the arched door.

I looked again at his bride through eyes that seemed to be failing me and yet again I swore that the Brides face was the face of my own beloved Godda

They were followed by smiling bridesmaids and a large knot of smiling, and chatting Knights with their ladies hanging onto their arms,

The Bride and Groom and the Knights and their ladies were all immediately festooned with clouds of rose petals from the throng of waiting Knights, men at arms and towns-folk who cheered so loudly that the noise triggered my headache again, sending booms which echoed inside my skull, causing me to lose consciousness again.

I wakened slowly for the second time within an hour, as my sight came and went with vivid flashes of lightening, which instantly turned into a blue cloudless sky, which suddenly turned as black as thunder, and then back into a sky full of wispy white clouds.

My vision cleared slowly, allowing me to gaze upward to the ceiling which caused me to realize that I was in my own room and I was lying on my own bed.

Ludmilla stood at the bottom of my bed and as she saw that I was waking, she walked towards the head of my bed and eased herself onto the bed beside me.

She gently took my hand in hers.

'Ah, there you are my Lord.'

'I had feared I had lost you.'

'We were all shocked when you fainted, as the Medic and my-self both thought that you were well on the way to recovery.'

'The Greek says that the fever has returned.'
'Neither the Medic or My-self can think of the cause.'
'Nor will you. 'I thought to my-self, as I saw the face of Godda swim across my vision.
'Did the King make any comment to you about disrupting his wedding?' I asked.
'No. My Lord. He did not, but he did threaten that if you did not make a full recovery, then I would immediately join you in your journey to the afterlife.'
'Then we had better make sure that you do not enter the afterlife.' I said wearily.
'You are much too young to go there.' I said as I attempted to force my lips into a smile.
'Indeed my Lord,' she said quietly.
This time, my recovery was far slower than it had been when I had initially been wounded by my own incompetence, taking six slow annoying weeks, for I have never been sick in my entire life, and I hated losing a single day, when I should have been up and doing one of the dozens of tasks that flooded my mind.
The thought of losing precious days of my life left me fuming with anger.
Ludmilla kept me informed about most things, but I felt sure that she only told me of the good things which were happening outside the perimeters of my fortress, and refrained from informing me of anything bad or difficult.
My suspicions were confirmed when King Richard burst into my room early one morning like a gale from the North.

'Well Sir Edric,' he boomed. 'I have heard that you are well on the way to recovery.'

'How are you feeling today?' He asked in a loud voice.

'Much better your Majesty.' I answered.

'Good. Good, Good. He said. 'But I doubt you will be fit enough to accompany me to the Holy-Land?' He said in a quieter voice.

I did not answer.

The news of him sailing for the Holy Land was something of a shock to me.

Ludmilla had certainly given me no hint that the King was leaving Cyprus.

'We leave on tomorrow's ebb tide.' He said.

'Your Majesty.' I mumbled.

'Whilst I would love to go with you, I do think that I would be more of a hindrance than a help in your task of clearing the Heathens from Jerusalem.'

'No. I thought so.' He said, 'but I shall be taking at least half of your men with me'.

'Including that boy, 'Cnut.'

'I think he could grow up into a new Alexander the Great.' He added.

I was shocked and spluttered, finding it difficult to breath, let alone talk about 'Cnut.'

'You Cannot take 'Cnut,' I mumbled almost under my breath.

I don't like.' But I was not allowed to continue, as the King interrupted me.

'What?' He spat.

'What do you not like?' he spat again, and I felt his spittle splatter my face.

'Is it the fact that I will be taking him as well as a lot of your men?' He shouted.
'Well. No. Well. Yes.' I coughed.
'Yes. No. Come on man.'
'Out with it.' He shouted.
'My Lord.' I said,
 I could see no escape route out of my predicament and I realised that I simply had to tell the King the truth about little Cnut, for if Cnut did go off with the King, then at some-time somewhere, the King would find out, one way or another that Cnut was a girl.
'It is Cnut my Lord.' I managed to blurt out but I was prevented from continuing when the obviously irritated King cut me short.
'Oh, for the love of the holy saints. What is it?
'Is the boy a genius with the sword or is he not?'
'Yes. Yes my Lord. SHE is.' I stuttered, for I had visions of my own head looking down at me from the top of a long spear.
'Well then?' he spat and then stopped in mid-sentence.
'What the devil is wrong with you Edric?' (That was the first time he had addressed me as such.)
'I think that knock on your head has addled your brain.'
'What do you mean She?' He spat. 'You are speaking in riddles.'
'That is what my problem is my Lord King.' I gulped and blurted out.
'Cnut is not Cnut at all, my Lord. He" She is a Girl, my King.'

I halted for a moment as I looked into his face, and all I could see was a large man with his mouth wide open as his brain tried to struggle with this unexpected snippet of news.

 I took the opportunity of trying to explain to him and said. 'I did not find out until a few days ago, your Majesty, who he, I mean. Who she is.'

 She was sick in the infirmary, and the medic saw her body.'

 He rudely interrupted me. 'Who else knows?' He asked.

 'As far as I know my Lord, it was only when Ludmilla discovered it when she nursed him, I mean her, just Ludmilla and myself.'

 'Well, that's the end of that. I suppose,' said the King glumly.

 'I can't take a young girl with me to the Holy-Land.' he added,

 'Why not?' I found myself saying.

 He turned his head towards me and gave me a funny look.

 'Why not? you ask?

 'Why bloody not?'

 'Well she is a young inexperienced girl for a start, and if my warriors found out that she is nought but a silly girl, then half of them would desert whilst the other half would probably want to rape the child, and that would be the end of that.'

 'That is not necessarily so, my Lord King.' I said boldly.

 'How so?' He asked curtly, as he gave me yet another of his strange enquiring looks.

'My King.' I answered, as my mind flew to find a good reason for being so stupid as to gainsaying a King.
'Your Majesty.' I said. 'Cnut has lived with men for as long as I have known her and as far as I know, no single man has yet to discover her secret.'
'However. 'He,' oops, sorry your Majesty, I think I must now get used to call her a 'SHE.'
'Please excuse me for saying, your Majesty,' I said.
'My People. The Angles. The Saxons and especially the Norsemen always had 'Shield maidens in their armies, and you must remember that many of my Englishmen's ancestors are not long removed from their Viking ancestors, and she is still the most skilled and savage warrior of all the men we brought here from England.'
'I think we should cease trying to hide her true identity.'
'We should flaunt the fact that she is a mere maiden before our entire army.'
I have been told that the Saracens dread fighting women, for if they are slain by a woman, they are turned away from the gates of Paradise and their souls are doomed to wander in darkness for eternity.
'We could dress her in the clothes of a maiden. Perhaps our black-smiths could forge a suit of armour for her and she could fight half a dozen men.'
'Maybe some of those bearded wonders who are still locked up in my dungeons here in Limassol.'
'After all.' I added.
'They are all condemned men awaiting execution are they not?'

'We could provide them with weapons and shields. Helmets and breastplates and allow her to slay them in front of half our men.'

'Slay them you say. What if she is the one who is slain?'

'What then?' He stabbed my chest with the hilt of his eating knife.

'My King. I answered with a confidence that I did not really feel. 'You yourself said that you had never seen anything like it, when you witnessed her slaughter those two assassins who broke ranks and attacked you before this very door.'

'Do you not think she could prevail?' I asked with a little sarcasm in my voice.

' MMmm. Yes,' answered the King.

'I think she could win, but as we both know that many things can happen in a battle.'

'I have seen groom slice the head off a fully armoured knight, and I have also seen a hundred mounted knights run for their lives after being attacked by a naked man with a single spear.'

Our lives are at the beck and call of the Gods when we enter their gory realm of war.

'What is the real name of this damned girl who is causing us so much consternation?' He suddenly asked.

'Her name? I repeated as his change of tactics had caught me off guard.

'Her real name is 'Brungilda.'

'Brungilda,' he said aloud. 'That name alone would put a man off looking at her.'

'That bloody awful name must be one of the most outlandish Saxon names I have heard in the past ten years.

'Knock the 'Brun' off and call her. 'Gilda' He said forcefully,' and introduce her to our troops as 'Gilda the lioness.'

'That sounds good my lord King.' I agreed, for I was only too happy that the King was ready to accept my plan.

'Yes, I too think that your plan might work.'

'You have the warped mind of a genius.'

'Guards.' He roared at the top of his voice.

'Four guards burst through the doors with their shields to the fore and their spears ready to meet anything before them.

'Oh. There is no need for that.' The King said loudly.

'You.' He pointed to one of the Guards.

'Have the drummer beat the drum to call my officers to attend me here now.'

'You.' He said to the other man.

'Find the Saxon warrior Cnut and send him here immediately.

'And bring Hugo.' I said quietly in the Kings ear.

He turned and glanced at me with a question on his face, which I had anticipated and answered his unasked question.

'So sorry, my King, but Cnut will not go anywhere without her friend Hugo.'

The King turned and bellowed at the top of his voice, for the guard was about to disappear around the corner.

'Bring the Giant, Hugo, as well.'
Hugo arrived before Cnut and lingered near the door, as if he was afraid to enter and see the King by himself, but his courage seemed to return when the diminutive Cnut entered the hallway.

They knocked rather gently on the door and entered the room together.

'Ah. There you are,' said the King loudly as he rose from the table and walked over to study these two strange English warriors.

'You two have sworn an oath to serve me? Have you not?' he said with a voice that only a King should, but rarely did possess.

The Giant and the small figure of Cnut looked at on another, slightly bemused to have been asked such a strange question.

'We have my Lord King.' Cnut said in a voice that she had rehearsed so many times that it did sound like the voice of a teen-aged boy.

'Good.' He said, and then he added.

'I have brought you hear to inform you that both of you will be joining me and my army when we sail to the Holy-Land in two days' time.'

They looked again at one another and both of them raised their eyebrows and rolled their eyes, for the rumour had long been rife in the army that the King and his army were to sail on the early tide on Wednesday next, so their brains asked themselves why had this strange Norman King called us, two normal spearmen into his presence, to tell us stale news which everyman and his dog had known about for the past two weeks.

I could see that the King was struggling, so I thought I might help him out.

I stepped forward and said to the King, 'May I my Lord King?' He nodded his consent.

'Cnut,' I said. 'I have been forced to tell the King that your real name is 'Brungilda' and that you are not a young man at all.'

'I have told him the truth and explained to him that you are a Maiden.'

The face of Brungilda reddened, but the face of Hugo was obviously not shocked.

His lips formed the shape of a smile, telling me that he already knew she was a girl.

'You knew?' I said, as my own face hovered near the giants chin.

'Oh yes Lord Edric.'

'All the lads from Wolf-Hall knew, but we have always kept that bit of news secret.'

The King breathed a loud sigh of relief, for I think he had expected this meeting to go badly for him, which could have thwarted his plans.

He cleared his throat and stepped towards the three of us.

'I have decided that you are henceforth to be called 'Gilda the Lioness.'

'Lord Edric has devised a plan which will allow you to cast away the clothes of a lad and allow you to wear the clothes of a maiden.'

Both the King and I could see that both Gilda and Hugo were about to object, so we both went into detail about our plans

 Gilda's face began to light up when the King told her that he was to arrange a combat between herself and a dozen of Saracen prisoner's, she began hopping around, totally elated that she could, at long last pitch her own skills against the skills of Saracen warriors and kill a few of them.

 Her elation abated a little when I informed her that it would be necessary for her to wear a maidens dress over her body armour and that her face and hair should be shown in order to allow the audience to see that she was a Maiden and not a famous warrior in disguise.

CHAPTER SIXTEEN

The mid-day sun blazed onto the hard baked sand of the arena.
It crunched under the steel boots of the heavily bearded prisoner's as they walked, bunched together until they eventually reached the centre of the old Roman arena.
They stood with the shields to the fore and their weapons ready as if they were about to be attacked.
The arena had not been used since Komnenos had twenty Christians slain and eaten by lions and hyenas, some five years ago.
Each of the Saracens had been clothed in a steel helmet and a breast-plate.
They wore steel shoulder and arm-plates, Leg and shin-pads.
Most of the men had chosen scimitars and shields.
One man had a spear and shield whilst three other men carried axes of different types.
The stood in the centre and gazed at the two gates which lay at each end of the oval arena.
Nothing happened for several minutes and the crowd who had been shouting abuse at the Saracens slowly became silent and restive.
At least half of the crowd was made up from King Richards's army, who had never experienced anything like a gladiatorial combat during their staid and quiet existence in England and northern Europe, and whilst maybe half of those men had heard rumours about

Cnut, the remaining warriors had no idea of what to expect

'GET ON WITH IT.' A drunken spectator bellowed who was standing in the stalls.

'WHY ARE WE WAITING?' Roared another wit, and the song was taken up by more and more of the audience, until the sound was so loud that it cascaded over the walls and into the hills beyond the town.

One of the gates opened, causing the crowd to cease their noise.

There was yet another minute of waiting.

One of the waiting contestants looked down in disgust as he pissed himself and shivered in disgust and shame as he soaked his own leg and both of his steel boots.

The tiny figure of a girl emerged through the gate.

She was not wearing a helmet but she wore a blue dress that was wide open, exposing a shining new breast-plate.

Her red hair that had been bleached by the sun into a reddish gold colour hung loosely onto her shoulders and was tied with a blue ribbon which matched her dress.

Her legs were covered in green leather leggings whilst her footwear seemed to be the kind of boots that a maiden might wear when she went riding.

The crowd hooted and hollered and slapped each other on their backs as they laughed and pointed to the tiny girl who was striding confidently up towards the waiting group of contestants.

The Saracens stared glumly at the girl as she walked up to them, fully expecting someone or something else to emerge through the still open gate, but sighed with relief as they saw the gate close.

'It is just a slip of a girl.' The largest man and most heavily bearded man amongst them snarled.

'That's all very well,' said another man, 'but she does carry a short sword and it would be well to remember that if any one of us is slain by a woman, then we will not be allowed to enter paradise.'

Two or three of the other men nodded and grunted their agreements with him.

'Don't let that concern you my friend.' The large man said.

'I will sort her out,' and he strode out of the group towards the advancing maiden.

'I'll chop the stupid little bitch in half with this new sword of mine,' as he turned to face his comrades.

He waved the sword at them, shouting 'This sword is twice as good as that piece of rusty iron which I threw in the pile when old Komnenos surrendered.'

The fact that he had momentarily turned to face his comrades was rather a silly thing to do for such an experienced warrior, especially so for a man who had fought in no less than three major battles and had never suffered so much as a scratch.

He turned to face Gilda at the exact moment that she threw her Saex the ten feet that separated them, so that as the bearded warrior turned back to face her, the Saex embedded itself into the warriors left eye.

He was dead before his heavy body reached the ground.

Gilda strolled past his body, casually retrieving her Saex as she did so.

'That's one less.' She muttered to herself as she approached the remaining men.

The Saracens waited in a line for her, with their shields and weapons to the fore.

'Pure luck.' Said one of the men as he turned his head towards his friend, who he had known since they were children in Persia, where they had fished together in the winter and swam in the river Euphrates to cool off in the summer.

'If the stupid sod hadn't turned to wave that stupid sword of his at us she would never have caught him out like that.'

'Pure luck.' He said again.'

Gilda walked slowly towards the left of the line but the line of men simply turned so that whichever way she went she always remained in the centre.

All of a sudden she pounced as silent and as quickly as a cat, striking the man in the centre a blow that almost severed his head from his torso, but the man's body seemed to stand still with the half severed head hanging to one side, for what seemed like minutes but was probably no more than a few seconds, before the body toppled over and re-joined the head as it fell backwards to the ground.

I have seen many a man slain and hover upright before falling and in almost all of those cases, the slayers of those men have always stepped away and had usually joined their fellow warriors in the shield-wall, but to my surprise, Gilda did none of the usual things.

In fact she veered to her left and like an avenging angel, allowing me to see the wide grin that stretched across her rather pretty face, she sliced the right arm off the next man with her razor sharp Saex and as the shocked man realised he had lost his arm, she thrust her short sword into the man's armpit and dashed on towards the next man.

This man had retreated towards his three companions, for the movements of this child warrior had been far too quick for him to even follow, let alone to allow him time to counter-attack her.

The Saracens stood with their backs touching and facing in all directions with their shields to the fore and their two axes and swords to the fore, they could well have thought themselves to be invulnerable.

But no man alive had ever fought against this child amazon, who simply walked the few paces and stooped to pick one of the fallen man's spear and with a movement that was so fast that even I could not have believed it possible.

The spear flew so fast and so straight that in the blink of an eye it was embedded in the eye of one of the axemen.

Apparently, I learned later, for I had never witnessed, or any of the men who told me the story, had witnessed, a duel like this before, and especially so with a maiden.

The Officer who stood beside me told me that according to legend, the Greek Goddess Athena, who we are told dwells on mount Olympus, had promised to return to the world of men and strike dead six blasphemers whilst the rest of the world looked on.

The man swore that the young woman in the arena was the Goddess 'Athena' herself.

Gilda stung the remaining men like a hornet worrying a herd of stationery cows, until most men simply collapsed onto the ground from the numerous cuts and slashes that she had inflicted on them.

She picked up the two discarded spears and with deadly accuracy the spear flew so fast and so deadly that each spear was embedded in the body of one of her adversaries.

I have never seen a warrior, be it man or woman move so fast and by the noise made by the crowd, neither had the whole mob of screaming spectators.

The crowd went wild as she danced around their bodies.

She played to the audience until with two seemingly like casual slashes; she detached both of their heads from their bodies and almost casually marched proudly out of the arena.

*   *   *

Gilda and Hugo left with the fleet in the pre-dawn light of the following day, leaving the town and my fortress silent, with the exception of the crowing of the cockerels and the occasional lowing from a cow who needed milking.

I had barely finished my breakfast when Ludmilla entered the dining hall, followed by the figure of Alaina, who had obviously been crying and stood with her head bowed and her hands clasped below her abdomen.

'My dear Ludmilla,' I said to her as I was slightly perturbed to have to deal with yet another problem coming from the servants.

'What is it now?' I asked with a slight sigh in my voice.

'Lord Edric.' She said in a quiet voice.

'Pray forgive me for interrupting you in your dining hall, but a matter of dire importance has arisen,'

'I would like to have a quiet word with you in private.' She said.

The servants had just finished clearing the table so I ordered them to leave, adding 'And I do not want to be disturbed until I call you in again.'

The room quickly emptied.

'Sit.' I ordered and Ludmilla sat on a vacant chair at the table.

'You too Alaina.' I said, and she sat near to Ludmilla.

'Well Ludmilla what is so important that you must see me so urgently?' I asked.

'My Lord.' She answered slowly, and I could see that she was struggling in choosing the right words, which was very unusual for her, as she had always been very verbal and forthright when speaking to me and more so when dealing with the household staff.

'My Lord.' She started again.

'You see my Lord, it is like this.' And then she halted again.

'It is Alaina here. Well, my Lord. You see,' and she stopped again and looked hesitatingly towards Alaina who still had not uttered a word.

'Alaina here. Well, my Lord. She is pregnant.'

'So? Ludmilla.' I said, for I was quickly losing interest in the conversation.

'Women have been pregnant before and I dare say that she will not be the last,'
I said in a rather offend way.

'Quite so, my Lord. Quite so, but you see my Lord, she says the child is yours.'

Now that did make me sit up and take notice, but I poo poo'd her allegation saying.

'The child cannot be mine my dear Ludmilla, for she and I have never mated.'

'Forgive me again my Lord.' She said rather quietly, as if only she and I could hear.

'But as you probably know my Lord, I have numerous spies both here and in the fortress, as well as in the town and the countryside, and I do recall one of them reporting to me some three months ago that Alaina had crept into your bed-chamber and did not leave until the dawn.'

I was aghast, but before I could say anything as my own mind flew back over the past few months, and I knew for a fact that I had not had sex with anyone since I left Wolf-Hall.

She intervened upon my befuddled thoughts saying. 'I can assure you my Lord Edric that Alaina is a chaste and good person and when I was a servant with that old rascal Komnenos, I personally checked her virginity, and I know for a fact that the old King did not touch her.'

'She has told me that during the night she spent with you, you apparently called her some strange name like Gorra or Gedda or something else that had an 'A' at the end of it.'

I can swear on the Bible and on the Koran that she has not lain with any man before or after you.'

I really did not hear the last words that Ludmilla said to me, although I think I heard her mention the Bible, as my mind could think of nothing but 'Godda' which was almost certainly the word that Alaina had heard.

To say I was shocked is an understatement, for I already had two grown up son's back in England and I had never given a thought of having more children, indeed I could not even visualise the thought of having more screaming babies about me.

I reached for a bottle and poured myself a large glass of my finest wine.

Turning to Alaina I asked. 'And how do you feel about this?'

'I am happy my Lord.' She said as she faced me and gave me a radiant smile.

I was trying to think of something else to say to this pregnant girl who I suddenly realised must be about half my own age.

She looked me in the face for the first time since she had entered the room and said, 'I have always admired you my Lord and I swear on the holy Bible that something or somebody drove me to your room on that night.'

My own sister swears that I sleepwalk but if I do, I have never been aware of it.'

'Lord Edric.' Ludmilla said quietly, 'I thought this matter to be so important for both yourself, Alaina and the baby, because our lord, King Richard is such a pious man.'

'Indeed, in my own opinion, he is almost what I would call a religious fanatic, and if he were to discover that you had sired an illegitimate child with a slave or one of your household, God alone what he would do.'

Indeed, it is rumoured that he has crucified Knights of high standing for siring children with common women.'

I was shocked with her statement, for I had not even thought of the King, or what his reaction would be if he were to hear of my infidelity.

'Find a priest.' I ordered her.

Ludmilla immediately walked as quickly as she could to the door and struck the gong.

The door opened and a servant walked two paces and stood in the room.

'Find a Priest.' I said sternly,

The servant bowed his head. Uttered 'Yes my Lord,' and exited the room.

'Alaina,' I said. 'I want you to go to Ludmilla's quarters, where she will find you attire that befits a young Bride to be, and return here within the hour, so that we can take our marriage vows and become man and wife'.

We were married an hour before mid-day.

My Brides sister 'Edith,' 'Ludmilla' and one of my trusted Knights acted as witnesses and signed the Priests book.

We all had a small wedding feast of cold chicken, cold pork, newly baked bread and hot cakes, swilled down with a bottle of red wine that I had been hoarding for some special occasion.

I escorted the Priest to the Door, placed ten silver coins into his sweaty hand, and thanked him for his services before I bade him farewell.

I allowed my new bride to be escorted to my quarters, telling her that I would be joining her in a few minutes, and when she had gone I walked over to the window to see if any new ships had entered the harbour.

It was a habit I rather enjoyed. I could stand by the window for an hour at a time whenever I had a brief respite from my duties. I was fascinated whilst I watched the Ships and fishing boats enter and leave the Harbour.

This afternoon I could see a new ship entering the Harbour. It flew an English flag, and was tacking against the tide as she slowly entered the bay.

I watched as she finally dropped anchor and lowered her one and only long-boat.

 When the Long-boat reached the shore, I watched as a well-dressed passenger stepped onto the shore, and as the Longboat-men began to un-load the few cases of cargo it carried, I was intrigued as I watched the passenger walk unsteadily up the beach and into the town.

 I was about to enter my sleeping quarters when a lot of shouting and other noises caused me to run down the stairway and open the door to see what all the noise was about.

 Ludmilla was standing outside the door with one of her famous writing pads in her hands.

 'What's all the fuss?' I asked.

 'I am not sure my Lord,' she answered.

 'But I think it is your friend Edward, at least he was the one shouting a few minutes ago.'

 Edward eventually emerged out of a crowd of men with his one arm around the shoulders of another man.

 He guided the other man towards me and despite the fact that I thought the man's face was familiar, I did not recognise him.

 He had a dark blue woollen hat on that hid everything above his eyes.

 The two men halted two paces away from me and a beaming Edward turned to the other man and said to him, 'for god's sake Bernard, take that silly hat off and allow our friend Edric to see who you are.'

The man pulled his hat off revealing a shock of blond hair.

God's blood.' Bernard.' I exclaimed.

'What a surprise. It is really good to see you of all people.'

'I thought you swore you would never venture further than the edge of the border of Wolf Hall.'

The two brothers walked towards me and both men threw their arms about me and gave me a much unexpected embrace which lasted for many moments.

'Well. Here we are.'

'The three of us are all together again.' Bernard said.

Both Edward and my-self nodded and smile at each other, but despite the warm welcome and the embrace, I could not help questioning the arrival of Bernard, thinking to myself that the last time the three of us were together, the circumstances had been rather different.

At that time, the two brothers were Lords of 'Wolf-Hall' and I was a mere lackey. Whilst at the present time, I am now the Lord of a huge Island and they will now be at MY beck and call.

My mind also questioned the real reason that Bernard had made such a long and arduous journey, for when Edward and I had left 'Wolf-Hall', Bernard was destined to be the 'Lord of Wolf-Hall,' where he could have remained safe and secure with land, servants and bondsmen under him, ready and willing to obey their new master.

'Take a seat,' I offered and Bernard and Edward sat at the table.

'I sat close to them and filled the silver goblets with the red wine, which I had acquired a liking for.

'Now my dear friend,' I said to Bernard.

'May I ask the reason for you to have travelled half way across the world to seek us out here in Cyprus?'

'I would not have thought of you as a Holy warrior who has come here to join the King's army?' I asked.

'You are quite right Lord Edric, I am no Crusader.' He said, although I did detect a slight reluctance in his voice when he uttered the word 'Lord.'

'I have sought you out as an emissary, in order to issue you with a proposal of marriage.' He said rather slowly, with an eyebrow that rose as he finished speaking.

'My thanks to you, my friend.' I replied, but you are not really my type,' I jested, 'for I was not only startled by his statement.' I was totally bewildered.

'Ah, you jest sir.' He said seriously.

'But it is not me who you are to marry.'

'It is my Lady Mother.' 'The Lady Ella.'

Now that really was a shock, for when I left Wolf-Hall, Ella, (as I used to call her) and I were on excellent terms.

She had even stood on the battlements and waved me off as we left for the Crusade,

'Was she not the very person who had sent me and some of her other men on this Crusade?'

'Nay Sire,' I said.

'It is you who jests, for it is true that your mother and I were friends, and I left Wolf-Hall. I left her as a good friend, with no clouds behind me.'

'And I went on this crusade on your Mothers own behest.' I added.

'Ah, but you are not correct there my Lord Edric,' he said as a slight sneer crossed his clean shaven face.

'You are quite wrong when you say that you did not leave a cloud behind you, but what you did leave was a little ray of sunshine in the form of a healthy son, who my Mother swears is your prodigy.'

'The boy, who my Mother has Christened 'Edric,' was born eight months after you left, but the Church and the local noblemen refuse to acknowledge the child, as my mother is unmarried and as such, she is shunned and shamed by her peers.

Hence I have travelled here to see you and to insist that you do the honourable thing and marry my Mother. By proxy if need-be.'

'But marry her you must.'

'I have the papers here,' he said quietly as pointed to a small satchel which lay on the floor.

The two brothers emptied their goblets and stood facing me with their right hands on the hilt of their weapons.

That alone did not bother me, for I knew that even at my age I could slay both of them in the blink of an eye.

I was in such an agitated state that I could not decide whether I was 54, 55 or even 56 years of age.

Not that it mattered what age I was, for whilst the thought of another son gave my heart a boost, the fact that I would probably never see the boy, or even have any say in his upbringing and would be unable to teach him the ways of a warrior did concern me.

Oh, the day had started well enough, but Alaina's pregnancy and then our marriage had been an unexpected twist. (I presumed Alaina was still waiting up in my bedroom for me,) and now, I had just discovered that I also had a son who was perhaps or four or five years of age?'

My mind was in a state of turmoil.

Thus, I had obtained two new children and a new wife in the space of a morning.

What in the name of the Gods would happen the evening? My mind asked me.

I looked at Ludmilla for a lifeline or some way out of my dilemma.

She smiled back at me.

Ludmilla was the most astute and clever person I had ever known, and her knowledge and experience of living with the devious and clever Komnenos had taught her so much of this world of ours in the Mediterranean, as well as the fact that she had also worked with the equally cunning Eunuchs who guarded the Harem, who had probably taught her tricks and plots that would have boggled my own simple mind.

'Lord Edric.' She whispered as she ushered me into the corner of the room.

'No one other than myself, Alaina's sister and the Priest and of course yourself know that you married Alaina this morning.

'I suggest that we keep Alaina and her sister locked up in her room, under the pretence of her being pregnant, and the fact that you would like her stay in her room in order that she can rest and take life easy.'

'I will tell her and you are so delighted and concerned with her wellbeing that you have ordered her to rest as much as possible, in order that she and her baby come to no harm.'

'I will personally take her favourite meals to her, with a decanter of watered down wine, in which I will allow a drop or two of my special medicine to be mixed.'

'That will send both ladies into a blissful sleep, which will not allow them to wake until the coming morning.'

I suggest that you send a troop of your men to find the Priest who married you this morning. Bring him back here and place him under house-arrest until such time as you see fit to release him.'

'Tell the brothers that you will marry their Mother by proxy.

'Apparently Bernard has brought the necessary papers with him, and you will go through the ceremony this evening with the Priest and both of the brothers.'

'You will ALL sign the papers this evening and in doing so, you will, in their eyes and in the eyes of their Mother and the Priests in England, be legally married and the true Father of your new son in England.'

'What of Alaina and her sister Edith.'

'Will Alaina still be my Wife?

'Of course she will,' answered Ludmilla.

'Neither Alaina or her sister will ever hear of your sham marriage to this lady in England.'

I will bribe the Priest to keep his mouth shut with enough silver for him to set up his own Monastery, and I will threaten the old toad with a horrible death if he utters a single word about this second proxy marriage, which will take place this evening.'

'You can send both of the brothers back to England on the same ship Bernard came on this morning.

'I know that the ship is still anchored in the bay and is waiting for the morning tide.'

'I suggest it would be wise to send a troop of ten men to act as body-guards and to escort the brothers to the ship in order that both the brothers and their signed affidavit will be on their way home by noon tomorrow.'

'What think you my Lord?' she asked, as a sly grin creased her already heavily lined face.

'Bloody wonderful' dear lady.' I said.

'Bloody wonderful.'

'Can I leave the details to you?' I asked.

'Of course you can my Lord.' It will be done.'

'I suggest you keep the two brothers in the house for the rest of the day,' She said. '

'I will arrange the ceremony to take place this evening.

* * *

The Priest, Ludmilla, Bernard. Edward and I sat around the table.
  The Priest earned his money that evening, for he laboriously read out the terms and conditions of the marriage, whilst the rest of us looked on, bored by the tirade of words that fell from his mouth like a never-ending torrent of rain.
  We sipped our glasses of red wine and nibbled sparingly at the cold food which had been left on the table, as we had all eaten our fill not an hour since.
  The Priest finished his reading and we all gave a sigh of relief and we all rose from the table in order to sign the affidavit, but we were forced to sit again as he clasped his hands across his chest, closed his eyes and allowed his head to drop, as he went into another long and boring prayer, wishing my bride in England and myself a long and prosperous marriage, which would, he prayed, be blessed with numerous sons to join the other son who I had produced some years ago.
  'That could be funny,' I smiled to myself, thinking that more sons by this particular lady might be difficult for I would probably never see her again.'
  I was the first man to sign the affidavit, to be followed by the two brothers and then the priest who all verified my signature.
  I then pulled the ring of office off my finger.
  It was the first time that the ring which King Richards's goldsmith had made especially for me as the first Governor of the island, had left my finger,

and after pouring a liberal amount of sealing wax upon the folded velum, I sealed it with my ring.
 The household was up and busy before first light on the following morning.
 Bernard and Edward did not want to miss the one and only ship that was likely to leave the island before the coming winter weather reached us, which would make the long Journey back to Northern France and England even more precarious than usual.
 I rode alongside the brothers and the escorted of ten of my own men, down to the shoreline, and I gave a loud sigh of relief as they boarded the Ship.
 They both waved vigorously as the anchor stone was hauled up and the sails spread to take advantage of the generous breeze which normally blew off-shore at this time of the year.
 Ludmilla joined me on the dock, as we watched the ship slowly disappear into the morning haze.
 She struggled as she attempted to step down out of the small cart which had carried her from the castle.
 'Get down and help the Lady,' I bawled at the driver, who was merely sitting in his habitual position, gazing into space, holding the whip in one hand and the ponies' reins in the other. 'Or you will feel the lash of your own whip across your lazy hide.'
 The driver was a dark skinned individual who seemed to have a permanent scowl on his unwashed swarthy looking face, slowly descended from his seat and after taking the arm of Ludmilla; he gently helped her to the ground.

She steadied herself with the additional aid of an ornately carved walking stick.

We stood on the shoreline for a considerable amount of time before we turned to return home.

I rode my favourite stallion alongside the cart that carried Ludmilla back up to the castle, enjoying the day for a change, as most of my worries about the King and his marriage to the Basque princess had passed off reasonably well, with the exception of my vision of Godda and my collapse in the church.

The ruse which Ludmilla and my-self had successfully pulled off with the brothers Bernard and Edward had also sailed off into the sunset.

I breathed another loud sigh of relief.

My sigh was so loud that Ludmilla looked up at me from her carriage and with a shake of her head she said loudly. 'There is no relief for you Lord of Cyprus,' she chuckled as she spoke, 'for you still have one long outstanding problem.'

'Oh. 'And what might that be?' I said with a long and very loud yawn.

'The Lady Alaina.' She said loudly.

'Who?' I countered, for I had not heard of a Lady Alaina, and for a brief moment I did not realise who she was talking about.

'Your Wife, my Lord.' Ludmilla said.

'She, who you have confined to her room for the past two days.'

'Oh My God. Ah yes. Alaina. Of course.'' I stuttered.

'I had not really forgotten her.'

'I have merely put my most pressing problems to the fore and had not forgotten that she was still safely locked up in her room.

'I will visit her the moment we reach home.' I said glumly, as it really had been in the back of my mind for the past two days, but I had been putting off the fateful moment when I would need to enter her room and confront her.

When we reached the courtyard, Ludmilla hobbled off towards her own quarters, whilst I manfully strode to my own sleeping quarters where my new wife and her sister still reigned supreme, for whilst I am a brave man on the battlefield, some may speak of me as a Hero, but when it came to a situation like this, I felt a like a child who had been naughty and needed to come clean and face his angry Mother.

I puffed up my chest, took a deep breath and walked into her room.

Alaina was lying on a sheepskin which was draped over the single bed which I had used for the past year.

Her sister Edith was standing by the window, and gave a slight yelp as she saw me enter the room.

'That will be all for the moment Edith,' I said and stood silently as she walked, head held high out of the room.

'Pray forgive me Alaina,' I said, 'but the King and his marriage had to take priority over our own situation these past two days, but I am pleased to say that the Marriage went well and the King and his Bride have now left Cyprus.'

'The King has taken many of my own men with him to swell his army in the Holy-Land, whilst Berengaria and her retinue have taken a separate ship to return to her Kingdom of Navarre.'

Alaina said nothing, but by her silence and the smile that crossed her face, she gave me the impression that she was both pleased and relieved that we were at last alone, and in the same room, speaking relatively pleasantly to each other.

I joined her on the bed and took her hand in mine.

'So Alaina,' I said to her.

'It seems that you and I are fated to be together, and I do think that I should assure you that despite my age, and the experience which I have gained over my lifetime thus far, I will treat you with the love and consideration you deserve and I will be as good a husband as I can be.'

She gave my hand a gentle squeeze and said in a voice which I had not heard before, and in truth. It was a voice that rather startled me, for it was a deep soothing voice, almost the voice of an old man, slow and distinct and yet somehow restful.

'Thank you my Lord.' She said.

'I too will assure you that I will be a good and obedient wife to you, but in all honesty I do feel the need to explain to you that for all of my lifetime, I have been cosseted and spoiled by my Mother and all of my many servants.

Apart from my own Father and my younger brother, 'YOU are the only person of the opposite sex who I have ever been alone with, or indeed the only man who I have ever spoken to.'

'It was probably something about keeping me chaste and innocent, in order to be able to demand a large dowry which my Father expected to get for me when I married.'

'He was a demanding and devious man who was always ranting and raving about the necessity of 'Planning ahead.'

Yet again I really did not know what to say, so I rose from the bed and walked over to the door.

I opened the door and spoke to the guard.

I turned and walked back to the bed.

'I have just ordered the guard to bring another bed into the room, as you are pregnant and I am a restless sleeper.'

'I think it best that we use separate beds until such time as the baby is born, or if you desire it, you may chose a time when you ask me to join you in your own bed.'

That time did not come during the first night, neither did it occur in the second night, nor did it happen during the first week or during the following two months.

It may never have happened at all, had it not been for the fact that I was wakened early in the half light of a hot and hazy morning, when Alaina screamed out in pain, sending the erotic dream I was having out of my mind, to be replaced by something resembling panic, for my immediate thoughts were that an intruder had entered the room and was in the process of strangling my new wife.

 I leapt out of my bed, snatching my Saex as I did so, and raced over to Alaina's bed to find her wide awake and staring up at me with eyes that were so very blue that each time I looked at them, they resembled the eyes of 'The love of my life.' The beautiful 'Godda,' who I still believed was the lady who I had seen in the Church marrying my liege Lord. 'King Richard.'

 'What is it?' I asked. 'Are you hurt?'

 'No.' she said in a husky voice.

 'I am well,' and she pushed the sheep-skin rug off her shoulders and held both of her arms aloft.

 'Come my Lord.' She uttered. 'Join me.'

 I clambered into her bed and lay along-side her with my one arm across her body.

 'I think I had a nasty dream and I yearned for your warmth to console me.' She said.

 'I too had a dream.' I said, 'but it was a good dream. It was about you.' I lied. Well, I half lied, for indeed the dream which had been cut short by her scream.

 She stretched up and kissed me on my lips.

 That is the first kiss we have ever had.' I said.

 'Not so, My Lord,' she said. 'I tend to recall many more passionate and longer kisses when we made this baby here.' She gently patted her exposed stomach.

 'Ah,' I coughed slightly, for my mind was now bewitched with this lovely naked lady who lay by me, causing me momentarily to forget our previous meeting when I had thought her to be 'Godda.'

The passion that took place during the following hour took me up-to and beyond what I thought the normal restraints of an average man could possibly experience when making love to a pregnant woman.

Alaina made up for my restraint with a passion of her own, which both shocked and pleased me, leaving both of us and the bed wet with perspiration.

Before I left the room for my breakfast, I had pushed both of the beds together and said to my still shy bride. 'Now we will be able to sleep together which is the correct and proper thing that a man and his wife to do.

CHAPTER SEVENTEEN

'Thanks be to Allah this day is over,' swore 'Hussein'.
 'If I am forced to do any more sword-work with this new scimitar of mine, I swear I will lop off the head of the next bloody infidel I see.'
 'Stop moaning you silly old fool.' Saif growled.
 'Don't you realise that the only sod who will benefit from your sword practice will be you.'
 'You are probably the best swordsman of us all, and will soon be better than any bloody infidel you are likely to meet in battle.'
 'That's right,' said the third man in the trio. 'Old Komnenos never gave us any training. Did he?'
 'That silly old fool just gave us an old shield and a rusty old sword and expected us to die for him.' He spat into the dust.
 'Ah, but he was a true believer was he not? Added 'Zahid,' whose name meant 'Devout or pious.' Zahid was a man who had especially been given that particular name by his Parents, because both of them were ardent believers in the faith of Islam.
 'I think that old Tyrant was a true believer in himself and no other man alive, 'cos he never did me any favours did he?' replied 'Saif' whose own name meant 'man of the sword.'
 'Saif' was a man reborn since these stupid Christians had furnished him with a new helmet and a new sword, which in latter days, only a Prince or a nobleman would have been able to afford.

Saif revelled in the drill, especially the new moves that the Sergeant revealed to his new recruits.

The Sergeant was a swordsman of some note and had been a man who had fought against a people called the Burgundians, although the suspicious 'Saif' doubted that there was, or had ever been a tribe called Burgundians, for his logical brain questioned the name, and he doubted that no one but an idiot would call themselves by such a ridiculous name.

As the three men walked towards their sleeping quarters, they were joined by two other men, the brothers 'Mahid' and 'Walid.'

'Any-way these damned Christians made me shave off my beard.' Mahid grumbled.

'I loved that bloody beard.'

'It took me bloody years to grow the thing and they made me shave it off.'

'The bastards.' He swore,

'Better lose your beard than let them take off your right arm wasn't it?' countered 'Hussein.' Anyway that damned moustache of yours would have passed for a good sized beard.' He added.

'That's all very well say, but The Holy Koran says we should keep our beards or we will not be allowed into paradise when we die.'

'How do you know that's true?' 'Hussein' asked.

'The 'Imam' says so,' answered 'Mahdi.'

'Have you seen it in the 'Koran?' asked 'Hussein?'

'Well no. I haven't.'

'Anyway, you know I can't read. Neither can you. And that old 'Imam' would have told a man anything for a jug of wine.'

'He must be the biggest blasphemer this side of paradise.'

'I think we should change the subject,' added 'Hussein,' who was the only real man with an active brain among this group of ignorant peasants, despite the fact his own upbringing had consisted of nothing other than being a herder of goats before he had been forced to join the old Kings army.

Since that time he had developed an enquiring mind and had already earned the respect of the other men.

They sat around a small table in their quarters, which was situated at the far end of the room, well away from the prying eyes and ears of their room-mates.

'Hussein' spoke first, purposely leaning forward towards the other men and began to speak in a hushed tone.

'There are only five of us, but I think that we should try to recruit more men as I think that most of these men here are well on the way towards being Christians, and if we can convince them to remaining true believers of the faith, then we had better do so before the weaklings amongst them get converted into the faith of the Christian God, and then before you know it the whole army will be Christians and we will have lost the complete island of Cyprus.'

The other men nodded and grunted their approval.

'What have you got in mind 'Saif?' asked 'Hussein?'

'I have given this much thought,' answered 'Hussein,' 'for I have foreseen many things in my dreams.'

'Whilst there are still only five of us here, who are still true believers in the faith, I think that there must be dozens if not hundreds of men in the army who could join us if they only knew about us.'

'The trick would be to find them without allowing the weaklings to realise what we are doing.'

'That is true 'Hussein,' 'Walid' said as he looked towards his brother 'Zahid, who was sitting cross legged on the floor.

'But how could we do that?' he asked.

'Well,' answered 'Hussein.' 'I am sure that each of us must know at least one true believer who is hovering between believing in the Christ Child and Allah.'

'So what?' 'Zahid' asked.

'If each of us were to approach one waverer, and quietly convert him back to us in the next couple of weeks, then our numbers would be doubled, and if we can persuade that man to recruit another man to our cause in the next two weeks then our numbers would double again and if we continue to do that for the next six months, then we would soon find that half the army would be on our side and we would then be strong enough to challenge these Christians, and take back Cyprus for the true faith.'

'Will you be with us on this recruitment campaign? Zahid asked Hussein.

'I will indeed, but first I must carry out a service for Allah which I have promised him and myself many moons ago.'

'What service is that?' asked the ever suspicious 'Zahid?'
'I have thought long and hard about this and have come to the conclusion that it is no good cutting the tail off the snake, for it will only grow back. Will it not?'
'What we must do is cut the head off the thing.'
'What on earth are you going on about?' asked the bemused 'Zahid.'
'We are talking about bloody people, not sodding snakes.'
'You have not quite followed me my dear 'Zahid,' 'Hussein' said patiently.
'The head of the snake is that damned infidel.'
'The one they call Sir Edric.
'That is correct 'Zahid.'
'I must slay Sir Edric, and then the rest of them will fall to us like ripe plums.'
'What I want you to do, is to ponder over the people you know and chose at least one of them who I would like you to casually bump into in the morning and make that man your best friend.'
'He must be a man who is unhappy with his lot here in this Christian army, and he must be a man who you think, may be persuaded to join our cause.'
'You must spend no more than a week trying to get him to join us, and if he has not committed himself to us by the end of that week, then you must waste no more time on him and move on to your next target.'
'Is that clear?'

The men nodded and grunted their consent before they turned towards their beds, where they could lie and consider who they would target in the coming days and weeks.

CHAPTER EIGHTEEN

 Over the following weeks I made a determined effort to locate and appoint three new Greek Physicians.
 I also ordered my master builder, the devious 'Clushto,' to design and oversee the construction of an addition medical centre within the walls of the fortress, where my sick and injured warriors could be treated.
 However, acting on Ludmilla's advice, I let it be known that the townspeople could also bring their sick to be treated by my physicians.
 She thought that by allowing the local people to be treated by my medics then it would not only give my Physicians additional practice, but it would also be another way to win their hearts and minds, as well as the respect of the towns-folk, many of whom, both Ludmilla and myself knew, had not yet taken to the path of Christianity, and as such could still pose a threat to their new Christian masters.
 I still took a troop of twenty horsemen into the countryside for one or two days each week in order to familiarise myself and my men with the terrain, as well as the locals who inhabited the villages and farmsteads in and around the foothills of the Troodos Mountains.
 I ordered my men to cease their old habits of looting and raping.'
 We always left Limassol with ample food and water for my men, so that we would not have to rely on

robbing the farmsteads and peasantry for food and water.

The other reason was that in varying my routes, was that it enabled me to arrive unexpectedly into areas where I suspected anti-Christian practices may be performed, and from time to time we did see many men on their knees as we rounded a hill-top or appeared suddenly out of one of the many patches of woodland, but I also noticed that those men who we had seen from perhaps half a mile away, had disappeared by the time we reached them.

Oft times their prayer mats had been left behind in their haste to disappear before we reached their Holy place.

I always tried to remember that I too, was not really a dedicated Christian, and I often spoke to Thor and Odin as well as the Christ child when I was alone.

I had little option other than to allow these farmers and peasants to continue to worship to their own God, but I usually remained with them for a while and tried my best to treat them in a friendly way.

After allowing my troop to rest for a short period of time in the shade of their farmsteads, we would mount our horses and move on.

I would usually order my troop onwards and upwards into the more remote valleys and hillsides.

Most of my patrols were peaceful and productive, with many of the farmers and cottagers greeting us with friendly words and gestures, whilst the number of them would provide us with fresh water and flat baked cakes, which seemed to be the usual fare in these remote areas.

The summer season with its sweltering hot days and hot sleepless nights had ended, as the so called autumn began with the cooler winds wafting in from the sea.

It was a warm morning when I led my men out of the Fortress and towards the Mountains.

The faint trail took us over the two crests of several hills and through a number of forested valleys.

I urged my stallion upwards, but the horse hesitated for a brief moment before he mounted a steep rise.

I glance down and saw what I thought looked like an old badgers sett that had been abandoned many years ago, for it was covered with closely cropped grass, but at the precise moment that I stooped down, an arrow thudded into the trunk of a tree I was about to ride pass, causing me to hesitate and my horse to snort in alarm and prance about nervously.

'That was lucky.' I mumbled to myself.

The man who was behind me grunted in agreement and we both stared in the direction to where we thought the archer may be hidden, but as I turned to look, I was struck in the arm by a second arrow which knocked me off my horse, where I lay for a moment, or it could have been for more than a moment as I writhed with pain holding my injured arm.

Two of my men dismounted and aided me up into a sitting position whilst a third man began to rip the sleeve of my tunic in order to examine the shaft.

Through my pain I heard the thunder of hooves and looked up fully expecting us to be attacked by the archer and his friends, but I was rather relieved to see that my 'Sergeant at arms' had taken control of my troop and had organised them into a line that was strung out along the side of the mountain and my men were already riding up the hill in order to find the hidden bowman.

I was brought back to the present moment as a surge of pain shot through my body.

One of my men took hold of the shaft of the arrow, which he was about to pull out of my arm.

'Hold hard young fellow.' I said.

'Are you a Medic?'

'No. Not really my Lord,' he answered.

'But I have done this before.' He assured me.

'Oh.' I said.

'How many times?'

'Three times. My Lord.' He said, but then he continued.

'I was successful on two of those occasions but with the third man, the arrow had cut the main artery and I'm afraid he bled to death.

'Yours looks to be fine my Lord, but if I do not remove the arrow right away it will probably fester long before we reach home, and then you will either lose your arm or your life.'

'In that case, you had better go ahead.' I said with a voice that appeared to be filled with courage and bravado, whilst in truth I felt neither brave or courageous.

'Hold him firm.' The young man said.

Three men knelt down beside me and the man gripped me with what felt like hands of steel.

The young man held the shaft of the arrow and cut it off two inches from my arm.

He then opened his flask and saturated it on the shaft on the front of my arm and shuffled around to my back and emptied his flask on the part of the arrow that protruded out of the back of my arm.

'Wine.' He said gruffly. 'That should prevent it from infection.'

'Are you ready my Lord?' He asked.

'As ready as I'll ever be.' I said, and before the words were finished, he whacked the front end of the shaft with a large flat stone, which he had thus far hidden from my sight, causing me to utter a stifled groan and sending stars and then blackness coursing through my head, forcing me into blissful painless sleep.

I'm not sure how long I was unconscious but when I had wakened, I was in a lot of pain and looked down at my shoulder where I could see that the wound had been bandaged and my arm was hooked around my neck in a sling.

My troop were standing and sitting around me.

There were mutterings of joy and approval as they looked my way and as I gazed at them I could see that they held a man captive who was standing between two of my men with his hands tied behind his back.

I was shocked to see the huge frame of 'Sigard', who was one of the twins who I had brought with me all the way from Wolf-Hall.

'Sigard.' I exclaimed in astonishment for he was probably one of the last men who I had expected to see on this, or indeed on any occasion.

'Oh my God.' I exclaimed. My hand flew up to my mouth.

I forced myself to look again as I could not believe my own eyes.

'I gasped as I recognised him as one of the men who I had personally trained, and who had followed me all the way from Wolf-Hall.

'Sigard.' I said angrily.

'Why you?' What did I do to you? To earn me this? I glanced down to my wounded shoulder.

'Is your brother 'Frithoft' in this with you?' I spat.

'No he is not.' 'Sigard' lied venomously. 'He knows nothing of this.'

I was sure he was lying and I shouted to my men. 'He has a twin brother called 'Frithoft' and he is probably hiding somewhere around here.'

'Find him.' And most of my men scattered in all directions riding their horses in every direction in an attempt to find the missing brother.

'He is a very big fellow, so watch out for him.' I groaned.

'He's dangerous.' I said in the strongest voice I could muster.

Within minutes my men were gone, leaving just myself, 'Sigard' and his two guards plus three other men who had sworn to stay by my side.

'Why would you and your brother want to kill me?' I asked the captive.

He merely hung his head and avoided looking at me.
'Who put you up to this?'
'No one did. I just wanted to be known as the man who slew the famous 'Wild Edric.' He smiled and spat.

I did not believe him, for I had known the man for nigh on three years and I knew that there was more to this that a couple of idiots putting their own lives at risk for the sake of having the dubious reputation of assassinating me.

We shall see if you can recall a name when you have one less eye, or perhaps one less hand, for if I am not mistaken, an archer needs both of his eyes and both of his hands to pull a long-bow.'

'Which would you prefer to lose first? A Hand, or an Eye?'

'Bring him over to the fire.' I ordered his guards.

The guards dragged the protesting prisoner over to the fire.

'Sit him down.' I ordered.

They pushed Sigard down and stood over him while I was assisted to my feet and I stooped down and searched the fire, looking for a good strong branch with a burning end.

Bringing a strong burning branch out of the fire, I grasped the burning branch and with the help of one of my men I hobbled over to Sigard.

I held it up and blew, it so that the ember burst into flames, and I brought the flames up to within six inches of his left eye.

'The eye first then?' I asked, as I looked into the sweating wide eyed prisoner who was doing his best to turn his face away from the flame, but was prevented from moving by the strong restraining arms of his captors.

The glowing ember hovered two inches away from his left eye and as I watched in horror I could see his eye-lashes begin to shrivel, he blurted out 'It was Lady Ella, she ordered us to kill you.'

'She said she would reward us with a purse of silver if we brought back your ring to prove that we had slain you.'

'It was her.'

'I swear to you my Lord Edric.'

'It was the Lady Ella.'

'Lady Ella?' I queried. Finding it difficult to believe that Lady Ella meant to do me harm.

She was the lady who had entered my bed.

She had been a lady who had obviously looked upon me as a man fit and noble enough to be intimate with.

She had always treated me as an equal and with fairness.

Surely, I thought, she could have no reason whatsoever to wish me dead.

I had just married the bloody woman.

Did she know she was pregnant with my child when she sent me off to the Crusades? I asked my-self?

'Perhaps she did,' I thought, and that could have been her reasoning?

My mind was in a complete turmoil.

It was alive with questions and possible answers which I would probably never know. I flung the burning stick back into the fire.

'Hang him.' I said and his two guards heaved him back onto his feet and dragged the screaming man towards the nearest tree.

I felt angry and repentant as I watched my men string him up and strain on the rope, causing him to rise about three feet off the ground where his body writhed and strained for a few minutes, before it ceased its shaking, and his body simply hung there, swaying in the breeze with his head on his chest causing his dead eyes to stare down into my own eyes.

'Perhaps I should have just taken an eye or a hand and let him go, but a one eyed man or a man with one arm can still wield a weapon and if I had let him go then I would forever be looking over my shoulder,' I mumbled to my-self as I tried to convince my-self that I had done the right thing.

'He has tried to kill me before, and if I had let him loose he would have tried again and, who knows he could have succeeded next time.' I told my-self.

Another pair of eyes had witnessed the scene from within his hiding place, a mere twenty paces away from the fire.

'Frithoft' shook with terror mingled with rage, as he stared out of the tiny hole he had drilled through the wall of the 'badger sett, where he was hiding.

The tears ran down out of his eyes to mingle with the mucus and dribble which saturated his grubby, unwashed beard.

He lay in the same position for a good hour after the killers of his brother had left, before he struggled out of the hole, and he remained in the same position for many minutes before his stiff body allowed his limbs to enable him to rise to his feet.

He staggered down towards the tree where the body of his brother hung limply in the warm almost windless air.

He dropped onto his knees as his muddled mind struggled to allow him to accept the fact that it was really the body of his beloved brother that dangled a few inches above his head.

He struggled to his feet again and looked into the face that had shared almost every waking moment of his life with him.

They had been born within an hour of each other.

Their wet-nurse had suckled them at the same time.

They had learned how to walk within moments of each other. They had eaten off the same plate. Learned how to fight each other and assisted one another when one twin had been bullied or had looked like he had been in need of help.

They had lain with the same girl. Even felt each other's pain and discomfort.

He stared at his twin brother, hanging a foot above his head with those pale blue eyes of his, staring, unseeing, down into his own similar coloured eyes.

His mind refused to accept what had happened.

He giggled with the silly voice of an imbecile, and trudged his way up the slight incline uncaring and unknowing where he was going, with a brain that was as addled as last year's egg.

CHAPTER NINETEEN

'Hussein' smiled slyly to himself as he realised that finally his plan to assassinate that damned Christian Sir Edric, was about to become a reality.

For the past six months Hussein had left the barracks before day-light, each and every Wednesday and Thursday morning, in order to follow his target and his small troop of horsemen, who trotted merrily through the fortress gates each and every Wednesday and Thursday, as they made their way out into the countryside on patrol, looking for bandits and ruffians.

He had been frustrated time and time again when the Christians had varied their routes, causing him to have lost them on several occasions, forcing him to ride his borrowed donkey back to its owner after yet another wasted day.

However, today was the fourth Thursday they had taken the same route and had, as usual paused for a good half hour near to a lagoon, which the morning tide had left amongst the rocks.

Not only had these stupid Christians halted at the same place again today, but they had, as usual, stripped naked, leaving a solitary sentry to guard their clothing and weapons, whilst the rest of the men splashed and bathed in the lagoon.

They returned to eat their food and drink a little of the wine that these Christian blasphemers seemed to be addicted to, before they mounted their horses and carried on with their patrol.

As usual, he had followed them on his donkey.

Today he was dressed as a beggar, carrying a single bundle of rags and a half empty earthenware jug of water, but in the past he had disguised himself as a normal Muslim woman, dressed in black from head to foot, whilst on other occasions he had dressed as a wealthy man riding a jet black horse, which he had borrowed from a sympathiser.

He talked quietly to himself as he rode home, telling himself that he must bring at least two crossbowmen with him on his next Thursday trip, as well as his band of men, which now consisted of no less than eighteen believers.

'I will hack the head off this new Christian usurper next Thursday, or maybe the following Thursday and restore the Island to the true God.'

'God is great.' He shouted aloud into the clear blue sky and the empty hills, as he made his way back to his evening quarters.

During the following evening of the day that the Christians had named 'Wednesday,' after some obnoxious heathen God, he gathered his men in a darkened glade, just outside the town and told them of his plans, explaining to them, that each of them must assemble in the darkness, just after mid-night, on the following morning.

'Each of you must wear your chain mail which you need to cover with a shirt, but do not bring your helmets,' He told them, 'for helmets can glow in the moonlight AND in the morning sun.

We will hide in the spot which I have chosen for the trap.
'I do not want any of you to be seen by our prey.'
'Is that clear?' He asked.
Grunts of approval came from his zealots, whilst some of them merely grunted and stared at their leader in admiration.
'Remember.' He hissed.
'You are the huntsmen.'
'You are the Killers of our enemies.
'Follow my orders, especially you crossbowmen, and we will all be famous.'
'I fully expect to slaughter them all as they bathe in the pool, for they will all be unarmed and naked'
'I don't believe that any of us will die, but should that happen, then we must welcome death with open arms, for then we will ascend to paradise and enjoy wealth an happiness for a thousand years to come.

*   *   *

The Huge frame of Frithoft shrank during the first four weeks of wandering through the mountains, for his large body needed much more food than an average man.
The image of his brother's body swaying gently in the wind clouded his already warped mind during large parts of each day and night.

He trudged up-hill, following the only stream that still had flowing water, causing him to halt many times during the hours of daylight in order to drink copious amounts of water which was the only thing that passed through his lips since the death of his Brother.

He was still mumbling the name of his dead brother when he reached the source of the stream and he wandered into the deep pool until the depth of the water reached his chest.

Something in his clouded mind told him to halt.

He ceased wading through the water and gazed around the pool, slowly turning his head to study the surrounding hillside, where he could see the outline of a small farmstead that had been built in the centre of four small grassy fields.

His empty body knew that where there was habitation there must be food, so he turned his weary body in the direction of the farmstead and forced himself to thrust through the water and onto the bank of the pool towards the building.

He walked through a small flock of goats which fled in all directions, causing him to halt for a moment as his clouded mind told him to catch one of the goats and eat it raw, but something in his mind persuaded him that better and easier food awaited him a few short steps away.

He staggered past two barns and a shed before he reached the Farmstead.

Without knocking, he burst through the door to confront three men and an old lady sitting at a table.

He ignored the people as his eyes fell upon the food and a large earthenware jug which lay on the table.

He thrust the oldest of the three men to the floor in his eagerness to reach the food, grabbing the remains of a half uneaten loaf of bread with one hand and the jug with his other hand.

He filled his mouth with bread but was prevented from drinking when one of the other men placed both of his hands around his arm, thus preventing the jug from reaching his mouth.

Frithoft turned his head to see the third man making his way towards him carrying a scimitar.

The other young was hanging onto Frithoft with his other hand, but Frithoft refused to release the half eaten loaf of bread, and brought his own forehead downward with such force that he simply head-butted the man, sending him unconscious to the floor.

The man with the Scimitar hesitated for a brief second and glanced down towards the prone form of his brother.

The slight hesitation was his undoing, for Frithoft had been schooled, had he not by the fiend who had killed his brother when they had lived a peaceful and good life at Wolf-Hall? He simply kicked the man in his groin, causing the man to double up in pain.

Frithoft then brought the half empty jug down on the back of the man's head sending him to join his brother on the floor.

The old man had regained his seat and sat at the table with his wife, as they were still shocked by this foreign giant who had invaded their home and knocked both of their sons to the floor.

'Fahad' shook his head in disgust and amazement and said to his wife. 'I am ashamed of 'Aryan.'

'He is the eldest of our brood and he should have done better.'

'If I had been his age and had my old scimitar in my hand I would have lopped this foreign brutes head off before the stupid oaf knew what was happening.'

'You are quite right my beloved, 'Safia' whispered quietly.

'After all,' she added, 'he was one of old Komnenos's personal bodyguards and he should have done better.'

'Cut out that chatter.' Frithoft snapped, as the food, drink and the fight seemed to have brought his befuddled mind back to something reassembling normality.

There was a loud groan from the floor as the youngest of the brothers' regained consciousness. He rose to a sitting position and noticed his brother 'Ayan' lying a few feet away.

He looked up towards his mother and asked 'Is he dead?'

'I don't think so.' She whispered as if she was afraid of disturbing the brute of a foreigner from devouring every morsel of food and every last drop of 'watered down wine' that remained in their clay pots.

'Imran' bent over the prone body of his brother and grasped his shoulders shook them. 'Aryan.' 'Aryan' he repeated.

'Wake up. Come on. For God's sake. 'Wake up.'
'Hand me a cup of water.' He ordered his mother.
'There is none.' She answered quietly in case this large foreign oaf heard her.
'Go and get some.' He snapped.
His Mother rose to her feet and pointed to her empty pot, which she turned upside down to show the man that it was empty and needed filling.
Frithoft looked at her and seemed to understand her, and allowed her to pick up three empty pots and walk out of the room.
She returned and hurried over to her sons and handed a pot to 'Imran,' who snatched the pot out of her hands and splashed it over his brother's face.
The eyes of 'Aryan' fluttered and opened.
He stared into 'Imran's' face for a long moment before he realised what had happened and rose to a sitting position looking around the room as the events of the past few minutes came back to him.
'Frithoft' stood and watched with caution as the two brothers also stood. He stooped and picked up the fallen scimitar from the floor.
He flourished the sword as if he was assessing its balance and said in a gruff voice. 'You have more?' He asked as he nodded towards the sword.
The two brothers shook their heads to deny that this was their only sword, and when he stared at their parents he noted with acceptance when they also shook their heads.
'You have more. I kill you?' Frithoft snarled.

The three men smiled, but the woman dashed to the corner of the room, where she opened up a wooden trunk and stooped to bring out three long knives and a war-axe that Aryan had brought back with him when he had deserted from the Kings Guards.

'Oh yes. 'Fahad' lied. 'I had forgotten them.'

His lie cost him his two teeth in his head, as he reeled from a punch from the fist of 'Frithoft.'

'More?' 'Frithoft' snarled as took the weapons out of the woman's arms.

He then made a speedy inspection of the farmhouse, leaving the shocked family alone for a few minutes, quickly returning and walking past them and paused for a second to turn and inform them that he intended to enter the room.

'Mine.' He said as he pointed to his huge chest, and he scooped up the weapons off the table and strode into his room, loudly bolting the door behind him.

The food and drink seemed to do wonders for 'Frithoft' who, apart from the two occasions that he roused himself from his bed during the night, in order to reassure himself that all four members of the family were there and asleep by the dying fire, he had the best night's sleep he had experienced for the past four months.

Frithoft had not undressed at night and had, as usual slept in the clothes which he wore during the daytime He walked boldly through the door, and out of his room to the overpowering aroma of bacon sizzling on a pan and the smell of fresh bread which 'Safia' had recently removed from the oven and was sitting on a wooden platter on the freshly scrubbed table.

Frithoft plonked himself down on a chair and wrenched a large chunk of the bread from the loaf, which he immediately cut in half with his 'Saex' and stared at 'Safia.'

'Bacon. Woman.' He snarled.

'It's not ready yet.' She said in a harsh voice, forgetting for a moment that she was not speaking to her husband or her two sons.

'Bacon.' 'Frithoft' demanded again in an even louder voice.

'Oh. If you must insist.' 'Safia' grumbled and pulled two slices of half cooked bacon out of the pan with a pair of wooden tongs and plonked them onto his wooden platter.

Half cooked or not. Frithoft put the sizzling hot bacon between his two slices of bread and despite the fact that he burned both his tongue and his lips. In the days ahead he told people time and time again, that his bacon sandwich was the finest meal he had ever eaten.

He was still living with the family six months later, but he had not been idle during those six months. He had regained all of the weight he lost following the death of his brother. He had trained not only himself, but he had also instructed 'Aryan' and his younger brother 'Imran' in the ways of war.

Although he found it hard to believe, he racked his brain in an attempt to recall each and every move which Edric had unsuccessfully tried to thrust into his thick head when he had been teaching him and the other men at Wolf-Hall the ways of war.

He revelled in the fact that it was he who was the leader and the instructor of his two new recruits and he totally enjoyed the long bouts of swordplay with the two brothers, who were both learning so fast, that during half of their long practices with him, one or other of the brothers would actually win the bout.

The main thing that was always on his mind, was to actually decide which of the many ways of killing a man, he would use to kill Edric.

He knew that in order to beat Edric in a fight, he would need to train and practice with the two brothers until he could easily beat both of them together.

He considered an arrow in the back but discarded that idea as he sorely wanted to see the face of the man as he breathed his last breath on this earth.

A spear in the back was discarded for the same reason.

Much as he would like to kill him with a sword, he knew that despite the days and weeks of practice he still knew that he had not reached the skill which Edric seemed to possess as if was as simple as the smirk that crossed his face when he would disarm his opponent with a simple flick of his wrist.

He reached that point within a period of six months when he could out-match both of the brothers with sword and axe, but even then, his warped mind told him that he would still need to be super-fit to win against such a famous killer of men as Edric.

'But he is an old man.' He told him-self time and time again.' He must be at least sixty years of age by now.' he muttered to him-self smugly.

He trained every single day with the brothers until late in the afternoon, when he dismissed them in order that they could attend to their duties of looking after the farm and the animals.

He would then walk into the nearby woodland until he reached his favourite glade, where he would lift a heavy log, which he had cut especially for the purpose of hefting it onto his shoulders. He then ran up and down a well-worn path in the woodland until the sun faded away over the top of the mountains.

He assisted the family to harvest the single crop of oats and the two fields of hay.

'To-morrow we leave.' He announced at the supper table.

'Who leaves?' Asked 'Fahad.'

'Not you old man.' Frithoft said.

'Just me and the two boys.'

He rose from the table and stuffed the last chunk of cheese in his mouth.

'Aryan.' 'Imran.' 'Get your war gear cleaned and have your weapons ready so that we can leave first thing in the morning.'

He left the room and the family heard the bolt clang shut, as usual.

'It's all very well for him to say have your weapons ready when we all know that all the weapons are locked up tight every night before we go to bed.'

CHAPTER TWENTY

Gilda thoroughly enjoyed the voyage.
 She had learned to love the sea and totally enjoyed the voyage.
 She laughed at the antics of the fish and especially the pod of Dolphins that raced in front and alongside the ship, as the ship made its way through the calm, silvery blue waters of the Mediterranean Sea.
 She chuckled when a member of the crew stumbled over a rope that has been carelessly left in a bundle.
 Her laughter and her jolly mood transferred itself to the two clumps of warriors who were seated in the only two spaces that they were allowed to inhabit, being the 'fore' and 'aft' parts of the ship.
 The breeze was with them and carried the wide merchant ship across the sea to the port of Latakia, which, according to the Captain was where he had been ordered to drop off his cargo of men and supplies.
 Hugo had known of Gilda's sexuality from day one, and for the past twelve years he had been her constant friend and protector, not that she needed his protection now, for despite the fact that she was a girl and half his size, over the past few years she had slowly developed from being extremely good into a formidable warrior who was virtually un-beatable and could probably slay her gigantic friend in the blink of an eye.

However, at the present time, the titanic Hugo was in no state to defend himself, let alone anyone else, because from the moment he had set foot of this leaky old trading ship, his face had turned into a pallid shade of green, whilst the ship was still in dock, and every morsel of food he had eaten over the past four days had been returned to the fishes.

His aching belly had never felt so empty and so bloody sore.

Gilda screamed with joy as she watched a dolphin leap clear out of the water and turn a somersault before it returned to the sea without so much as a splash.

Hugo turned his head towards his small friend and gave a half-hearted smile before he sank back against the ships planks, wishing he was either dead or anywhere else on earth, as long as that piece of earth was not moving from side to side and up and down at the same time.

'Land Ahoy,' shouted one of the crewmen and pointed to a point in the distance.

The shout itself caused everyone on the ship to look.

'Where away?' Bellowed the Captain?

'Off the port bow.' The man answered, as he pointed towards a blur of grey, which seemed to rise out of the very sea itself.

'Thank the good Lord for that.' Mumbled Hugo, as he bent, yet again over the side of the ship and retched, fetching up nought but yellow bile which dribbled down his greying beard and onto his filthy smeared jerkin.

It seemed to Hugo that it took a full day for the ship to actually reach the port, which turned out to be a single wooden plank that protruded out into the sea from a township that consisted of a few mud huts which lay half hidden in a cluster of sand-dunes.

He was the first man off the ship and stepped off the ship onto the so called pier, which wobbled so much that he would have fallen into the clear blue water, had it not been for the quick thinking of a sturdy crewman who grabbed one of his arms and steadied him. He shrugged himself free, and without a word of thanks, he waded his way shakily onto dry land.

Gilda on the other hand was rather sad to see the end of the voyage.

She was rather reluctant to leave the ship, but still jumped onto the pier, and then hopped daintily down the shaky pier.

She performed one of her famous summersaults and landed daintily onto the shoreline beside Hugo.

'That was fun.' She said loudly in that funny voice of hers.

'Maybe it was fun for you.' Hugo grunted.

'I would call it Hell,' he added, 'and I hope I never see a bloody ship or a bloody ocean again in my life.'

The twenty seven other men slowly joined them on the beach, where they all waited until dusk had fallen.

They were eventually met by a single Knight who, despite the fact that he was dressed for riding, arrived on foot and looked to be totally exhausted.

He stood on a small patch of grass that had managed to find root amongst the sandy soil.

'Men, He shouted in a loud voice in order to be heard above the noise which the assembled men were making.

'I am named Sir Alan of Mercia, and the King has sent me here to meet with you, and to guide you to a place where the rest of your fellow warriors will be waiting for you.'

'I have been ordered to lead you and the other men to join the King's army.'

'As we speak the King is marching towards Jerusalem.'

'He intends to conquer the city before Christmas day of this year.'

Hugo and Gilda looked at one another.

Hugo grimaced and said gruffly 'That will mean more bloody fighting.'

'Great,' said Gilda loudly.

'The sooner we get to it the better.'

'Much as I enjoyed the voyage I can't wait to kill a dozen or so of these ugly looking Savages.' She added.

'God's own blood.' Hugo said, as he cleared his throat of the dust and spat in the sand. 'You really are a blood-thirsty little sod. Aren't you?'

'What's wrong with that?' she countered.

'That's why we are here in this hot horrible land isn't it?'

'Follow me.' Shouted Sir Alan, and he walked towards the town.

Hugo and Gilda walked behind Sir Alan as he led them through the township itself and then along an overgrown cart-track for at least two miles.

They eventually reached a sheltered valley that was so green that it stood out like a green oasis which had been placed in the centre of a dry and barren desert.

Camped along-side a large lagoon were hundreds of weathered leather tents, which had been spaced out and set in orderly rows.

Hundreds of men sat around a large number of fires, which sent spirals of smoke up into the hot dry air.

'Here we are,' Sighed Sir Alan and he led his newcomers down the slight slope and into the camp.

He halted and said to his assembled men.

'I have arranged this single row of tents.

'Each of the tents will take two men and I want you all to follow this man here,' and he nodded towards a youngster who appeared to be sixteen or seventeen years of age.

'He will take you to the quarter-master who will fit you out with everything you will need for the coming campaign.'

'You will then return to your tents, where you will sleep, but you must all be up and be ready to march by dawn on the morrow, and do not forget to pack your tents as neatly as you can for they will be your sole responsibility and will probably be your living quarters for the coming weeks, or if things do not go well for us, then the tents could be your homes for much, much longer.'

Hugo was shocked out of a deep slumber an hour before dawn as Gilda shook him awake and shouted 'Up you get old chap.' She shouted in his ear.

'The camp is awake and if you don't shift your big bum, you will not have time to have a bite to eat before we march.'

The assembled Army marched hour later.

They heading southward as they followed Sir Alan and his two Arab guides along what they called 'The Coast road' but the so called 'coast road' was little more than a rutted track, which soon became a barely visible track that appeared and disappeared at irregular intervals in and out of the drifting sand.

Arab horsemen appeared along the dunes by mid-morning and their numbers increased as the day wore on, so much so that at times it seemed to the marching Christians that the horizon itself was moving with swarms of white robed men.

Many of these Saracens rode Camels, which was a beast that few Christian men had ever seen, whilst another separate body of men thundered up and down the sand-dunes on magnificent looking horses.

But both the riders of Horses and Camels were soon out-numbered by hundreds of foot soldiers who tramped doggedly through the sand. These foot soldiers marched some three hundred paces away on a course parallel to the marching Christians.

Sir Alan halted his small army and rode up and down the line of sweating men.

'Men.' He shouted loudly.

'Fear not at this multitude of Saracens who are dogging our footsteps.'

'They are shepherds and farmers and are not warriors of note.'

'They may rush up to us and shoot a few arrows at us, but we can put up with a few pin-pricks to hasten us on our way.

'But,' he shouted.

'Just in case there are a few warriors amongst them, I want you to carry your shields on your shoulders as we march along, so that none of their arrows can damage us, and I want you archers to march to the left of our column, just in case any of those idiots should get near enough, then a volley or two from you bow-men will tell them that we are the true warriors, and send those idiotic shepherds and camel drivers back home to their stinking tents.'

Sir Alan stood up on the stirrups of his horse and stretched his neck as he looked at the series of sand-dunes where the Saracens were assembling.

'Now those chaps up there look a little more serious,' he said aloud.

Gilda and Hugo, who were standing just below him, heard his comment.

They exchanged looks and both turned their heads to gaze in awe at the antics which some of the Saracen riders were performing in order impress both their friends and their foes.

Hugo had acquired a new breast-plate, which had been cobbled together by a local black-smith.

The aged smith had found two old Breast-plates that had been rusting away in a leaky old shed, and he had converted them into a single shiny new Breastplate which was not only large enough to encompass Hugo's huge chest, but due to the skilful manner in which the smith had constructed the item, he had overlapped each of the old pieces of metal together in order to give its wearer ample protection to withstand anything other than the charge of an wild elephant.

Gilda had also altered her appearance.

She had been ill at ease when the King had ordered her to wear girl's clothes and had left them in a heap, an hour after the King had set sail for the Holy land.

She now wore a chain-link shirt which encompassed both her front and back.

The only other three items which she now wore were a white silken shirt and a pair of tight black leather trousers that were tucked into her new ankle-length camel skin boots.

It seemed obvious to Sir Alan that an order had been given, for a large contingent of riders suddenly broke off from the main army of Saracens and charged towards the stationary Christians, who had remained strung out, still in their 'order of March.'

'Quickly now,' Sir Alan bellowed.

'Spearmen.' He shouted. 'To the front.'

'Archers. Gather around those three carts.'

There were many long moments of confusion as the men ran to carry out their leaders order.

The Saracen horsemen led the charge, leaving the camels a few paces to their rear, (for these camels were not racing camels, which in many cases can out-run horses) they were merely, run of the mill ordinary camels. Never-the-less, both camels and horses speedily crossed the distance between the two forces of men.

The Saracen horsemen were the first to shoot, and they loosed a ragged volley of arrows.

Many of the arrows fell short, or over the bulk of the waiting Christians, but maybe a third of them splattered onto the Christians, striking a few unfortunate souls who had not raised their shields in time to avoid the missiles.

'Loose,' Sir Alan bellowed to his archers, causing a cloud of arrows to be released from their taut strings, and with a loud swishing sound, the deadly arrows soared over their fellow warriors and fell upon the tightly packed Saracens, sending men, horses and Camels screaming to the ground.

'Left flank. Advance.' Sir Alan shouted who was hoping to encircle the riders.

He then cupped his hands to his mouth and shouted as loud as he could.

'Right flank. Advance.' He ordered, causing both sides of his small army to advance.

The men in the centre, which included the archers, remained stationary and continued to shower the Saracens with clouds of arrows, causing mayhem amongst their enemies.

Sir Alan then ordered the centre of his army to advance, for he was intent upon catching the screaming camel and horse riders in a pincer movement, which he hoped would eliminate them from the fray, whilst the enemy foot soldiers who were no more than three or four hundred paces away, could do nought but watch as their comrades were slaughtered.

Gilda and Hugo were in the fore of the centre of the Christian army.

Gilda had never carried a shield, and always sheltered behind the huge shield belonging to her gigantic friend

In the stories and saga's that have been told in the past, when warriors were sitting around their camp-fires on cold winter nights, or when they were on campaign during the fighting season, the collisions between warring armies were nearly always described like the clashing's of titans, sending noises like thunder-claps echoing across the valleys as shield met shield, before the real work of killing began.

This meeting between these particular Christians and Saracens was not at all like that, for as the Christians quickly advanced behind their shields, they were met by a tangle of dead and maimed horsemen and their animals, which had been transfixed by the Christian arrow storm.

Hugo and Gilda speedily passed through this tangle of men and animals towards a solid phalanx of undamaged Saracen warriors, who stood in a solid shield-wall with their shields and weapons to the fore.

Gilda scurried behind Hugo, who had stormed ahead of her and the other men, and with a huge swipe of his huge long staved, battle-Hammer, he attacked the man who stood directly in front of him.

His Battle-hammer crashed through the man's shield, sending both the Saracens arm and his shattered shield to the ground.

The dazed man stood and stared at his arm which lay before him.

Before he had a moment to collect what remained of his wits, Gilda had dashed in and sliced off the man's left leg, and then as the man fell, she slashed his head from his body.

Hugo and Gilda led their men through the gap which the man had left, hacking and slashing as they went, slaying man after man with what, to their opponents, looked like casual ease, leaving a trail of dead and dying warriors in their wake, causing dismay and confusion amongst the Saracens who were in a position to witness the destruction of their friends.

Hugo was akin to a battering ram, as he crashed into Saracen after Saracen, either bowling them over or simply slaying them with his huge Hammer, whilst Gilda followed him, dashing into man after man so quickly that Sir Alan thought she was more like a miniature tiger, striking each man she attacked so speedily that they were either dead or mortally wounded before they realised they were actually being attacked.

The mayhem that they left in their wake caused many of their Saracen enemies to turn tail and run, whilst a large number of their comrades simply threw down their shields and weapons and knelt down with their heads bowed, before these two awesome killing machines, who continued to advance remorselessly through them.

Sir Alan was a mere step or two behind Hugo and Gilda, and he paused for a moment to rest the point of his battle-sword on the grounds and he watched these two awesome warriors carry on slaying man after man.

'If I hadn't seen that with my very own eyes I simply would not have believed it.' He said aloud.

Hugo and Gilda had reached a space where no living enemies remained in front of them and simply ambled back to the waiting Sir Alan.

'YOU, Hugo and your little friend here have just slain more than a dozen or more enemy warriors, and captured or put to flight more than a hundred Saracens by yourselves.' Said the still amazed Sir Alan.

'I think your actions have been so noteworthy that I shall have to mention them to the King.'

'I would rather you didn't.' Said the blood smeared Gilda in her child-like voice.

'Why ever not?' He queried.

'Well, my Lord. If the King knows about us, he may well split us up, or even send us home.'

'Especially now that he knows that I am a girl.'

'Oh I am sure he wouldn't do that.' Sir Alan assured her.

'You two are too valuable in his plans to conquer Jerusalem.'

'He will want every fighting man with him here if he is to conquer the Holy-land and the city of Jerusalem.'

'That is exactly my point my Lord, if you will excuse me for saying.'

'He is an avid believer in Christian values and I know that he is aware that I am a mere girl, and as such, he may think that it could dishearten his men to be outfought by a young girl.'

'Then perhaps it would be wise to merely tell him of your bravery and not to stress the point that you are a girl.' He said as he toyed with his thick blonde moustache.

Sir Alan was forced to turn his head towards his rear where something resembling a brawl was taking place between four or five of his men who seemed to be squabbling over a piece of looted silver that one of them had found.

'What's going on here? He bellowed as he strode down towards the scene.

Before he reached the scene of the fight, he could see that two of the men had their short swords in their right hands and the face of one of them was already covered in blood.

Sir Alan also noted that a number of his men in the act of looting and killing the remaining Saracens who had been wounded in the fight.

The men were also slaughtering the wounded and un-wounded horses and camels which still remained by the bodies of their former owners.

'Halt.' He shouted at the top of his voice, causing all of the men to cease their slaughter and looting and stand and turn their faces towards him.

'Stop your killing NOW. He shouted.

'We cannot obtain information from dead men and we can use some of those animals who are not wounded.

'We may be able to save a few who only have superficial wounds.'

'Sergeants-at-Arms. He shouted.

'Take control of your men.'

'Stop the idiots from killing each other, and have them cut off all the pieces of edible meat from those dead Horses and Camels.'

'That meat will provide us all with a decent meal tonight. He bellowed.

'Quickly now, and you can tell them that I will allow them to continue to loot the bodies of our enemies, for I have seen scenes like this before and I know full well that if our own men are prevented from looting the dead, then dozens of local peasants will arrive during the night and they will strip the dead of anything of value before the coming dawn.'

'Have the prisoners brought down to me by the water wagons.'

'Sergeants,' he shouted again, for he whilst he was delighted at the way that the battle had gone so far, he was still aware of the horde of Saracen foot soldiers who still stood a few hundred paces away on the first ridge of sand dunes.

Or at least, they HAD stood on a ridge of sand dunes a few minutes ago when he had last looked, but when he turned his head again to judge the numbers of his adversaries who still opposed him, he saw nothing but empty sand dunes and the backs of the white robed figures disappearing over the next ridge.

He stared in amazement, and within a few fleeting minutes the second ridge of sand dunes were as empty as the first.

'Stand down men.' He shouted at the top of his voice. And then in a quieter voice he said, almost to himself.

'It seems as if we have won. Does it not?'

'Sergeants at arms,' he shouted again.

'As soon as you have allowed the men loot the bodies of the slain, have them assembled and ready to commence our march. '

'These Saracens carry their wealth with them,' he mumbled to him-self, so I assume that many a man will be wealthy before the sun sets today.'

He turned to his Sergeants again and said in a loud voice. 'I also want you to assign a squad of men to seek out those camels and horses with flesh wounds, and have the surgeons save as many of them as they can.'

'We still have a long way to go and those animals that are fit enough to make the journey will be of value to us.'

'That man there.' He pointed to a sergeant who appeared to be standing around, doing nothing.

'Assemble a squad of men and lead them to salvage all of our arrows that are re-usable, and pick up all the Saracen weapons you and your men can find.'

'I have a feeling we are going to need them.'

'Hurry up man.' He shouted.

'We have less than two hours of daylight left and we need to reach the next source of water before nightfall.

Sir Alan led his weary army down the coastal road towards the town of Haifa.

During the following fifty years the Saracens spoke with awe about a gigantic Christian and a dwarf who fought like caged lions, slaughtering two complete regiments of true believers.

* * *

Hussein assembled his men at midnight as a full moon shone brightly out of a cloudless clear night sky.

He and his men had managed to recruit no fewer than seventeen men which included three experienced crossbow-men, who had served the late King.

All of his men had obeyed his orders, and each man was wearing black or dark leather jerkins and they had avoided wearing any shiny armour or helmets.

They were all eager to ambush this Christian upstart and his men, providing the man followed his usual pattern of halting for a rest at pool that was known locally as 'Cleopatra's pool'.

Instead of leading his men, as was the usual procedure for any Caliph or leader of men.

Hussein jog trotted at the rear of them, in order to ensure that no man fell behind, as he was fully aware that their numbers were about equal to those of the usual patrols which this Christian idiot led, and the loss of a single man, especially if that man happened to be a crossbowman, could easily turn his carefully devised plans into a disaster.

By the time they arrived at the sight he had chosen, his men and himself were totally exhausted, for he had not realised just how difficult it would be jogging or even walking quickly at night over the same terrain that he had covered a number of times over the previous weeks, but that had been during the hours of daylight and he had never previously covered the same terrain in darkness.

He had not lost a single man during the journey, but two of his men including one of his crossbowmen had twisted their ankles and limped up to the crystal clear pool in order to quench the raging thirsts they had all acquired during the arduous journey to reach Cleopatra's pool before dawn.

'Thanks be to 'God.' He said aloud as he bathed his feet in the cool, clear water.

'We have at least three or four hours to catch our breath and regain our strength before these idiots to walk into our trap.'

Hussein joined his men and knelt onto his tiny prayer mat, clasping his hands and touched the floor with his forehead as he muttered his morning prayer.

It was nearly an hour later before he rallied his men, and took each man to a position that he had chosen for them during the past two weeks.

He positioned most of his men at least fifty or sixty paces away from the pool, but he allocated the positions of his crossbowmen much nearer, in carefully dug camouflaged pits, which he had scooped out of the sandy soil some weeks ago.

He had scattered the soil far and wide, in order to remove all evidence that anyone or indeed any-thing had dug or disturbed the soil or the undergrowth in the past year.

His last act was to walk carefully around his trap site and view each of his men from a standing and a then from a sitting position around the pool.

He re-arranged the positions of two of his men until he was completely satisfied that they were totally invisible from prying eyes and would be in a more ideal position when the time came for them to vacate their hiding places and slaughter their enemies.

As he visited each man for the last time, he refilled their own drinking bags from his own water bottle, and left them hidden, before he walked carefully over to his own carefully chosen hiding place, brushing any sign of his passage with a leafy branch that he had broken off a small bush.

CHAPTER TWENTY-ONE

'I only learned about an epic battle that had taken place on the coastal road in the Holy land some six months after the battle had taken place.

It was told by an old sea Captain who had relayed the story to one of Ludmilla's spies, who was the manager (under Ludmilla's tuition) of a busy brothel in the town.

The Captain had told a story of a huge Christian Knight and his page-boy, who was apparently little more than a ten year old boy, who had single handed, ('with the help of a ten year old child") defeated a huge Saracen army of ten thousand hardened warriors.

My brain immediately jumped to the conclusion that these two Hero's must be non-other than 'Hugo' and 'Sven' (I still had the habit of calling her by her old name and had not yet brought myself to call her by her new name of 'Gilda.'

Of course, I took the figures of an army of ten thousand battle hardened warriors and the fact that this ten year old child had slain five hundred men with a large piece of salt, and doubted that the true figures were probably half that.

I immediately called Ludmilla into my presence and ordered her to find the Captain and have him brought to me, in order that I may be able to glean more details about these two Christian Hero's.

Three hours later Ludmilla escorted the man into my hall.

He had the looks of a typical old sea dog.

He wore a greasy woollen cap.

His grey speckled beard reached down to his wide leather belt, which with the help of a large brass buckle attempted, without success, to prevent his ample stomach from overlapping.

What I could see of the part of his face that was not covered with his greasy grey beard, was very flushed with vivid red veins that protruded almost to a point where they looked like they were about to burst.

He was obviously a man who liked his drink.

Ludmilla stood beside me and introduced the Captain to me.

'This is Captain 'Saad,' she said

'Welcome.' I said in an amiable tone and held my right hand out as a sign of friendship, as well as to show him that I carried no weapon in my sword hand.

He readily grasped my hand and with a smile which caused his beard and his moustache to part a little, he said. 'And what can I do for you my Lord?'

'Take a seat,' I offered him and indicated a chair at my table.

'Would you care for a drink?' I asked.

'That would be nice my Lord.' He answered.

'Would you like Beer or wine?' I asked.

'I am partial to the local red wine thank you My Lord.'

'Ludmilla.? I nodded towards Ludmilla who, in turn nodded to a serving wench who was positioned near the kegs of beer and wine that I kept in a locked cupboard in the Dining Hall for occasions such as this.

When the empty glasses of Ludmilla, the Captain and my own glass had been filled, I raised my glass, held it aloft and allowed the three glasses to touch.

'Captain Saad,' I said. 'I have been led to believe that you have been talking about a recent battle, which took place some six months ago, in which two Christians defeated a huge army of our enemies, and I would like you to tell me, in as much detail as you are able, about these two men, as well as the battle in which they fought.'

I could see that he was not expecting this, and surmised that perhaps he had come to my home, in order that I was about to offer him a lucrative contract for him and his ship.

'Ha, my Lord,' he said as he nearly chocked on the mouthful of wine that he had been savouring in the back of his throat. 'I thought you had summoned me here to offer me some deal which would make me a wealthy man.'

'Well wealthy enough to allow me to sell my old tub and purchase a bigger and better ship.'

'Let me put this to you Captain,' I said. 'If you please me and relay all the facts and figures on to me regarding the two Christians and the battle in which they fought, then I might, just might, reward you with enough silver to allow you to purchase a new ship.'

He nodded and attempted, but failed to smile through his copious beard, and he peered over the rim of his glass with suspicious eyes before he took another long drink out of his half-filled glass.

'My Lord.' He said, as he plonked his glass on the table so hard that I was amazed that the fragile Egyptian glass did not break.

'I only heard about it second hand like, from a man who heard it from another man, and this second man told of a Christian Army had been attacked by a Saracen army of ten thousand.'

'He said that the Christians were outnumbered by ten to one.'

He paused for a moment as he watched his glass being filled again and licked his lips. (I think, for I could not actually see his lips.)

'This man said that the Sheiks and the proven warriors charged into the Christian lines, and one of the Christian Knights, who was a giant of a man and had a boy of about ten or eleven years of age with him.'

'This huge Christian Knight slew the Saracen chieftain with a massive Hammer, the like of which they had never seen before, and simply slashed his way through rank after rank of proven warriors until he came through at the other end and he simply turned around and hacked his way back through them again.'

'What about the boy?' I asked.

'Oh, yes the boy.' He said. 'I had forgotten what he said about the boy, but I do recall that the child was like a wasp, or a hornet, for the child dashed in and killed any man who stood before him.'

'He said the child was like a streak of lightening, as fast as a cheetah he was, as if he had been sent by Allah himself to smite down those who annoyed him.'

'My thanks to you Captain,' I said to him as I stood up, as I had taken a dislike to the man and of course I knew that I had promised him silver, so I reached into my pouch and threw the purse full of silver, which I had already counted out prior to our meeting.

'Thank you for your time. You have answered my questions satisfactory.'

He emptied his glass of red wine, weighed the purse in his hand and stood, nodded his thanks, and was escorted out of my presence by one of the serving maidens.

I was satisfied that the two Christian warriors who the Captain had spoken about could be non-other than my old friends from Wolf-Hall. It had to be Hugo and Gilda.

That was the last time I heard about them.

It was over one year later when news came from the Holy-land, telling of our own King Richards success of capturing the holy city of Jerusalem.

'Did Hugo and Gilda survive the slaughter?' I asked myself?

No one seemed to know.

The story of the conquest of Jerusalem did not fill my chest with pride and happiness, for it was marred with the blood of innocents.

Whilst the taking of the heavily fortified city of Jerusalem was an achievement worthy of note, it was stained by the revengeful army of Crusaders, who slaughtered Greeks, Saracens, Jews and Christians.

They slaughtered every citizen they could find, man woman and child.

In their blood-lust, they killed every cow, goat and sheep until the once sweet smelling streets of the Holy city reeked with the stench of death and blood.

*   *   *

I had ceased my recruitment drive nearly six months ago, and I now had more trained warriors than I really needed, but after a recent meeting with Ludmilla's son 'Stavros' plus two of his senior officers. (I had promoted Stavros to be THE senior officer in our new army.) I had decided that the best way of preventing these marauding pirates and freebooters, who still plagued, not only the shores of Cyprus, but also continued to raid up and down the entire coast of the Mediterranean sea.

In order to deter these Pirates I had decided to use the same tactics that the ancient Romans had used to subdue the tribes they had conquered many long years ago.

I ordered my Generals that whilst they should not discontinue training our standing army in weapon practice and in the tactics of warfare. We should also use our man-power to construct roadways across our island for easy access.

I also ordered them to build stone towers along our complete coastline at regular intervals, in order to warn our populations that marauders were in the area or had been seen at sea. Thus, allowing us time and access to send large enough companies of our trained warriors to deal with these corsairs.

Stavros assigned his officers to their sectors of the Island, with the order to collect enough supplies of foodstuffs and tools which would enable them to march, or even ride to their assigned areas within the following few days, and repel any raiders who had the audacity to raid the island.

Ludmilla was rather concerned as she and a number of household servants watched Edric as he led his men out of the courtyard and through the gate on yet another patrol into the wooded hills and secret valleys of the Island.

Even she had not been told of the route which he would travel, but she did know from previous conversations that on days such as this, he did like to take his men to one of their favourite watering holes called 'Cleopatra's pool.'

'I have warned him.' She muttered to herself as she watched the last horseman ride through the gate.

She turned to re-enter the house in order to catch up on some urgent errand that had been concerning her for the past few days.

*   *   *

I rode through the township with my head held high, for I was reasonably proud of my achievements over the past year, and I was equally proud of the twenty men who rode behind me.

They were all chosen warriors who I had promoted to be my personal guards through one action or another.

They were not the normal run-of-the-mill men, but they were men had stood out from the crowd by doing or maybe simply by being something different.

And as I rode along, I thought of those differences which made these men special.

Most had not been, or were not particularly huge warriors or even outstanding men, but almost all of them were young and agile.

One young man was an excellent horseman and could do all manner of spectacular acts on horseback, whilst two of the men were experts with their crossbows and most of them were reasonably good with one weapon or another.

I know that Ludmilla's spies had told her that there was a plan afoot to attack either myself or one of my generals, but no one seemed to know who, when or where, so I had erred on the side of caution and added an extra two men to all of my patrols and, as is my way, I refused to worry about things that may or may not happen.

My old friend and mentor 'Vorta' who had taught my friends and myself the arts, and of the ways of war and warfare when we were untried children, living with him in a cave in the remote wilderness near the Welsh border.

He had often stressed to us that our destinies had already been written from the day we were born, and worrying about the future was totally pointless.

He had two phrases which seemed to explain every situation that ever existed.

One was. 'Happens.' which I think he learned when he himself was a child in the north of England.

The second was 'What will happen, will happen.'

And so with the memories of old Vorta and his wisdom ringing inside my head, I rode merrily along, ahead of my troop, up and through the sweet smelling thyme covered lowlands of this beautiful Island.

The further we rode, the more the countryside became less cultivated, causing us to ride through hillsides covered with orchards and grape-vines, which in turn led to more wooded and wilder terrain, for this was still a country of untamed beauty, containing Wild Boar, Bears and two species of Deer.

As we walked our mounts up the final hill before we reached a valley which in turn would take us to Cleopatra's pool, my thoughts turned back to the warning which Ludmilla had hissed at me, before I had mounted my horse to leave.

'Beware Lord Edric,' she had hissed. 'I have seen the signs and they are not good.'

As I reached the brow of the hill, I gazed across the valley to the slight mound where we usually halted for a rest and a drink from this famous pool.

I knew of course, that some of my men were looking forward to a soak and a splash in its cool clear water.

I thought, although I couldn't be sure that I caught a momentarily glimpse of metal shining in the mid-day sun.

I immediately retraced my steps and pulled my horse off the brow of the hill, and back a yard or so, colliding with the rest of my men who were following a few steps behind me.

One of the youngest of my men started to cuss and said 'What in the name of t.' and then said no more for he could see me standing a couple of feet away staring at him.

'Sorry my Lord,' he stammered. 'I didn't see you there.'

I allowed myself a slight smile but did not chastise him for I saw an image of myself in that very youngster many, long moons ago.

'I think we will go the pretty route today lads,' I said cheerfully.

'I have a feeling that the beautiful Cleopatra may have things other than cool clear water waiting for us in her bath-tub today.'

Young they may be, but most of them caught the drift of my words and I was pleased to note that most of the men's right hands flew quickly to the hilts of their weapons.

We retraced our steps, walking our horses for more than half a mile until I gave the order to mount and I led them at a gentle trot southwards, along a narrow grassy valley.

After we had covered a further mile southwards, I veered back in the direction of the small hillock where I knew Cleopatra's pool was situated.

I knew full-well that our detour had put us at least an hour and a half behind the usual time when we would normally have reached the pool.

 I also realised that if there were armed men waiting for us at the pool, then they too may well have realised that we were late and that knowledge would make them anxious and uneasy.

 From my own past experience when, many long years ago when I had been lying in wait for a deer or a boar to walk into my trap.

 I knew that anxiety and tension could cause men to do unexpected and unwise things, and with a bit of good fortune, our detour and delay just might encourage men who have been waiting for hours in the hope that their prey may simply blunder into their trap, could well be tempted to get up and stretch their weary bodies.

 It took us the best part of an additional hour to reach the top of the hill, which over-looked the pool of fame, and much to my disappointment, the hill below us and the pool itself, which shone through the branches of the two trees that hid it from the sun, were completely empty.

 I have always been a man who is not easily convinced.

 I studied the sloping hillside before me in detail and I still could see no sign of man or beast.

 'If there are men down there lying in wait then they are very well hidden.' I muttered quietly to the young warrior who stood beside me.

'I can't see anyone either my Lord.' He said in a low tone.

'And yet my instinct is telling me that something is just not quite right.' I said.

I had actually made two steps to lead my men down the hill, when a medium sized bush of wild thyme seemed to jump to one side of its own accord.

A man rose and stood as he stared down the hill, in the opposite direction of my men and my-self, who were standing totally shocked some ten feet away from him.

I stepped forward a single pace and brought the hilt of my Saex down on his head.

I caught him before he hit the ground and eased him to the ground without making a sound. I could just have easily killed the man, but somehow my English upbringing stepped in and prevented me from carrying out such a cowardly act.

I turned to my men and placed my fore-finger to my lips, saying in a whisper. 'Where there is one there must be more.'

'Shields' I ordered and watched as the men swung their shields off their backs and placed them onto their left arms.

'Tie the horses to that tree and follow me.' I ordered, nodding towards a tree that was a few feet away down the slope we had just climbed.

'Form a line.' I said quietly, 'and I want you three bowmen to space yourselves out.

'I want one of you on each end, and one in the middle. Quickly now.'

We all stood for a moment until we were ready to walk down the rise towards the pool.

'Slowly now my lads.' I said.

'Jab your swords into the bushes before you move on.'

'The man had been named 'Zahid the pious' by his own zealot of a father.'

'Zahid' heard a slight noise and rose from his hole.

He turned and hurled his spear at his nearest enemy.

It was a good cast for he had rehearsed it a hundred times and more, and indeed the spear did speed fast and true and embedded itself just below the rim of the shield belonging to Joseph, who was a Greek Christian and the second youngest man in the troop.

The force of the blow thrust the metal rim of Joseph's shield backwards and upwards into his face, shattering two teeth and leaving a red scar in the form of a crescent across the left hand side of his face.

Zahid instantly fell to the ground with two crossbow bolts embedded in his chest.

As he fell, men began to pop up all over the hillside, causing my men to bunch up and generate towards the centre of their line, but I could see their mistake and shouted 'Stay where you are men. 'Put your shields forward and continue to follow me downward and slay any man we meet.'

'Slowly now.' 'There could be more men hiding in their holes, so keep on prodding the bushes so that we can get all of them.'

'Saif,' whose name means 'man of the sword,' had never been a man to wait for things to happen to him, and he was tired, angry and was determined not to lie here in the earth merely to wait until one of these heathens reached him and thrust their sword into him.

He leapt out of his hole with his sword to the fore and his small, round metal shield in his left hand.

He ran the few paces up the slope to confront the nearest Christian who he hoped would be the leader of these infidels.

'Saif' ran as fast as he could towards the man he sworn to send to Hell.

The man directly in front of him was my-self, the leader of the Christians who 'Saif' had hoped it would be, and as I waited for him to reach me I drew my broad-sword from its scabbard on my back and waited for him to reach me.

I allowed his first wild swipe to sail a foot away from my chin and then caught his backward cut with my own sword, which was a famous blade that I had acquired long ago, and I had been assured that it was a blade which had been forged by a master in the Spanish city of Toledo, over one hundred years ago.

The two blades met with a clash and my own sword shattered the inferior blade of 'Saif' allowing my own blade to continue its way and meet with the body of my opponent, where it lodged itself half way through his body.

The blow was so savage that it wrenched my sword out of my hands and sent my own sword and 'Saif's' body tumbling down the hillside.

'Hussein', whose name means 'The Beautiful,' as he had indeed been a beautiful baby, and had been a good looking boy who had grown up to become a handsome young man, so much so that he had four lovely wives and nine children waiting for him at home, but as he stood on this hillside amongst the gentle breeze that smelled of wild Thyme and lavender as well as the steaming guts that oozed out of a man who lay three feet away from him, he did not feel beautiful.

'God is great,' he screamed, as he plucked up his courage and raced up the slope towards the line of hated Christians, crashing into the shield of one man, who was knocked backwards a pace.

Edric's well trained man countered the blow with a swipe of his own sword which narrowly missed its target.

'Hussein' grinned to himself, but the grin left his face as suddenly as it had reached it, for he felt a great weight in his belly which halted his forward movement, and as he gazed down at his abdomen, he could see a Christian sword protruding out of it causing his legs to suddenly weaken. He fell face forward onto the man who had delivered the killing blow.

Several other crossbow bolts thudded into the shields of my men and I noticed with pleasure that my own crossbowmen were busy sending their own shafts into the unprotected bodies of our-would be assassins.

The grunts and screams of men killing one another slowly ceased leaving the hillside silent, apart from the gasps and pants that came from my own men, who were with a single exception, standing with their hands on their knees, gasping for breath.

The one exception and our only loss was a young warrior who was lying face down on the dusty ground with two crossbow bolts protruding from his back.

I looked behind my line and I could not see a man standing, neither could I see the body of a man who had been slain.

'With me men,' I shouted. 'I think we have a live one up here

'Form a line and follow me back up the hill,' I said and began to retrace our tracks back up the hillside.

'Careful now lads.' I said loudly. 'This sod seems to be a bit smarter than the rest.'

'Look for anything that looks to be out of place, like a hole that could be large enough to allow a crossbow bolt to be shot out of it.'

I led them up the slight rise which contained no real trees but did have a number of bushes and tussock's of herbs and dried grass, which dotted the rise.

We had almost reached the top when one of my men who stood about fifteen feet away from me shouted. 'Here my Lord.'

'I want the rest of you to stay exactly where you are whilst I will look what he's found.' I shouted to the men, and I walked over to where the man stood, pointing to the ground with his sword.

I looked at the ground where he was pointing and saw nothing except a small round hole which was about the size of a medium sized coin, and was about to dismiss it as a false alarm, due to the fact that there were a number of small raised mounds of earth in the area, which indicated to me that the hole was probably the result of an active mole.

I stared at the spot and for a brief moment, and my mind flew back to the moles we used to catch in the woodlands and fields near Wentnor, where the local mole catcher had always referred to the mounds as 'Unti tumps.' (Mole hills)

The silly grin, which I am sure I wore at that precise moment, much to the amusement of my men, suddenly changed to astonishment, when I noticed the shiny inch long point of a bolt protruding out of the moss.

'Stand clear men.' I shouted causing the two nearest men to step away.

'Give that bush a tug.' I ordered, and the nearest man stepped forward and with a hefty heave, he pulled the bush out of the ground, revealing the startled face of a youth of perhaps seventeen or eighteen years of age, who simply remained static as we, in turn, gazed down at him.

'To me men,' I shouted, and the rest of my men ran over towards me and gathered in a ring to see what we had found.

'Haul him out of his hole.' I ordered, and the nearest men bent down and hauled the man out of his hole.

I snatched the crossbow out of the man's hands and looked into the youngsters hate-filled eyes.

'What's your name?' I asked like a fool for his name was totally irrelevant, for both he and myself knew that the best he could ask for would be to lose at least one of his hands, whilst the worst and more probable outcome would be a hanging by a woman, for he had been told by Hussein and the local Imam that if he was killed by a woman then he would be refused to enter into paradise and would wander the night skies for eternity.

'Walid,' he spat. My name is 'Walid,' and my name means 'Reborn' and I shall be reborn when I enter paradise.'

'I also knew something of your teachings' and said.

'That may be so Walid, but not if I assign a woman to kill you.'

Many of my men smiled and one or two of them laughed aloud for some of them had been believers in the false God before they had been converted to Christianity.

One of the men laughed and said. 'Well in all fairness, he did look like something being reborn when he was hauled out of that pit of his.'

I ordered one of the men to tie his hands behind his back, and as that was being done. I looked down again into his hiding place which had been cleverly chopped out of the hillside. The task itself must have taken at least one man a considerable time to dig the hole, as well as to carry the soil away without leaving any trace of his digging.

It took my men and our prisoner the remaining daylight hours and all of the following morning to bury the dead.

We ate a hasty lunch and had our last splash and drink in the famous pool.
 I insisted on loading our two young prisoners with as many of the captured weapons they could carry and commenced out return journey home.
 I was met by a worried looking Ludmilla as I entered the house.
 'Oh my Lord Edric,' she said as she rose from the chair in the hallway where she had been waiting from me.
 'Dire news my Lord,' she said clutching her hands together in front of her corpulent belly. 'News arrived on the yesterday that our good King Richard is besieged by a huge Saracen army which outnumber him by ten to one, and he has ordered every man you can spare from Cyprus to sail to Jerusalem immediately.'
 'When did you say you received this news?' I asked.
 'I heard it in the evening of yesterday. My Lord.'
 'I have his documents and his seal here.' She said as she handed them to me.
 I took the documents from her and broke the seal.
 I read its contents twice to make sure that I fully understood what was written and with a heavy heart I concluded that the document was genuine and the seal and signature all looked to be in order.
 'Ah.' I said quietly. 'Then if the rider had left Jerusalem early enough to catch the tide the following day, he would have needed to ride for at least a day. Then, providing there had been a ship available, and IF the weather had been kind and the winds

favourable, the voyage to Cyprus would have taken another four or five days.'

'So,' I added. Your urgent news must have taken at least six days to reach us.

I will send riders immediately to Sir Thomas in Larnica and to his nephew Robert in Nicosia, with orders to them that they must gather their men in the east of the island, whilst I will send riders out in this and the western areas of Cyprus.

That will probably take up another two days.'

'Then there will be provisions needed for the voyage and for the journey to Jerusalem when the ships arrive, which will mean that the earliest we could arrive to assist him would be around fourteen or fifteen days.'

'Fear not my dear Ludmilla,' I tried to reassure her, but in truth, it may be that it was I who needed the reassurance, for I had fought in many a battle.

Some of those battles had been won or lost in the space of an hour, whilst others had taken days or even weeks or months in mindless confrontation before something important had happened.

Maybe this new leader of the Saracens, whose name sounded like 'Saladin,' would settle for a compromise rather than to risk all on one single battle.

Perhaps this fabled army of his was no more than a crowd of goat herders or shepherds.

Perhaps the numbers had been wild exaggerated.

I really did not know and my agile mind leapt from one possibility to another like a flea that was unable to make its mind up as to which of the donkeys ears or his tail, or his buttock, would be the tastiest.

*   *   *

I had literally torn up all of my plans regarding the building of roads and ordered that the constructions of my towers must be halted, in order to collect all the men the King required.
 I organised that Sir Thomas should take temporary control of the island whilst I was away.
 I had also gathered most of the men from his own Castle and the Castle of his nephew as well as my own, leaving skeleton garrisons to man the three Castles and to continue to patrol the rest of the island.
 I stood on the Jetty amongst squads of men, small groups of horses, several small flocks of sheep and a half a dozen milking cows waiting for the first ship of my small fleet of twelve ships to reach the Jetty, in order that we could begin loading in readiness for the voyage.
 Both of the roads that led to the Jetty were clogged up with men and provisions, and I could just see the beginnings of the town, which was also solidly choked with men waiting for their turn to file towards the Jetty and board their ships.
 As I looked for the umpteenth time towards the town, I noticed that a lot of noise was coming from

that area and I could see men begin to move aside in order to allow a horse and a carriage to pass.

I watched with interest as the carriage slowly made its way through the crowds until, after half an hour or so of progress, it slowed to a halt a few paces away from me.

I was unable to see over the heads of the waiting warriors who was in the carriage, but as I hurried towards it, I made out the figures of three fully armed warriors, whilst in the front I saw the small figure of what looked like a woman, whose smaller figure was hidden behind the large frame of the driver.

'Ludmilla.' ! I exclaimed as she stood between not two, but four warriors.

'Good Lord Ludmilla,' I said loudly, for she was the last person I had expected to see amongst all these noisy men, noisy animals and this muddle of confusion.

'What on earth are you doing here?'

'My Lord,' she said as she wrung her hands together, 'Oh My Lord' she repeated, 'I am so very, very sorry my Lord.'

'Please forgive me?'

'Forgive you? 'I asked.

'What in Heavens name am I to forgive you for?'

'It is entirely my fault my Lord,' she said, and I could see tears running down her lined cheeks.

'What is entirely your fault?' I asked angrily, for I was getting slightly annoyed that this silly old woman who had, in all fairness taught me so much, and who was now crying and screaming about something or nothing, that was all her fault.

'This my Lord,' she wept, and she swept her hands about wildly in all directions,

'This is all my fault my Lord.'

'They fooled me my Lord. They fooled me. Me' she screamed and tore out a handful of her long white hair. 'Me. With my vast network of spies.'

'Me! 'I should have known better.'

'The parchment. The signature. The seal. They were all forgeries.'

'These men. These animals. These ships. My Lord.' They are all entirely my fault.'

'It was all a ruse.'

'There is no Saladin. Well, yes! There is a Saladin, but he has no vast army.'

'He is still sitting in his villa in Syria.'

'They know my Lord. They know.'

'Know what for goodness sake woman. Tell me what they know?'

'It was all an elaborate hoax, my Lord.'

'They have spies my Lord.'

'They had found out that you have a trained an army here in Cyprus, and they know that you are building roads and are construction stone fortresses across the island.

'Their spies have spread rumours throughout the island that King Richard is facing destruction in the holy land, and have dreamed up a lie, knowing that if you were to receive a sealed writ from the King, ordering you to leave the island virtually undefended, you would have no option other than obey. That would have allowed them to walk into Cyprus virtually unopposed and retake the Island from you and your Christians.'

'Thus with one fell swoop, he would eliminate Cyprus from what to Saladin believes has become 'Sword of Damascus' which he believes is hanging over the head.'

'It was all lies, my Lord. The Envoy himself was an actor playing a part.'

'The parchment. 'The story.' 'The great Seal.' 'They were all lies.'

'How can you ever forgive me?'

I shook my head in order to absorb all that she was telling me.

'And these men here?' I asked, as I pointed to the three prisoners who stood between the two armoured warriors.

'The middle one is the Envoy who confessed to me.' My Lord. She said.

'He thought that by confessing, that you would be merciful, and spare his life.'

'The other two are spies. They were mingling with our own men here in Limassol.'

'They were spreading lies about Saladin and his fake army to everyone they met. What of them?' She asked.

'Hang them.' I said, for to show mercy would also show weakness to my enemies who remained on the island

I called the nearest officer over to me.

'This whole thing has been part of a test.' I lied.
'It has been an elaborate exercise in order to show me just how prepared we are, should the real thing happened.'
'Now.' I muttered to myself.
'I had better do a spot of quick thinking and make some sort of success of this mess.
I called the officer over and we walked along the sea front for a moment
'What you must do is fill up the first five ships with men and supplies,' I said to him.
'I want you to order the Ships Captains to sail to the city of 'Acre' in the Holy land on the next tide, and once you are there, you must march to Jerusalem where you and your men will reinforce King Richards's army.'
The shocked officer saluted and marched away, delighted to think that he, who a few moments ago, had been a middle ranking officer, with little or no prospects of promotion, was now a man who had been in charge of three hundred warriors, and a man who would be received by the King himself in the fabled city of Jerusalem.

CHAPTER TWENTY-TWO.

Alaina gave birth to a healthy son on the first day of Spring, in which the mid-wife informed me had been a speedy and an easy birth, but to me it appeared to be a long difficult and noisy process for Alaina who shouted, grunted and bellowed like a 'bull,' (or maybe I should say like a 'cow,' but that may be a little unkind,) and no sooner had she ceased her creaming, than my son took over and shouted like a new-born calf, which I swear kept the whole garrison awake until reveille sounded, calling them out of their beds for morning roll-call.

I took the my new-born son from the midwife and held him close to my chest, noting that his eyes were blue, whilst what little damp hair he possessed was the colour of bracken in the autumn.

I gazed in awe at the child, who was the fourth child I had sired.

I had been at the birth of my eldest son Godwin and Aelnoth, but the new son I had recently been informed about, who had been born far away in the small fortress of Wolf-Hall, some four or five years ago, was the son who I realised that I was unlikely to meet unless, either I returned to England, or perhaps that particular son were to venture into my domain in the Mediterranean some day in the years to come.

I blinked and brought my mind back to reality as I looked down again at my son, shocking me back to the present time.'

I handed the child back to his nursemaid

I informed Alaina that with her approval, I would like to name our new child 'Tito.'

Despite the euphoria of having a new son, I still found it difficult to sleep without my mind turning to my lost love 'Godda,' and in my mind, I still found it difficult to believe that the face that I had seen beyond the veil at King Richards wedding was really the face of my beloved 'Godda.

I tried to convince my-self that at the Kings wedding to Berengaria, when I had seen the face of Godda behind the Brides veil, I had still been suffering from a fever which had been the result of my self-inflicted wound, causing my befuddled brain to think that the face behind the veil was that of my wife Godda.

Slowly I had been forced to accept that 'Alaina' was also a beautiful woman.

She was kind and considerate towards me.

She was also an intelligent woman who treated me with respect, and that alone was something difficult to find in this present and violent world we live in.

Thus, as the days turned into weeks and then into months, our little 'Tito' grew from a squealing babe into a chuckling toddler who won the hearts of each and every man woman and child who dwelt within the walls of our keep. I began to realise that I was happy, and found myself laughing and smiling, which was a feeling that I had thought lost many a long year since.

The relationship between Alaina and I blossomed from liking each other into a kind of love that I had not hereto experienced, and I found myself seeking her out on numerous occasions for a Hug and a Kiss, and from time to time I needed to seek her advice on a difficult problem that I had been mulling over without reaching a decision.

Bernard and Edward had informed me that their mother had given the boy my own name.

She had named my child 'Edric'. (Presumably after my-self.)

The very thought of Wolf-Hall and my old manor of Wentnor flooded back into my mind, causing me to hear the songs of a thousand of birds, whose medley of the dawn chorus used to rouse me from my sleep in the cool springtime mornings.

My thoughts took me into those sweet smelling meadows, yellow with buttercups.

I imagined my-self walking through woodlands that were blue with vast swathes of bluebells, whilst the canopy of great oaks and stately beech trees above glistened in the evening sun with the numerous shades of green.

I blinked and brought my mind back to reality and looked again at my son, shocking me back to the present time.'

I returned the babe to his nursemaid and walked out of the door, into the courtyard.

The two guards at the gate must have thought that their Lord had gone mad, as I passed them, as I was muttering to myself, for my mind was jumping about in my head as I thought about my old life in England, which I had just begun to compare with my life here in Cyprus.

It was something which I had never really thought about before.

'Yes.' I agreed with myself.

'All was not roses back in England, as I reminisced about England, and my mind flew back to the dark, freezing days of winter, and of the days, weeks and sometimes months when it appeared that the sun had deserted the land of mankind, making every man woman and child as damp and as miserable as the cold and flooded countryside itself.

The rain and the dull, dark days left people afflicted with all kinds of ailments.

Indeed I recalled my own Mother mentioning what she had called the mental illness of 'Nordic gloom' which afflicts us people of the north and demoralised many people in our northern climes, so much so that some people sank into the darkness and ended their own lives.

'And yet,' I said aloud to myself, 'here I am.'

'I am a Lord of this beautiful Island.'

'Whilst I live here, I am bathed in sunshine, even in the winter.'

'Many people die of starvation during the winters in England, and yet, here in my Island, starvation is unknown and no one starves simply because they have not stocked up enough food to see them safely through the winter.

Of course we do have ice and snow in the mountains but hardly anyone lives up there.

'Cyprus has an abundance of grain and fruit.'

'There are so many fish in the sea that surrounds our Island that it would be impossible for any sane man to starve here.'

'I have a beautiful new wife and a new son, and we will soon be living a life of luxury in my newly renovated Roman villa.'

I suddenly realised that during my long tirades of mutterings, 'I had been referring to Cyprus as 'My' Island and 'Our' Island.'

I ceased my walking and stood in front of a Chrystal clear pool of water.

Above the pool was a small waterfall which cascaded into a narrow rock strewn stream as it flowed from the mountains towards the sea?

In the past, I had merely taken each day that Woden or perhaps the White Christ had given me, as a thing that had simply happened. Good or bad. It mattered not to me, for whatever happened, had already happened, and if it had happened then it could not be reversed, and then the person who it happened to, simply has no option other than to accept it.

I felt muddled, and the thought suddenly struck me that if there had been anyone within hearing distance listening to my ramblings, then they must have assumed that I was stark staring mad.

I nodded and agreed with myself as I continued my mutterings as I walked slowly back towards the town, waving my arms and nodding my head as if I was alone, and in the great forest of Clun, back in England.

'I shall move out of the fortress,' I said aloud to myself.'

'I will get Clushto to rebuild that old Roman villa for me, and I will move Alaina and the household there.'

'I will order him to construct quarters in my villa, to house a dozen guards just for safety's sake.'

I walked past the guards on the gate, still chuntering away to my-self, totally unaware of their presence.

'Ludmilla. 'I bellowed, as I walked through the front door.

As if my magic, the stooped figure of Ludmilla appeared out of the dining hall.

'Send a servant out to find that old reprobate Clushto for me.' I ordered, and she turned to do my bidding.

I did not cease my planning whilst I was in my house.

I strode backwards and forwards as I planned the extensive alterations to the Castle as well as the old Roman Villa.

'I am wealthy enough now.' I told myself, 'for as the lord of Limassol, every household and farmer in the town and the district pay me taxes each and every month.'

These taxes were individually quite small, but when Ludmilla and her scribe added the taxes up, they amounted to a considerable sum of silver that was paid into my coffers on a monthly basis.

Oh, I have never considered myself to be a dishonest man, for during my lifetime I have known many such men and I abhor them for being liars, cheats and nithings.

I also dislike them for the unseen damage they do to more innocent and less clever people than themselves.

But neither am I a fool? And over the years my coffers have been filled to overflowing with gifts which have been forced upon me for favours that I have done for wealthy and greedy people.

It was almost always silver coin that had been forced upon me by rich men for the simple task of reaching a decision which I would probably have reached anyway without a bribe of any kind.

However I did not always side with the rich and famous, and over the years I had gained the reputation of being a good judge and an honest Governor.

As such, there have been numerous times that I my judgements have fallen on the side of the poor and the oppressed, often earning a basket of eggs or a leg of mutton, or maybe nothing at all for my decision, other than a happy peasant.

I ate a frugal meal of large chunks of cheese, wild onions that had been soaked in vinegar and freshly baked bread, but as I was savouring my final onion, my solitude and my thoughts were interrupted by a loud knock on my dining hall door.

'Come.' I said in a loud voice.

The guard appeared in the doorway, followed by Clushto.

'Ah Clushto, here you are.' I said stating the obvious.

'Come on in and sit here and enjoy a glass of wine with me,'

Clushto was never a man to pass up on a free glass of wine, for he was a person who loved his drink.

He was also a man with an astute mind and he knew full well that this particular glass of wine would come with a price.

He smiled and joined me at the table.

He gazed at me over the rim of his glass, he raised an eyebrow, asking the question 'why' whilst a cool mouthful of his favourite wine trickled slowly down his gullet.

'I will tell you my dear Clushto, why I have invited you here into my home and into my dining hall to share a glass or two with me today.'

'I am weary of living in this huge castle and yearn for something a little cosier to rest my old bones in during the coming years.'

'Now I know you have announced that you have retired from your role of master builder of the Island, but I have also heard that you are not only a lover of good wine but you also like to hear the clink of silver as it drops into your nearly empty chest.'

'If you carry out a small task for me, then I will reward you with enough silver to fill that chest of yours to a point where it is overflowing onto that new Persian carpet which your wife has recently purchased from Ahmed the dealer, here in Limassol.'

A slight change in his face showed me that the information which Ludmilla had given me a mere hour ago, had shocked him, and had told him that I knew about the brand new, very expensive Persian carpet which two of his servants had struggled to carry into his home from the market on the yesterday.

The astute mind of Clushto also told him that I most probably also knew of the blazing argument which he had with his wife this very morning, when he had threatened to divorce her and send her back to the slave market, from whence he had purchased her a mere five years ago, but of course, both she and he knew that would not happen, for they also knew that he was head over heels in love with her.

'This small task,' I continued, shocking him back to reality.

'Would not mean that you needed to lift a single finger in actual work, but it would entail you to employ a large number of skilled and unskilled workmen, who would renovate that old Roman Villa near this fortress for me.

'You will need to purchase and then demolish these five houses here.'

I pointed to a map which I had placed on the table, 'in order to extend the Villa to my specifications here.' I stabbed the map again, indicating to him where the extension would take place.

'Pay the owners of the five houses double the going rate for their homes.'

'I want the existing wall reinforced to double its girth and it needs to be ten feet higher.'

'Finally, I want your men to dig a ditch fifteen feet deep and eight feet wide around this new villa and this fortress.'

'I want you to employ a squad of labourers to dig a secret tunnel from my new Villa to the Fortress which must be four feet wide and six feet high.'

'It must be faced in stone with stone lentils, so that it will last for a hundred years.

'I need this last request (order) to be carried out during the hours of darkness and the tunnel and the spoil from the workings must be disposed of during the hours of darkness.

'In other words, this tunnel, for that is what it will be when it is finished, must be kept secret by you and the men who will be working on it.'

'You must employ only men you can trust and in reward for their silence, you will be allowed to pay them double, nay. Let us say treble the rate of your unskilled workmen.'

'Thank you for your offer my Lord Edric,' Clushto said, 'But I had intended to spend my retirement fishing in the new boat which I bought a few weeks ago, but all this time and work that you have so generously offered me, will mean that I will be unable to go fishing for a month or two and be rewarded by merely giving me three times my usual wage.'

I nodded and said, 'Did I say three times old friend?' I said, with a smile.

'Perhaps your ears have started to clog up in your old age.' I said, as I coughed a slight cough and added. 'I could swear I said five times your usual salary.'

'Six has a nicer ring to it.' He said, but I could also see his eyes widen a smidgen as a sign of fear or shock crossed his face, and from my past experience when I had dealt with such men, I was able to read that sign as a signal that he thought he may have overstepped the mark just a little.

'Aha,' I thought. 'He is talking money. 'I have him!'
I was about to haggle with him to meet his outrageous figure 'half way' but thought 'what the Hell,' and we shook on the deal.

*   *   *

Despite his still muddled and grieving mind, Frithoft had planned this morning's raid meticulously.
He had ordered his usual drink at the same Tavern early each morning for the past ten days, lingering and watching the sun as it reached its zenith. He made a mental note that the so called 'Lord Edric' passed the Tavern at more or less at the same time each and every day as his mortal enemy made his way towards the docks.
Frithoft's long, tangled black beard and his grubby turban made him resemble one of the many vagrants who inhabited this part of the township, and nothing at all like his old self, who had been a man who spent numerous long days and months with Edric.
He habitually sat hunched over his half empty earthenware cup and always turned his head away as soon as he caught a glimpse of Edric appearing at the far end of the street.
'The town is better than the countryside,' he had told 'Imran' and 'Aryan,' as he had ridden with Lord Edric on a number of his patrols into the countryside, and he knew that from the moment the patrols left

the town, Lord Edric's men had always been ordered to be on the alert and to scrutinize each and every bush and possible hiding place that could hide an assassin.

'Frithoft' had ordered the two brothers to start a fight on the corner of the street as soon as they saw him he rise from his table and walk down the two steps that led into the street.

'Don't hurt yourselves, but you must make it look realistic, and then when Lord Edric steps in to stop the fight, as I am sure he will, because he is that sort of an idiot, you must both join with me, and we can hack the bugger to pieces.'

They grunted acceptance to his order.

He left them on the corner of the street and he walked towards the Tavern.

This particular morning the sun was blazing hot causing Frithoft to pull his turban down over his forehead to protect his forehead.

He was beginning to think that Lord Edric was not going to arrive, when he noticed the familiar brilliantly white cloak which he had seen him wear before.

As soon as his intended victim passed him, Frithoft emptied his cup and casually rose and strolled down the two steps.

He allowed the man to walk ten or fifteen feet in front of him as he walked slowly behind him.

Frithoft noted with pleasure that his victim appeared to have no weapons, other than a short sword, which he recognised as being a Saex, but then no man other than a penniless vagabond walked the streets of Limassol without a knife of one sort or another.

He smiled to him-self when his fellow conspirators started to slap and punch one another across their faces, causing a small crowd of onlookers to stop and form a loose circle around the two squabbling brothers.

Frithoft joined the circle, and edged his way to the front.

He watched with pleasure when 'Aryan' punched his younger brother twice on his body and then landed a sweeping haymaker on his chin, sending him to the floor, but his glee became annoyance when Edric made no attempt to step in and stop the fight.

In fact his annoyance turned to a seething rage when he saw Edric smile and shout 'Get up and fight the sod,' he called to 'Imran' who still lay on the floor, rubbing his already reddened chin.

'Leave the youngster alone.' An elderly looking man who stood in the front shouted.

'Can't you see the poor boy has had enough?'

'Leave him alone.' He said harshly and took a couple of steps forward, holding his hand out to help 'Imran' to his feet.

The dazed younger brother allowed the old man to help him up and stood facing his brother.

The disappointed crowd began to disintegrate.

Not only did the two brothers realize that their plan had gone awry, but the fuming, frustrated and red faced Frithoft also knew it.

Edric was standing slightly to his right and although Edric was aware of the large fellow standing to his left, he had not recognised the grubby looking Saracen as being one of his old sparring partners from Wolf-Hall. However, as he turned to leave and to continue his journey to the dockyards, he became aware that the big man's hand had already reached the hilt of the scimitar that hung at his waist and was in the act of being withdrawn from its scabbard.

His own hand flew to the hilt of his Saex but he did not draw it, not knowing if the big man was going to attack him or somebody else.

He walked two paces away before he turned to face the man.

It was not a moment too soon, because had he walked another single step, the scimitar would have lopped his head from his shoulders.

Edric stepped back and faced the man with his Saex in his right hand.

He stared at the big man and although he thought that there was something familiar about him, his brain was refusing to tell him what or when he had seen the man before.

The scimitar sliced through the air again forcing Edric to sway backwards to avoid the cut, but that single slice told Edric that it was a clumsy use of such a fine weapon, that caused him to stare into the face of his opponent more closely.

It was almost as if a ray of light a shaft of light flew through Edric's brain as he suddenly recognised who it was.

'Frithoft.' He gasped aloud, causing a sinister smile to cross the face of his opponent who neither acknowledged nor denied Edric's statement.

Frithoft slashed the scimitar once, twice and yet a third time at Edric, hitting nothing but thin air.

'So! You have come to avenge the death of 'Sigard?' Edric said in a loud voice.

The very mention of his brother's name seemed to infuriate him to such a point that his rage appeared to take over both his brain and his large body and he literally strode towards Edric, forcing Edric to retreat as he backed away from this maniac until he felt his back halt as it met the front of a wooden shop.

The owner of the shop had watched with awe and fascination as he saw the man who he knew to be 'Lord Edric' retreat before a man who was clearly unhinged.

Many of the onlookers also knew that the famous 'lord Edric' could slay this mad-man whenever he chose to do so.

Edric also knew that Poor Frithoft had clearly lost his mind and that he could easily kill the poor fellow whenever he wanted to, but now Edric had his back to the wall (so to speak) and was being showered with wild cuts from a man who was mad with rage.

He now had no option other than disarm the man or put him out of his misery.

'I will just wound him.' He muttered under his breath, but the situation suddenly took an unexpected turn, as Frithoft's muddled brain told him that his futile swipes with his scimitar were doing nothing other than tiring him out.

He threw whatever caution remained in him to the wind.

He dropped his scimitar to the floor and flung his huge body at his enemy crushing Edric against the wooden walls of the house.

Edric remained crushed up for many minutes, but then he looked upwards at the face of his old friend to see that the man's lifeless eyes were gazing, unseeingly over the top of his own head.

He then realised that his own hand was wet and warm.

It was only after he had managed to heave the body of Frithoft off him that he could see his own Saex was firmly embedded in the dead man's chest.

CHAPTER TWENTY-THREE.

 The years seemed to speed by, almost too quickly to be noticed, as I dwelt on this sunny Island that had been bestowed to me by King Richard.
 One day in early spring I walked over to the window of my new Villa which overlooked the bay, accompanied with little Tito, who held my hand, and I reached down and heaved him up into my arms, and then I raised him shoulder high so that he could see the ships in the bay.
 I recalled the time when I first came to Cyprus and had often stood in the main tower of the fortress to gaze at the ships, hoping for a sighting of a school of dolphins or a solitary whale that occasionally ventured into the bay.
 The novelty of watching the ships coming and going had long been lost to me, but little Tito loved to watch them and often growled with annoyance when I was particularly busy and refused to hold him high to see the bay.
 This day seemed to be no more than an ordinary day as we watched the arrival of a single merchantman that took the place of two other ships who had weighed anchor and were now well out to sea.
 I carried Tito out of the room and down the stairway, depositing him in the great hall where his mother and her sister Edith were working away with the long needles which they needed to embroider the large tapestry they were working on.

It was a lovely sunny morning with a little wind blowing down from the hills, causing me to decide that it would be such a shame to waste such a lovely morning doing nothing in particular, so I thought that a ride into the lowlands of the Troodos mountains, to search for a particularly large wild boar that had been seen in the area.

Dressed in my leather riding gear and carrying a sturdy boar spear, I opened the door with the intention of walking the few steps to collect my horse, only to find my-self confronted by a young man who was standing on my portal, with his mailed fist about to knock on my door.

'Yes young man.' I said. 'Can I help you?'

'Indeed you may, I am looking for Sir Edric.' was the reply

'You have found him.' I answered.

'Wonderful.' He said with a sigh of relief and a smile that broke out of his almost beardless face.

'And how can I help you?' I asked again.

'I am Godwin.'

'Ha, Godwin,' I said.

'It is nice to meet you, but what brings you to my door on this sunny morning?'

My mind immediately flew to my Brother. Harald, but that thought quickly left my mind for it has always been one of the most common names amongst us English.

'I am the son of Harold.' He said.

'I know many men of that name.'

'Which Harold is your Father?' I asked.

I was getting rather annoyed at being waylaid by this stranger, who was preventing me from riding to the hunt.

'I am the son of your own brother my Lord.' He spluttered as he too was becoming a little annoyed at this delay in his uncle recognising who he was.

'Hal.' I am from the township of Walford.' He said.

I stood back a pace, for it was so long that I had thought of my brother Hal, let alone heard any news of him, that I had almost forgotten that I had a brother.

The memories of my brother were so vague that I had almost forgotten the circumstances of our second meeting.

At that particular time I had thought of him as one of the children who had been slain by Madoc the Lucky, The savage Welsh Chieftain who had attacked and burned my Fathers Fortress to the ground, and then I recalled finding my only brother many years later.

He had been half-dead and hanging from a skewer in the dungeon of Madoc's own fortress in Wales.

'Hal' had been ill for many months after that ordeal, but he had eventually recovered his health and had married one of my wife's maidens.

They had built a new Keep a few miles upstream, near 'The Red-lake River.'

Hal had built his own Fortress a few short miles from my own Fortress.

And now, here, standing at my own portal, hundreds of miles away from my beloved boarder-lands, stood Hal's son, seeking my patronage.

I stepped forward and clasped him around his shoulders.

'Welcome to my Keep Godwin, son of Hal. '

'You are most welcome.

'Come, come,' I repeated, 'Let me take your baggage and we will drink a toast of red wine to welcome you to my Island of Cyprus.'

'By the way.' I said over my shoulder.

'How is my brother?'

I noticed that my young visitor had suddenly halted and looked around at him.

'Is something amiss?' I asked.

'My! My Father is dead.' He said with a voice that choked with emotion.

'Dead!' I exclaimed in shock.

'Dead. How? When?'

'It was many years ago,' answered the youth.

'He was gored by a cow.'

'God's blood. A cow! How could a cow of all things, kill a grown man?'

I almost ate my own words as I said them, because I knew just how dangerous a cow could be.

I had been no more than a stripling when I had experienced of being chased by cow.

We always said that the cow had been bitten by the Bree fly, although for the love of me, I never seen and certainly did not know what a Bree fly looked like.

'She had just given birth to a bull calf,' said Godwin, 'and my Lord, as I am sure you know. Bull calves are of no use to us unless we intend to grow them up to maturity, so that they can service the cows, so we took the calf off her.'

'She went mad and before any of us could stop her she had gored my Father and trampled him to death.'

I was thrown into one of my moods of melancholy and I stumbled across to my chair by the hearth and plonked myself down, remembering my younger brother and of the pranks and stupid things that we did, and indeed most children do to when they are young and foolish.

I was brought out of my dreams of days gone by, when I saw young Godwin walk towards me and stand directly in front of me.

'Uncle Edric.' He said in a stern voice that I had not hereto heard before.

'I am afraid I am the bringer of more bad news.'

'Godwin.' Your eldest son.

'He, who I have been named after.'

'He is also dead.'

'He was slain by a Norman, who was given your Keep of Wentnor by the first King William, and that family of Normans occupied Wentnor for many years, before Aelnoth returned from Constantinople and took it back.'

'By Thor's golden balls.' I exclaimed.

I jumped to my feet, not really knowing what to do.

'I cannot believe it. Godwin was my eldest and my hope for the future.'

'Did he leave Sons?' 'Or even daughters behind?' I asked, for that was the only thing I could think to say.

'Nay Sire. He was unmarried.'

'Did he not leave a bastard or two lying about in the villages?'

'Not that I know my Lord. He was a clean living man,'

'Aelnoth is still there my Lord.' Godwin added.

'He returned from the east a wealthy man, and he married a local maiden.

'I believe they have five children, who are all hale and hearty?'

'Thank the good lord for that.' I said.

'It is good that you have brought me SOME good news.' I emphasized the word some, almost sarcastically.

'So young Godwin,' I said.

'Have you travelled all this way simply to bring me news of our family?'

'No. Not really Uncle.' He said.

'I have taken the cross, and I am on my way to join King Richard in his quest to wrestle the Holy Land from the Saracens.'

'Why not join me?' He asked?

CHAPTER TWENTY-FOUR.

The dreadful decision as to whether or not I should join young Godwin and journey to the Holy land was made for me a mere hour later by an invasion into my Villa by a middle-aged well-dressed man, who barged his way into my house and confronted me in my own dining hall.
 He was followed by four heavily armoured and armed Knights, who stood directly behind him as their leader stood in front of me,
 'I am Guy of Lusignan,' he said in a flamboyant manner as he threw his chest out and thumped his chest with his right hand, 'and I am the new owner of this island.'
 'And I am Sir Edric.' I said as I advanced in an aggressive manner towards the man who I had taken an instant dislike to, and dare I ask,' I said in a very aggressive voice,
 'Just who had entered MY Villa without MY permission, and who is now standing in MY dining hall issuing his orders to me?'
 'And I am the Governor of this Island and you are standing in MY villa without the manners to even knock on my bloody door,' I said loudly, and I advance a single step towards him and stared into his pock marked face which was now two inches away from my own.
 The four Knights dashed forward towards me and the nearest of the four placed his hand upon my shoulder in order to restrain me, but as he did so I brought my

right hand across and grabbed his hand and with the help of my thumb I bent his hand forwards, disabling the man and forcing him to his knees.

The Knight directly behind him dashed forward but was met by the hilt of my Saex which caught him under his chin knocking the man to the floor, where he remained.

The two other men halted abruptly and looked towards their master for instruction, but their master was still in my grip of my left hand, squirming in pain.

I released the pressure on the wrist of Guy who groaned as he stood upright, massaging his damaged wrist as he did so.

'How now Guy of, where did you say you came from?' I asked in a friendlier manner.

'Lusignan,' He said as he continued to rub his wrist.

'Well. 'Guy of Lusignan,' perhaps you would be good enough to sit at my table and partake of a glass of good Cypriot wine, and explain to me in a gentlemanly way, the reason that you have barged your way into my home?'

'Thank you my Lord,' he said in a more civil tone, 'and do forgive me for my rudeness.'

'It is a fault I was born with, and I seem unable to break the habit of a lifetime,' he said as the faint hint of a smile swept over his corpulent face.

'You had better break the habit before someone breaks your neck.' I countered half in joke and half in sincerity.

I stood and collected two glasses and a goblet of wine from the far end of the table and poured out two glasses of wine before I sat down on the opposite side of the table to my opponent.

He was about to speak when I noticed that three of Guys Knights were attempting to lift their fourth companion to his feet.

'You four! Out.' I said gruffly and nodded towards the door.

As soon as we were alone, Guy started to speak.

'Again, my Lord Cedric.'

'Edric!' I intervened angrliy.

Oh. Yes. Edric. Sorry.' He stuttered.

'It is just that King Richard has sold the island of Cyprus to me.

'He needed the cash to fund his crusade and I had the silver with me, so without going into the gory details, after a lot of haggling, he sold Cyprus to me, so that he could continue his crusade against the infidels and convert the east to Christianity.'

He sat back and took a long drink out of his goblet.

'What about documents of sale? I asked.

'Do you have any documents signed and sealed by the King that will prove to me that he really has sold the Island to you?'

'Oh yes. Indeed I have the very document with me.' He said eagerly as he opened the large wallet that was tied to a cord to his belt.

He pulled out a fresh scroll which he untied and placed it on the table before me.

I bent over the scroll. I read the wordings and studied the seal.

'Well Sir Guy,' I said.

'It is a bitter pill to swallow, but I am forced to admit that it does appear to be in order.'

I saw a look of relief pass over his face.

He rolled the scroll up and was about to return it to his wallet when I added. 'However whilst the scroll describes that you are in possession of the Island and its inhabitants, I did not see any mention of his existing Governors of the Island or of their families, so I assume that the King, and your good-self will allow us to retain our personal belongings and remain In Cyprus as your personal representatives?'

'Er' Yes. Well no. Not really.' He spluttered.

'The King has decreed that Sir Robert and his Nephew Thomas are both to remain here in Cyprus in order that they can continue their good work here, but he told me that he values your Knightly skills too highly to allow you to remain here, in this backwater. (His words. Not mine)

He told me that he sorely needs your skill and your strong right arm, as well as half of your Cypriot warriors to assist him in his conquest of the Holy Land.'

'Do you have those requests in writing?' I asked warily, for in truth, I did not trust the man.

'Of course I do Sir Edric,' he said and I noticed that his hand quickly flew to his leather wallet and he pulled out a much smaller parchment with the seal intact,

'Here, my Lord.' he said smugly. 'I have not allowed the seal to be broken, so that you can see that all I say is quite genuine.'

I didn't remark upon his statement but I did think to myself, that if all was as genuine as it seemed, then why in the name of Odin, did he not show me the parchments in the first place?

I nodded my thanks to him and broke the seal.

Despite the fact that the parchment was small and the sentences were short and well written. I studied each word and every line, and although I was hoping to find an error or a single word that felt wrong to me, I was forced to agree with him that all seemed to be in order.

'I will have my scribe copy the document, in order that I will be able to take a copy to take with me, when I leave for the holy land.'

'I will be leaving my wife and child in my Villa here in Cyprus.' I said sternly.

'They will be safe here will they not?' I asked.

He nodded and grunted. 'Of course they will my Lord.'

I forced my-self to smile at the man and nodded my consent.

'I will return the original document to you within a couple of days.' I said.

'In the meantime I think it would be wise if you and your men were to reside here, in the Castle for the time being, whilst I make preparations' to leave.'

'Walk with me.' I said and I made my way towards the door.

Sir Guy followed me.

He was in turn followed by his four Knights.

As I led them into the courtyard, I said to Sir Guy. 'I will leave my personal assistant Ludmilla with you.'
 'Should you need any advice as to the workings of the Castle and the finances and running of the Island, then I suggest you ask her.'
 'I have found her to be extremely helpful over the past five years.'
 'She knows every man of importance on the Island, and she has a network of spies and informers who tell her about the Saracen spies and of the intentions of their masters.
 'Come,' I said, 'I will show you into your quarters in the Castle and then I will introduce you to the General who is in charge of the army.'
 'His name is Stavros and he a Christian Cypriot and the son of Ludmilla.'
 'Both Ludmilla and her son are totally trustworthy and I would recommend that you, as a stranger to the Island, seek their advice before making any drastic changes here.'

*   *   *

I thought that in the present circumstances I had been rather over-polite towards Sir Guy, for he had, had he not? Arrived in the island and entered into my home without so much as a please or a thank-you?

He had already usurped my position as the Chief Governor and Lord of Cyprus, simply by purchasing the Island from our permanently cash- strapped King?

Alaina was frantic with grief when I told her that I had been ordered to take half of my warriors and sail to join King Richard in the Holy-land.

'What will happen to me and little Tito?' She wailed.

'We cannot be expected to stay here while you are off fighting in the Holy land.'

'There now my dearest.' I said. 'Try not to worry.'

'I have arranged for my guards to stay with you in the Villa.'

'They will keep you safe.'

'I have also asked Ludmilla and Stavros to watch over you.'

'How will they be able to look after us,' she screamed.

'Ludmilla is an old woman and Stavros could be anywhere on the island, or even be ordered to join you in the Holy land.'

'You will both be 'fine.' I tried to assured her, finding it difficult to reassure here that everything would really be 'fine' for her and Tito, whilst my own mind was seething with doubts.

I continued packing the few additional clothes which I thought I might need into my bag, and after I could cram nothing more into the bulging satchel, I walked over and held my son high above my head, and then I placed the laughing child onto the floor and gave him a final hug.

'Now my precious boy.' I said to Tito.

He stood in front of me as if he was a soldier standing on parade?
  'I shall be going away for a while' I said and then I faltered a little and almost sobbed, for I dearly loved this cheeky little son of mine.
  'I do not know when I shall return to Cyprus, but I will return as soon as I can.'
  'Whilst I am gone, I want you to be a dutiful son to your Mother and keep her and yourself safe from harm.'
  'Obey her orders and learn all you can from your Tutors and from my good friend Stavros.'
  I stood and felt tears in my eyes trickle down my face and into my beard.
  I snatched up my satchel and walked, stiff backed out of the room.
  I knew that I had left Alaina and Tito a couple of hours sooner than I had needed to leave, but I have always advocated to others that if a person has a difficult task to do, then it has always been better to do it immediately, rather than to leave it to do another day and allow oneself time to stew and worry about it for hours or even days on end.
  I walked over to Georgios who I had assigned to be my companion for this trip.
  I examined the tightness of the leather straps which he had used to secure our provisions onto the horse and the two mules we were taking with us.
  Both Giorgios's and my own suit of armour were securely packed on one of the mules, which assured me that all would be well and that none of our

provisions would slip off the animals backs on our short journey down to the waiting ships.

Georgios was the eldest son of Stavros, and had been trained in warfare by Stavros himself long before I had been introduced to Stavros and his family some five years ago.

Georgios was as strong as an ox and excelled in all manner of weaponry, especially his crossbow which he always carried in a home-made case that was strapped onto his back.

The two of us mounted our steeds and a steward led the mules out of the castle and down towards the waiting ships.

We were met by my nephew Godwin who was chatting to a servant as they sat in the sun on the three bundles of baggage, which they had carried with them from England.

I had assigned one of my own ships to join the small armada of ships that the King had sent, in order that my warriors and my-self could be shipped over to the holy-land together.

We assisted the ten man crew to load our animals and baggage onto my ship, and after we three men and our servants were aboard, we loaded my ship with fifteen other warriors and as many of the other provisions necessary to sustain ourselves during the voyage.

The sea was kind to us, and with the help of a following wind, we arrived three days later at the friendly port of 'Acre.'

The Captain informed me that the city of 'Acre' had been taken from the Saracens some eight years ago.
 On entering the bay, I viewed the city from the stern of the ship, assessing it to be about the size of one tenth the size of one our old English roods, but as I gazed across the bay, I thought that it was one of the prettiest little cities I had ever seen.
 'It is now thought of as a Christian city.' The Captain said in a sullen manner and from his tone and the length of his beard, I surmised that he was not a Christian and was not too happy about the fact Acre belonged to the King of England.
 The city contained two stone built Churches, which girted the harbour.
 The high stone towers of the Churches also served as Castles, or Keeps, in order to protect the city, should the need arise.
 I stood by the Captain as he steered the ship into the bay.
 'Captain.' I said.
 'Please accept my thanks for a safe and pleasant voyage.'
 'If you would be so kind, I would like to ask you something that has been on my mind for many years, and that is to ask you how do you seafarers seem to sail unerringly across miles of featureless seas, to find tiny dots like this city of Acre?'
 'It is not that difficult my Lord Edric,' answered the Captain.

'Both my-self and my young assistant here,' he clapped a boy of eleven or twelve years of age on his shoulder.

'We use the sun in the daytime and navigate by the stars during the hours of darkness, but as far as this short trip is concerned. Well.' He said with a shrug of his shoulders. 'I have been to Acre before, you know?' he said.

I knew many of the stars and a few of the constellation's but I did more or less understand what he had said, it was still something of a mystery to me, so I nodded and grunted before I joined my three friends on the Dock-side.

CHAPTER TWENTY-FIVE.

Our ships were speedily unloaded, and the men, animals and wagons that were assembled along the sea-front into squads of one hundred men, interspaced by a column of archers guarding a dozen or so wagons, who were in turn guarded by a thin screen of riders who rode along-side the column.

Within a few minutes we had left the township of Acre and entered into a world of sand and stones.

I actually picked up one of the shiny stones in order to examine it and noted with distain that it was almost too hot to hold.

The sun blazed down onto the unprotected heads of our men who, in most cases had taken off their plate armour and chain-mail shirts which they either carried with them, or else had been fortunate enough to have found space for their armour on one of the nearby wagons.

Every man had been ordered to retain his shields and weapons.

By the evening we had reached the relative shade of the few sparse buildings and palm trees which made up the village of Arsuf.

We were told we were about ten miles away from the Crusader stronghold of Jaffa.

The few fresh-water wells and watering holes we came across were quickly emptied by men and beasts alike.

The donkeys, camels and dogs belonging to the Saracens who inhabited the town were quickly slain and butchered by the Crusaders, who had been ordered to collect all the skins and innards from the slain animals in order to provide water bags that were to be filled during the hours of darkness from the waterholes and wells which, we were assured, would refilled themselves during the night from underground springs.

Georgio, Godwin and my-self spent a restless night amongst the hundred men of our squad who either seemed to be enjoying a good night's sleep, or maybe they were immune to the swarms of mosquitoes that made my own sleep almost impossible.

We had been joined during the hours of darkness by King Richard and the rest of his Norman, Burgundian and English Army.

The men, the horses, donkeys and camels of the Kings army were exhausted by their night march, so much so that many men dropped to the floor with fatigue.

However King Richard, who appeared to be unaffected by the vigour's of the night march, roused his senior Knights and assembled them near the centre of the town.

As I was classed as one of the aforesaid Knights, I was ordered to join the King and I trudged wearily through the soft sand towards his large marquee.

The Guards allowed me to pass and enter into the Kings marquee where I joined eight other Barons and Lords who had already formed a huddle of men perusing a map, which had been stretched over a small portable campaign table.

I pushed myself into the huddle and was in time to hear King Richard say. 'This is where we are, in this excuse for a town called 'Arsuf.'

'This spot here,' He stabbed his finger onto a point in the map. 'Is our Crusader fortress of 'Jaffa.'

King Richard stood out from the throng of Lords and Knights, not only by his tall stature, but also by his red-golden mane of hair, which shone in the light from the oil lantern which hung from the centre of the ceiling.

'Gentlemen,' he said in a loud cultured voice. 'As you are aware, we were fortunate enough to have captured most of the Saracen fleet when we landed here, and I intend to have this captured fleet sail up the coast with our own ships in order to carry water and supplies for our army when we march up the coast towards Jaffa.'

'I have been informed by our spies that 'Saladin' and his army, who outnumber us by two to one, have positioned themselves somewhere on the road between us and the city of Jaffa.'

'They will try to prevent us from reaching Jaffa.' He added.

'Can we outflank them?' asked one Knight.

'No!' the King answered.

'We have the sea on one side and the desert on the other, and they are familiar with the desert and they know where to find water, whilst we, on the other hand, would be hampered by our enemies, who would do everything in their power to keep us from water, so if we tried to march out into the desert in an attempt to out-flank them, we would almost certainly be lost, and die in a sea of sand.'

'It might be wise to march at night?' I said boldly.

'Ah. Now that is a thought.' The King said.

'Who said that?' He asked.

'Come forward.'

I nudged my way to the fore.

'Ah, it is you,' exclaimed the King, as a grim smile crossed his face.

'It is my favourite Englishman. In fact it is the only Englishman in this army worthy of serving in my army who I am actually fond of.'

'Now that did anger me to such a point that my temper nearly got the better of me as there were several hundred Englishmen who were here fighting for him and quite a number of us have already died for him and his cause.

However I managed to curb my rage a little, and felt that his remark had been totally uncalled for.

I also knew I was not expected to reply, but I did say boldly. 'Perhaps my Lord King, our enemies have yet to feel the weight of an arrow storm falling on their heads, sent by your English archers.'

There were gasps and shouts from around the table, and I noticed that many right hands belonging to the Knights immediately shot to their empty scabbards.

The King merely stood and looked directly into my eyes and I could see something resembling either a sneer or a smile crossed his suntanned face.

'Gentlemen,' he said slowly. 'I would like you to meet Sir Edric of Wentnor.'

'Sir Edric has been acting as the Lord of Cyprus for me during the past five years.'

'During those five years he has subdued the Island and he has persuaded most of its inhabitants to convert to our Christian way of life.

He has also trained and sent over a thousand men from Cyprus to fight against the Saracens.'

'What he says about me not having to experience the weight of an arrow storm is quite right, for I have been fighting here in the Holy-Land for many years and have yet to experience clouds of arrows appearing out of the sun.'

'But the Saracens have slain many of our men with their arrows.' One Knight said.

'True. True,' Thee King consented. 'But they have been mere light showers.'

'They have never been a full blown Storm.' He added, as he shook his mailed finger at the man.

'However.' I said loudly. 'The Saracens still block our road to Jaffa and I, for one, cannot think of any way around them, therefore I think that the only way forward is to go right through them.'

'Quite right.' The King said. 'The only way to reach the port of Jaffa is to fight our way through.'

'Sir Edric suggested that we march during the hours of darkness, and I concur that we will do just that.'

'I will send a screen of horsemen ahead of us and to the east,so that we are prepared for an ambush and are not caught off guard.'

King Richard spent the following hour in finalising his order of March before we were interrupted when a lady who was veiled and clothed in silk, entered the Marquee.

'Ah, there you are my dear,' the King said. 'Do come in.'

'I think you know my guests, do you not?'

'I do your Majesty,' the Lady said quietly.

Alas, I did not recognise the lady, despite something inside my brain told me that I should.

'I am afraid I am not acquainted with the lady.' I said, as I made a slight bow as I held my hand out towards her.

My hand was grasped in a vice like grip, which should have told me something, yet it did not.

I gazed in awe at the beautiful creature, which looked back at me through her veil.

'Come now Sir Edric,' said the voice from beyond the veil, and it was in that very moment that I realised that I did recognise the voice, and I knew instantly that the Lady behind the veil was none other than little 'Gilda.' The warrior child who I had sent off to the Holy Land five years ago.

She was no longer the little farm girl who had watched us practice at Wolf-Hall, as her stance was different. Her head was held high and she stood with her shoulders back with her breasts thrust forward with a pride that she had acquired since I had last seen her.

Her hair, which had been a tangled mass of dark red hair had been turned by the Mediterranean sun, as well as a personal hairdresser, into a carefully combed mane of golden hair that contained streaks of sun-bleached white blonde hair.

I was dumbfounded, for I could still not believe my own eyes.

I managed to blurt out one word. 'Gilda?'

'The same.' She confirmed, 'but I am a wiser and older Gilda after spending five years in this land of blazing sun and boiling hot sand.'

'Good gracious I didn't recognise you.' I said, 'And dressed in such finery too.'

'I have promoted her to be the Sergeant of my personal body-guards.' The King said.

'And I do not wear these clothes when I am on duty.' Gilda added with a smile.

'Is our old friend Hugo still with you?' I asked.

'No. I'm afraid not. He was slain three years ago.' She said.

'Oh!' I said. 'I am sad to hear that.' And

'I used to think that he was invincible.

'How did it happen?' I asked.

'He was just unlucky.' She said. 'A stray arrow took him in the throat.'

'I held his hand for over an hour before he passed to Heaven,' she added as she raised her hand to her veil and then she raised the veil and threw it onto the top of her head, where it rested and fluttered very slightly in the gentle breeze that had suddenly started to blow in from the Sea.

I looked again at the beautiful face that had once belonged to the most feared and fierce warrior I had ever fought alongside, and as I compared that face with the face of the child warrior, I recognised the features of the child warrior who I had sent to war some five years ago.

She walked the three paces that separated us and stood by me.

'I have donned this finery just for you my Lord.'
She said with a smile, 'but do not be dismayed.'
'I can still thrust and cut with the best of them.'
'Indeed she can,' the King said.
'I am aware that one of my Knights ladies had given 'Gilda' one of her dresses,' the King muttered, ' but I have never known her wear it, and to be honest with you my Sax' 'er,' English friend. I hardly recognised her when she walked into the room.'

I nodded, and looked again at 'Gilda,' finding it very difficult to recall the grubby red-haired ruffian who had posed as a boy for so long, who had now been reincarnated into this beautiful young lady who looked so stunning in her 'Brand New, Second Hand Dress.'

'Gilda' turned her head away from The King and Sir Edric for a moment and smiled craftily, knowing full well that this was not really the first time she had worn the dress.

She had actually been given the dress at least a month ago by one of the Ladies who escorted one of the Kings senior Knights on this particular Crusade.

'Gilda' knew that this march towards Jerusalem would take King Richard and his army into a confrontation with this new leader of the Saracens, but the thought of the coming Battle caused her some excitement that was mingled with a smidgen of doubt that had entered into her brain.

It was no more than a smidgen of a doubt which had never entered her head before, but it was lodged somewhere in the back of her mind and was unwilling to go away.

After all, she mused, even her huge friend 'Hugo,' who she had thought of as being indestructible, had been slain by a single arrow.

Was it the death of Hugo that had caused this sliver of doubt to crawl a little further into her Brain? She asked herself?'

'Without Hugo's huge shield to hide behind during the next 'Battle,' I will be just as vulnerable as the next man,' she muttered so loud, that a man standing next to her, turned his head and looked at her.

The King dismissed his senior Knights.

The Knights including Edric and Gilda made their way out of his Marquee and went their separate ways.

As Gilda lay on her cot that evening, she began to reflect her life, realising that whilst she had lived at 'Wolf Hall' she had always been thought of and had acted as a boy.

'But now every man and his dog know I am a woman,' she mumbled to herself, 'but when the men thought I was a boy, they were always bragging about their sexual exploits, and how wonderful sex was, and how exciting it was to do this and that,

'Yet, here I am nearly twenty years of age and I am still a virgin.'

'I have never enjoyed lying with a man.'

'I wonder if it really is as good as the men say? Or was it all 'Big talk, and Bragging?'

'Still,' she said aloud to the emptiness of her tent.

'If I am to be slain on the morrow without ever knowing the pleasures of having a man, I would have to walk amongst the shadows in the afterlife for ever and a day in the guise of a virgin.'

She leapt out of her cot and put her dress on.

As she was walking down the street towards the centre of the town, she pushed her way through the crowds, visualising the man she would choose to give her the thrill of her life.

'I wonder if it will give me the same buzz that I get when I kill a man?' she mused.

'He must be young and fit.' She thought.

'I would want him to be aged between 25 and 30, with a mop of dark or even red hair.(To match my own?) She mused.'

He must be spotlessly clean and strong and have the weird sense of humour that will sweep me off my feet.' She smiled inwardly.

The crowds were so dense that she was forced to walk at a snail's pace in order to pass through them, but that was good, (she thought,) 'for it will give me time to study each likely looking man, and I will have enough time to choose the right one.'

She reached the end of the street where the crowds thinned out until they ceased all-together, causing her to stare into the blackness of the countryside.

She had actually turned and had begun to make the return journey when a voice out of the darkness said. 'Didn't you find what you are looking for little lady?'

She halted and turned again towards the darkness, to see the figure of a young man emerge from the shadows.

She said nothing and allowed him to amble casually over towards her.

'Could I be of help?' He asked in a deep pleasant enough voice?

'I doubt it.' She answered, as he appeared in the light of a lantern which hung near the doorway on one of the final houses in the street.

As the man stood by her, she noticed that he was a young man with a short well cropped beard.

Alas, His clothing announced him to be either a peasant or perhaps a fisherman.

He is certainly NOT the Nobleman or the Adonis I am looking for. She mused.

'But HE IS young.' She thought, 'although he is a bit scruffy and I was hoping to find someone with a bit more class.'

As if the man had read her thoughts, he said. 'My name is 'Yannis' and I live just there.' He pointed into the darkness.

'It's close to the shore so that I can watch the tides and go fishing when the mood takes me.'

He walked the two paces which separated them and placed his hand on her arm.

'Come.' He said. 'I will show you my house.'

This was not quite how she had planned things, but for some inexplicable reason she allow herself to be escorted out of the light and into the darkness where, after her eyes had adjusted to the darkness, she could see two shabby buildings that each contained a boat and a bundle of nets that were hanging over wooden frames.

'This house is mine. 'Yannis' said as he guided her up the one step and into the front door.

He followed her in and stooped to light a lamp from the single candle which stood on an upturned crate by the side of his bed.

Gilda reeved her nose up a little at the unmade bed and the dirty clothes which lay around the room.

'I don't particularly like this.' Gilda thought, but she consoled herself as her orderly mind counteracted her thoughts, by telling her-self that she had lived among men for many years and had slain more men like this than she could recall.

'Yannis' sat down on the bed and pulled her to him, placing his arms around her waist and drawing her towards him so that his face was nestled below her breasts.

'This feels alright.' She thought and she placed her right hand on his shoulder, 'but I don't feel any stirrings in my loin, or anywhere else for that matter.'

He roughly turned her over and fumbled with the cords at the back of her dress'

He pulled her dress off and flung it onto the bed behind her.

She allowed him lea-way, which was very unlike her, hoping to experience the thrill she had heard the men speak of, longing to feel the elation and the tingling they had spoken of in hushed whispers.

He grasped her breast and squeezed it, causing a bolt of pain to shoot through her chest, which did not feel either erotic, or even pleasant.

His knee forced itself between her legs until they were open wide, and then he yanked his own trousers down and with a grunt and a heave, he plunged into her.

The pain was unexpected and unlike anything she had previously experienced.

'If this is it, then it is a waste of time. Her confused brain told her.

I am I not enjoying this. '

The overpowering smell of fish and rancid perspiration seemed to ooze out of his sweaty body and his greasy hair, which fell onto her face, began to revolt her.

The movement of his buttocks not only annoyed her, but caused a bolt of pain to shoot through her body each time he crashed down upon her, causing her to knot her stomach muscles up into a bunch, whilst her right hand fumbled on the bed, where she had flung her belt.

Her hand finally fell onto the handle of her Saex.

She silently withdrew the Saex from its sheath and plunged it savagely into his side.

He grunted, stiffened, and then he fell onto the floor, allowing his lifeblood to spread in an ever growing pool across the grubby earthen floor.

'That was a bloody waste of time.' She said aloud, as she rose from the bed.

She casually gazed at the body on the floor without any emotion or regret.

'I can't see what all the fuss was about.' She muttered.

She casually dressed and walked back through the thinning crowds towards her tent, where she lay down satisfied that all the lies and boastings of the men she had heard bragging about their conquests and their love life, were just another way of those stupid men-folk trying to impress their friends.

She pulled the sheep-skin cover over her shoulders, and mumbled to herself.

'Well that was the waste of a bloody evening,' and she turned over and slept like a log until dawn.

CHAPTER TWENTY-SIX.

The King assigned three of his heavily armoured Knights to spearhead his army, ordering them to ride a little way ahead of his front ranks.

Lord Conrad and the Duke of Burgundy led one hundred fully armed Hospitallers who were hidden behind the first four ranks of his army.

They marched alongside their squires who held their steeds in readiness to assist their Lords to mount their restless war-horses.

There was no sign of man or beast during the first five miles of our march, but when the spearhead of our army made its way around one particularly large mound of sand-dunes, the whole army came to an abrupt halt.

We were ordered to advance a little further along the sandy track that served as a main road, in order to allow the majority of our army to enter the level stretch of scrubland.

Although I stood in the sixth rank of our army, I was able to see the vast horde of white robed Saracens who stood before us, like a white cloud of snow upon the wide, sandy valley in front of us.

The order of 'March' which the King had ordered, had been made in order to prepare each body of our men ready to meet exactly the kind of a delay which now stood before us.

I was not alone as I looked at the faces of some of the men who surrounded me, as we stared unbelieving at our enemies, who despite our screen of scouts, had suddenly appeared in front of us.

However, The Duke of Burgundy rode his black charger in front of our men and within a few short minutes, he and his aides had calmed the murmurs and confusion, so that after a few orders, our ranks stiffened and we became prepared to meet our enemies.

The huge mass of the enemy stood before us, barring our way into the tiny village of 'Baha-al-Din.' Thus in one simple move they had prevented us from reaching the vital water which oozed out of the two wells which had turned the village into a green oasis amongst this sea of sand.

I looked inland, where I could see that we were confronted by rows of Saracens who stood silently on the sand dunes to our west, in readiness to race forward and eliminate us.

My own men from Cyprus were positioned directly behind Lord Conrad and the Duke of Burgundy, in readiness to fill the gap which they would create once they had left the army and had charged, (successfully we hoped,) into the bulk of the Saracen army.

The sun was almost directly above us, indicating that it was nearing mid-day, causing man and beast to stand, sweating profusely, and wait for the battle to commence.

'The longer we stand here and sweat,' I thought to my-self. 'Then the greater will be the advantage we will be giving to our enemies'

'These Saracens have been born and bred to stand heat such as this.' I remarked to Godwin who was standing beside me and who I could see was wringing wet with perspiration.

'Have a drink from this, as I handed him my own water bottle and said to him, Hold on for a little while.' I said to him. 'I am sure we will soon be moving.'

Someone else must have reached the same conclusion for no sooner had the words left my head than I heard the order to advance.

Almost as one man we moved forward.

Our advance guard halted some two hundred paces from the army of Saracens.

Our army was ordered to form into the pre-arranged shape of a spear-headed shaped formation.

I knew from experience that the range of our long-bows could outshoot the Saracens small bows in both the number of arrows loosed in the space of a minute.

I was not at all surprised when a dark cloud of arrows soared from within our ranks and fell upon the Saracens like a hailstorm, killing and maiming men and horses, causing mayhem amongst the ranks our enemies.

Before they had time to recover, our front lines opened up, as planned, and the King un-leashed 'The Duke of Burgundy' and his heavily armoured Hospitallers Knights, who spurred their armoured Steeds out of our own ranks and into the ranks of our enemies, so that within the space that it takes a man to take ten breaths, they had crashed into the unprepared Saracens and causing havoc and confusion in their ranks.

Most of the Knights had found a target with their lances, and almost immediately they had discarded their shattered lances and had drawn their swords and maces.

Their savage war-horses spun around in an arc, as they had been trained to do and the Iron shod stallions and the Knights who rode them, slew any enemy who came within reach.

Someone near me shouted the word 'Shields,' and the men around me joined me as we held our shields up to protect ourselves against the thousands of enemy arrows that had been launched from the high sand dune, where the thousands of enemies had been standing.

They were not standing on the dunes now, for they had launched their arrow storm just the one time. They had discarded their bows and were now racing down the sand-dunes, screaming as they sprd across a flat portion of about one hundred paces that lay between our two armies.

The screaming Saracens swept onto our warriors and in some cases over us, as they swamped us with their sheer weight of numbers.

Some of the braver ones or maybe the most foolhardy ones were tossed over our front ranks by standing on a shield that was being held by two of their friends,

However, most of our warriors wore chain-mail under their leather jerkins. The leathers had been boiled twice and hardened to such an extent that they could withstand a stab or a sword cut.

Few of the Saracens appeared to wear armour, preferring not to be weighed down with metal, which has been known to boil a man alive if he is unfortunate enough to stay in the mid-day sun too long in this land of the extremes.

Our men rallied, and the onrush that the Saracens had appeared to be relying on was halted.

Our men began to retake the ground which they had recently lost a few minutes ago, leaving dead and dying Saracens in their wake.

The Crusaders main body of cavalry, which the King had ordered to march a mile behind his army, suddenly thundered up the sandy road and encircled the Saracen foot soldiers, hemming them in between ourselves and our cavalry, allowing us to slay and maim at will, until the surviving Saracens took flight and ran back up the large sand-dune from whence they had emerged less than half an hour before.

I turned to face the other part of the battle which was being fought between our two main armies and was slightly dismayed to see that most of our Hospitallers Knights had vanished in a sea of Saracens.

I thought to my-self. 'Their horses have tired and they have been un-horsed, or perhaps, and I hoped that the Knights had abandoned their tired steeds and had chosen to fight on foot.'

'Then, almost as if my thoughts had been read out aloud. I saw one single Hospitaller horseman become suddenly surrounded by enemies, who hauled him off his steed and pounced upon him, constantly stabbing him until they seemed to lose interest in stabbing a dead body and moved away looking for another victim.

Although strictly speaking, I was not the real leader of this portion of the Kings army. I did feel that I needed to do something other than sit in the centre of this throng of Christian warriors who were doing nothing other than standing and watching other men fighting and dying for them.

'Forward.' I bellowed and I strode across the gap of seven paces which lay between the battling Crusaders and Saracens.

The Saracen ranks, which had encompassed the Crusaders suddenly opened and three white robed figures stepped out to meet me.

I could see by their attire and their bearing that these three men were not merely lowly peasants, for their heads were circled by what looked like several rows of pearls whilst the weapon carried by the tallest man, who was in the middle, was encrusted with an ivory handle that was embedded with jewels of many colours.

Had I been the man who had landed in Cyprus nearly six years ago, then I would not have recognised the type of weapon he carried, but since that date, I had encountered many such weapons which I now knew bore the title of a 'Scimitar.'

Indeed, the collection of weapons had become a hobby of mine and there were six Scimitars in my collection back home in Cyprus.

But alas, no sword in my collection could compare with the blade that I now faced, for to say that it, 'shone in the sun,' would not do it justice, for it gleamed like burnished gold, and I am certain that any adversary would quiver with fear, and would see his own death in this wide blade as it swept before his eyes.

The two men to the left and to his right of this man advanced towards me as he stood leaning upon the hilt of his scimitar.

The warrior on the left swung his iron club in an arc so fast that it actually shaved my sparse beard as it zoomed past my head.

I countered with a slice of my broad-sword which was parried by his iron shield, whichcaused a dent in my favourite sword and also causing a sly smirk to break across the man's weathered face.

Of course my slice had been nothing other than a ploy, and the true intent of my move came when my opponent staggered backwards with my Saex stuck in his throat.

He was still trying to smile as he fell to the ground.

I stooped down to retrieve my Saex and as I did so, I noticed that the Saracen to my right had leapt forward.

My Kite shaped shield prevented his scimitar from taking off my left leg and I stepped backwards quickly in order to avoid his next stroke, which would have been to lop off my sword arm.

I parried the blow with my Saex and countered with a huge downward slash, that caught him on his right shoulder, which I knew from experience, would break his shoulder bone unless he was wearing the strongest of armour.

His piercing scream was followed by a dull thud as he crashed to the ground.

'I yield. I yield.' He repeated holding his left hand in the air.

I looked down at him and then I looked into the face of the third man, who had not moved so much as an inch since I had fought and bested his two companions.

'Well,' he said in a pleasant tone.

'Are you going to kill him or not?' He asked.

'I shall spare him,' I said, 'although I fear that he will probably die from a wound like that.'

'He is blood kin of mine.'

'I shall allow my surgeon to heal him.' The man said confidently.

'He may live,' I countered, 'but only If I allow YOU to live long enough?' I said, for I knew that this man who had been in the centre of the trio would be my next opponent.

'Are you ready?' He asked politely in the same pleasant tone as before.

I stood and regained my stance, waiting in a chivalrous way for him to confront me.

'I am now.' I answered, as I flexed my shoulders and my neck, for in truth, my body was hotter than I could ever remember it being, before this moment in time.

Now that was interesting.' He said, as if he had just supped a glass of new wine and was swilling it around in his mouth in order to assess it's vintage.

'On guard.' He said. Not in Norman/French, as is the norm, but in the language of the English.

'English.?' I spluttered. 'Now that is another surprise.' I added.

'Oh, I have other surprises for you,' he said as he stepped forward and jabbed his Scimitar at me, which in itself is surprising, for a Scimitar is a slashing sword and hardly ever used as a thrust.

I had hardly finished speaking the words, 'I am' before his face loomed before my own face and he head-butted me, sending me backwards and causing me to land on my back like an upturned lobster.

Thankfully, His 'head-butt' had been a crash of helmet against helmet and I could feel that my own helmet had been dented, and could see that the helmet of my new opponent also had a dent in it.

I could also see that both of us were slightly dazed, which surprised me some-what, for I knew that he must have planned the move, whilst the head-butt had been a complete surprise to me.

I stood and regained my stance, waiting in a chivalrous way for him to confront me.

His Scimitar had merely touched my chest and I deemed that the move had merely been made in order to tell its owner what manner of armour I was wearing.

'Chain-mail,' he said pleasantly.

I had been right in my assumption.

I suddenly thrust my shield forward deflecting his raised Scimitar in order to jab him with my broadsword which clanged against his armoured chest.

'Plate iron?' I stated. 'You must be cooking inside that.' I added.

He smiled again.

'This sod smiles a lot.' I muttered to myself.

'I think I need to take that smile off your face.' I said aloud, as I swung my sword high where it was blocked by his round iron shield and then I switched my stance and sliced at his ankles but he simply danced over the cut and thrust his Scimitar at my right arm which was stretched to the full.

I leapt backwards to avoid his counter backstroke, and in doing so, I nearly tripped backwards over the body of the man I had just slain.

My opponent speedily stepped forward to take the advantage I had given him and raised his Scimitar to strike again, but before he could bring his curved sword down I leapt to my feet and struck him on the side of his helmet with my broad-sword, sending him to the ground where he lay in a helpless heap.

I placed the tip of my Broadsword at his naked throat, which lay exposed between the lower side of his helmet and his sheet armour.

He still attempted to smile as he looked, first at the sword and then up into my face.

'It seems to me that I am at your mercy messire.' He said.

'It may be a mistake to slay me now, for I am a rich man. He added.

'My name is Osman-Padi-shah-ben-Hafsa,' he said as he regained his feet, leaving his scimitar on the sand as he bowed to me, and then he stood upright and as he looked into my eyes he touched his forehead and then his heart with his right hand.

'If you spare me,' he said, then you must ask a ransom for my safe return, and the silver which you would gain would make you into a rich man.'

He again dropped to one knee and looked up at me.

I shall not ransom you Sire.' I said with more than a little reluctance.

'You have fought well and I think there has been too much blood spilt on this sand today.'

'What I will do is to spare your life and escort you through my own men and into the company of your own kind, who, by the way, appear to be retreating.'

His smile seemed to have passed and he exhaled a loud breath of relief as I plunged the blade of my sword into the sand and held my right hand out to him.

After a slight hesitation he held his hand upwards towards me and gave me yet another radiant smile as he rose to his feet and shook my hand.

He stooped to the ground to retrieve his Scimitar which he then held by its blade and offered the hilt to me.

'The laws of chivalry and of conquest demand that I offer you my sword in surrender.'

'This sword has been in my family since the time of my grandfather's grandfather. (May Allah rest their souls)' he said with a sigh, as he thrust the hilt towards me.

I had noted. Indeed. I had envied him this spectacular weapon even before he had stepped forward to challenge me, and as I stared down at it I knew I could not accept such a treasured gift.

'Keep the sword.' I said as if it was nothing other than an ordinary 'run of the mill' weapon, being offered to me by a nithing.

'I already have a sword,' I added as I sheathed my own broadsword.

'Come now. Follow me through my men or one of my bowmen will scavenge the sword from your dead body.'

I walked before him through the remnants of our Crusader army shoving no less than three crusaders who attacked him to the ground and escorted him into the area of 'No-man's land,' which lay between our two warring armies.

'Go now.' I said to him, 'and maybe we can share a cup of wine when this madness has been put behind us.'

He nodded his head and shook my hand again.

'Thank you my friend.' He said as his famous smile returned to his face.

'I will remember you.'

The words, 'My Friend,' hit a soft spot. Causing me think that I may just be able to count on one of my hands the number of people who had called me such in the past ten or even twenty years.

He turned, and within the space of twenty heartbeats he entered the ranks of his own people and was gone.

As the gap between the remains of the Saracen army and the army of the Christians widened, I could see the bodies of the warriors who had been cut down during the battle and could not fail to notice that the white robed bodies of the Saracens far outnumbered the bodies of the Christians by at least two to one.

I also noticed that whilst the bulk of our warriors were retiring towards our encampment, there were many of our men who had abandoned the ranks of their friends and were, even as I looked, stooping over the bodies of friends and foes alike in order to relieve them of any jewels or armaments they could salvage from them.

Of course I knew that loot was the only reason that many of the men had joined this crusade, for the finding of a single jewel or an object of value could easily mean that that single item of booty could turn a man from a peasant into a Nobleman once he returned home with his loot.

However, I turned away in disgust and walked slowly back towards my own ranks.

I walked towards a group of my own warriors who had been waiting for me.

I was feeling totally exhausted and rather stupid, for not accepting the man's priceless Scimitar, as well as the huge ransom which I could have obtained, had I been wise enough to hold him for ransom.

I managed to reach my tent with the help of my men and stood in its shade as my squire helped me to shed my armour and most of my clothing.

I lay on a sheep-skin rug feeling more fatigued than I could ever recall and drank two leather water bottle's full of water before I began to recover a little, as I felt my energy slowly returning to me.

'Overall,' I muttered my-self. 'I did not fare too badly.'

'I have beaten three Saracen Knights, who were not nithings or even normal warriors, but they were Warriors, men of the sword, like my-self.

They were men who had been trained from childhood in the ways of war.' I mumbled.

'And that must be good for many a man of fifty five years of age.'

'Fifty-nine.' I said out loud, and then I tried hard to remember exactly how old I was.

I simply could not remember just how many summers I had lived.

I thought it might be fifty. 'No' I said out loud. 'It is probably nearer to sixty five.'

I eventually fell into a deep sleep.

CHAPTER TWENTY-SEVEN.

Despite our fears, no second army of Saracens barred our way to the city of Jaffa and after three weary days, (or rather three weary nights,) of travel, as the leaders of our army had followed my suggestion of travelling in the cool of the night, rather than enduring the scorching sun of the daytime, which had previously sent many of our men, especially the blonde and fair skinned men of northern Europe, to the ground with sun-stroke and dehydration.

We entered the open gates of the city to cheers and the banging of drums from the citizens' and Crusaders alike, who treated us as conquering Hero's.

My section of the army was assigned to a small area of the western side of the city, close to the shoreline, where we could enjoy the cooling gentle breeze which came from the Mediterranean Sea.

I spent the following few days recuperating from the strains of the march and of my brief moments of fighting, enjoying my leisure by sitting in a cool spot where I could see most of my Warriors swimming and splashing about in the water, as if they didn't have a care in the world.

Never-the-less. Rumours were rife in the camp.

One day we were supposed to make ready to march to Jerusalem, but on the following day we were told that the march had been called off, due to the fact that Saladin was about to assault Jaffa with an army of one hundred thousand men.

I abided by the old adage of, 'If in doubt. Do nout.' So I remained sitting under my palm tree, watching a pod of Dolphin's splash about, fifty feet away in the sparkling blue Sea.

It was not another rumour, nor was it an order to prepare for battle that caused me to leap up and stand in the seething hot noonday sun, but my lethargy was shaken into action when a Greek messenger and whispered in my ear.

'Lord Edric.' He said excitedly.

'I have been ordered by The Duke of Burgundy to inform you that as from this moment in time. The Duke will be leading the army, since King Richard and his immediate retinue of Knights are sailing to Cyprus on the next tide, providing they can replenished their ships with supplies before the tide turns.

'Apparently, they will sail on some urgent business to France.'

The Duke of Burgundy arrived unexpectedly at the hovel I had commandeered, and demanded entry from the two sentries, who I had ordered to guard the door.

The two men were part of my Cypriot division and they did not recognise the Duke as he wore the cool attire of the Saracens, causing their initial refusal to allow him entry.

My two guards received two heavy clouts from the Mace's of his body-guards, who then simply escorted their Lord over the unconscious bodies of my guards.

I leapt out of my chair and snatched up my Broad-sword which lay beside me before I recognised the

Duke, causing me to slam the blade of my sword back into its sheath.

'Forgive me my Lord Duke?' I said as I held out my right hand to greet him.

'You startled me.' I spluttered.

'So I see.' He said in his snooty Burgundian accent.

'I believe you are English?' he inquired.

'I am. My Lord.' I said bluntly, for I had taken an immediate dislike to the man.

'Am I correct in thinking that you are also the man who advised the King to march in the cool of the evening as well as the hours of darkness?'

'I did my Lord. Was that wrong?' I asked.

'No. No. Not at all.' He said gruffly.

'Are you also the man who slew two Saracen Noblemen and allowed another to walk free after you had disarmed him?' he asked in a more sinister tone?

'I am my Lord, but it was a fair fight and I thought that he was too good a man to slay, so I escorted him through our own lines towards his own people.

'YOU THOUGHT. YOU THOUGHT' He bellowed so loud that his highly pitched voice made his words echo in my head.

'That's just typical of you bloody Saxons. You don't think. You just think you can do what you want, and you don't take your superiors orders into consideration.'

'Do you know who that bloody man you let go was?' He screamed again as he hopped up and down in his fury.

'Do you bloody well know who the ugly bugger was?' He shouted.

I was about to answer, but I was thwarted by the rage of this so called nobleman, causing my hand to go down to the hilt of my Saex, but before I could either answer or draw my Saex, he screamed.

'He was only bloody 'Osman-Ben-Hafsa.''

'That's who he was, and due to your stupidity you have let Bloody 'Osman-Ben-Hafsa' go.'

'You have allowed the man who is only second in command to bloody Saladin himself to walk free.'

'Walk free. Do you hear me?'

'Walk bloody free, with no ransom.'

'No promises of peace. No bloody thing.'

He raised his face to the sky. 'Walk bloody free.' He screamed loud enough for half the camp to hear.

'No bloody nothing.'

'What sort of a bloody Saxon fool are you?'

I had just about had enough of this silly old fart of a Duke shouting at me when he was interrupted by a messenger who had barged past my still dazed sentries and halted as he stood in the small space which separated me from the Duke.

'My Lord Duke.' He said interrupting the Duke who was just about to continue his tirade of abuse towards me.

'What the hell do you want?' the Duke screamed into the face of the startled messenger.

'I have urgent news for you my Lord Duke.' The man stammered.

'Well man? Well? '

'What is it that is so bloody urgent that you have the audacity to interrupt me when I am about to have this stupid Old Saxon beheaded?'

'Great news my Lord from our master spy in the court of Saladin himself.'

'We have just heard the news that Saladin and his army are retreating all the way to 'Baghdad' and he has ordered his second in command, who is, as you know, a man called 'Osman-Ben-Hafsa' to vacate and demolish the Saracen fortresses of 'Ascalon'. 'Gaza.' 'Blanch-Garde' and 'Ramleh,' which, according to the news we have received.

These fortresses will now all be too weak to withstand our forces, due to the losses they suffered in the recent battle of Arsuf.

The Duke of Burgundy stood with his mouth open and his right hand raised high in the air, as if he was going to strike me, as his simple mind attempted to digest the news he had just heard.

'The fortress of 'Blanch-Garde' and 'Ramleh?' He queried.

'Yes my Lord Duke, and 'Ascalon' as well as the fortress of 'Gaza.''

'By the blood of Jesus! The Duke said quietly, as if he had not believed the news.

'It was a resounding victory was it not?' He said in a rather meek voice.

'Forgive me for my outburst Lord Edric?' he asked.

'It does seem that by releasing Osman-Ben-Hafsa you have bought us the peace we all desire, as well as half a dozen fortresses which would have cost us dearly in time and casualties, had we been forced to storm and conquer them .

Pray forgive me for this temper of mine?

'You see. I lost my good friend 'James D'avesnes' at the battle of Arsuf and I do miss him so, for he had a wicked sense of humour.

I understand that he fought like a lion, and slew no less than sixteen Saracen cavalrymen before his horse was shot from under him and he was slain.

'Non-the-less,' he said. 'We did slay three other Saracen noblemen.'

'We slew 'Musak,' who was the Grand Emir of the Kurds, and a famous warrior named 'Lighush,' as well as 'Kaimaz-el-Adeli.'

I listened of this man who I had come to dislike more and more as he tried to worm his way out of the abuse he had rained upon my head a few moments ago, and I wondered to myself exactly who 'HE' had personally slain during the battle, and the more he went on about who 'WE' had slain, the more convinced I became that he had probably been tucked safely away, out of harm's way behind his personal iron clad body-guards somewhere in the centre or even the rear of our army.

He suddenly seemed to have pulled himself together as he straightened his shoulders and placed his right hand on my shoulder.

'Again Lord Edric, I ask your indulgence for my recent outburst of anger.'

'My old Mother used to say to me when I was a boy. 'Eustace my boy, she used to say. 'Eustace, that temper of yours will get you killed one day.'

'She may have been right.' He muttered, as he spun around on his heel and left.

I made no comment but knew full well that his Mother's prophecy had almost been fulfilled a few moments ago.

CHAPTER TWENTY-EIGHT.

 The Sea-lion took on food and water for the voyage, plus ten heavy bales of cloth which the Captain had assured the King would sell for treble the price in England.
 The sea was as calm as a mill-pond as the Captain eased the ship out of the tiny waves towards the headland, whereupon, once he had reached the headland he steered the ship north by north-east along the coast of Cyprus, staying within sight of the enchanted island of Cyprus until it disappeared over the horizon and the ship sailed down the Mediterranean and into the calm azure blue of the Adriatic sea.
  The Captain steered the ship by his acquired knowledge of the stars which shone in a cloudless night sky, and sparkled like a ladies dress made of light blue silk that had been embedded with a million diamonds.
 The sea and the weather remained calm as the ship sailed effortlessly on its way during the first night and the second day, but during the night of the third day, a sudden storm erupted out of the norther sky causing the 'Sea-lion' to be buffeted by massive waves which, despite the heroic efforts of the captain and his crew, overwhelmed the Sea-lion, soaking the sails which had been lowered and stacked aboard the ship, and saturating the precious bales of cloth, causing the ship to wallow in the huge waves and crash into a

cluster of rocks a hundred and fifty paces off the shore.

King Richard had been resting on his bunk in the small private cabin that had been set aside for him.

He was dressed in his nightshirt and was half asleep when the ship was driven onto the rocks with a sickeningly crash, causing him to leap to his feet and step quickly out onto the deck of the doomed ship.

He could see three of the members of the crew run to the port side and leap overboard into the sea, where they immediately began to swim to the shore.

Two of the men seemed to be strong swimmers but the third man was not, and the King watched in dismay as the man threw his hands up into the air and suddenly disappeared under the waves.

He also saw that a small number of his personal guard who were attempting to rid themselves of their heavy chain mail shirts, in the hope that they would not suffer the same fate of four other members of the guard, who had been thrown into the sea as a result of the Sea-lion's collision onto the rocks, where they had just seen their friends disappear under the water due to their heavy chain-mail shirts.

The King watch in horror as he saw two other members of the crew swamped by a huge wave which seemed to devour them and they too followed his doomed guards to a watery grave.

The ship was pounded relentlessly by the enormous waves which flung the remains of the wrecked ship time and time again against the rocks, causing some of the valuable bales of material to be washed away and disappear under the surging waves to follow a number of his crew and guards to the bottom of the sea-bed.

Gilda watched the scene in dismay and staggered down the remaining decking of the wrecked ship with the intent of assisting the King, but as she neared him, she gasped in disbelief as she saw him walk unsteadily to the edge of the ship and without a moment's hesitation, he dived head first into the boiling waves.

Gilda made her way to the spot where she had last seen the King and hurled herself into the water in order to save him.

Fortunately, King Richard and Gilder were both strong swimmers and within the space of twenty minutes, both swimmers were floundering on the beach, gasping for breath.

'Well, that's the end of that.' The King gasped as he stood up and held his hand out in order to haul Gilda to her feet.

'It is indeed your Majesty.' She agreed as she hugged her own body and attempted to stop shivering.

'I see some of my men made it,' The King said as he nodded in the direction of the southern end of the beach, where Gilda could see two small bundles of men sprawled out on the saturated sand, half in and half out of the waves that still washed over the feet and the lower parts of two or three of the men.

'Follow me.' He ordered and began to trudge through the wet sand towards the men.

Gilda followed him and struggled to keep with him, as he was a very tall man and for each stride he took, she took two or even three.

As they reached the first group of men, she could see that there were four of them and although their uniforms were missing, they all had their army belts around their waists, including their short swords, identifying them as members of the Kings bodyguard.

'Well done men. Are there any more of you?' The King asked.

The four men rose unsteadily to their feet and the man who answered the Kings question said 'None your Majesty. 'I was. I mean I am your Sergeant at Arms and I think that we four are the only survivors out of our squad of ten men.'

'Oh.' The King said as he viewed the beach.

'And those men there?' he queried as he nodded towards the five other men who were huddled close together farther along the beach.

'They are members of the crew your Majesty.'

'Did the Captain survive?' He asked.

'I don't think so your Majesty.' The Sergeant said.

'Go and see.' The King said to Gilda.

'And if he isn't there your Majesty? Shall I kill the rest?' She asked.

'I don't think they are Christians.'

'Gods holy blood.' Spat the King. NO! Do NOT kill them, you bloodthirsty little bitch.'

Christians or Heathens. They are all my subjects and I am sure I can find a good use for them.'

'Heaven knows. If we are attacked by hordes of tribesmen on this God- forsaken beach, then we will need every man who can handle a weapon to help us defend our-selves.'

'In fact,' the King added. I think it may be unwise to send you to those heathens over there.

'Sergeant.' He said, as he turned to the Sergeant.

'Send one of your men to those sea-men and order them to gather together and join you and walk along the shore-line to see if they you can find any weapons or food that has been washed ashore by the waves.'

'You never know.' He said, 'you may be lucky enough to find something of value.'

'If the storm continues like this, then there will be little or nothing left of the ship by morning, so providing we survive the night here, we can scavenge along the beach again at first light.'

'Gilda, I want you to walk up into the dunes and collect any dry wood or kindling you can find and we may be able to find a shaded place where we can light a fire and spend the night.'

'We will join you as soon as the sergeant and his men have scoured the beach for weapons.'

Gilda trudged up the beach towards the dunes muttering to her-self. 'Fetch the bloody sticks. Light a bloody fire.'

'I am the warrior here, not those shabby sea-men.'

'They are the bloody serfs here. Not me.'

'I should be the one to find a sword or two 'cos they wouldn't know what to do with the damned thing even if they found one.'

The fire fizzled and smoked for a few hours during the first two hours of the night, but did little to dry out the survivors.

The King noticed that the clouds appeared to disappear sometime in the early hours of the morning and the sound of the waves crashing against the shoreline seemed to abate a little, before he dropped off to snatch a couple of hours of sleep.

He was wakened by Gilda who touched his still sodden shoulder.

'Tis morning your Majesty,' she said quietly, causing him to open his eyes and stare up at her for a few moments, before he rose to his feet and stretched his lean frame, emitting a loud groan as his body rebelled against his iron will, warning him that another difficult and stressful day lay before him.

'Come.' He shouted loudly as he kicked the nearest man to him.

'Up you get you lazy laggards.'

'We have nothing to eat, so I suggest you all get up and follow me to the beach where I am sure we will find something edible, and, hopefully a few of our weapons that my guts tell me we shall be needing before this day is out.'

Gilda walked out of the sand dunes with the King and they were followed by the rest of the men who had survived the shipwreck.

The shoreline was littered with all manner of flotsam, which mostly appeared to be shattered and broken shards of wood.

King Richard stared at the rocks that had ended their voyage so suddenly.

He could see no sign of the ship except a section of the mast which lay on the largest section of the rocks, half in and half out of the water.

'Follow me lads,' he shouted and began to wade out towards the rocks through a sea which had no semblance of the raging torrent he had experienced on the previous day.

They all reached the rocks, and walked carefully along the slippery seaweed covered rocks until they reached the end, where the remains of the mast rocked gently as the outgoing tide ebbed.

'Ah.' The King grunted as if was a man who had just discovered an ingot of gold.

'I can see the ship, or at least I can see what remains of our ship down there.' He corrected himself.

'Can any of you swim underwater?' He asked.

Three of the crewmembers nodded and joined him on the edge.

'What about you?' he asked his four bodyguards.

'I've never tried.' One man said.

'Me neither my Lord.' A second man said, whilst the other two guards and the remaining crewmen gazed at their feet and said nothing.

'Right men.' The King said. 'You men, (he indicated the three seamen and the two guards) and you, Gilda, can join me and we will dive down to the wreck.'

We will bring up anything we can find to you men who can't swim and you can carry whatever we salvage to the beach.'

We must salvage anything we can that may be of use to us. Especially weapons and food, although I think that if we do find food it will probably be spoiled by now.'

'Oh,' he added. 'Try to find our helmets and chain-mail if you can and keep your eyes open for sharks. They may have been lured here by the smell of our men who drowned in yesterday's gale.'

'Off you go.' He ordered.

'You stay with me Gilda.'

'I want you to keep a look-out for sharks and help me find my chest which contains a goodly amount of silver.'

'I feel we will need all the silver we can carry if we are to make our way across half of Europe to reach home.

He then dived into the water and was immediately followed by Gilda, who dived in a split second later.

Fortunately the wreck lay in no more than ten feet of water and swayed slowly with the outgoing tide.

The King reached the wreck first, and pulled himself along the ships remaining spars to the spot where the small hut-like dwelling where he had spent much of his time.

Gilda swallowed in alarm when she saw that the hut had completely disappeared.

However, King Richard seemed to be unconcerned and dived down onto the few boards that remained and forced his knife between two of the boards and strained to lever them up.

He left the knife where it was and sped to the surface to breathe.

He was speedily followed by Gilda who also rose above the surface to join him, gasping for breath.

They dived again and returned to the wreck where the King grasped the knife again and levered the boards loose, revealing a foot long box which he grabbed and shot to the surface again.

'I've got it.' He shouted with relief.

Gilda was pleased although she was not sure what the box contained.

She dived again to join the rest of the men who were all in the act of scavenging along the seabed searching, or else making their way to the surface with their finds or returning to the seabed after depositing their finds to the men on the rocks.

As she spotted a spear-head protruding from under the litter of wrecked spars, a flash of a large object caught her eye just in time to allow her to snatch up the spear from its hiding place and thrust it forward into the gaping mouth of a shark which was intent on striking a fellow diver.

The man, who she recognised as being one of the Kings guards, was about to rise to the surface carrying a crossbow in one hand and a leather bundle of crossbow bolts which he had looped over his shoulder.

The man dropped the crossbow and after a brief wide-eyed stare at Gilda he simply shot to the surface.

Gilda hung on to the spear as if her dear life depended on it, surprised at her own strength and determination.

She had listened many times to stories about these assassins of the deep, and she tried to stay clear from the rows of white teeth which seemed determined to reach her.

She also realized that she and the rest of the Kings party were desperately hungry and knew that this monster of the deep would provide them all with a much needed meal, if only she could just hang on to the dying fish and bring it ashore.

Prey and predator struggled with each other and fortunately rose to the surface in a cascade of splashes which allowed Gilda to gulp down a lungful of much needed air before she followed the massive fish as it dragged her under the water again.

The Sharks convulsions eased and then ceased altogether, allowing Gilda to reach the surface again.

She swam, not towards the rocks that were close to her, but towards the shoreline which was over a hundred paces away.

King Richard abandoned his treasure box on the rocks and dived off the rocks into the water, in order to help her, and together they managed to haul the huge fish, which was as big as the King, onto the shoreline, where two other men ran to them and assisted them to drag the Shark towards their camp.

'You look after the fish.' The King said to the men, 'and stoke up the fire whilst I go back to collect my box and gather the rest of the men.'

'We can all look at what we have salvaged and have a good meal.'

King Richard gathered the large haul of their findings on the ground before him whilst the large Shark steaks sizzled on a spit which one of the seamen had constructed over the fire.

He chose to wrench a steak off the spit and despite the fact that the shark meat burned his mouth; he continued to devour it, whilst Gilda and the men looked on.

'What are you waiting for?' He bellowed, as he reached out for another steak.

'Help yourselves. You must be starving.'

As he continued to eat, the King picked up an items from the pile of their labours, he quickly assessed the item, be it a weapon, a chain-mail shirt or a piece of clothing and threw the item to the man he had thought would make the best use of the item.

He made sure that each of the chain-mail vests went to his guardsmen, but he also allocated one to a seaman and one to Gilda.

Gilda immediately threw it back to the King. 'I fight better without that thing.' She snorted.

'It is much too heavy for me to fight in'.

The King merely snorted in disgust and threw the shirt to another seaman.

Each of the survivors, including Gilda were eventually kitted out with weapons and clothing, whilst the King himself retained his own broadsword and armour which had been fortunate enough to salvage from the wreck.

After a hasty breakfast of shark steak, the King allocated a portion of the fish that remained to each person in the group, before he led them out of the dunes and into the lush green countryside.

Gilda was not alone in trying to keep up with the long legged King.

She trotted alongside him as he strode ahead, and as she glance back, she could see both the Kings Body-guards and the surviving members of the crew panting and puffing as they too struggled to keep up with their King.

They made their way northwards along pathways and tracks, that more or less followed the coastline of the Adriatic Sea, pausing at farmsteads and small villages in order to find a man, who would be able and willing to guide them through the peaks and passes of the mountains that the King assured them lay ahead.

It was not until mid-day on the third day of their march when they had halted at a large house, that Gilda thought looked something like and English manor house, where the King met with the minor nobleman who owned the house.

The man invited King Richard into his abode.

Gilda and the rest of the men were treated to a rare meal of roast lamb and a goodly amount of reasonably good red wine, which they ate and drank as they rested in a nearby barn.

He did not return until he and his retinue had broken their fast in the morning and appeared at the barn with a broad grin on his weather-beaten face.

Gilda and the men stood and greeted him with some enthusiasm, as many of the men had feared that his absence had been caused by foul play.

'Fear not my friends,' Said the King, 'for I have found a new ally here in my friend 'Ferdinand' who has provided me with a guide who will show us a way through yonder mountains.'

He pointed to the snow-capped mountains which we could see in the distance.

'He has not only agreed to guide us, but he has also sold me eleven mounts and two mules, which will allow us all to reach home in the space of a few short weeks.'

'Our steeds did not come cheap.' He added as he touched his purse.

'So you will all see just how important it was that I retrieved my chest from the wreck.' He said loudly as he rattled the almost empty leather satchel aloft for all to see.

The guide appeared on foot, leading a string of horses and two mules pulling two wagons, causing a flurry of activity as each man collected a horse and loaded each of the wagons with our weapons, armour, blankets, food and bedding, that we hoped would sustain us on our journey up to, and then through the mountains towards Normandie and England.

The journey to the foothills of the mountains turned out to be reasonably easy, unless one considers the blisters and raw thighs that pretty well each person suffered, with the exception of King Richard.

The guide turned out to be a pleasant enough fellow who had travelled through these mountains in his youth.

He spoke a few words of French which he had learned many years ago, but he had not spoken a word of that language for nigh on thirty years, causing the King and most of his men to smile, and even have the occasional laugh at his accent and the natural slip-ups he made as he tried to explain things to them.

They followed the guide through the foot-hills which seemed to go on for perhaps ten or fifteen miles, before they reached the foot of the snow-capped peaks of the mountains that seemed to stretch before them into what seemed like infinity.

He led them down valleys which were so narrow that the packages that had been tied onto the backs of the Mules actually scraped the walls of the canyons as they wrenched their way through, whilst other valleys contained wide meadows full of colourful flowers, the like of which they were alien to them.

The King, and indeed Gilda and all four the Kings guardsmen feared being ambushed in these narrow confinements but no such happenings took place, allowing all concerned to breathe a sigh of relief as they spread out into a wide valley, which contained two small meadows that were watered by a crystal clear stream that cascaded down the mountain-side and along the valley floor.

When they were half way down the valley the King held up his hand and shouted.

'Halt men. We will rest here for a whi.' He did not complete his order, due to the fact that a single man had suddenly appeared a mere fifty feet in front of him.

Whilst the appearance of a single man should not have daunted the King of England, the sudden appearance of what looked like over a hundred other men, who also rose from the stream-bed to join the man, did rather dumbfound him.

'Grab your weapons.' King Richard bellowed, causing all the men and the King himself to run to the wagons to collect their shields and weapons.

None of the Kings men had time to pull their chain-mail shirts on, and looked in a mixture of fear and awe as their opponents trudged silently through the damp grass towards them.

Gilda glanced back the way they had come, only to find that the Valley entrance, which they had just passed through, had suddenly been filled with another group of warriors, who in turn were also advancing towards them.

King Richard looked around in despair.

He looked back at his own men he said aloud. 'Ten men and me, plus one girl, against nearly two hundred fully armed men.'

His gaze turned again towards the advancing men, causing him to note that they all had helmets and chain-mail, except half a dozen men who strode forward ahead of the main group.

These six men wore expensive plate mail.

They carried a variety of weapons, which included broad-swords, double headed axes, except one huge warrior who carried what looks like a metal hammer which was attached to a long metal shaft.

King Richard strode two paces forward and halted before he plunged his broad-sword into the damp earth.

He shouted an order to the heavily armoured men who appeared to be the leaders of his opponents.

'Who are you?' The King asked in an aggressive way. 'What do you want?'

'We want you!' The giant in the plate-armour said in a loud voice.

'Why?' The King asked in an equally loud voice.

'We are nought but innocent Pilgrims who have been shipwrecked, and we are making our way back to Normandy.'

'We have nothing of value and can offer you nought but blood and death if you stand in our way.'

The huge warrior answered our King's warning with a warning of his own.

'We are one hundred and eight-seven men,' he said loudly, 'and you dare, with your pitiful ten men to stand against us.'

'The blood and death will be yours if you do not yield to our arms and bestow all that you possess upon us within the course of the next few minutes.

'I must warn you.' The King said in a loud voice that carried not only to his own men, but also to many of his opponents who stood around the Giant.

'We are all Crusaders and have fought many battles with the heathens such as you.'

'Each and every man here is worth ten of your milk-maiden's, and if you ask me to prove it I will send you this maiden here.' (He pulled Gilda to the fore.)

'Pah!' Spat the Giant.
'We do not have time for this nonsense.'
'We have you surrounded and outnumbered.'
'Surrender to us this instant or we will slaughter the lot of you.'
'As you will!' The King answered.
'But first, I will send this maiden out to slay a few of you, and then perhaps we will talk again,' and he gave Gilda a pat on her shoulder, which was a pre-arranged signal to shoot, causing her to lift her crossbow, in an almost casual way, she pulled the trigger.
The bolt plunged into the eye of the Giant almost before anyone realised the bolt had been shot and the Kings enemies watched in shock and amazement as the Giant toppled backwards crashing to the ground with his right hand straining to withdraw the iron projectile out of his eye.
'How did you know that this man was not our Lord?' asked another man who stepped out of a small bunch of iron clad men.
'I too am a Lord.' The King answered, 'and I know these things.'
The man nodded. 'And is this the maiden who you say we should be afraid of?' he asked.
'And you say that she can beat ten of my men in a fair fight?' He asked.
'She can.'
'So be it.' The man said.
'Let her step forward.'
'And when she wins?' The King asked.

'Then we will escort you all safely through our territory.'

'But if she does not win, then you will all be at my mercy to do what I will with you.'

Gilda stood by the King and looked up at him.

'Ten is rather a lot!' She said.

'It is.' The King agreed.

'But I am sure you can manage ten puny men?'

'Well I haven't slain anyone for a week or two, so a little practice will be good,' she added as she walked forward.

The leader of her opponents took a few minutes to select her opponents, who ambled casually out of the crush of the men, and walked the few paces towards her, stopping about ten feet away from her.

They were all grinning at what they saw, and what they saw was a pretty enough young woman who wore the clothes of a sea-man that were several sizes too big for her.

She had her reddish/blonde hair tied at the back with a leather strap.

They were even more surprised as they watched her plunge her short sword into the earth and untie her shirt, which she then dropped to the ground and they bellowed with laughter as they watched her pull down the trousers which she had managed to wrench off a dead man near the wreck of the Sea-lion.

They hooted and doubled up in laughter as they pointed their weapons at this nearly naked girl who simply stood before them in a pair of sea-man's pants, looking like a young girl who did not have the strength to swat a fly.

'Bloody idiots,' muttered Gilda, as she touched her left hand with the blade of her Saex.

'They have no bloody idea just how fast I can be without all those bloody clothes.'

The leader, plus two heavily armoured warriors walked towards Gilda.

'Forward,' ordered the Leader and the two warriors each side of him placed their shields forward and took one additional pace towards Gilda.

She sped towards the one on the left with the speed of a striking leopard and as she swept past him, she turned her body in mid-air and struck at the bottom piece of the man's helmet where the helmet met his iron shirt, leaving a red spurt of blood which burst out of the shocked man's neck, sending him to the ground.

Not satisfied with her-self, she then spun around on her toes and was behind the leader aiming her Saex at the legs of the second man who screamed aloud as he tumbled, but before his body reached the ground Gilda had sped past him leaving her Saex sticking out of his face.

The leader was so shocked at seeing both of his companions slain by this blood covered girl, that he unintentionally stepped backwards a pace and looked down in horror at the bodies of his own Uncle and a man who had been his personal bodyguard, who he had fought alongside and protected him for more than eight years.

Gilda stooped and retrieved her Saex from her last victim, and as she rose to her full height of five feet, she gaped in awe at the face of the leader who, a few seconds before, had worn his visor down, which had partially covered his face.

He had already plunged his sword blade first into the ground, and with both of his hands he had reached up and removed his helmet.

The young man who stood before her looked exactly like one of the Greek and Roman statues of the Gods she had seen in Cyprus.

He had their short cropped fair hair that was curled untidily upon his noble head, whilst his startling blue eyes stared at her from the most tanned, utterly handsome face she had ever seen on the face of a human being.

Standing before her was the man of her dreams.

Her jaw dropped. Her hands fell to her hips and as she stood a pace away from him.

She simply stood and gazed with her mouth wide open at this young Adonis.

He reached down and withdrew his sword out of the ground and suddenly thrust his sword forward, stabbing her in the centre of her chest, sending her dead to the floor.

She was still smiling in adoration into the beautiful face of her killer, despite seeing a brief image of the smiling face of 'Yannis' the fisherman swim before her body reached the ground.

'By Gods holy blood.' King Richard screamed.

'What in the name of Christ did the stupid bitch do that for?'
'I've see her kill twice that number of men without getting out of breathe.'
'The idiotic, stupid little cow.' He raved. 'I should have done the job myself.' He added, knowing full well, that he was as good as any man he had ever known with a sword, but he also knew that Gilda would easily have out-classed him in a matter of seconds.
'Your Sword Sir?' 'Oh.! Oh yes.' Said King Richard and he placed the blade over his bent arm and offered the sword, hilt forward to the leader.
'Pity.' He said almost to himself. 'She was the best killing machine any King could wish for.'
'King?' the man questioned. 'You claim to be a King?'
'What manner of King are you? Who bring this rag-tag band of beggars and a maiden through this lawless countryside?'
'I am the King of England and the Duke of Normandy.'
'And who, may I ask, are you?'
I am Lord 'Archibald' and I am the nephew of 'Duke Leopold' of Austria' the man said, 'and I have been given the task of governing this lawless territory by my uncle, who has recently conquered this land, and has annexed the whole of this area to his own Dukedom of Austria.'
King Richard was shocked to the core, and although he made no remark, as he was not aware that this stripling knew about the dislike that Leopold and himself had for one another, due to the fact that when

they were in the Holy land, Leopold had cast down King Richards colours from the walls of 'Acre.'

He was racked with despair, as he and Léopold of Austria had argued and had almost come to blows over some long forgotten petty item that had caused the two men to become sworn enemies when they had been Crusading in the Holy-land.

Archibald waved his left arm in the air, causing his men to advance and encircle King Richards's small band of survivors, who were immediately disarmed and held with their hands tied behind their backs.

However, King Richards's hands were not tied and he was allowed to retain his side arms, on condition that he swore to Archibald that he would not attempt to escape on the coming journey back to Austria.

The King was still shocked at the death of Gilda, but as he stood before his captor he placed his hand on his heart and gave his parole, swearing that he would not attempt to escape, despite the fact that he knew that he had already planned to allow himself to be safely escorted through the treacherous countryside that he knew lay ahead.

'Oh,' He thought to himself. 'I shall keep my word, but only until this silly young fool reaches a point when the territory of the Count of Austria is near to the French border, and then I will break my parole and escape from the clutches of this child-like Nephew of Duke Leopold of.'

He watched silently as his four bodyguards and the seamen were forced to kneel and were executed before his eyes.

CHAPTER TWENTY-NINE.

I had watched with dismay at the disintegration of our army of Crusaders over the past three months, as one after another, the Lords of the different contingents of our army packed their gear and left our encampment.
Our own King Richard of England had not been seen for over a month and no one seemed to know where he was.
The Sergeants at arms and the few Norman/French Lords who I did managed to speak to, gave me different answers.
One Nobleman said King Richard had returned to England, whilst his colleague argued that he had left to assist the King of France to quell a rising in Brittany.
Another man told me he had been killed by an assassin, whilst his colleague informed me that he had died an honourable death in battle with Saladin himself.
I had been informed that many other noblemen who had joined the Crusades with family relations and friends from their own domains in Northern Europe, intended to make their way back to their homes in Europe, whilst the majority of the Lords said that they were going to make their way across the barren terrain of the Holy-land towards the deserted Strongholds and Castles that the retreating Saracens had left vacant, with the intentions of turning the

vacant Castles into Crusader Fortresses, to become Lords or even Kings in their own rights of the vast estates they had usurped in the Holy Land.

The thought had already crossed my own mind as I saw other, lesser men than my-self, head off into the hills with groups of warriors varying from a dozen men to several hundreds, in the hope of carving their own estates out of these empty lands.

I had more or less disregarded it, for although I was still in command of nearly one hundred men who I had brought over with me from Cyprus. I reminded myself that I was still the Lord of Wentnor, back in England and I owned a large estate in Cyprus and longed to see my newly born son again.

'Tito' I said aloud.

'He must be five or even six years old by now,' and with the thought of 'Tito' on my mind, I had abandoned all thoughts of carving out a domain for myself in this hot, sandy country.

Our English army had been reduced in numbers to about a quarter of its original strength since our own leader, King Richard had left us, and with each day that passed, more and more men disappeared.

I assembled my men and led them out of our half empty encampment one moon-lit night'

We headed towards the coast, with the intention of reaching the Port of 'Acre' by making a forced march each and every evening for three consecutive nights, halting every morning at an assigned oasis, which I had marked on the crude map that I had purchased from one of the so called friendly Bedouin's.

Fortunately, this particular Bedouin turned out to be an honourable man and the map which I had purchased from him, was more or less correct, except for the fact that the distances between the 'Wells' and the 'Oasis's' that were marked on the map turned out to be much farther apart than I had calculated, forcing us to trudge through the scorching sand for the best part of five nights and not the original three nights I had planned for.

The small township and the Harbour of 'Acre' was literally seething with men who appeared to me to be deserters from the Crusaders army, to such an extent that I was compelled to leave my exhausted men near a small Oasis and force my way through the crowds of townspeople, animals and armed warriors, who shouted and spoke in so many different languages that this crushing amount of people and the noise from this hubbub of humanity and animals caused me to barge into and through knots of people who refused to move out of the way and allow me to pass towards the Docks.

I did eventually reach the Dockside, which was choked with all manner of ships,.

I had planned to find a Ship's Captain who would be willing to transport us back home to Cyprus.

Fortunately, I still had the purse containing a large amount of silver, which I had brought with me from the time I had been the Governor on the Island of Cyprus.

Despite the fact that I mentioned that I possessed enough silver to actually purchase a ship, let alone hire one to take my men and I to Cyprus, not one of the Captains I met seemed to be interested.

I was rather despondent as I walked towards the final Ship that was docked in the bay and I approached the Captain, who seemed to be a jovial enough fellow.

I asked him the same question that I had asked at least a dozen other Captains before him.

'Nay my old friend,' he said aloud in a jovial way.

'That small purse-full of silver of yours would not buy a single berth on a ship, let alone your small army of seventy or eighty men.'

'Look you here,' he said as he leaned down and removed a cover from a crate that lay on the deck before him.

I looked down at the crate which was about three feet in length and two feet deep, and I gasped in wonder at the crate, for it was full to the brim with all manner of gold silver and jewels.

'Loot.' The Captain said, 'and this lot is the price of a passage to France for just one man, his lady and four of his Knights.'

I was dumbfounded and merely stared down in awe at the wealth.

My thoughts were interrupted by the Captain who said. 'He had two more of these with him.'

'He said he was going to buy a Castle in France and live in luxury for the rest of his life.'

'As will I.' He added as he closed the lid of his box.

'You seem a nice enough old fellow.' He added, 'so I will say to you, that you may just have enough silver in that purse of yours to catch a ship home, if you were to march southwards for a couple of miles, into the next bay and help an old seadog friend of mine, whose ship was driven onto the rocks in the last storm.'

If you could help him get his ship off the rocks and repair it, then he might, just might be grateful enough to accept your piddling amount of silver and give you passage to France.'

'Cyprus.' I said.

'We want to go to Cyprus.'

'Oh. Cyprus then. That isn't too far.'

'Tell him you are a friend of 'Leonardo.'

'That's me.' He added and turned his back on me as if to say. 'Off you go?'

I was back with my men within the hour and I had them organised and marching southwards by early evening.

We trudged along the coastal road in the cool of the evening.

I was fully convinced that we would reach the village of Al-Hiada before daybreak, but alas, as the sun rose over the flat desert that confronted us, we had not reached anything other than a lone traveller who was making his way in the opposite direction.

The only other sign of human habitation I could see were the ruins of a mud hut that was in such a state that it looked like it had been abandoned when Adam was a lad.

'Take heart men.' I shouted to the stragglers who had been lagging behind the main party of my men.

'It can't be far now.'

'It is probably around the next hill.'

But it was not. Neither was it around the next bend in the dunes.

Nor was it around the next bend, or the next.

My men were flagging in the heat of the day and many were staggering and falling with heat-stroke and fatigue, causing me to think that the friendly Captain Leonardo had lied to me just to get rid of me, but when we rounded the next ridge of sand dunes, a vision which I can only describe as a miracle appeared before us.

I would not describe it as a large town or even a good sized village, but it was a village, and it was situated in a small green valley, with dozens of large date trees towering over the huddle of houses and mud cottages, which nestled around a small crystal clear pool of WATER.

Most of my men reached the pool by themselves, but it was necessary for me to collect some of the stronger of the men who, once they had been allowed to drink at the pool followed me to help and carry the men who had fallen by the wayside.

As soon as my horde of Crusaders had appeared, the villagers had scampered into their houses, where they remained behind their locked doors.

I decided to settle my men down in the shade of the trees before I tried to find the Captain of the ship, which I could see on the rocks, a mere fifty feet off the shore.

I summoned one of my Greek/Cypriot men, who introduced himself as 'Marius from Nicosia.'

'Marius' spoke a few words of the Saracen language and we walked into the village and began banging on the locked doors.

The first three houses produced nothing other than the shaking of heads, but when we pounded on the door of a house that was larger than the average dwelling in the village, a large fellow, who wore the wooden collar of a slave around his neck, answered the door.

'Have them come in,' a loud voice shouted from within the dwelling.

The slave stood to one side and bowed his head slightly as he waved us in.

We followed him through one large airy room, which in turn led to an enclosed patio that contained two men.

The men were sitting at a table, near to a small fountain.

The silence of this sanctuary was only broken by the water from the fountain which bubbled and gurgled as a small stream of clear water, gurgling out of the mouth of a stone lion into a pool that contained a single white lily which moved slightly on the surface of the water.

'Come in my friend. Come in!' said the younger of the two men.

'We have been expecting you.'

'Come now and join my friend and my-self.'

'We have a refreshing glass of orange juice waiting for you.'

We both walked up to the two men who remained seated and I sat on a chair made of reeds, whilst Marius remained standing under the shade of a tree.

The man clapped his hands and a few moments later the same slave who had ushered us into the house appeared, carrying a tray with a glazed jug and two expensive looking goblets, which seemed to be the normal ware used by the wealthy noblemen of the Holy-land.

Marius and I speedily drank our juice, which I found to be both delicious and refreshing.

The elder of the two men stood and bowed his head to me.

I am called 'Ashmaha,' and I am the Sheik of this small Oasis of 'Mahalla,' but I suspect that you are seeking the owner of yonder ship that has met its death on the rocks in our beautiful bay.

'It is Gods will that the very man you seek is here, sitting at my table.'

'May I introduce you to my very good friend Captain Begrum, who is the owner of 'The Whale.'

'The Whale?' I said rather stupidly.

'Yes.' He answered.

'The Ship that is dying on the rocks!'

'Of course.' I said, but Captain Begrum interrupted me before I could add to my statement, as he rose to his feet and held his right hand towards me, saying.

'Indeed, I too consider it to be God's will, that your own and my destiny have always been that we were to meet here and now, at a time that he selected when we were both in the wombs of our Mothers.

'Tell me Northman. How are you called?' he asked pleasantly.
'I am Edric of Wentnor.'
'Well met, Edric of Wentnor.' He said.
'Is Wentnor part of your name or is it a country?' he asked.
'It is a village in England.' I said.
'Ah. I have heard of England.' He added with a smile.
'I have also heard that it rains each and every day there. Is that not so?'
'If it is so, then I would wish to live in England, for it only rains here for a few hours each year, but then I have known many years when it rains not at all.'
I eventually managed to release my right hand from his grip and attempted to change the subject from rain back to destiny.
'My God is a God of the North,' I said, 'and we also believe that we are born with our destinies already foretold.'
'Once our fate has been decided, it can never be altered.'
'Quite so. Quite so.' He repeated.
'So Edric of Wentnor, what has our fate got in store for us this day?' he asked.
'Captain,' I answered. 'I am a blunt man and I do not enjoy fancy words or the so called art of haggling like fishwives over the head of a mackerel, so I will ask you a straight question,' as I withdrew my small purse of silver coin and plonked it onto the table before him.
'If I give you this purse of silver and help you re-float your ship off those rocks and have my crew repair

your ship, will you deliver us safely to our homes in Cyprus?'

Without a moment's hesitation he grasped me by my shoulders and bellowed loudly in my ear.

'So it has been written.' He said with a smile.

'AGREED.'

'Let's go.' He said loudly.

'What? Now? I asked? 'as I knew that my men were tired after the trials of the past few days.

'There is no time like the present.' He said.

'Believe me Edric of Wentnor. I am a man of the sea, and the sea is a mistress with many moods, and whilst she is calm and kindly this afternoon, by the morrow she can blow up a gale that could completely wreck 'The Whale' and destroy this very village in the blink of an eye.'

In less than an hour, seventy three of the fittest of my men and myself joined the Captain and his three crewmen on the rocks with ropes and tackle and we were hauling for all we were worth to wrench the stricken ship off the slippery rocks.

The incoming tide helped a little, as the small waves appeared to give 'The Whale' a little additional lift each time they reached the stern of the ship.

Captain Begrum shouted to the men. 'Hold her there men and don't haul again until the seventh wave.'

Now, the seventh wave meant little or nothing to me, but as I watched him count the waves as they reached the stern of the ship, I realised that each and every seventh wave appeared to be just a little higher and a little longer than the others.

We waited until the seventh wave swept in and as it reached the ship.

The Captain shouted. 'Pull.' And each of the seventy or so men hauled in unison.

The ship creaked and groaned as if she was a milking cow giving birth and with a mighty heave from seventy seven men she slid reluctantly and smoothly off the seaweed covered rocks.

We cheered loudly at our own success, but I did feel a little disheartened as I saw her settle on the sea-bed full to the gunnels with sea-water.

'I can see by your face that you are not a happy man.' The Captain said to me as he stooped to sooth his gnarled hands in the surf.

'Fear not Edric,' he said.

'The tide will turn around mid-night and by the time we wake in the morning, the tide will have deserted her and she will be high and dry.'

'I will need your men by day-break, when she will be ready to be hauled up, beyond the shelf, where we can try to repair her.'

I met Captain Begrum a few minutes after the sun had appeared over the eastern horizon, to find him standing on the side of the wrecked ship bellowing orders as if there was no tomorrow, sending men hither and thither to do certain tasks.

He paused for a moment as I approached him and greeted me with a friendly nod.

'Ah, here you are Lord Edric,' he said in a quieter voice.

'You are just in time to see us bail out the last of the water and I have just ordered your men to knock the dowel out of the mast so that we can turn her over on her back, in order to allow me to see if it is possible to repair her.

We watched for a few minutes until the last of the water was ladled out of the bilge, allowing one man to scale up the remaining side of 'The Whale,' and leap down onto the sand in readiness to join the rest of my men and the Captains remaining crewmen, who were waiting in position to heave the ship over, in order for the Captain to inspect the hull of 'The Whale.'

At the Captains command, we all strained our muscles to heave the stranded ship up and over, causing her to land with a loud crunch with her hull high in the dry sunny morning air.

Dark liquid oozed from her rotting looking timbers.

'The Hull looks rotten?' I said to the Captain.

He did not answer me but he walked up to the Hull and pulled a small knife from his thick black belt.

He stabbed the knife into the black rotten looking planks a couple of times.

'Yes.' He said. 'They do look a little ripe, don't they?

'But they are a good three inches thick, and my knife only went in about half an inch, so they should be sound enough for another couple of years before I need to check her again.'

'My only problem now is to find a good sized load of suitable timber.'

'I did send my Boson to Acre with a few silver coins last night.

'I just hope he can sniff out some suitable wood.'
'He's a good man, so he should be able to locate some.' He added.
'And what happens if he doesn't?' I asked.
'Well let us hope that doesn't happen, but if he can't find the wood I want, then I shall be forced to go back to the skill I learned in my boyhood on the Nile.'
'The Nile?' I queried for although I had heard of the river Nile, I had never seen it, but I was intrigued as to what skill the Captain had learned as a child on the Nile.
'What kind of skill was that?' I asked.
'Well,' he answered as he stroked his long, white speckled beard for a long moment as if he was reluctant to tell me his secret.
'Most of the boats on the Nile are made from reeds.' He said.
'Oh, the Pharaoh and the Lords can afford wood, which is brought down the river in its annual flood, or even felled in the upper Kingdom and floated downstream by the Pharaoh's own servants.'
'You see.' He added. 'The Pharaoh owns all of the lands of 'Upper Egypt' as well as the land that you know of as 'Egypt.'
'It's complicated.' He said as he strode manfully away from me towards something or someone who had caught his eye.
The Boson arrived by mid-morning with four camels carrying planks of wood.

Although I did not do much work on the ship, the repairs on the ship seemed to be proceeding at a good pace.

So much so that after three days I thought that The Whale' was pretty well ready to be to be rolled down to the sea on the rollers, which had been cut and prepared for that particular event.

However, when I queried it with Captain Begrum, he told me in no uncertain manner that in his opinion, the ship should not be launched until the Hull had been given one addition coating of the slimy black oil which seemed to seep out from one of the many bubbling pits that festooned the area.

I bowed to his experience and reluctantly turned away.

That evening I experienced one of those doom and gloom feelings that seemed to affect me from time to time, which usually seemed to be followed by difficult or dark events.

I awoke from a very fitful night's sleep, not to the noise of our usual noisy bustling camp, but to a stony silent camp, causing me to rush out of my tent half clothed and still in the act of slinging the strap of my Broad-sword over my head.

I was halted as I bumped into one of my men who simply stood and allowed me to crash into him.

'What the Hell,' I shouted angrily, but said no more as I followed his gaze to the perimeter of the camp.

Every other man in our silent camp was also standing and staring in the same direction.

I automatically completed tying the strap on my sword, as I too saw what they were all staring at.

The bodies of our two sentries were lying on the ground in front of a huge army of silent, white robed Saracens.

My logical mind quickly assessed the chances that my seventy five men had of successfully defeating this mass of enemies, or turning 'The Whale' over and reaching the sea before we were swamped and slain by the Saracens.

I immediately reached the conclusion within a few meagre heart-beats, that we had NO chance whatsoever.

'Arm yourselves.' I shouted, 'and join me in a defensive ring around the ship.'

'My men shook themselves out of their stupor and dashed to their respective tents and sleeping mats to obey me, but I felt sure that they, like myself, knew that we could only put up a token resistance that would last for no more than a few brief minutes before we were overcome by the huge numbers of our enemies, if we were forced to fight.

I did not see or hear the order, but it must have been given, because the Saracen army moved forward.

More and more men erupted slowly out of the sand-dunes until the entire beach was full of savage looking, white robed warriors.

They continued to advance until they halted a spears throw away, obviously awaiting the order to attack.

Long silent minutes passed.

With our shields held to the front and our weapons ready, we stood together, two deep around the black greasy Hull of 'The Whale.'

The centre ranks of the silent mass of Saracens moved aside to allow three white robed figures to emerge from their ranks.

Two of the three were dressed in the normal white robes that the Saracens always seemed to favour, but the centre figure, who was slightly taller than his companions, wore an elaborate helmet with a silver lined visor.

The Visor was down.

The three men halted ten paces from me, and I watched with bated breath as the Knight in the centre plunged the point of his sword into the sand and raised both his hands high into the air, shouting something into the sharp morning air.

He then brought both of his hands down upon his helmet and lifted the heavy metal helmet off his head.

I had been caught off guard for a moment, as my eyes seemed to be transfixed upon the expensive looking sword that he had plunged into the ground in front of me.

Something told me that I was looking at someone or something that I ought to recognise, but the man's voice interrupted my thoughts as it said in the tongue of England.

'Well my English friend, it is the will of Allah that we meet again.

I stared unbelieving into the smiling face of Osman-Ben-Hafsa.

CHAPTER THIRTY.

I was speechless for longer than I can recall, as I had fully expected to be attacked by the overwhelming numbers of these silent white robed figures who stood before me.

I had also been surprised when the leader of these men had plunged his sword into the sand rather than attack me, and found it difficult to comprehend that the man who was now in the act of embracing me had been the very man who I had been prepared to fight and slay, before his numerous white robed warriors could race down the few paces that separated us and kill me.

How wrong could I have been, as my shock turned into joy and I returned his greeting by patting him roughly on his shoulder?

'Sheik Hafsa' I said.

'You are the last person I expected to see on this desolate shore.'

'Osman.' he said rather sternly.

'My friends call me 'Osman.' He added, 'and surely you must be one of the small group of men who I can call friend' for if it were not so, then you would have slain me two years ago and had you done so, then Allah would not have wanted me to be here and save you from this horde of Holy warriors behind me.'

I glanced behind him towards the thousands of Saracens who stood behind him.

'I will say this quietly,' he said quietly, 'so that these two Sheiks behind me cannot hear, and if you do agree with me, then please do as I suggest.'

He moved a little closer and whispered.

'My two friends here, and the majority of my warriors would like me to slay all of you here and now, but If they see you kneel before me and pretend to swear allegiance to me and to 'Allah,' then they will leave this place completely satisfied that I have converted seventy–five heathens into our faith.'

And then they will leave this place singing their praises to god and to my-self.'

'As you are kneeling, you do not have to say one single word.'

'Just go through the motions and they will be satisfied.' He added.

I called Captain Begrum over to us.

I stood as he reached us and I took him a few paces away from the Sheiks servant and said quietly to him.

'You are a Moslem are you not?'

'I am my Lord,' he replied.

'Now, I am going to ask you to do something that may prevent those friends of yours from attacking us, and save our lives.'

'You may say No to my suggestion, but if you do, it may well cost the lives of all of us, including you.'

'I will do whatever is necessary my Lord.' He said quietly, as he looked towards the horde of Saracens who had begun to grumble and shout due to the lack of an order to eliminate us and their eagerness to move on.

'Good man,' I said and outlined my plan to him.

He nodded and followed me a few paces down the beach towards our men who were waiting by 'The Whale.'

'Men,' I said, loud enough to be heard but not quite loud enough for my voice to carry towards the horde of white robed warriors who waited a hundred or so paces away.

Captain Begrum has agreed to help me to pretend to convert all of you to 'Islam.'

A chorus of grunts of disapproval and growls came from my men.

I held my hand aloft to quieten them and said. 'Don't be afraid. It is only a sham and no Saracens up there will be close enough to hear what the Captain says, so his words will not be binding.'

What I am saying will meaning that you will not really be converted, but you will remain with the same Gods who you wish to be with.'

'Just kneel when I kneel and kiss my sword I want you to kneel and kiss your swords.'

'Mumble something that sounds like you are agreeing, and those Saracens up there will be under the impression that you have sworn to follow their faith.

'I believe that will save us from being over-run by those Saracens who are like a pack of hounds standing up there, baying for our blood.'

Grunts of approval came from the majority of my men but there were four or five men who were reluctant to comply with my suggestion, and needed their fellow warriors to persuade them to kneel with them.

I purposely stepped backwards a pace and knelt before 'Osman.'

'Osman' muttered a few sentences which I could not understand and nodded to me.

I kissed the blade of my sword before I stood up.

My own men knelt, kissed their weapons and after mumbling loudly as if they were swearing their allegiance to 'Allah' they also rose to their feet.

The Horde of Saracens cheered and left their ranks as they held their weapons in the air and danced as they cheered for many long minutes.

My men who remained near the upturned ship, looking on in amazement as the vast army of Saracens began to stream back into the Sand dunes and vanish into the distance.

A Saracen, who was dressed in the robes of a nobleman in the Saracen army, rode a white mare that was accompanied by a pure white stallion towards Osman and my-self.

He reined both horses up in front of us in a flurry of sand.

'Aha,' Osman said. 'I can now stay with you for a short while and catch up with my men before nightfall.'

Captain Begrum interrupted Osman and my-self as we were resting in the shade drinking our second cup of juice which his servant had made for us.

Lord Edric,' said the Captain as he bowed towards Osman, 'Please forgive me for interrupting you but we have completed all the repairs we were able to do on 'The Whale,' and we now need to turn her over before the tide turns, in order to complete the repairs needed on the top-side.'

I drained the drop of juice which remained in my silver cup and stood.

'Forgive me Sheik Osman,' I said, 'But I think I am needed to assist my men with our wrecked ship.'

'It shouldn't take long and hopefully, if all goes to plan, I should be back with you in a short time.'

'No need my dear Edric,' Osman answered.

'I am in need of a little exercise and would enjoy assisting you in your endeavour.'

He rose to his feet and joined the Captain and my-self as we walked down the sandy shore-line towards the ship.

Captain Begrum had already assigned each man around one side of the ship and without further delay he gave a long sturdy pole to Sheik Osman and my-self and escorted us towards the other side of the ship to join a dozen or more men who carried similar poles and were standing in a group.

'Sixty five of us should be enough to push her upright but I think that we will need your muscle on the port side of the ship to steady her or she will come crashing down, which would probably turn her into a pile of wood that would never take to the water again.'

'I need you and your men here to steady her with your poles, as she reaches her zenith and lower her gently to the ground.'

We nodded and grunted our approval, before we spread out along the length of the ship and stood with our poles in readiness to prevent her from crashing down onto the hard packed sand and splitting asunder.

I could not see what was happening on the other side of the ship but I could hear a lot of groaning and the sound of men straining but could see no sign of the heavy hulk moving.

As I was the third man from the stern on our side of the ship I flung my pole down and indicated to the man next to me to join me and called to the two men nearest the bow of the ship to join me as we raced around to the other side of the ship to lend our muscle power to them in order to lift the ship.

At the order of the Captain, we all stooped down in unison to lift the ship, which after what appeared to me to be a final act of defiance 'The Whale' actually moved to knee height.

"The Bloody Whale is the right name for the bloody thing,' one of my men said as he inhaled a breath of fresh air into his lungs in readiness for the next order.

At a second command from the Captain, the ship was hoisted to the height of our shoulders and with a final command it was held high.

After the next command and with the assistance of a number of men who had long poles pushed the heavy ship to its apex where it hovered for a few seconds before it commenced its way downward.

My-self and another man from the stern, who I now recognised as being Sheik Osman, ran the few paces around the falling ship, just in time to add our poles to assist the remaining men who had already placed their poles into the top ridges of the falling ship, forcing us to strain our already aching muscles, in order to allow the ship to descend as gently as possible to the ground.

A feeble cheer arose from the few men who were not actually bending over with their hands on their knees, in order to recover from their strenuous efforts.

Captain Begrum joined Sheik Osman and my-self near the bow of the ship.

'That went well?' I suggested.

'Yes.' He answered with a little hesitation.

'Although there is still a lot of work to be done before she is sea-worthy.'

'How long will it take?' I asked.

'A good day and a half, if we are lucky.' He answered with a shake of his head,

He ambled off towards his ship, whilst Sheik Osman and I walked up to a rather large tent which had been erected by his servant who was waiting for us beside an array of cushions, plus a folding table that had been covered with an embroidered cloth, which contained a silver decanter and two silver cups.

We sat at the table on two large cushions and drank the deliciously flavoured water whilst we watched the scene of my men working away at their tasks of repairing 'The Whale.'

We spent an hour enjoying pleasant small-talk about the weather and the beautiful scenery but avoided speaking about 'The War' or of 'The Religious' beliefs of our two opposing forces.

I knew that our parting was imminent the moment he rose to his feet.

I held out my right hand and said 'Osman my friend.'

'It has been good to see you again and despite our differences, I do wish you a successful, long and happy life.

He took my right hand in his and we knew that our friendship must end here and now.

Both of us realised that the possibility of ever meeting again was extremely unlikely, but as we were both sensible and practical men, and we both knew that if our destiny brought us together again, then it would be as enemies and not as friends.

He turned and mounted his white charger and without a wave or a backward glance he spurred the horse and he and his servant quickly disappeared into the distance.

I walked away from his abandoned tent with its contents and joined Captain Begrum at the ship. Seventy five men can achieve a lot working on a forty foot long ship, and true to his word the Captain and our men carried out the repairs necessary to make 'The Whale' as seaworthy as she was ever going to be, under the circumstances.

We had very few personal belongings but we had managed to salvage half a dozen floating barrels from the wreck and had filled them with fresh water.

When I mentioned that we had no food to the Captain, he simply shrugged his shoulders and mumbled to me. 'The sea is full of fish and I did manage to salvage the nets, so we will all have full bellies before nightfall.'

It seemed to me that our run of bad luck was a thing of the past.

'The Whale' had been rolled over the logs we had placed in front of the ship and launched into the sea. She floated without any serious leaking.

The Captain eased the ship out of the bay on the morning tide and within an hour we had hauled in a heavy net-full of fish.

Some of the men were so hungry that they ate and apparently enjoyed the raw fish, whilst the majority of the men, including the Captain and my-self waited eagerly for our fish to be grilled over the single fire which had been constructed with stones to make a passable galley-kitchen.

It had taken the Captain and his remaining crewmen many hours to weave a sail which they constructed out of the stalks of 'reeds' and much to my amazement the improvised sail caught the prevailing wind, and within the space of an hour, it had dried out, sending 'The Whale' speeding over the sea towards Cyprus.

The Whale enjoyed a night of calm seas and a slight breeze, speeding her gently towards our goal, but two hours after day-break I heard the shout from one of the crew.'

'Sail ahoy.'

We all looked to a point in the horizon where the seaman was pointing, where we could see the outline of a ship.
  The ship appeared to be heading directly towards us.
  An hour later the Captain shouted. 'She looks as if she is a trader out of Constantinople, so we should be safe enough, causing the helmsman to adjust his steering and continue on our old course.
  The other ship appeared to have altered its course a little, making me think that we seemed to be on a collision course, but I breathed a sigh of relief when I eventually realised that she would sail past us with maybe a hundred yards between the two ships.

*   *   *

  In 'The Dolphin,' the Varangian guards could relax now that the danger of being captured by The Emperor of Constantinople's fleet seemed to have passed, and 'Aelnoth' was leaning against the bow of the ship speaking to 'Olaf' the big Icelander who had become his constant companion.
  'Have you decided how you are going to reach home after we reach England?' Aelnoth asked.'
  'No. Not really, but with a bit of luck I am hoping to find a trading ship that is heading for Iceland, and I will purchase a passage on her.' Olaf said.
  'You once told me that you had lost both your Father and your Mother.' Olaf asked?
  'Were they both killed by the Normans?'
  'No.' Aelnoth said.

'Neither of them were killed, and certainly not by our so called Norman friends.'

'Oh. What happened to them then?' Olaf queried.

'Now that is the question, and to be honest. nobody really knows.' answered Aelnoth.

'My Mother, who was named 'Godda' was said to be a Princess of the 'Light Elves,' although many thought her to be nought but a Welsh Princess.'

'That's nothing too special.' Olaf intervened.

'There must be a Welsh King with a dozen daughters in every one of the six or seven Kingdoms in Wales.

Aelnoth ignored his remark and continued with his story.

'My Father was called 'Edric the Savage,' by the Normans in their famous 'Doomsday book,' but he was named 'Wild Edric,' by us English folk, due to the fact that he once avenged the killing of his first wife by a troop of Norman marauders, by slaying the complete troop of twenty-two men.'

Olaf felt a shiver of fear surge through his body. Not because Aelnoth's Father had slain twenty-two men. (Which in itself was a mighty deed,) but because he had been bred and reared in the treeless land of Iceland, and from his earliest of his childhood memories, he had always held a terror of Elves, Goblins and the creatures who dwelt in the dark English forests.

'Twenty-two?' He uttered with a voice that had a little doubt in it, mixed with the sound of awe.

'So they say.' Aelnoth answered.

'Well, after a blazing argument with one of her sisters who was lodging with us, my Mother stormed out of the house and we never saw her again.

My Father was so distraught about losing her, that he saddled up his old war-horse which was a stallion that he had named. 'Chieftain' and he disappeared into the vast forest of 'Clunn' looking for her.'

'He did not return whilst I was there, but he must have returned many years ago, with or without her.'

'And then, to rub salt into the wound, a band of bloody Normans attacked us in the early hours of a morning about six or seven years ago.

One of their woman-folk sneaked up behind my Brother 'Garth' and plunged a spear in his back, and they drove me out of our fortress.'

'My old Dad is now probably sitting in front of a big log fire in our Manor house at Wentnor.'

He was about to finish his story and inform Olaf that his Father had almost certainly retaken his fortress, when one of the sailors shouted. 'Ship ahoy.'

'Where away?' The Captain shouted.

The man pointed to the west and all eyes stared to the west, where the outline of a sail slowly emerged out of the morning sea-mist.

As the sun reached its zenith 'The Whale' and 'The Dolphin' appeared to be on a collision course, but both of the Captains were men who had spent most of their lives at sea, and were both curious as to what type of ship they were approaching.

Both Captains had assessed correctly that both ships were simply trading Vessels, dispite the fact that the

Dolphin's crew contained a goodly number of men who were dressed in the blood-red cloaks of Constantinople's feared 'Varangian Guards,' whilst the Whale was crammed with armed men.

The two ships sailed alongside each other for a few minutes.

What ship are you? Captain Begrum shouted at the top of his voice?

'The Dolphin, out of Constantinople,' was the answer.

'Where are you heading?'

'England, and Scania.'

'What about you?'

'My ship is the Whale out of Acre.'

'Where are you heading?' The Captain of The Dolphin shouted.

'Cyprus,' Captain Begrum shouted back.

'The Dolphin' began to surge ahead.

My head shot up when I heard the word 'England,' and my mind was hurled backwards almost in despair, as I if I could feel the cool winds and smell the damp green meadows of my home-land.

'Damn and blast those bloody Varangian's.' The Captain said aloud.

'They are probably loaded down with silver and gold they've looted from Constantinople and will be too keen to get home to give us any help.'

He altered his own course in order to continue to sail in the direction of Cyprus.

The gap widened between the two ships and the gap between 'Edric' and his son 'Aelnoth' became wider and wider, until both ships disappeared from sight in the vast expanse of the Mediterranean Sea.

Aelnoth sat on the side of The Dolphin and dreamed of re-claiming his birthright as soon as he reached England, whilst Edric's thoughts were of meeting his new son 'Tito' again in his luxurious Villa in Cyprus.

Neither Edric nor his son Aelnoth were aware of being a few short yards apart, except from an uncanny and weird sensation that seemed to surge through both of their bodies.

Aelnoth had never really taken to the new religion of Christianity and he smiled to himself, for despite the fact that he sometimes prayed to the White Christ, he had never really deserted the old Gods of Thor and Woden.

'Loki.' Who was the Northern God of 'Tricks' and of 'Revenge.' The Father of 'Hel' and of the Wolf God 'Fenrir' was splitting his sides with laughter, as he sat in his fortress in 'Asgard,' watching the two miserable, puny humans go their separate ways.

'Of course' thought Edric, I know of 'Loki' the trickster' although I could not hear his laughter, neither was I aware of what was amusing him.

I merely sat near the prow of the ship and dreamed of England, and Godda.

CHAPTER THIRTY-ONE.

King Richard and his captor, the young nephew of the Duke of Austria, rode ahead of the main body of the Austrians troops, as they travelled up the deep valleys and foothills of the only alpine track that traversed the main trail through and over the mountains that lay in their way.

They halted near the bottom of a huge mountain.

'Why are we stopping here?' Richard queried.

'We need to go up here together.' Archibald answered.

'Why ? We have not seen a single man for at least two days. Richard said.

'We wait here until my men catch up. Archibald said in a stern voice.

'This is the very route that Hannibal took when he marched into Italy,' Archibald explained, 'and he was attacked by tribesmen on the top of this very ridge and lost half of his army to his attackers.'

'I too have been schooled in the wars between the Romans and the Carthaginians,   and I have been led to believe that Hannibal lost most of his elephants and thousands of his men from starvation and frost-bite.' King Richard countered.

The King stared into the face of Archibald and they both smiled.

Richard had become fond of his captor to such an extent that he was beginning to think of him as his own son.

He had noted with some satisfaction that Archibald was, despite his young age, a stern but fair leader.
He was also a man who led his men from the front and did not ask them to perform any acts which he, himself declined to do.

'I know that Hannibal was attacked during his journey over the Alps, King Richard said, 'but that was many hundreds of years ago.'

'Do YOU expect an attack during our climb up there?' King Richard asked, knowing full well that Archibald rode within a ring of scouts, in the front and to the rear of his party.'

'Nothing would surprise me. 'Archibald answered.

'We have made this journey only once before,' he added, 'and we saw neither hide nor hair of any tribesmen, except a few stray arrows that landed amongst us from time to time.'

'And yet you did not see anyone?' the King persisted.

'Not a thing, your Majesty.'

'But we should be safe on this journey,' Archibald added. 'I have over two hundred men with me this time and we are travelling within a screen of scouts.'

The King mumbled something under his breath and gazed up to the pass and along the sides of the sheer mountains which rose into infinity on both sides of the pass.

'Fear not your Majesty.' Archibald said loudly. 'I can see your concern and may I assure you that I can also see the dangers of entering into valleys such as this, but I have already sent scouts up to the top and if you look carefully you will be able to see them standing on the top, so they have passed safely enough and they will remain there until we join them.'

'Forward.' He bellowed at the top of his voice and began to lead the way up the steep slope.

His men including King Richard followed the leader commenced their trek up yet another forbidding snowfield.

Six men had been assigned to escort, defend and protect 'The King of England,' as well as being given the unenviable task of preventing him from escaping, which, if such a disaster would occur, could deprive his Uncle from demanding, and from obtaining a 'King's ransom' for the Kings release, formed a protective ring of warriors around him as they began to make their way up the mountainside.

Archibald was fully aware that if he did not deliver King Richard alive and unharmed to his Uncle, it would bring untold wrath or even execution upon him, despite the fact that he was the only son of the brother of the powerful Arch-Duke of Austria.

King Richard and his entourage climbed up the slippery snow filled gully behind Archibald and his own personal guards.

The King halted for a moment and looked behind him, noting that Archibald's entire force, which included a large baggage train of mules and servants, which carried all the necessary trappings that a Noblemen of importance claimed to be essential for such expeditions such as this.

Archibald's retinue lagged behind him in a string of men and animals that stretched right down to the bottom of the pass.

The King looked upwards at the sheer snow covered cliffs which rose on both sides of the pass, but could see no sign of life and no obvious way that men could reach the peaks that disappeared into the white clouds above.

He then looked ahead of him and realised that even this short pause from the climb had left a gap between his own party and the people who were ahead of him.

He put his head down into the wind and speedily continued his way upwards.

The higher he climbed, the lower the sides of the mountains on each side of the pass became, causing the King, who had been schooled since an early age on the ways of war, to mumble to him-self. 'Now is the time I would launch my attack he muttered under his breath,' but no attack came, and he and a number of other men lingered at the summit of the pass, waiting for the remainder of Archibald's men and the baggage train to reach the top.

The King gazed down the pass, which had been used by mankind and animals alike for hundreds of years as it meandered from the peak into the snow laden foot-hills below.

'There you are, your Highness.' Archibald said loudly.
'I did say that we would not be attacked.' Did I not?' He said in a scornful tone.

He turned to his men, and said. 'I will lead the way down.'

'You men follow me,' he added.

'And you men who are looking after the King. Make sure he comes to no harm.' He growled.

'It will be slippery on the way down and my Uncle will not be happy to receive a King with a broken neck.'

The way down was just as dangerous or perhaps even more dangerous that the ascent, as the sun had melted the top layer of snow causing men and animals to slip and slide leading to the death of one mule and the broken leg of one of Archibald's guards.

The King breathed a sigh of relief as he joined Archibald who was waiting on the level ground of what looked like a peaceful alpine meadow.

Ever cautious, the King ambled slowly to the edge of the group and stared at the snow, searching for the tracks of men or animals, or in fact anything else that looked out of place in this silent, snow covered meadow.

He was both pleased and yet a little disappointed that he found no sign of anything, other than the straight line of a fox that had probably patrolled the valley during the hours of darkness, looking for an alpine hare or a ptarmigan to stave off its hunger.

The King ambled slowly around the group of men who were looking up the pass that they had recently descended, urging the laggards to hurry up, with jests and shouts of encouragement.

He reached the other side of the men, and stared along the other side of the meadow and then he looked up the side of the mountain, finding nothing other than white, unbroken snow.

He then turned his gaze to the meadow itself, which stretched about half a mile into the distance, showing nothing other than a white landscape, which was interspersed with half a dozen stunted, leafless trees.

Something moved about twenty feet away, causing his eyes to stare at the spot for a brief moment, and yet he could not see anything other than more snow.

He looked again as his eyes focused on the area where he had seen a movement.

'Pah. There's nothing there,' he said aloud.

'I must be going mad.'

'There is nothing there but a twig, blowing in the wind,' and he was about to turn away when the stick moved again.

The King ambled slowly towards the stick, gazing casually to his left and to his right in order to allay any suspicious from an enemy.

Had not his tutors drilled into him time and time again, that he must always be on the lookout for assassins or felons wherever he happened to be and whenever he was alone?

He was within three feet of the stick when he finally looked down, and what he saw did not actually shock him but rather pleased him, for he could see that the stick itself was hollow and the slight warmth that had emitted from the stick had thawed a small ring of melted snow about the base of the stick.

As he examined the area, he could see that the snow around the stick had been carefully arranged as if it had been driven into slight ridges by the wind.

In an instant he withdrew his sword from its scabbard and plunged the blade into the snow an inch away from the stick.

A scream pierced the air as a man rose in a shower of snow, holding his neck which had been opened up by the Kings sword.

The King swung his sword and severed the man's hand and his head with a single massive blow, sending the three separate parts of the man into the reddening snow.

Momentarily forgetting that he was not in charge of this small army of men, he shouted 'Shields up.'

He noted with a little pleasure that most of the men around him followed his order and swung the shields around off their backs, to resume the standard position of a man awaiting attack from the front.

It was now the Kings turn to be shocked as a man rose out of a snow drift two feet in front of him waving a long dagger in his right hand and a small round shield in his other hand.

'Archibald', who was standing alongside the King, plunged his own sword into the man's chest sending the dying man to the ground.

King Richard could see men emerging out of snow drifts all along the valley until the entire valley seemed to be full of attackers who were all racing as fast as they could towards him.

'Gather around me men.' He roared as he chopped his battle-sword down through the shoulder of an attacker who was in the process of thrusting his spear at 'Archibald.'

'Form a shield-wall around me and the wagons.' He roared as he stepped back a pace in order to join the line of 'Archibald's' men who rushed to form a ring about the two wagons that had, fortunately been parked beside each other.

The ring had been completed a mere moment before the first crowd of attackers reached it, where they found their progress halted by a ring of shields and a strong force of trained, grim faced warriors waiting for them.

The King noticed that most of the attackers' wielded either Knives or spears.

Only one or two of them had helmets or chain-mail.

'They are only peasants and farm boys.' He bellowed over the screams and shouting that was echoing in his ears.

'Kill them.' He shouted, as he brought his huge battle-sword down onto the unprotected shoulder of an attacker in front of him.

The attackers began to waver after seeing their friends and family members fall dead or wounded, after attacking and failing to break through the shield-wall of this determined, battle hardened warriors, who sent man after man to the afterlife.

Several of the attackers stepped back, white faced and shaking after the horror of the Shield-wall, and then they turned and ran.

They, in turn were followed by tens and then by dozens of their fellow attackers leaving the valley silent except for the moans and groans of half a dozen men who had been wounded and lay on the ground of this blood reddened snow filled valley.

'Archibald' walked around the wagons studying his men, speaking to the three men who were suffering from wounds, none of which looked to be serious enough to warrant more than a stitch or two.

However, when he reached the bodies of two of his men who had been slain, he recognised them as belonging to the ever growing number of deaths out of his original squad of twenty men who he had brought with him from Austria.

'That makes eleven.' He said in a muted voice.

'Eleven what?' The King asked.

'Eleven men killed out of the twenty who I brought out here from my estate in Austria.' Archibald said quietly, as he turned his head away from the King in order that the King of England could not see the tear that trickled out of his right eye and down into his neatly trimmed beard.

He noticed one of Archibald's men robbing the dead and wounded men, and after he had finished his looting, he plunged his sword into the bodies of the slain and wounded before he moved on to the next man.

'You there!' He shouted, causing the man to rise to his feet and look towards the King.

'Loot them if you must,' King Richard shouted, 'but I think there has been enough killing for one day, so you can cut that out.'

The man shrugged and walked over to the next body, which lay a few feet away.

King Richard could see that the man was still alive and he also noted that the wounded man was one of the very few of their attackers who wore a helmet and a chain-mail shirt.

He raced over to the man, just in time to see the looter heave the man over onto his back and raise his sword to kill the man.

Richard reached him in time to grasp his arm as it began its downward journey in his iron grip and struck the man across his face with his other hand.

'Did you not hear me you Knave?' He shouted in the man's ear as the man fell sideways.

The looter speedily rose to his feet and with his sword in his right hand and turned to face the King, only to find him-self staring into the Kings broad-sword that prodded his unprotected throat.

King Richard shook his head from side to side and with a flick of his wrist he slashed the flat of his sword across the arm of the man, sending the man's sword flying.

The king then kicked the man in the groin sending him flying into the snow some six feet away.

He then knelt by the wounded man and raised his head a little.

'Do you speak the language of the Franks?' he asked.

The man nodded.

'Good,' the King said.
'Where are you hurt?' he asked.
The man hesitated for a moment and then he brought his right hand up to the side of his head.
'Here I think,' the man said, and then he winched and brought his hand down to rest in the snow, 'and my shoulder,' he added.
The King placed both of his hands on the man's helmet and as gently as he was able he lifted the helmet off the man's head and studied the Helmet.'
'It has been struck with a sword here.' He announced, 'and the sword blow probably glanced off your Helmet and hit your shoulder.'
'Are you bleeding?' He asked.
'I'm not sure.' The man answered.
The King placed his hand in the top of the man's chain-mail and pulled it out in order to peer under the shirt to see if the sword had penetrated the shirt and cut him.
'Mmm, nothing more than a few bruises,' he said in a voice full of disgust.
'Get him up.' Archibald said.
'Now Kill him.' He added as he turned to walk away.
'One minute. The King said, and he stepped and stayed the hand of the warrior, who was about to bring his sword down on the prisoners head.
'He may be able to help us through this warren of valleys and speak to the tribesmen who we may encounter on our journey.'
'Take him then,' said Archibald, 'but I shall have his life at the first sign of betrayal.'

'Let us be on our way and get out of this valley before those vultures up there start their meal.

Several of the men looked up into the cloudless sky to watch the ever growing flock of vultures circling overhead in anticipation of a good meal.

As the prisoner was still unable to walk, the King ordered his two body-guards to lift him and carry him over to the supplies wagon and the King walked slowly behind the slow moving cart.

'What Tribe are you from?' he asked.

'Venetetic'. The man mumbled.

'Now I don't know much about the tribes in this area.' Said the King, 'but I do know that the 'Venetetic' are not really a tribe but the word Venetetic means a group of tribes.'

'So, which tribe are you from?'

Are you 'Selassi' or 'Raeti?' He asked

'I was 'Selassi' but I am now of the Venetetic.

'We are all Venetetic now.' The man reiterated.

'We are all one now after the Romans conquered us and made us one.'

'And are you a Chieftain amongst the Venetetic?' asked the King.

'No.' The main mumbled. 'I am not a chief.'

'I am what you heathens would call a Holy-man.'

My name is 'Dakpe' of 'Giba Clan' he added.

'Ah. That is good.' Said the King, 'it means that your people should not attack us again as they will not be willing to endanger one of their own, especially if that man happens to be a Holy-man.'

'If they attack you,' the prisoner mumbled. 'Which is certainly what will happen, for the news of your journey through our territory has been known for many weeks, then perhaps you, my smart-assed captor, will tell me how they will know of my capture before you all die under a shower of my peoples arrows?'

'I will tell you how my friend.' The king answered. 'As soon as you have recovered enough to sit on a horse, you and I will ride a hundred paces in front of our men, so that your rag-tag gang of so called warriors will be able to see who is leading us through your mountains.

The following morning the prisoner 'Dakpe' and King Richard rode together one hundred paces in front of Archibald's cavalcade, through snow which varied in depths from mere inches to drifts of twenty feet high.

They made their way through valleys where the snow had been driven off the sparse tufts of hardy grass to reach the exits of the valleys where Archibald's men were compelled to dig their way through snow blocked passes which were higher than four men standing on each other's shoulders.

Tired men struggled through snow day after weary day, which stretched into week after week until after the seventh week there appeared to be a little less snow than the previous day.

Men breathed a sigh of relief, believing that they had left the mountains behind them and were safe from any further attacks by the tribesmen who dwelt in this snow-covered wilderness.

The King felt certain that the daylight hours were becoming longer and the snow clouds, which had obliterated the sun for so long, were becoming fewer, causing the days to actually appear to be a little brighter.

Archibald still lost men and animals who succumbed to the severe frosts and the howling storms that seemed to penetrate through the sheep-skin sleeping blankets and into the very bones of sleeping men, who, when Archibald viewed the frost covered hair and faces of his dead comrades, could do nothing other than to shake his head in amazement that these frail men had survived so long before succumbing to the silence of death.

The animals who succumbed to the cold were eaten by the hungry survivors, whilst the dead men were prayed over and laid to rest in the deep snowdrifts, leaving a trail of bones and bodies in the wake of their long march.

Archibald's ragged and weary band received nothing other than hard stares and blunt refusals from the few crofts and villages they passed through.

The faint trail took the survivors over what seemed to be an endless landscape of high mountains and deep gorges, until late one morning, they halted on a ridge to stare, almost unbelievingly, into a valley that contained not only half a dozen green fields, but also a small village where they could see smoke rising horizontally into the clear morning air.

The village that had looked so near, took the slow moving survivors until mid-day before they reached the first house, which was situated about fifty paces away from the bulk of the cottages, which lay huddled together to form the small village.

Archibald's servant banged on the door with the hilt of his Poniard several times, to no avail.

'Try the next cottage.' Archibald said angrily.

They urged the three horses who had survived the journey towards the next cottage. However as they reached what had originally looked like a dip in the land, suddenly turned out to be a fast flowing torrent of water, which was six or seven feet wide.

The heads and shoulders of men carrying shields and spears appeared out of the dip in the land, which had been washed away by the flooded stream in years gone by.

King Richard noted that the numbers of the men opposing him were roughly the same as Archibald's men but whilst Archibald depleted band of perhaps fifty men were emancipated and exhausted from their journey, the men standing in front of him seemed to be fresh, healthy and well fed.

'Fear not my friend.' He said to Archibald.

'They are mere farm boys, whilst our own men are seasoned warriors who will wash over them as if they are unarmed children.

Archibald strode a few paces in front of his own men.

'Put down your weapons.' He shouted in a very loud voice.

'We mean you no harm.'

There was no response from the angry looking villagers who appeared to grip their weapons more fiercely and stare angrily at Archibald and his men.

'I am Lord Archibald, and I am the nephew of Duke Leopold of Austria,' Archibald shouted, 'and if you resist me or anger me in any way, then my uncle of Austria will descend upon you like an avenging Angel and wipe you and your village off the face of the earth.'

This statement did not fall upon deaf ears and King Richard saw the raised spear-heads immediately drop towards the ground.

A large man who sported a grey forked beard and a shock of white hair stepped out of the line of silent men.

'How do we know you are Duke Leopold's nephew?' shouted the man.

'Do you dare to doubt my word?' Archibald shouted back in anger.

'Well with the greatest of respect. You could be anyone coming out of the mountains claiming to be the Dukes nephew.' The man said in a more sombre tone.

Archibald turned to his servant.

'Fetch my colours and show this peasant who I am.' He ordered.

The man hastened to the rear of the column and opened one of the calf-skin bags which contained his Lordships personal effects.

He returned to Archibald within the space of fifty heartbeats.

'Show this peasant my colours.' He ordered, and the servant pulled out the intricately weaved silken colours of Duke Leopold out of its leather casing and held it aloft. He shook it, so that it unfurled and fluttered in the wind.

The village headman followed by his men walked the few paces up the slope and knelt with his head bowed in submission towards Archibald.

Archibald led his men towards the head-man who stood with his head still bowed.

'Forgive me my Lord,' he said. I did not know you were the nephew of our benefactor The Duke of Austria. 'But we have been raided by robbers more times that I can recall in my own lifetime, and we have developed a system of defence in order to protect us from most of the raiders.'

'That is acceptable.' Archibald said.

'It is pleasing to see that you are protecting my Uncle's domain so well.'

'Now,' he added. 'As you know, we have crossed the mountains and we are in dire need of food and shelter, and I must insist that you attend to our needs until such time as we are strong enough to continue our journey into Austria.'

'But my Lord,' the head-man said. 'You are already in Austria.'

Archibald nodded and gave the impression that he already knew he was in Austria, whilst in truth; he really had no idea where he was.

To King Richard, the news that they had actually reached Austria sent a jolt throughout his entire body.

The fact that he was already in Austria meant two things to him.

In the first instance, he realised that if he was to escape, then he must get away before Archibald delivered him to The Duke.

And secondly, if he failed to escape then he knew full well that he would be kept in chains, or at least in a foul smelling, damp dungeon until his brother John collected and delivered the enormous ransom that he expected The Duke of Austria to demand for his release.

King Richard was assigned to live in a large cottage with no fewer than six of Archibald's personal guards, and whilst the seven of them were well fed and were treated with the respect that their ranks demanded, King Richard was escorted by at least two guards wherever he went.

On the second day he had been politely, but firmly disarmed by Archibald's guards, who had taken his Broad-sword and his Poniard away from him.

As he lay on his straw mattress on the fourth night of their recuperation, the King muttered to himself 'I am forced to grant that Archibald is not the stupid boy I had thought him to be.'

'He, like my-self, knew that there was no possibility of escaping his clutches whilst we were still in the mountains, but as soon as we arrived in Austria, he has placed me under strict guard where I am closely watched by armed men by night and by day.'

'My only chance now is to grab a mount and make a run for it.' He mumbled.

CHAPTER THIRTY-TWO

It was late in the afternoon when we caught our first sighting of Cyprus, causing a feeble cheer to rise from the men who were crammed together in the belly of the ship.

'Will we reach land before nightfall?' I asked the Captain.

'No chance my Lord.' He answered. 'The tide is against us and I will need to tack, and that will probably mean that we will not make landfall before mid-night.

'That could be a blessing.' I said.

'I have been away for such a long time.'

'It has been many months since I have had any news of our homeland, so I do not really know what state Cyprus is in.'

There was little that I could do other than inform the men to gather their meagre belongings and to help each other to struggle into their chain-mail war shirts, just in case we were met by enemies.

I noticed that some of the men gave me a strange look when I gave the order, as if they were asking me if I knew something they did not know. Indeed, despite the fact that I had received no news from Cyprus for at least six months, I did have a strange feeling that all was not well on the Island.

After the long and tedious business of tacking, the ships prow eventually crunched onto a stony beach.

I ordered the men to wait for a few minutes before I dropped down into the ankle deep water which lapped gently onto the silent beach.

A lone owl hooted as the first sign of dawn fought against the darkness.

Nothing stirred in the tangle of bushes that vied with each other in a tangled mass in their quest for space.

I turned and signalled to the men to vacate the ship and join me on the shore.

My men and I willingly splashed into the shallow water, relieved to be free at last from the confinement of the ship and groaned as we stretched our limbs.

I gave the Captain the silver I had promised him, which he willingly took and immediately turned and ordered his three men to man the two oars which were needed in order to push the ship out of the shallows and back into the sea.

'Where do we go now my Lord?' asked one of my men.

'What I intend to do.' I answered, 'is to take you and our men to a safe place I know, which is not too far from here, and leave you there for a couple of days whilst I will contact my wife and learn how things are here in Cyprus.'

'Then I will return to you and if things are normal, I will dismiss you and allow you to return to your homes.'

'However,' I said in a lower voice. 'If all is not well here then I may need your strong right arms to rectify the situation.'

'It all depends on what I find in Limassol.'
I was on my way within the hour and I travelled speedily through the countryside that was waking to another warm and sunny day.

I met a few peasants who were on their way to Limassol, carrying their wares or driving their livestock to sell in the town, and I walked through the streets where the store-holders, were in the process of removing the shutters of their shops and stocking their empty shelves with all manner of produce, ranging from fruit and vegetables to clothing, carpets and a myriad of other things.

They all appeared to be far too busy to notice a grubby old man trudging slowly past, to pause for a moment and recognise me.

There were no guards on the gates which swung open at a touch and allowed me to walk casually across my own courtyard to the door of my Villa.

I gave the door a slight push, and to my surprise the door swung open to reveal the room and its furnishings that I had said my goodbye's to when I left my wife six years ago.

I entered the room very carefully, for I suspected foul play, and I drew my Saex in readiness to protect my-self, should the need arise.

The room was empty.

I walked through the kitchen and down the hallway, peering into rooms that appeared to have been vacated some considerable time ago, until I reached the large bedroom which Alaina and my- self had shared.

To my utter astonishment I gazed at the large Saracen type bed which we had especially made for us, to see the sleeping forms of two men who were obviously guards for they were wearing the uniform which I had supplied them with before I had left.

I was still holding my Saex in my right hand when I kicked the nearest man to me.

He jumped to his feet and his sword was half out of its scabbard before he recognised me, causing him to stay his hand and gape at me with his mouth open in amazement.

'My Lord Edric,' he gasped. 'We thought you were dead.'

He shook his friend who slowly opened his eyes, yawned and sat on the side of the bed.

He too looked at me as if he was seeing a ghost.

'My Lord.' He stammered, unable to believe that it was me.

He jumped off the bed and stood to attention in front of me.

'Where is the Lady Alaina and Tito?' I asked in a voice that sounded as if I was expecting to hear bad news.

'Are they dead?' I demanded.

'No. My Lord. No, they unharmed.'

'Things are not good here in Limassol.' The other guard said warily.

'Why is that?' I asked.

'Is Sir Guy of Lusignan not keeping the peace here?'

The two men looked at one-another, but I could not read, or even suspect what they were about to tell me.

'Sir Guy is dead.' They both said in unison.
'That is why Lady Alaina left, my Lord. He was hacked to pieces by the rebels my Lord, and Limassol has been ruled by them since he was killed.'
'Forget him for a moment.' I said loudly.
'Where are my wife and son? I demanded.
'The Lady Ludmilla took them to her son's castle in the Troodos Mountains.'
'Why did I find you asleep, when you should have been wide awake and guarding my property? I said angrily.
'The rebels carry out their attacks during the hours of darkness, my Lord. 'We have both been up all night making sure no one damages the Villa.'
'I will send two of my men to help you guard the Villa during the day and the night.'
'I am off to make sure the Lady Alaina and my son are safe but I will be back as quickly as I can.' I said and hurried away.
I was back with my men within the hour.
After I had assigned two men to join the two guards guarding my Villa, I assembled the rest of my men and they followed me up and into the hills towards the fortress belonging to Ludmilla's son.
It was a difficult march for all of us, as we had been cooped up in a ship for more days than I could recall, and the long up-hill trek over the rock strewn track caused even the hardiest of my men to struggle up towards the fortress where I hoped to find 'Ludmilla' and 'Tito.'

We stood before the gate as the final glow of the sun was dying in the west.

I must admit that I was dripping with sweat, which was blurring my vision as it trickled down my forehead and into my eyes.

'Your eyes are younger than mine.' I said to one of my younger Greek Cypriot men.

'Can you see who it is standing on the wall above the gate?'

'Yes my Lord.' He answered. 'It is Lord Stavros and your wife, the Lady Alaina.'

I smiled with relief but was slightly concerned as I had expected to see my son with his Mother.

The noise of the opening gate pleased me even more as the forms of upright figure of Stavros joined the bent figure of his mother Ludmilla stood in the entrance.

I led my men through the gate, standing aside to allow them to pass me as I spoke with Ludmilla and her son.

'My Lord Edric.' Stavros said. 'It is good to see you again.'

'We had no idea you had returned to Cyprus.'

We clasped hands and thumped each other on our shoulders in a show of friendship.

Ludmilla stretched upwards and smiled at me with one of those knowing smiles that had always been part of her charisma. 'Welcome home.' She said quietly, as if I had been out for a day's hunting and had not been away for six years fighting in the Holy-land.

I walked with them into the courtyard and was pleased to see Alaina and her sister descend from the ramparts and walk over to meet me.

She placed her arms around my neck and kissed me on my left cheek and then kissed my right, and whispered in my ear. 'Welcome home my Lord Edric, Jesus has answered my prayers and he has returned you to me, safe and sound.'

'It is good to be home and especially so to find you in good health but I do not see little Tito. I do hope that he also in good health.'

'Where is he?' I asked in a nervous voice.

Stavros intervened before she could answer. 'Come with me my Lord,' he said.

'You must be tired and hungry after your journey here and must be in need of food and drink.'

'My servants will see to the needs of your men whilst you join me in my dining hall.' 'There are things that I will need to tell you before you hear it from other men.'

As Stavros ushered me to his table, he placed his hand on my arm and said. 'Fear not Lord Edric, your son is safe and sound. He is merely out hunting for a wild boar that has been ruining the crops of one of my neighbours and they should be home soon.'

I followed Stavros into his dining hall where he told me in detail of the killing of Sir Guy, and as much as he could about the rebels, who under a leader had caused havoc amongst the islanders.

'He is hiding somewhere up in these mountains, and he strikes at our vulnerable and less guarded townships, before he disappears again like a puff of smoke.'

'What else do you know about him?' I asked.

'Does he have a name or a family?'

'I'm afraid not.' He answered. 'We know absolutely nothing about him.'

'I could find who he is.' Came a calm voice from a person who I had not noticed sitting on a large settle by the fireside.

I turned towards the fire and as I did so, the slight figure of Ludmilla stood and faced me.

'Then why haven't you?' I asked.

'Because this silly son of mine will not allow me to return to Limassol, where I could contact my spies and find out about him.' She answered demurely.

'Is that true?' I asked Stavros.

'Indeed it is.' He said. 'My Mother is an old woman, and I am sure that this new leader of the rebels will have spies of his own in the town and she would probably be slain within a couple of days.'

'Not if I was with her.' I said firmly.

'We could leave first thing in the morning.' Ludmilla said as a determined smile crossed her lined face.

'I see that I am fighting a losing battle.' Stavros said with a sigh, 'So it seems that I must agree but only on condition that you allow me and a few of my men to accompany us.'

'It is agreed.' I said. 'We will leave first thing in the morning.

I was about to rise from my seat when the door was suddenly thrust open to allow two mud splattered youngsters to enter the room.

'Ah, here you are at long last.' Said Stavros, who then turned to me and said 'Lord Edric, I would like you to meet my eldest son Joseph, and of course, you know the other ruffian who has just interrupted us.

I rose and shook the hand of Joseph, and turned my eyes to his companion.

'No, Lord Stavros,' I said. 'I think you must be mistaken for I am sure this young man and my-self have never met.'

'Forgive me my Lord.' Stavros said quietly. 'I did not realize that is so long ago since you left us. This mud splattered ruffian is none other than your son 'Tito.'

I was forced to retreat a pace in order to look at the face of my son who I had not seen for the past six years and found my-self staring into a pair of blue-green eyes that looked identical to the eyes of my long dead father, shocking me so much that I was forced to regain my seat at the table in order to prevent my head from spinning.

Tito approached me and held out his hand in a very grown up way and said. 'Forgive me Father but I'm afraid I did not recognise you. It is such a long time.'

'Did you get your wild pig?' I asked stupidly as it seemed to be the only thing I could think of at the time.

'No.' He answered. 'We could see where he had been and where he had wallowed, but other than that we had no sightings of him.'

Alaina saved me from making a further fool of myself as I was still shocked at the sight of my son.

She breezed into the room like a breath of spring sunshine, wearing a yellow dress which I had not seen before, but I did note that the colour of the dress matched her hair that seemed to have lightened in the seven years I had been away.

'Alaina,' I said loudly and walked over to meet her, taking her in my arms and giving her a long hug. 'It is so good to see you again.' I said. 'And you are looking so well.'

'How long is it?' I asked, and I answered my own question. 'It must six years?'

'Not so. My Lord. It is nearer to eight.' She said in that husky voice of hers, which sent a familiar shiver through my body, just like it did when I had first heard her speak.

'That must make little Tito here nine years old then?'

'I'm nearly ten.' Tito said in an indignant voice.

'Yes, my Lord.' She said. 'He will be ten in two months' time.'

She turned to her son and said. 'Off you go now and make sure you wash some of the mud off your face and put your new tunic on whilst I go and make sure I can rustle up some food and drink for your Father. He must be starving.'

'I will leave you with Stavros,' she said as she laid her hand on my arm, 'while I go into the kitchen and order the kitchen maidens to provide you with a special meal to welcome you home.'

She left Stavros, Ludmilla and myself at the table and walked out of the room.

'What I would like now.' I said. 'Is for you two to tell me exactly what has happened here since I left that has dragged the island down into what seems to me to be a state of anarchy'?

I listened to them for the best part of an hour before I called our meeting to a close.

I thanked them for their thoughts saying that I totally agreed with them, and that the mess in which I have found the island seemed to be brought about by a single agitator, who had stirred up the different factions in the island, causing them to rebel against our Christian rulings.

We ate a meal fit for kings which consisted of roast fowl and well hung venison with a large platter full of vegetables that we washed down with rich, red wine made from the grapes from Stavros's own vineyard.

Loud noises in the morning roused me from my sleep, causing me to rush over to the window, thinking that we had been invaded, which to my relief was not the case, as the noises coming from the courtyard, that was situated directly below my window, was being made by my own men, plus half a dozen pack donkeys who Stavros had assigned to follow us into Limassol that very morning.

I left twenty of my men to help protect the fortress and added my thirty-one warriors to the twenty men who Stavros had allocated to march with us, causing a little delay and confusion which meant that it was nearing mid-day before we commenced our journey.

After a slow but uneventful journey we reached Limassol by late afternoon.

I added ten extra men to join the four who already guarded my villa, before I joined Stavros in the empty courtyard of the castle.

We speedily quelled the noisy courtyard by ordering the two Sergeants at arms to take control of his men, who all appeared to be shouting as loud as they could at the men who Stavros had brought with him.

I eventually managed to leave the Sergeants to their duties and walked through my front door to the relative quiet of my Villa, where I joined Ludmilla, Alaina and Tito who were also dashing hither and thither as they ordered the household staff to arrange the interior of the dwelling to their liking.

By the time the sun began to sink beyond the eastern mountains I managed to find time to relax and enjoy a wonderful evening in relatively silence, as I sat with my wife and son and enjoyed our evening meal in peace.

I was sitting at the top of my table with Alaina and Tito sitting next to me and I knew that I should be talking to both of them, and yet whilst I was at ease with Alaina, talking about the mundane workings of the house and servants, I found that despite attempting to converse with my son, which was a thing I had dreamed about doing many times over the past seven years. His answers were a single nod, or sometimes a shake of his head or from time to time, or a mere word of agreement or a disagreement.

His silence told me that I had been absent from his life for far too long and as such, I had missed out on forming the kind of relationship that a father and son would normally build up during those vital adolescent years.

I too dropped into silence as I ate a small portion of my meal and cast my mind back to the days when Aelnoth and Godwin had been children and dispite my desperate need to recall all the things I did and enjoyed and helped them with during their childhood years, I found it impossible to remember a single item that I could honestly say was happy enough to make me smile.

I remembered my own Father, recalling the first time when he took me hunting and of the numerous trout that we had caught when we fished in the red Lake.

I recall how he thought me to string a bow and how to fletch an arrow, and of the many times that we sat together eating a freshly roasted partridge over an open fire when we camped on the heathlands of the great forest of Clunn.

Although I had taken Aelnoth and Godwin out hunting and fishing, there were so many other things that I regret not having enjoyed with them.

I could not recall singing with them after we had made a fire and roasted a bird or a hare over an open fire.

The few times I had taken them fishing had not really been for fun, but it had been an expedition of necessity, in order to provide enough meat for the Kitchen.

I reached the ugly conclusion that I had been, and still was a bad Father.

I had been nothing more than a provider of food and lodgings for them, existing only to ensure that they never went hungry, but for the early lives of all three of my sons, I felt that I had missed most of my their childhood making war.

Alaina touched my arm, shocking my muddled brain back to reality.

'What is amiss my Love?' She said in a quiet voice.

I stood and I walked over towards the fire place.

She took my arm and followed me, standing in front of me as I stood with my back to the fire.

'I am disappointed with Tito.' I said in a low voice.

'I have tried to talk to him and I can't seem to get through to him. I have a strong feeling that he hates me.'

'I think he resents me for barging into his life after so many years of freedom and taking over his role of being the man of the family.

'Give him time my Lord.' She said quietly.

'He has been without a father for many years and he has made a life for himself with his own circle of boys who all treat him as their friend as well as their leader.'

'They know he is the son of the most famous warrior on the island, and now that you have returned, they are forgetting your past deeds and your reputation and see nought but an old man before them.'

'Oh, forgive me?' she said quickly, 'I did not mean to offend you or indeed to say that you are an old man but I am trying to look at the situation from my own point of view, as well as through the eyes of a ten year old child.'

'I still look upon you as the love of my life.'

'Look at yourself in the mirror.' She said, pointing to the copper mirror that stood in the corner of the room.

I shook my head, for I had fallen into one of my blackest of moods.

'Then I will tell you what I see.' She said.

'I see a warrior of old.'

'I see a battle scarred Alexander who has returned from the wars.'

'Certainly, his beard has turned from the colour of Gold, into a regal shade of mottled grey, but his hair is still the hair of a thirty year old Adonis in his prime.

Just look around you when you walk through the town, and you will see men who are half your age, whose hair has retreated from their heads to their chins, where it hangs in long grey braids.'

'Either that,' she said in a sarcastic voice, 'or they are fat and bald headed, so when I compare you with them, I can only see the man I love and feel the need to make more babies with such a handsome and special man.

Her logic and her reasoning did sort of make sense, and as I looked back to the times when I had been in the Holy-Land, I was able to recall many instances when I had been marching with my men through the arid deserts or scrambling up rock faces or steep sand dunes, where despite my age, I had been able to keep up with and on many occasions, reach our objectives before men who were less than half my age had been left behind or indeed, had failed to reach our target at all.

I reached out and took her hand, drawing her towards me where we held each other in the sort of embrace that I had dreamed about more times than I could remember over the past seven years.

Her kind words and our embrace had lifted me out of my dark mood and we left the dying embers of the fire and walked to our cold bed-room.

We were both naked within minutes of entering the room and snuggled under our sheep-skin sleeping blanket, where we both made up for the loneliness that had been forced upon us during those long lonely years.

Alaina's passion thrilled me, so much so that it caused me to recall some of the recent words she had spoken to me when, she had spoken about babies.

'Well.' I said aloud, after I my breath had returned to something like normal. 'If that was not a baby making session, then I really don't know what was.'

*   *   *

After a hasty breakfast I walked down the tunnel that led into the cellar of the castle.

I looked through the spy-hole to assure my-self that the hall was unoccupied.

I entered the Hall and walked along it, emerging through the front door of the castle into another glorious sunlit morning.

I joined young Godwin who I had put in charge of organising the sergeants at arms to lead the troops of twenty men out of the fortress and into the town to show the towns-people that I. Lord Edric was back in Cyprus and in charge of a force of veteran warriors who would bring law, order and prosperity back to the island.

I personally led one troop whilst Godwin and Georgio. (Who was the son of Stavros) would lead the other two troops.

My own troop and the troop led by Georgio returned without an incident but Godwin's troop returned carrying the body of one of their men who had been slain by an arrow.

After consoling the men I asked Godwin. 'Did you see where the arrow came from?'

'Oh yes my Lord.' He answered.

'Then why did you not chase the assassin?' I asked angrily.

'Well, my Lord.' He said 'We did run to the corner of the street where the man was, but when we reached the corner he had disappeared and we could see no sign of the man.'

'It was in the slums of Limassol where all the beggars and cut-purses live.

 I feared we could be running into a trap, so I ordered my men back to the fortress.'

'Did you keep the arrow'? I asked.

'I did My Lord.' He answered.

'Good. Bring it with you in the morning and we will return to that area and see if we can find another arrow with the same markings on it.'

 Arrow-smiths and Archers usually have their mark on their own arrows so that they can claim the kill should the need arise.'

'Dismiss your men and meet me in the courtyard first thing in the morning.'

CHAPTER THIRTY-THREE.

My warriors had completely surrounded the town an hour after daybreak with armed men who I had positioned at regular intervals of one hundred paces apart.

My remaining men searched each and every House, Cottage and Shed in the town.

Before I had retired last night, I had ordered three men to collect scraps of leather and paint the leather with colours matching the arrow that had slain my warrior on the previous day.

I employed the three men as orderlies to paint the strips of leather.

These men were veterans who had been injured in our recent battles in the Holy-Land and despite the fact that they were no longer fit enough to continue to serve as warriors, I had kept them on my payroll due to the loyalty which they had previously given to me.

Each member of my search team carried the colours with them in the hope that they would find an arrow, or even an arrow-smith who could remember making arrows with corresponding colours.

It was mid-day when my men met in the centre of the town, and I could see by their faces that no-one had found the man we had been searching for.

I joined my men in the small square and was about to dismiss them when I saw 'Georgio' approaching me.

He was accompanied by a grubby looking individual, who he introduced me to.

'Lord Edric.' He said.

'This man is one of my Mothers agents, and he has just told me that he has discovered the name of the man who is causing all this trouble and he knows where we can find the man.

'Why hasn't he contacted your Mother before and told her?' I asked.

'He says that the Rebels have checked every man woman and child who left the town for the past month and have already slain three of his friends.'

'Can he be trusted?' I asked.

'Oh yes my Lord.' He answered. 'He is one of my Mothers most trusted informers.'

'He is from her-own village. She has known him since he was born.'

'Has he told you where they are?'

'He has my Lord.

'And?' I said in a stern voice.

'They are with their leader, who is a man called 'Argyles.' He lives in a farmstead at the foot of the Troodos Mountains.'

'Argyles' has a small farm called 'Glykpi-nerou.' Which I am sure you know, means the place with 'Fresh-water.'

'I think I know that place.' I said.

'I am sure I have stopped there on several occasions when I used to lead my troops up there, before I left for the Holy-Land.'

'If my memory is correct then 'Fresh-water' cannot be more than three or four miles from Limassol'. I said.

'My Lord.' Georgio said in an excited voice.
'It is a little over three miles. We could be there within the hour.'
'Make sure that all the men's water bottles are full and have them ready to march as soon as you can.' I ordered.

I selected one third of my men and we left Limassol an hour later, marching along the well-worn track which led to a number of Mountain villages.

I halted my men when we reached the valley some one quarter of a mile from the farmstead called 'Fresh-water,' and ordered half of them to go to the south under the leadership of my nephew Godwin, whilst I took the rest of my men to the northern side of the valley where our target was situated.

Both Godwin and my-self left two of our men at intervals at the apex of the hills that surrounded 'Fresh-water' we circled and advanced towards the farmstead.

The afternoon had turned hot and humid causing the few goats and the two milking cows to seek shelter beneath the few trees that surrounded the farmstead.

I could see no sign of sentries, in or around the two buildings which made up the Farmstead.

I signalled to the men to move forward, causing us all to walk down the slopes and into the valley towards our target.

No arrows met us on our way and we all reached the two buildings at more or less the same time.

I stood on one corner of the farmstead and took my Hunting horn from my waistband.

I made sure that all of my men were ready and blew hard on the horn to signal them to move into the house.

'Shields up.' I ordered loudly.

We all crashed through the back and front doors.

Our reception was not what I had expected, for as the first of my men crashed through the doors, and as the first two men rushed through the front door they were immediately impaled onto a trellis of wood which had been impregnated with sharp wooden spikes that crashed down from the ceiling, killing both of the startled men and halting the rest of my men, who stood aghast on the front porch way.

The first three men who crashed through the rear door suffered a similar fate, for as they stepped through the doorway the floor beneath them suddenly collapsed and the three men toppled down into a pit, where they too were impaled onto wooden spikes that had been driven into the ground.

I was totally shocked at this disastrous turn of events as I looked at my dead and dying men, most of whom had been my constant companions who had suffered the scorching heat of the Holy-land and the battles we had fought there.

The men from the rear of the house joined us at the front and I could see the shock and horror in the faces of my men as we all gathered around the front porch.

I heard a familiar hum and as I looked up I could see a cloud of arrows high in the air as they reached their arc and zoomed downwards towards us.

'Shields up.' I shouted at the top of my voice, noting as I sheltered under my own shield that all of my well trained warriors had obeyed me as they too huddled under the cover of their shields.

Arrows thudded down into our shields and thudded into ground around us.

'Where the hell did they come from?' I shouted.

'There.' Godwin screamed. He pointed at the hillside which we had crept down and left unguarded in our eagerness to reach the farmstead.

'They must have been hiding up there, and have occupied the hill

'How the Devil did we miss them?' I said angrily.

I was furious at leading my men into a trap.

I was enraged that this rebel, who I had considered to be little short of a peasant without a brain had out-thought me and had slain five of my best men, leaving me standing in open ground like a novice in range of his bowmen.

I had been so sure of my-self and of the bravery and training of my own men that I had not even bothered to bring a single Archer with me.

'What shall we do now my Lord?' Godwin asked in a low voice.

I realised that my men and my-self had been left standing in open ground like the proverbial 'Sitting Ducks,' waiting to be slain by a bunch of untrained peasants and if I wanted to salvage not only my reputation, but even more importantly, save the lives of my warriors who expected so much more from me, I needed to move, and to move fast.

'Shields up Men.' I shouted again, and as soon as the men had their shields up and had formed a line, I said loudly. 'Follow me.'

I took my place in the middle, and a single pace in front of our line, and led them up the hillside towards the large band of archers who loosed their arrows as speedily and as often as they could, peppering our line so often, that by the time we reached them our shields had been rendered almost useless due to the amount of arrows that protruded out of them.

Almost all of my men were seasoned warriors and brushed most of the arrows off their shields with their swords, but during that short respite when a warrior steps out from behind the protection of his shield, that man is left vulnerable from spears and arrows, and during that particular advance, three of my men fell to the constant volleys of arrows.

My usual habit of counting numbers was overlooked due to my intention to thrust my Saex through the slit between my own shield and the shield of Godwin into the foe who stood before me, but after the fight I did try to assess the number of the enemies who had stood before us and reckoned that they outnumbered my men by two to one, but I think that their leader had counted on their traps and their bowmen reducing my men by more than eight of my men who I had already lost and now that we had reached them and faced them in a shield-wall, the experience of my men made up for their superior numbers, and enemy after enemy fell before us as we advanced up the slight hill.

Almost all of our foes wore white turbans on their heads indicating that they were not either Greek Cypriots or Christians, and although many of them were brave men who fought and died where they stood, I thought that very few of them were probably not trained warriors, and would be Farm workers or trades-men, and these men fell in swathes before us as we continued our advance.

Their ragged line broke sending fugitive's in every direction as they fled down the reverse side of the slope, except for a small bunch of eleven men who stood on the very top of the hill.

Now that we had ceased our advance and the fighting had stopped, I had automatically counted their number.

These eleven men wore iron helmets and had expensive looking chain-mail.

They carried an assortment of weapons varying from Scimitars, Axes and Iron Maces.

I looked up the slope towards them and assessed them.

I noted that they all had the bearing and the confident look of warriors, but I more or less discounted all of them, except one huge man who stood in the centre of the group.

This man towered over his fellow warriors by a good head and a half and gazed down towards me with a look that I can only describe as 'utter arrogance.'

I have always been a confident man. I have always been confident of my own ability and proud of my record of overcoming the best of men who have challenged me.

 I recalled some of the men I had slain from 'Ivor half-face, and his twin brother,' to their leader, the mighty 'Madoc the Lucky,' when I had been little more than a youth.

 My mind sped back to many other warriors of note who had fallen to my skill with the sword during the many wars and battles I had fought, but this look of 'utter arrogance' somehow took me by complete surprise, and caused me to falter as I strode up towards these eleven men.

 My mind suddenly made me think that if I had been standing on a similar hill and looking down, then all I would be able to see would be a white bearded old man of perhaps sixty or more summers, struggling and puffing like a wounded pig, as he made his way slowly up towards his death.

 'Leave this silly old bugger to me.' 'Ahmed' shouted.'

 'Ahmed' was 'Argyles' second in command, and a man who had been 'Argyles' friend and constant companion since the day some ten years ago when he had met his leader, who was at time a Major-General in the ranks of the elite bodyguards of King Komnenos.

 'Ahmed' strode the few paces down the slope to reach me, and when he was near enough to strike, he brought his scimitar around in a wide sweep with the intent of taking the head off this 'silly old bugger,' but I simply ducked beneath the scimitar and used my own broad-sword in a move that my old mentor

'Vorta' had taught me when I had been a mere sixteen year old boy, and I simply sliced off both of my opponents ankles, sending the man tumbling down the hill in a screaming heap.

'Argyles' was shocked to the core to see his friend writhing on the ground screaming for help.

He could see that thirty or forty of his enemies were walking up the hill and had already reached 'Ahmed' and he knew from past experience that 'Ahmed' was already beyond help, as nothing or no-one on God's green earth could prevent him from bleeding to death within the next few minutes.

'Argyles' was furious and pushed his way through his fellow warriors and swaggered down towards 'Edric'.

'I was shocked to see just how tall this leader of the rebels was, for although I had been a tall man when I had been in my prime, I realised that as I had aged, my height had decreased, so much so, that I was now slightly smaller than most of my own men, but compared with this gigantic man who stood before me, caused me to feel decidedly inferior.

The fact that he was standing in a slightly more elevated position than my own, did nothing to boost my confidence.

I could see a more level piece of ground to my left, and I stepped back from him to reach it.

He gave me an evil smile, shook his head as if to tell me that my move would do nothing to save me and advanced towards me.

'Argyles' own men ambled down towards us, causing my own men to gather nearer to my opponent and my-self.

Both groups of men now stood some ten feet apart, in readiness either to attack or retreat, however the fight turned out.

'Argyles' was still hopping mad at the death of his friend, and although his enormous size and his former position of Major General in the Guards had given him an inflated ego. That ego and his bullying nature had allowed him to give orders to virtually everyone in the army of Komnenos.

The fact that he had achieved the habit of eating far too much good food, coupled with his laziness and bullying tactics, he had practiced with his weapon each and every day but he had not wielded a sword in anger for the past ten years.

He jumped towards me and lounged his scimitar at me, allowing me to parry his lunge and drive the rim of my steel lined shield into his stomach caused nothing other than a loud grunt from my opponent. 'Argyles' reached out with his left hand and caught hold of my jerkin. He then gave a loud grunt and with a mighty heave he wrenched me off my feet and threw me along the side of the hill, where I lay for a moment in a daze before I scrambled to my feet, just in time to avoid the iron clad boot of my adversary to crunch down onto the dusty surface of the hillside where my head had been a split second ago.

His friends hooted and cheered him on as he advanced towards me forcing me to step backwards with my battle-sword held in front of me as I parried and ducked the wide swipes of his scimitar.

His huge muscular body oozed strength and power as he followed me along the hillside, although I could sense his frustration and his anger of not slaying this old man who, despite his own power and skill, still stood before him, unharmed.

His lunges and swings became wilder and more savage.

I could see that I had outstayed the usual time limit of his previous combats and I began to take heart. His obvious weariness allowed me to use the skill and the knowledge of my many years of fighting and war-fare.

The cheers of his followers became less and less, until they stood in silence and watched their leader as he began to tire.

My long awaited opportunity came as he continued to advance and push me backwards, when his left foot stepped into a patch of sandy soil and a hole that had been dug out of the hillside by some animal. He half stumbled, causing his head to momentarily look down towards the thing that he had stumbled into, allowing me to thrust forward with my battle-sword, taking him in the throat.

I withdrew my sword and stood as I watched his face, as his eyes shot up skyward for a moment, showing just the white of his eyes before his huge torso crashed to the ground and rolled over just the one time before it lay still on the hillside.

It was now time for my men to cheer as they walked across to me and congratulated me on my win against the man who had boasted that he was the strongest and most famous man on the island.

I was too exhausted to celebrate and could do naught but lean on my sword in an attempt to catch my breath, whilst my men hooted and cheered and joined me around the body of my opponent.

Argyles few men who had watched the fight stood silently on the hillside as their weapons were taken from them.

Despite the fact that I was pretty well exhausted; I did need to appear to be strong and resolute. I could show no mercy to these men, so I ordered them to be stripped.

My men stripped the clothing off the prisoners, and looked to me for approval.

'Strip them of their pants and their shoes too.' I ordered angrily.

'This was done with the savagery of victors taking their revenge on their conquered enemies, leaving the captives completely naked, as they stood in their nakedness, with their heads bowed onto their chests.

'Bury my warriors who you have slain.' I ordered, indicating the bodies of my own men who they had killed during the battle.

I sat down for a rest with Godwin and my men whilst the prisoners dug holes, and after they had gently lowered my dead warriors in, they filled in the graves, and stood by the graves tired and sweating in the late afternoon heat.

I could see that the prisoners were wet with perspiration and badly in need of a drink, but I was determined to be harsh towards them, for I knew that I must use them as an example, in order to show the population that insurrections like this simply would not be tolerated.

'Godwin.' I said. 'I want you to take charge of the men.'

'Please order the prisoners to assist our wounded men onto the few horses and to carry the rest of their dead comrades.

Have our men drive the prisoners before us, as we make our way down to the town and drive them through the town to the town centre, where I want you to hang them on the large tree in the square.'

He nodded with a face which clearly displayed his dislike of the role I had given him, but I gave him a grim smile, which I thought told him that I too disliked what we were doing, but that he too, hopefully, realised that it was necessary.

'You and I will lead. You can take the roan whilst I will ride the black stallion.'

He nodded and walked towards our men who stood to await their orders.

People appeared at their doorways and stood in the streets, as we reached the outskirts of the town as we led our procession through the silent streets.

We made our way slowly past shops where the customers and stall holders stood and watched us, with many of them following us until we reached the town centre.

After the prisoners had piled the naked bodies of their dead at the base of the tree, our nine naked, and half dead prisoners were hung on the ancient olive tree that had given shade and succour to generations of the citizens of Limassol.

The stark warning of the tree's strange new fruit differed from its usual crop of rich berries and attracted naught but the eaters of carrion.

The new governor of Limassol had brought peace and order back to the island.

CHAPTER THIRTY-FOUR

In the glow of the candle, he watched as the sand clock emptied itself, indicating that two excruciatingly slow hours had passed since mid-night.

King Richard eased himself out of his bed and dressed, making no noise other than the slight rustle of the stiff leather as he eased himself into his heavy overcoat.

He knew that one of his guards would be sitting on a stool outside his door and eased the door open a mere inch in the hope that the guard would be asleep.

A sigh of relief was stifled as he silently crept past the sleeping man.

He stepped carefully over the other man, whose duty had been to oversee the three other men and to make sure that the King did not escape.

The King eased the outer door open just wide enough to allow him through and stepped out into the cold night air.

Many weeks ago he had chosen the strongest of the three horses that had survived the trek over the mountains, and after a few soothing words whispered into its ear; he saddled the horse and led it out of the compound.

He did not mount the horse until he reached the edge of the village, but once he had settled himself in the saddle, he automatically dug his spurs into the side of the horse, not realising that this particular horse was not one of his own warhorses which had been trained for war and was accustomed to the use of the spur, and as he dug the spur into the horse, it stood on its hind legs and let out a loud whiny.

As the unhappy horse landed on the ground the King spurred it savagely again, causing the horse to gallop along the track which led towards the end of the valley.

Upon reaching the end of the valley he eased the pace to a trot and they followed the track and the fast flowing stream down the one and only exit of the valley.

He stopped for a moment in order to turn and look back to see if there was any sign of pursuers and after a few moments he smiled to him-self and urged his horse forward at a fast trot.

He did not see the net that encased both the horse and its rider, forcing them to come to an abrupt stop, encased like flies in a cobweb that enmeshed them so tight that neither the horse nor the King could move.

What he did see out of the only eye that was functioning was a large, turf covered cottage, out of which emerged half a dozen men, who had obviously been wakened by the noise made by the trapped horse and the loud curses which emitted from the man trapped in their snare.

He heard one of the men ask. 'Well now. What have we got here?'

His question was answered by one of his companions. 'It's a horse and rider.' The voice said.

'Are you blind?'

'Leave the bugger there.' The man said.

'We can sort him out in the morning. I'm back to my bed.'

'No,' a third man said.

'I know this man. He is the so called King of somewhere or other, who Lord Archibald is taking to The Duke, and if this sod dies, then the Duke will hang the lot of us.'

'Get him out of the net.' The leader ordered in a loud voice.

Richard was shivering as the cold light of a grey morning loomed when they finally managed to untangle him from the thin clinging tentacles of the net, causing him to flop onto the damp ground like a landed trout.

He was hauled to his feet and frog-marched into the hut, where he was placed on a stool before a roaring fire, and given piping hot bowl of gruel.

'There you are my Lord,' the man said sarcastically as he handed the King a wooden bowl of gruel.

'That'll put hairs on yer chest.' He laughed at his own joke, as he walked back towards his own bunk.

The King had not quite finished the bowl of gruel when Archibald and half a dozen men burst through the opened door and crowded into the small room.

Archibald was furious.

The fact that King Richard had broken his parole and not only had he escaped, but he had stolen the only ridable horse, which Archibald had intended to ride the remaining thirty miles to his uncles Citadel.

'You have broken your parole.' He blurted out, 'and not only have you acted like a nithing, but you have stolen the only decent horse, and only your rank is preventing me from treating you like the felon you are and hanging you from the nearest tree.'

These were harsh words, which everyone in the room knew that he should not have used to address the King of the English in such a manner.

'Nevertheless,' he snarled. 'You have been caught like a bird in a snare and I do assure you that you will not be given a second chance.'

'Chain him.' He ordered.

Four of his men grabbed King Richard and heaved him upright out of his chair and he could do nothing other than struggle as he felt his hands wrenched behind his back and secured with iron chains.

'Prepare him for the journey.' He ordered before he stormed out of the room.

Archibald led his men out of the valley, marching at a brisk pace out of the foothills and into the lowlands of his uncle's realm.

Four weary days of travel and three nights of sleeping under the leaden clouds brought them to his Uncles Citadel of Saltzburg.

Whilst the climb up to the Citadel caused four of his men to succumb with fatigue, the climb was a triumph in itself as the citizens shouted and cheered them up the hill where they were met by the Duke.

The Duke greeted Archibald as if he was a conquering hero returning triumphantly from the wars, not like one of his sixteen nephews who had been lucky enough to be in the right place at the right time in capturing a man who was likely to make the Duke the wealthiest man in Europe.

He merely glanced at King Richard with pure hatred, and a sinister smile crossed his face as he saw the grubby travel weary image of the man who he had quarrelled with when he was crusading in the Holyland.

'Take him to his Cell.' He ordered.

'Take the chain off him, but leave the handcuffs on until you reach his quarters, and make sure you order the gaoler that he is to be well fed and well treated.'

'We must take care of such a valuable asset. Must we not?'

The Duke of Austria placed his arm around the shoulder of his now favourite Nephew and they walked through the door into the dining hall of his Citadel.

King Richard was unchained and escorted through a different door.

He had no other option other than to follow the jailor as he was escorted by his guards up the stone stairway and enter a large single room which possessed a small wooden bed, a small desk and a single chair.

The single door through which he had entered the room and a very small window with iron bars, were the only ways of entry and exit.

The four guards stood to one side whilst a fifth guard released his handcuffs.

The door was slammed shut behind him.

He flopped down onto the bed and his weary body succumbed to blessed sleep.

One dreary day followed another dreary day as the days stretched into months and then into years.

He gleaned small snippets of news from his sour faced guards, who had obviously been ordered not to to converse with their Noble Prisoner.

He paced his small cell for hours on end, in order to stretch his limbs.

He attempted to keep his mind active by composing sonnet's and poetry.

After demanding a quill and velum several times he was eventually supplied with a meagre supply of writing material which allowed him to write at least one poem and a short book depicting some of his thoughts, as well as his experiences of imprisonment.

After many alterations, he named the book = Ja Nuls Hons Pris or ja nuls om pres. (No man who is imprisoned) and was allowed to send both the book and his poetry to his half-sister. 'Maria de Champagne.'

Duke Leopold stormed into his cell one cold September morning, threatening to Hang Richard.

The Duke accused Richard of appealing to the 'Holy Roman Emperor, Pope Celestine III, asking for lenience, accusing Duke Leopold of the crime of 'Wrongful Imprisonment,' as at that particular time it was a crime to imprison a Crusader.' Thus forcing the Pope excommunicate Leopold.

Over his two years of imprisonment King Richard was moved to the castle of 'Trifels,' on the orders of the

Holy Roman Emperor. He was later taken to the Fortress of Speyer.

The Citadel of Speyer was a huge castle situated on a natural plateau overlooking the Rhine.

King Richard was eventually released after the enormous sum of ransom had been paid.

The huge amount of money paid for King Richards release virtually bankrupted the Kingdoms of England and Normandie.

He immediately returned to his two main loves. Hunting and warfare.

THE END.

AUTHORS NOTE.

Many of the characters, place names and battles in this novel are based on real people and actual events.
However, I have used 'Fictional Licence' in respect of the timing of events that do not coincide with true Historical facts, especially so with regards to 'Edric Sylvaticus,' (Wild Edric.) Who I feel was, and still is, such a local English Hero, who has been neglected by British Historians to such an extent, that NOT to include him in this novel would be a dis-honour to English history.
Edric Sylvaticus lived in the 11th Century, in the area of England that was at the time. 'The Ancient Kingdom or Mercia.' and is now the present day County of Shropshire.
He married a lady named 'Godda' and history tells us that they had one son who they called 'Aelnoth.'
Edric was a respected Land-owner who owned a large number of townships and settlements in what is now England and Wales.
He is locally known as 'Wild Edric 'but is described in the Norman 'Doomsday book,' as 'Aedric the Savage.'
There are still villages he owned in Shropshire, which still contain the word 'Savage' in their title'

We know far more about King Richard. (Couer-De-Leon.) Whose life consisted of little more than Intrigue and Warfare?

We have been led to believe that he was a brave and courageous warrior, who was one of the leaders of the third Crusade.

He was shipwrecked, captured and held for ransom for a little over two years by Duke Leopold of Austria, who he had fallen out with whilst on the Crusade.

Richards Brother, John, who was a much despised regent during his Brother's absence, and who later became King of England.) John bled the Kingdom of England dry by raising taxes to such an extent that he caused unrest and rebellion.

King Richard was killed by a bolt from a cross-bow whilst he was attacking the tiny Castle of 'Chalus-Chabrol in Limousine, supposedly due to the rumour that the Castle contained a fortune of Roman Gold.

The archer who slew the King was said to be either a boy or a cook.

King Richards's body was buried at the Abbey of Fontevraud but his heart was embalmed and buried at the Cathedral of Rouen in Normandy.

He left no Legitimate Heirs.

Printed in Poland
by Amazon Fulfillment
Poland Sp. z o.o., Wrocław